FARAWAY

MODERN CHINESE LITERATURE FROM TAIWAN

FARAWAY

A NOVEL

Lo Yi-Chin

TRANSLATED BY
JEREMY TIANG

Columbia University Press
New York

Sponsored by the Ministry of Culture, Republic of China (Taiwan)

Columbia University Press wishes to express its appreciation for assistance given by the Pushkin Fund in the publication of this book.

Columbia University Press wishes to express its appreciation for assistance given by the Chiang Ching-kuo Foundation for International Scholarly Exchange and Council for Cultural Affairs in the preparation of the translation and in the publication of this series.

NATIONAL ENDOWMENT for the ARTS
arts.gov

This project was supported in part by a Literary Translation Fellowship from the National Endowment for the Arts. To find out more about how National Endowment for the Arts grants impact individuals and communities, visit www.arts.gov.

Columbia University Press
Publishers Since 1893
New York   Chichester, West Sussex
cup.columbia.edu
Translation copyright © 2021 Jeremy Tiang
All rights reserved
Library of Congress Cataloging-in-Publication Data
Names: Luo, Yijun, 1967– author. | Tiang, Jeremy, translator.
Title: Faraway : a novel / Lo Yi-Chin ; translated by Jeremy Tiang.
Other titles: Yuanfang. English
Description: New York : Columbia University Press, [2021] | Series: Modern
    Chinese literature from Taiwan
Identifiers: LCCN 2021001274 (print) | LCCN 2021001275 (ebook) |
    ISBN 9780231193948 (hardback) | ISBN 9780231193955 (trade paperback) |
    ISBN 9780231550581 (ebook)
Classification: LCC PL2880.O2326 Y825 2021 (print) | LCC PL2880.O2326
    (ebook) | DDC 895.13/52—dc23
LC record available at https://lccn.loc.gov/2021001274
LC ebook record available at https://lccn.loc.gov/2021001275

♾

Columbia University Press books are printed on permanent and
    durable acid-free paper.
Printed in the United States of America

Cover design: Lisa Hamm
Cover image: digital composite, Jui Chieh Chang / EyeEM / via Getty Images

CONTENTS

FARAWAY 1

FARAWAY

Dear Miss Shih,

How are you? I'm Lo Yi-Chin, the person currently stuck in Jiujiang on the mainland because my father had a stroke. Thank you for your warm offer of assistance, which came just as I was at my most helpless. There are a few things I need to bring you up to date on:

First, today I had a discussion with Dr. Wan, the head of the neurological department here (Jiujiang First People's Hospital). He said that my father's condition is good, and as long as we have enough days to satisfy the requirement for an international flight, we can request that you start making arrangements to bring him back to Taiwan. (Of course, the medical team at your end will need to contact the hospital to sort out the details.)

Second, I want to remind you that my father weighs 95 kilos, and he's about 175 cm. Basically, he's fat, and you'll need to make sure to have an extra-large neck brace and so forth. I hope the medical personnel you send over will be able to cope with this tonnage.

Third, the hospital removed my dad's oxygen tank today.

Fourth, regarding the airline tickets for the return trip (how many people will you be sending?), here are copies of my and my mother's (Chang Pao-Chu) tickets, in case that's useful. The fax machines here seem pretty old.

Thank you very, very much for your help!

Our only wish right now is to bring my father safely back to Taiwan as quickly as possible.

Respectfully yours,
Lo Yi-Chin

August 2001

ONE

FALLEN LIGHT

I was strolling with my child along a roadside arcade. This street ran along the very edge of the small town where I'd spent my entire childhood. At the end of the road stood a bridge (fairly old) across Xindian Creek to Taipei. The ground seemed to drop away beneath my feet as I walked, but actually it was the bridge that was rising. Cars, scooters, and buses zoomed past my shoulders, then my head. I kept going. At the end of the arcade were a rundown tire shop, an animal hospital, an old-fashioned convenience store, and so on, and beyond them a high embankment. When we were kids, this was mounds of earth studded with goose-egg pebbles and covered in green moss. Now, the towering gray concrete wall of the highway, impassable to pedestrians, blocked the view of the river and opposite shore. I'd wandered all over this little town as a schoolboy, but never came here (the bridge spanning the divide between our small town and the modern metropolis) because it happened to be in the opposite direction from my daily commute, and hardly any of my schoolmates lived nearby. It was only after I'd moved out and started college that I stumbled upon this arcade on one of my twice-yearly visits (the other side of the road had remained exactly the same). Shop after shop with illuminated billboards such as *Yonghe Soy Milk King* with the usual tour buses outside (ferrying visitors from central and south Taiwan to sample the soy milk, sesame biscuits, and dough fritters?), then the mass incursion on the main road of McDonald's, KFC, Les Enphants, Panasonic, Lee Jeans, Kingstone. At one point, I began to believe this little town I'd spent my entire childhood drifting through would be stretched and pulled higher and wider without limit, reinventing itself constantly through human ingenuity. Japanese-style tar and wood houses replaced by cement buildings, those torn down to make way for condominiums, which in turn disappeared for skyscrapers to take their place. I even imagined this spot on the edge of my little town might one day resemble a street corner in Kowloon's Tsim Sha Tsui or Osaka's Midosuji. Within this tiny space, my futuristic imagination confidently erected fancy hotels, shopping malls, street markets, coffee shops, international banks. . . .

Gazing wide-eyed at the world, I once imagined my body would never stop growing, just as this little town would keep expanding. I didn't expect this firming of its boundaries, stopping its expansion at a certain point (at a mysteriously chosen moment). As if the urban body had produced some polluting cell that caused the whole organism to age and wither, a cancer that attacked and swallowed existing structures. And so on either side of that road, the arcades froze as if from a curse, still sporting placards from some long-ago general election, and the tangle of condominiums grew older and more badly maintained. The rusty aluminum rails of the central divider sprouted political banners and slogans when it came time to vote, but otherwise stood defeated and abandoned.

But why should such a street appear in my dreams, and more than once (though not, of course, in its present form)? In this calm, soporific dream rhythm, underscored by unspeakable anguish, I took the hand of the beloved, vital person next to me, as if I needed them as an eyewitness, and walked down that arcade past shop after shop.

(Look, this is a street I used to walk down during one period of my life.)

(It wasn't always the way you see it now, though it did later tumble irretrievably into decay and destruction.)

Many years ago, I dreamed I was leading my young wife silently past that arcade, though many details have now faded from memory. I felt we'd stumbled into a time before I was born: a dark storm drain (it was night in the dream) instead of the four-lane stream of traffic, clouds of dust on either side. We were in the aftermath of a disaster, an earthquake or typhoon, and more than half the wooden structures making up the arcade had crumbled, while the surviving shops (including a mainland-run breakfast place serving biscuits and fritters from a tar barrel and soy milk from an aluminum kettle) were bustling, the passing crowds silhouetted against the blazing generator-powered lights. A tiny storefront stacked high with enormous watermelons and nothing else lingered in my memory. The tank top-clad shop assistants dashed back and forth across the wooden board that spanned the gutter, with a handcart piled high with melons.

I remember at this moment (in the dream) I nudged my wife, reminding her to pay attention to this detail, a watermelon business from a bygone time.

The other arcade dream, the one with my child, took place closer to my own childhood, not late at night but, I would guess from the light, an hour or two before rush hour on a winter's afternoon. Buses stopped by the side of the road, raising clouds of gray dust that, together with the wheeze of their doors opening, all but brought tears to my eyes.

Into my ear came my father's weary, impatient voice: Son, that's where your dad lived as a little boy.

You could absorb this whole scene in ten seconds, but every shop in the row, every signboard, every shifting detail, every passerby who might well be the descendant of a former acquaintance, even the old place names on the bus-stop signs that had been replaced umpteen times—this street corner in a nonexistent city reconstructed my father's distress and entrapment.

In the dream, I brought the child to a shop, where we stared at a glass case that looked like a claw machine, but missing the mechanical grabber and pile of plush toys. This was bigger and filled with five or six live roosters strutting across a bed of chaff, shaking their bright red combs.

Next door, in a shop that looked like a temple, was an even larger case housing a colorful paper lantern (maybe the technical name is "paper craft"?) in the shape of a rooster, the sort you see on the last day of Spring Festival. Every bit of this creature, from its beak to its tail feathers and claws, was constructed of paper in many colors, glued together to produce a shimmering, ever-changing effect. Before it was a little bronze stove, studded with a few sticks of incense.

"Have they started worshiping roosters around these parts?" I wondered. A ragged old woman at the corner (I'd been about to tell my child those battered boxes in front of the lady were a candy store grab-bag like I'd had as a kid: fifty cents a time for green bean cakes, candied sweet potatoes, *Brother Liu and Brother Wang on the Road in Taiwan*, goldfish-caught-through-ice, chocolate toothpaste . . .) opened her mouth and said, "That's my son, the rooster constellation."

And with a jolt, I woke up.

My mouth was dry, my head ready to split in two. My pillow, blanket, mattress pad, and T-shirt were soaked in sweat, as if I'd been plunged in water.

What just happened? A question floated in my brain, its vagueness tinged with something like regret: how had my mind come up with "That's my son, the rooster constellation"? I ought to have asked: Then where's my son from? What group of stars or celestial being was he originally? What destiny links my child and yours? What creature is my son, if yours is a giant rooster?

At the same time, the melancholy memory of reading *Journey to the West* as a child: the rooster constellation appearing when the Monkey God and his master ventured into the fake Taoist temple conjured up by a demon, where they ingested poisoned tea, leading to an epic battle between Wukong and the false priest, who refused to yield but shrugged off his robes and lifted his arms so a thousand eyes blinked open on his torso, each shooting golden light. I was terrified out of my skin, and even the mighty Wukong was rooted to the spot by the thousand eyes that could "dazzle the eye, and obscure the sun and moon." Finally, Sun Wukong appealed to a bodhisattva for help, and her embroidery needle flew through the air to pierce the creature's eyes. It turned out to be a centipede demon; the needle was forged in the sun eyes of the bodhisattva's son.

Wukong asked, "Who is your son?"

The bodhisattva replied, "My son is the rooster constellation."

Each time I woke up, sadness assaulted me as I panned futilely through the slurry but could not hold on to the fragmentary images in my mind, nor summon any more details. The darkness of that final image, the vastness of the tragedy, was like choking down mercury or paraffin wax and feeling it shift around my body.

Something awful must have happened.

Otherwise that face in the final image, the one that shifted for several seconds before freezing (sometimes it was mine), wouldn't have stared so long at me where I stood beyond the dream, like the shadow lines of a woodblock print.

For a time, I drove a long way every day (my son beside me, strapped into his harness like a fighter jet's ejector seat) across the elevated gray cement highway to the old hospital on Guandu Plain, where we'd visit my father who lay paralyzed, his mind in retreat. As for what that place was called, the remnants of my memory are like pages in an art catalogue I once absentmind-edly flipped through: the mysterious burbling frenzy of man-groves producing future generations beyond the sea wall in the darkness of a moonless night; or the Guandu Forces concealed in some unknown location on this plain in grass-green camou-flage, tanks and trucks stippled in the same green paint; or the tents in front of Guandu Temple housing salted-egg and century-egg vendors, and in the temple a dark tunnel like the one in *Journey to the Center of the Earth*, surrounded by statues of demons and spirits, gods and monsters.

I never thought that someday, like a broken clock, my father would be abandoned in such a building—as if a faraway nuclear explosion had removed the weight of time. Doctors and nurses in stained white uniforms walked distractedly down these cor-ridors, and each ward held a pair of old people lolling in their beds, their bodies twisted and destroyed, entirely without dig-nity, like sullied or damaged chrysalises, stuffed into cell after cell of that gigantic hive.

Much later, I had this thought: during that time of daily driv-ing to the hospital, just me and my two-year-old child, we hardly exchanged a word (at a time when he should have been chattering away, acquiring language skills). I was even careless enough to play cassettes of the most mournful Scottish bagpipe dirges, rather than something more appropriate like nursery rhymes or the alphabet song.

(Could it be that my own father being so cruelly felled left me uncertain how to assume the role of a father in front of you?)

For all I knew, the day might come when my child would ask, "What kind of person was your father?" How would I answer? "Oh, he was a good man." And the same thing would happen to him, when he got to my age. When I was old enough to be asked that question, there ought to have been something pure and beautiful in it, something to stir the soul, but I don't know what happened, time churned and churned, like a rumbling cement mixer flinging me around till my body felt ready to break apart, tumbling uncontrollably in gunk that clung to me and hardened around my limbs. The child would surely forget there'd been a time in his life when every single day, he'd have his hair combed and get dressed up like an imperial courtesan, snoozing as his father drove him a long distance to sing and dance (just for a moment) in front of a dying old man's bed, after which he'd be rewarded with a Anpanman or Baikinman cartoon character lollipop, then stumble blearily back to the car. In this way, I brought my child all the way to visit my father in the hospital, as if we were a wandering father-and-son minstrel troupe, performing our show by his bedside (the lead actor naturally being the two-year-old). "Come, Bai, recite the little mouse poem for Grandpa, quickly now. How does it go? Little mouse . . ."

"Little mouse, climbs the lamp, licks the wick, can't come down. Calls for Dad, Dad won't come, calls for Mom, Mom won't come. Crash and bang, he tumbles down."

"Excellent, give yourself a hand!" (The child applauds himself.)

"Good. Next, Grandpa, Bai will recite a Tang dynasty poem . . ."

"Qingming Festival brings light rain, dead souls roam the earth again. Ask him where an inn is found, the cowherd points to Xinghua Town."

"Give yourself a hand."

"The cow has come, the horse has come, and big sister Chang has also come. The cow has gone, the horse has gone, and big sister Chang has also gone."

"Very good, give yourself a hand."

But gradually, the child grew impatient with the empty pleasure of singing and performing on his own. Like a melting candy, he began to slide from my encircling arms, out of the plastic bedside chair. My father resembled a gigantic overturned lizard, wrinkled eyelids open only a slit, eyeballs darting from side to side. Was he sunk deep in dreams? He was so far gone, those twin eye slits gazed toward the other end of an unimaginably long tunnel. Could he still hear me half coaxing, half forcing my son to continue his awkward recital?

The boy had begun to not recognize this old man, so stuffed full of tubes, like a fossilized crawling bug. (I complained to my wife, in helpless anguish, "See, such a heartless child.") After that, cajoling him to sing and dance by the bedside (at times I wondered whether this was more akin to a Maori battle dance or a child medium writhing to summon spirits) grew harder and harder. Like someone trying to quench thirst with poison, I found myself stopping on the way to the hospital for a Fujiya chocolate lollipop or motorcar candy or other vending machine treat, trying to facilitate the dialogue between grandfather and grandson by the hospital bedside, not just the child stammering impatiently through some Tang poem or childish song, but for him to ask (scripted by me), "Grandpa, what kind of candy can I eat afterward? Grandpa, can I ride the little bee and motorbike?" (Downstairs from the hospital, in front of a flyblown shop, were a couple of kiddy rides that, for ten dollars, would jolt you up and down to a jaunty tune.)

The strange thing was, even sunk in dreams, my father would nod weakly in response to these requests.

One time, I led the child from the old hospital building (after a chaotic performance part threatened, part coaxed out of him), and we stood for a moment in the vicious dry wind outside the automatic doors. For a moment, I couldn't remember where I was, which moment in which journey. (I was standing by a hospital built on a sinking marsh, a building containing a thousand old people, gasping and waiting for death like beached mudskippers.) For the first time, I didn't tell my son no, but brought him to the nearby public park to play. The existence of this green space could only have been some sort of installation or performance art to illustrate life withering away. One by one, Indonesian aides wheeled old people out into the park, lining them up like prehistoric crustaceans basking in the sun. On the stone benches opposite them, piss-soaked elderly vagrants slumbered beneath old newspapers. Throughout this park, the trash cans full to the point of bursting, the stone tables and seats in the pavilion, the paths studded with goose-egg pebbles for foot reflexology, the children's playground with its cement elephant slide and seesaws—everything was covered with sticky black grime that wrecked your mood down to the bottom of your heart. I quickly deduced this was the residue of the urine dribbled by all the people passing back and forth. An absolutely disgusting sight. (One dark night, an old vagrant rouses himself from among his drowsing compatriots, sways his way to the top of the elephant slide, pulls out his filthy dick, and gushes pee down the smooth cement slope.)

My child scurried over to the three playground rides, a motorcar, a seal, and a snail on springs, clambering over each of them in turn. This might have been his one moment of pleasure in the whole dull journey. Next, he dashed to what might be imagined as a castle but was actually a metal structure painted red (like a giant Rubik's Cube). Burrowing into a compartment, he knelt down as if in a real fortress and called out (one of the few bits of dialogue between us during this time that felt authentically father-and-son), "You can't see me, Daddy."

I replied: "Yes, I can't see you, where have you gone?" Just at that moment, I saw another boy, maybe two years older than my child, the only living thing in this park other than us and the old people, swinging energetically as a gibbon across the monkey bars. He spotted my child and swiftly lowered himself down into the metal grid.

My child smiled at this boy in the neighboring segment and said, "You can't see me." The boy stood, eyes spinning in confusion. I tried to explain, "He said you can't see him."

Suddenly, as if to prove that there was nothing but empty air between them (rather than reinforced glass or brick), the other boy punched my child. Without a word, he hit my child's head and smacked his left ear, then yanked his hair so his skull crashed against the metal bar. Before I had time to react or my son could recover from his shock enough to cry out, he'd slithered just as quickly from the metal frame.

In that moment, the complex structure holding up the whole world snapped and crumbled. Like the panther with its ever-morphing body that wanders through dreams taking on their different colors, once every feature has been so deformed from time-travel that it can no longer be recognized, only a gigantic rage can tear through the hardening syrup enveloping its form. I shoved my howling child back into the metal frame behind me, and with my muscles at their most carnivorous and explosive, I sprang forward to tackle the other boy in his hiding place beneath the cement elephant's belly. An anguished lament poured from my mouth, no longer resembling human speech. And then, in front of the old men—stationary as giant chess pieces, as if they'd been petrified by a curse—my fist came down again and again into his flesh, savagely hitting that stranger, that tiny specimen of humanity.

two

ON THE WAY

always hear people (the families left behind after plane crashes, car accidents, or terrorist attacks) say dully: "Yes, that day as he left the house, I noticed the weather was unusually good. If only I'd told him to stay home."

Yes. Because it's sealed off and impossible to express, what ends up being remembered tends not to be the event itself but glimpses from around that time, mouths opening and closing like a silent film, or a 360-degree panorama of the surroundings, astonishing and alluring, every detail of every object visible.

And in the days to come, the film loop plays over and over, gnawing at your remorse and wariness.

I remember how that morning, my elder brother and I gave Father a lift to the meeting point. Father sat beside me in the passenger seat, unable to conceal his excitement, like a fat child about to set off on an expedition.

Over and over, I urged him to be careful, and he made the right noises as if trying to humor me. "No problem, the others in the tour group will take care of me!" On the other hand, he was very insistent that as soon as my brother had some spare time, he should go prune the longan tree in his garden.

As we helped him up the high steps of the tour bus, I saw that the "old people" on board (the agency had informed me most of their clients were elderly) were clearly at least a decade younger than my father. They gazed at us expressionlessly but sternly, as if thinking, "How could they send such a frail old man out of the country on his own?" (Isn't this a bit like that film *The Ballad of Narayama*, where the old lady hikes into the mountains so she won't be a burden on her family?)

At the time, my heart contained only anxiety and frustration. Would he, as had become his habit these last few years, latch on to someone in the group, babbling about old grudges that ought to have been forgotten long ago?

% % %

And just like that, silently, the man who seemed to have lost his wits half a lifetime ago unbelievably "saw" (he couldn't understand that this was sound, making contact with his battered eardrums) amid the vast and gleaming glass screens a faint and distant tremor, like the merest ripple in water, shimmering its way toward him.

Just like that, his eyes perked up, bathed in intense light.

You have no idea what you'll hear when that tone, like the *ching* of a high-quality crystal glass, hits your aural nerves. Or what has happened. At the time, I'd brought my wife—a month away from her due date—and our two-year-old child to the heated indoor pool of the hotel in Hualien where we were staying, all glass walls and domed roof. We'd been planning this trip for a long time (as the first stage of a railway journey through anonymous small towns, though that would never come to fruition). All had been going smoothly, pleasurably. We enjoyed the free buffet breakfast at the hotel restaurant; then my wife suggested we check out the pool.

At the time (later, when telling the story, I'd always mistakenly skip ahead to "And that's when it happened") I was in the water, feeling like I ought to stand up and leave. What was up? I was uneasy, wary, but still I stayed, hands groping in front of me, body submerged. With uncoordinated strokes, I swung my arms and kicked, blowing water off my brow, my nose, my cheeks. I could feel all the joints, muscles, and fat deposits in my body straining and twisting.

Could it really be that nothing had happened?

In my ear was the dull crashing of the water, the murmur of surface tension being broken.

Apart from me, the swimming pool contained only two old people (their torsos disproportionately broad compared to their truncated lower bodies) moving fluidly, their postures correct, as if determined to prove themselves, gliding up and down the fifty-meter length. I thrashed clumsily under the center line as if it were a volleyball net, snorting and twisting my head, jerking upright then gathering my courage to plunge back in, crossing the pool in several bursts.

From time to time, I heard my far-off wife (in her maternity swimsuit), playing with our two-year-old in the elephant-shaped plastic paddling pool. The child giggled shrilly, surprised and delighted each time he plunged into the water at the end of the slide.

Several times I climbed out, sidling awkwardly past the lifeguard in his deck chair. (It had been more than a decade since I'd exposed my sagging middle-aged body to such public scrutiny.) Approaching my wife and child, I saw her focusing the V8 camera, trying to capture our cub splashing away. I stammered, unable to think of any words to share with them, and finally slunk away, shoulders hunched and gut sucked in, jumping back into the water.

I struggled through maybe four or five laps, completely buoyed up by water (it had been many years since this strange sensation of both feet leaving the ground), the stink of chlorine, the joyous light all around me so bright I couldn't open my eyes, the icy oddness of tiles beneath my toes.

Then I said to my wife, "Let's go back upstairs!" I brought the child to the men's changing room, complete with sauna, shower, and spa (the hotel had designed this with the stark, science-fiction feel of an airport corridor lined with equipment). I wiped both our bodies dry with a huge towel, then part cajoled, part forced him to submit to the hair dryer. After wriggling a Q-tip into his ear, I scooped him back into shorts and flip-flops.

We left the pool area to find my wife smilingly waiting for us in the elevator lobby.

Back in our room, the phone was ringing as we walked in. It was my wife's little sister, calling from Taipei. "Where've you been? Why weren't your cell phones on? The travel agency called. Uncle Lo's had a massive brain hemorrhage in Jiujiang. It's serious."

THE CHILD

In Kenzaburō Ōe's *Theories of the Novel*, chapter 9—"The Image System of Fantastic Realism"—he quotes from the section of *The Brothers Karamazov* in which Ivan, tormented by demonic thoughts, says to the saintlike Aloysha, "If children, too, suffer terribly on earth, it is, of course, for their fathers; they are punished for their fathers who ate the apple . . . Listen: if everyone must suffer, in order to buy eternal harmony with their suffering, pray tell me what have children got to do with it? It's quite incomprehensible why they should have to suffer, and why they should buy harmony with their suffering."

In making the point that "mythological saviors frequently appear in the form of a small child," Ōe lists four "preconditions for the infant as divine image": terror of abandonment, lack of enmity, double consciousness, and "the child being the organic combination of life and death."

Let me try to expand on that fourth point. Ōe says, "Children represent the start and finish. They are a new life, a reincarnation, but also an end point—a subliminal part of being alive is you can foresee the state of existence after death. Children are lives that spring from the entirety of the unconscious, and so represent the 'beginning and end.'" This passage fills the reader with terror; it's as unfamiliar as science fiction. It reminds me of this tale from the Qing dynasty compendium, *Close Observations from a Thatched Cottage*: "There was a baby who, as soon as he was born, could speak like an adult and had the eyes of an old man. He spoke vividly about the events of his past life. By the age of four, he'd begun to forget all this, and soon seemed no different from any other child. Some busybody made secret inquiries about the things he'd said as a baby and found that sure enough, there really had been such a family in such a town. Everyone was exactly as described, and when they heard what the visitor had to say, burst into tears. 'Our patriarch died this year,' they sobbed, 'but we never imagined he'd still remember us in his new incarnation.'" I thought of how, in a cemetery in the Sagano Hills to the west of Kyoto, I once came across the grave of a small child and felt a surge of great sorrow from the bottom of my heart.

The death of a child and the death of an old person. The two states of grief these call up rely on two entirely different conceptions of time. The old person's death causes us to mourn the entire landscape of a life, even if this is in the form of an extraordinarily long film reel, screened at high speed. But with the child, it is the innocence that makes us sad, that pure state before its existence changes and grows outward.

When I was first learning to write fiction, I would create drama by having my father die violently in my stories, or else showily bookend a piece with a tale of rescuing him like in a video game (battling my way through demon realms until I could bring his soul back to the world of the living), inserting a turning point into his ridiculous life. In the last few years, my father now so petrified he might as well have been a prehistoric animal, he would cling to me with such stubborn sorrow, meticulously describing a particular memory from this or that period of his life. He even started flipping through my novels and no longer grew furious, as he had just a few years before, that the willful twists and turns of my narration made him appear foolish. (He no longer shared his reminiscences with anyone but me.)

I remember something like confusion and rage brewing inside me: Why was he hurling these memories into the cavern of my soul, like bucket after bucket of nuclear waste? What about my own life, the years slipping away like water? All the people I'd known in my youth?

In this way, I prematurely took on the role of "the child who saves his father" in my stories. Then the day came when it happened in reality, with the old man and the unconscious child switching positions. I really would have to hurry to a strange city to bring my father back. My wife was a month away from giving birth. Like muttering the words of an incantation to preserve ourselves, my mother and I each bought emergency coverage worth eight million at the airport. (If something happened to me abroad, as it had to my father, neither my two-year-old nor the fetus in my wife's belly would be capable of strapping on a rucksack, as I was doing now, and coming to my rescue.)

What did it mean to "rescue my father"? (Was I Mulian, banging on the gates of hell armed with nothing but hope and a monk's staff?) I felt as if I were frantically trying to save a flickering film projector from a steadily sinking ship, a piece of machinery so outmoded the images it sent out were yellowish and moldy, giving off an ominous scorched stench as if it might stop working at any moment.

There was no backup. The reel, the projector, the cinema, and every single event in the film would be completely destroyed as soon as the screening was over.

I imagine that's the sensation of "a child rescuing his father." He'd be unwilling to believe that the end was arriving, that we were on the very last reel.

RECEIPTS

An entire bag of receipts. We'd checked the lucky draw serial numbers, but none of them had won. Usually they'd go straight into the bin after this (lines and lines of numbers, shriveled as if coated with anthrax). I kept several of them in order to have a record of the date, or the address of the shop, or the goods we'd bought, picking them out of the pile with infinite grief and tenderness.

The first one was dated August 15th, 7:27 p.m., from the parking lot at Taipei train station, for $50 (an hour's stay).

The second was dated August 16th, 9:38 a.m., from Zhengxing Convenience Store, for I-Mei real fruit juice gummy sweets (grape flavor), three bottles of H_2O water, AirWaves ultra-cool chewing gum, Wishing beef jerky, Triko lychee coconut jelly, and two packets of Takoaka seaweed.

These are the lines of motion captured in those frozen moments: the first thing we did was rush to Taipei train station to buy a ticket to Hualien on the Ziqiang line early the next morning (an express route with only three stops). But after struggling through traffic jams on Zongxiao West, Zhengzhou Road, and Chongqing North, we finally made it to the parking lot on the west side of the train station and stumbled clumsily through the empty foyer, child in tow, only to have the counter clerk inform us they only sold tickets for the day of travel, and we'd need to call to book advance tickets. So, absurdly, we found a phone booth in the vastness of that building and dialed 104 to ask directory inquiries for the ticket hotline.

In a rage, I abruptly decided we should drive to Hualien (damn the railways and their trunk lines). The next morning, before setting off down Beiyi Freeway, I stopped off at Zhengxing for snacks to keep me alert while driving.

The third receipt was dated August 16th, 3:28 p.m., from Taroko Convenience Store, for Cartier Ultra-Mild 0.1 cigarettes, a two-liter bottle of More Water, a pack of balloons, Wei Lih instant ramen (spicy dandan flavor), Jin Jin cartoon chewy candy, a Kabuchi strawberry lollipop, a Shengxiangzhen fruit bar (tangerine flavor), Tai Bu angelica duck noodles, a can of Heineken, dried mango strips from the Philippines, and a tube of Pringles (sour cream and onion flavor).

That's a complete representation of our state of mind after six hours heading down first Beiyi then Suhua Freeway, stopping for a break just before Taroko Gorge. That jumble of bright-packaged snacks is exactly what a couple of young parents with limited finances would buy to pacify their son before bringing him inside a fancy hotel that they themselves didn't feel comfortable in, trying to create a sort of holiday atmosphere, as well as the petty consideration of making sure we had enough food for dinner and bar snacks rather than subjecting ourselves to the no doubt inflated prices of a mountain resort.

The fourth receipt was dated August 16th, 3:29 p.m., a minute after the previous one, from the same shop, for a mini bottle of Choya plum wine. Just what you'd expect from a man who'd gotten into the car with a bag full of snacks, only to turn to his wife and mutter, "We should try to relax—let's have a couple of drinks tonight," then bolt back to the refrigerated cabinet.

The fifth receipt was a day later, 1:08 p.m., from the same store, for a bottle of Canbet 200P, three bottles of H_2O water, a fresh cream baumkuchen, and AirWaves ultra-cool chewing gum.

Could an onlooker deduce the vast transformation that had taken place between this receipt and the previous one? That we'd received a phone call and learned that my father was in danger, that I'd called home to comfort my mother and decided to head back to Taipei, so the next day my mother and I could get the first plane to Jiangxi (the travel agency was helping us sort out tickets and travel permits)? After hurriedly checking out, I still needed to bring my pregnant wife and child safely on that winding, dangerous mountain road, to get us through the next six or seven hours.

I remember those hours like sleepwalking, as I took great swerves along those tight bends, enormous trucks honking at us from time to time. Everything ahead of me looked gray, drained of color. The gray chimneys of a gray cement factory, gray roads, and the gray sea in the distance.

Exhausted, I clung to the steering wheel, turning left, turning right, navigating along the white painted lines of that narrow cliff road, unable to see through the gloom, only one thought circling around in my head: *Father, who'd have thought this is how I enter your time of death, in such a joyless spiral.*

※ ※ ※

As time passed, the event of "Father collapsing with a loud thud" transformed from the sharp blow of "Father's sudden illness in a distant place, which we heard about while vacationing in the eastern hills" into a complicated, drawn-out series of scenes. But I still retain the first, simplest memories of this event, driving through an endless gray fog, so dizzy I wanted to throw up. In this image, the lines of my face are stiff, as if I'm trying to resist a strong urge to sleep. (Keep turning, turning.) In the back seat, my wife wrapped her arms around her protruding belly, while our son slumbered like someone had flicked his off switch. I couldn't see their faces.

"Stay awake, dammit," I muttered to myself.

Finally we arrived in Su'ao Township. More grayness: the metal towers of the cement company, the industrial chimneys, the heaps of lime and gravel. Away from the hills, my phone recovered its signal, and calls came in one by one. First my sister, asking where we were. Then my mother-in-law—my wife began sobbing in the back seat as they talked—and then my sister again, letting me know my brother couldn't find his Hong Kong visa and mainland travel permit, and the travel agency wanted to know if mine were still valid. My wife and I struggled to remember; my Hong Kong visa was fine, but the travel permit was in a safe deposit box (it had been five or six years since we'd been to China) and the bank was closed for the weekend—but we needed to leave for Nanchang first thing in the morning. We'd have to find another way. My sister called the travel agency again, then called back to say our brother had decided to stay put (to take care of our grandmother). As for me, Mr. Chen from the agency said I could get a travel permit on arrival at Hainan Island. Or perhaps Mr. Chen would come with Mother and me to Hong Kong, and then the two of them would get the noon flight to Nanchang while I'd go to Hainan for my visa-on-arrival before catching the four o'clock to Nanchang. That was how we left it. I asked my sister how our mother was doing and she said not too bad, she was being very strong.

Just as we were entering Yilan City, my wife's little sister called to say they (my mother-in-law, her uncle, and she) had just been to the Yonghe house to see my mother (her condolences, she added), and they'd given her five thousand dollars. Apparently, Mother was unable to speak two sentences without bursting into tears. My sister-in-law wanted my wife to make sure I had plenty of medicine on me, plus everyone's phone numbers, spare clothes in my carry-on, and American dollars. She worried that Mother might be fragile and confused, and besides, we didn't know the situation on the mainland. (Later, at the airport, Mother would open her bag to show me its contents: a copy of the *Diamond Sutra*, the *Sutra of Ksitigarbha Bodhisattva*, water and blanket of Great Compassion, a set of Father's clothes—to wear in his coffin?—and a black-and-white passport photo of him, as well as a piece of sandalwood to ward off evil. Also the things she needed for herself: a few changes of clothes and kneepads.)

So we went into a Watsons on Yilan High Street and bought a dozen pairs of disposable underwear and socks, travel toothpaste and toothbrush, Panadol cold tablets, Seirogan digestive pills, a box of headache pills, bandages, plus rehydration salts for heatstroke. I also grabbed some Centrum multivitamins.

(Perhaps Mother and I were in silent agreement in our refusal to imagine the duration of this trip—whether its purpose was to deal with Father's remains or to witness his miraculous recovery—in terms of the number of days Mother had taken off work or the time till my wife's delivery date, but it surely wouldn't be much more than a week, ten days at most. Of course, things would turn out to be far more complicated than we'd imagined.)

Then my wife suddenly remembered her sister-in-law had once told her about a fifty-year-old food stall with the most delicious rice vermicelli and pork broth noodles, down an alleyway off the very street we were driving on. We turned onto the alley, which was crammed full of people hawking plastic stools; pots and stainless steel woks; plastic buckets full of roses, sunflowers, lilies, and pale purple bellflowers; all kinds of fruits; incense;

and hell money for the dead. We parked in front of an after-school center, by the end of an arcade building, and found the narrow old noodle shop. An elderly couple stood before a pot of boiling water, swirling noodles with bamboo ladles, while a colorful assortment of pig innards lay on the aluminum counter. My wife ordered some vermicelli and pork noodles, plus some shark meat, starchy sausage, and lung membrane. The shop barely occupied nine square meters, which fit just three folding tables. Sitting around us were men and women the same age as the stall owners, in their seventies.

I've always wanted to find a simple mathematical structure to delineate the light and shade of my separate worlds, to fully describe the fractured state of being a son to my father and mother and a husband to my wife and in-laws. But then I realized my prime years had been spent wandering around this crowded city, searching for scenes from other people's memories or the "former existences" they'd describe to me, proffering evidence. And just like that, my days had flashed past. Then suddenly Father collapsed in the middle of his vacation. Once again I found myself among elderly folk speaking a different language to Father, unable to join in but completely understanding what they were saying. I sat there, feeling shaky. Directly opposite the noodle stall was a half-built student activity center in the yard of an elementary school, reaching toward the sky. Blue-and-white striped canvas hung off the scaffolding, rustling as the wind filled it. Two laborers in white hard hats sat bare-chested, high up on a protruding bit of metal girder, turning a blowtorch on something. From this distance, the intense blue and white flame seemed to quickly shatter into tiny red sparks, scattering toward the ground. I remember when I was a child, whenever we walked by metalworkers by the roadside with their welding masks, pointing a flame at some window frame or bit of machinery, Mother would always tell me to turn my face away, not allowing me to look into the brightness, "otherwise you'll get glaucoma." As if suddenly thinking of something, I now told my son to look away, rather than gazing like me with curiosity at the far-off fires guttering in those tiny hands.

This scene was both familiar and foreign. The old people around us chatted happily, comfortably (so certain this place was their hometown), their voices full of childlike wonder and mischief, their words jabbing back and forth, refusing to settle into a background hum. I remembered how I'd almost agreed to write a regular newspaper column and came up with a plan to produce a year's worth of content: each week, I'd board a train with no destination in mind, get off at a random station, and describe my impressions of the small town, quaint as a black-and-white photo or woodcut print. Then the column evaporated into thin air, and I never got to put the plan into action.

I was about to embark on a long journey. I couldn't stop thinking that this was a farewell dinner with my wife and son. Perhaps I would soon be the head of this little clan. But what did that even mean? I felt I ought to say something to my wife, like "When I'm not around . . ." or "Be sure to take care of yourself," or "When you move back in with your parents, try not to fight with so-and-so," or be on time for your obstetrician appointments, or when you go into labor, don't forget to ask my brother to feed our dog Niuniu, or could you help me phone these people and tell them what happened. . . . All these little things. Several times I opened my mouth, but stopped myself. My wife quietly lifted greasy noodles with her chopsticks from the broth with fried shallots floating on its surface, wound them into a clump, and encouraged our bleary-eyed child to take small mouthfuls. Her belly was enormous. Now and then, she'd dab a corner of the child's mouth with a pink napkin, then rub at the soup stains on her bulging maternity dress. The three of us must have appeared helpless and scruffy sitting in that dark little shop (with old people all around us).

Yet I no longer felt part of this scene, because something fatal had happened, and although my journey hadn't started yet, I'd prematurely gotten on the road, no way to turn back, my body already inhabiting other scenarios, incomplete from lack of understanding and perception.

ON THE WAY

This wasn't how I'd imagined my father's death.

Crowds moving like goblins through the sunlit streets. Hunched over three-wheeled scooters. Women in inexpensive summer dresses, showing off tanned shoulders, legs, and bellies. Fruit stalls. Oddly shaped melons. Piles of coconuts, husked and looking like ostrich eggs. One kilogram of Asian pears for one-fifty, of grapes for one-sixty. More variation between these fruits than in the bare arms and cleavage on display in the street, or the faces of men on the prowl.

The road was straight as a runway, and for a long time I saw no taxis other than the one we were in. Coconut groves swayed on either side, but you couldn't tell what lay beyond them. This was the highway from the airport, forcing its way through the jungle. No turnoffs, no traffic lights. Lonely, unbending, monotonous, forging straight ahead.

The sun blazed hot enough to melt rubber, but our driver, in his pale blue and white Hawaiian shirt, refused to turn on the air conditioning. Two speakers blared behind Mother and me, lashing the backs of our heads with a treacly, unctuous tune (hard to imagine) imitating Teresa Teng's nasal voice, "Three hundred and sixty-five days are so hard to get through, if I'm not in your heart. Return my true love to me . . ."

Haikou Airport on Hainan Island, a border crossing. My travel permit had expired, and there hadn't been time to get a new one in Hong Kong, so Mr. Chen from the tour company (the same one that organized Father's vacation) decided at the last minute to fly from Hong Kong to Hainan (where it was possible to get one on arrival). But when we got to the drab counter (which reminded me of the military police outpost in a corner of Taichung Railway Station years ago) before immigration and went through the paperwork with a man and woman in People's Liberation Army uniforms, we found that none of us had any Chinese money to pay the hundred-yuan administration fee. My money pouch held only crisp American hundreds, changed earlier at Taoyuan Airport. Finally we decided that Mr. Chen would go through customs and come back with renminbi for us. A complicated and tedious process, but there was no way to skip it.

I found myself thinking: *We're journeying to the scene of a death. Right now, Father is in a dilapidated hospital in some strange, distant town, all alone, slowly dying. Yet unlike in an actual nightmare, we have no way of jumping straight to the next scene.* No way to avoid the exhausting, byzantine bureaucracy. We had to get on the plane and tell the smiling stewardess no thank you, I don't want a meal, out one gate, in another, a standby ticket, changing money, waiting forever in a departure lounge for our next flight as the air conditioning sucked every drop of moisture from our bodies.

Earlier, as we'd sat in silence on the plane, a time machine bringing us to Father's death, some kids flung rubber balls with a glowing red light inside them toward the back rows; in front of us, a mainland businessman got out his cell phone and began an animated conversation; a whole line of people stood squashed in the aisle, waiting for the bathroom, just like any public toilet (at least no one lit a cigarette). The stewardess appeared, handing out packets of beef jerky like the sort I used to get from the convenience store as a kid, a dollar a packet (my playmates told me it was pickled tree bark). Everything felt like I was a child again, accompanying Father (still in the prime of life) on a long bus ride. We'd hoped to quickly get through the blank span of time in the middle, but a gentle female voice came over the airport public address system: "We regret to inform you that due to mechanical failure, the flight originally scheduled to depart for Beijing via Nanchang has been delayed, and will now leave at seven-thirty." So we'd be there a whole seven hours.

Mr. Chen took us in a taxi to dinner at a Haikou City restaurant (to burn away those extra hours, sprung from nowhere). The blue-floral-shirted driver, possibly Indonesian, laid siege to us in that overheated, loud interior (after Teresa Teng came an even more incongruous folk song, "The maidens of Ali Hill are beautiful as the lake . . . ee-yah-na-lu-he-hai-ya . . .") with his chatter, but was summarily and rather overbearingly shut down by Mr. Chen. That probably put the guy in a temper, which might be why, as we sped down that blinding, arrow-straight, deserted road to the city, he pointed at a military food truck in the next lane and announced, "Look, getting ready for war." "What do you mean?" Mr. Chen snapped. "Like our government said," came the reply, "Taiwan can't be independent. If they try, we'll whack them."

The taxi sped past the restaurant Mr. Chen had named, but our driver refused to stop. "This one won't do, it's no good at all." He said he'd bring us somewhere he knew, guaranteed to be delicious. And from god knows where, I found an enormous surge of rage, my voice coarsening into a roar: "He said stop, so stop. Why are you still driving?"

I'd thought Mr. Chen would send him away and we'd get another taxi back (his frustration and rage as he squabbled with the driver had left me certain he was staunchly pro-Taiwanese independence), but instead they launched into another fevered round of bargaining, finally deciding that for an additional fifty yuan, the driver would wait for us. To be honest, as Mr. Chen led the two of us into the restaurant, which had a mirror on each wall with a carved, gilt-painted frame, the sympathy with which he'd approached us in the arrivals hall ("Mrs. Lo? Such a terrible thing to happen. We're all so sorry . . ."), that expression calibrated for grieving families (or widows?), solemn and restrained, filled with some sort of tension, suddenly seemed overcooked, sodden, and spongy, ready to fall apart. The restaurant was completely empty apart from us, the heavily fragranced air carrying a hint that this place might be the closest this impoverished town could come to sultry charm. But how greasy the tabletops were, how dim the lights. Mr. Chen seemed to be a regular here. The waitresses roused themselves from afternoon naps, peeping out from behind screens or rising from pulled-together chairs, smoothing their wrinkled stockings beneath their high-slit cheongsams. One of them slinked over. "Oh dear, Mr. Chen, it's been *such* a long time since you've come to see us." The sort of girls I could imagine bewitching American GIs during the Vietnam War, so cheap and yet so beautiful. Plucked from their previous jobs selling rotten fruit from a street stall, their young frames still unused to these close-fitting dresses, well-cut bodices and tight skirts or flapping cheongsams that revealed their legs. And beneath these garments were immature bodies, still reeking of little girl, obediently submitting to the unequal demands of capitalism and allowing their placid limbs to writhe wantonly.

I slowly pieced together how they were connected: Mr. Chen, the driver in the Hawaiian shirt, these girls in uniform. Each of them hated and despised the others. But there was also a sort of crude acceptance of fellow sufferers. This flyblown restaurant, the taxi that refused to turn on its air conditioning, the perpetually delayed plane—to Mother and me, these were just a dreamscape, the people in it no more than props scattered around each setting. But to Mr. Chen, they were family. He had to keep reliving this nightmare, returning every month or two to see them again. He wearily ordered more than ten dishes (although Mother kept protesting that neither of us had any appetite at all), and we watched in silence as he chewed through those great plates of shrimp and shellfish, washing them down with ice-cold local beer. The lines of his face settled into pure rage, and he kept calling over the long-limbed girls. "How long ago was this chicken cooked? It's rancid." (They apologized indifferently.) Each dish was discarded after a few mouthfuls. I grew agitated, watching him putting on airs to destroy his opponents. The man who, in Taoyuan Airport, had appeared mundane and middle-aged from every angle was completely puffed up by some unseen energy. He told us, "I've been cheated too many times by mainlanders." But by that point, I'd stopped listening.

※ ※ ※

With this delay, my congealed grief stretched out, staring blankly, killing time.

I recalled the day before, rushing home from Hualien after hearing the bad news. On the Xiaogetou stretch of Beiyi Freeway (just after Pinglin district), we turned onto a little road winding through the hills down to the Wutu Caves. In the past (about ten years ago, I guess), when Father's legs were still strong enough, he used to like walking up this road from the caves and resting at an Earth God temple along the way. I made the trek with him quite a few times. He'd point at the slopes above and say a local had told him if you followed this road all the way to the top, you'd reach Beiyi Freeway.

When I passed the Earth God temple this time, I stopped the car and told my wife and son to wait while I squeezed myself into the dilapidated little building, no bigger than a sedan chair, and lit three sticks of incense. Three Earth God figures smiled up at me from the altar (strange not to have the usual trinity of Fortune, Prosperity, and Longevity, but the same deity in triplicate).

I remember walking out of the temple, sitting at the foot of the slope, and lighting a cigarette, muttering possibly to myself and possibly to these three low-level gods, old acquaintances of my father's, "Now I'm just a fatherless child."

THE TOUR GUIDE

It was very late by the time we got to the hospital. Changing planes, getting a visa at Hainan Island, a delayed flight . . . and when we finally got to Nanchang's Changbei Airport, it was still another two hours' drive to Jiujiang. The travel agency's local office sent a newish air-conditioned nine-seater van to meet us. It was only later that I found out our driver was the agency boss, and the middle-aged woman next to him was the tour guide who'd led the group up Mount Lu. My first impression was that these two mainlanders were putting on a good front, warmly saying things like, "My god, what a thing to happen, you must be worried to death," "What a long journey you've had, you must have left Taiwan first thing in the morning," "No question about it, as soon as the old gentleman finds out his wife and son came all this way to see him, it will do him a world of good. Maybe he'll be on his feet and walking around by tomorrow." After all that fruitless waiting at the airport, all that time without any updates about Father's condition (all we had was the travel company's notification from the day before: massive cerebellar hemorrhage, critical condition), all those things stuffed into my mother's rucksack—copies of the *Pure Land Rebirth Dhāraṇī*, blanket, purified water, temple chimes, sandalwood, black-and-white passport photo of my dad—ready for use at his funeral, encountering such kindness and sympathy from strangers in a foreign land was almost enough to move me to tears. Though perhaps we appeared silent and sinister by contrast, the unknowable, rapidly approaching reality of death having left us fearful and adrift.

I looked out the minibus window at the deep, still dark. This was completely unlike the highway and bright streetlamps on the way from Taipei airport. You had no idea what was lurking in this blackness your eyes couldn't penetrate. I wanted to prize more information about my father from these two mainlanders (Is he conscious? Is there any hope? How are the medical facilities here? Will he need surgery? Can you people even carry out brain surgery? What happened? How did an artery in his brain burst just like that?) but I quickly realized that their polite words were just words—they were actually terrified to have had something like this happen on their watch.

In a place where the rule of law wasn't clearly demarcated, the calculations and conflict of human interaction relied on a primeval yet intricate system of connections and power differentials (threats accompanied by a smiling face, socializing and bonding, stuffing alcohol or cigarettes into someone's hands, or else the chaos of arbitration); in this harsh, untamed nation, the urgent treatment of a dying old man (a Taiwanese compatriot) might not be as much of a priority as how to receive his Taiwanese family without angering them (which would set in motion a complex legal system they had no means of navigating). Of course, this only became clear to me much later on, from the ridiculous situations I found myself in when I actually had to interact with them.

The middle-aged woman looked quick-witted and dignified, and spoke with confidence, reminding me of certain principals and teachers I'd had in elementary school, generally recent immigrants from the mainland with round faces and large eyes, whose low, hoarse voices sounded like they'd spent a long time training themselves to eliminate every last trace of femininity from their speech. They had a solid quality that indicated loyalty, but also lacked a sense of humor. Their taste in clothing was generally middle-of-the-road, in dark shades that made the people around them feel melancholy for reasons they couldn't pinpoint. This type of human being was slowly approaching extinction in my city. Who would have thought that so many years later, I'd encounter a specimen in this distant land, as if in a dream or something out of time?

She said, "The elder Mr. Lo" (this also felt like something in a dream—how long had it been since I'd heard someone refer to him like that?) "has quite a temper! My god, he's lying there screaming at everyone. Cursing the doctors, saying what kind of treatment is this, he's dying of pain. Scolding his son and nephews" (my father's son and nephews from his mainland family, all elderly now. My half-brother and four cousins had come from Nanjing to Jiujiang to see my father, and in fact some of the cousins only arrived on the day of the incident, on the river ferry). "He was shouting, 'Help me up, help me get dressed, I want to go home!' When I tried to talk him out of it, he punched me.

"The elder Mr. Lo is so well educated. We went to a gallery of Bada Shanren paintings, and he told us all about them, as if they were his own family heirlooms. Then at Chiang Kai-Shek's and Chou En-Lai's villas, wow! He regaled us with anecdotes from their lives. Even the college student who was taking us around hadn't heard some of them before."

In the dark, I was blushing to the tips of my ears and almost let out a moan of pain. Before my eyes appeared the image of my father, like a broken wind-up toy, spouting off in public whether or not it was of interest to anyone. (Like when I brought him to that Picasso exhibit, or at the post office, or on the bus, all those moments he'd made me so embarrassed I wanted to die.)

FIRST ENCOUNTER

Although we'd been chatting and laughing on the way, as our minibus approached the People's Hospital, everyone fell silent. To this day I have no recollection of what the city looked like by night, between the highway turnoff and the hospital entrance. It was like something from a fairy tale, wobbling along dizzyingly on a little raft paddled by water sprites, so dark I couldn't see my hand before my face, only hearing the splash of oars until we finally reached the King of Hell's palace (where my father was bound in iron chains).

The harsh headlights hit a tall metal gate, and a guard came running out, shielding his eyes with both hands. He yelled at the driver in the local dialect, and the travel company boss yelled back, then muttered, "Fuck it." He yanked the gearshift, reversed, and with a mighty swing of the wheel, turned the vehicle toward the hospital's other entrance. The guard there drowsily opened the gate for us.

⁂

It was almost midnight, a good seven or eight hours later than our planned arrival time, and the hospital lay in darkness. At the last minute, the guide bragged that she knew a heart surgeon at some hospital in Nanchang, and if necessary she could ask him about getting "the elder Mr. Lo" transferred there for his procedure. (Were the facilities here inadequate?) My mother and I naturally expressed abundant gratitude. Under cover of darkness, we tried to stuff an American hundred-dollar bill into the hand of Mr. Chen (from the Taiwanese travel company), but he firmly refused. "Spend your money on the surgery. We can work something out back in Taiwan." Remembering past experiences traveling on the mainland, I shrewdly asked if we ought to give the locals a few hundred yuan. He thought about it seriously, with the typical pose of a highly ranked employee, and said, "Not yet. Let's wait till we really need their help." I began to dimly sense that we were about to face a large tangle of trouble, with many blockages to be cleared. He was reminding me that each of these would need to be carefully negotiated, and we couldn't allow ourselves to be flayed willy-nilly, or they'd see us as fat lambs ready for the slaughter.

He said, "Wait till you see the attending physician, and give him a hundred American dollars (no less than that). When they've confirmed which surgeon is going to carry out the operation, give him a hundred too. Don't waste your money on the others."

The minibus stopped by the terrace of an old building. The old men seated there rose and walked toward us, looking solemn and anxious. I recognized one of them: my eldest brother, Yiming. Then one by one, my cousins Fourth Brother, Second Brother, Third Brother.

Yiming took my luggage from the van (embarrassingly, this contained *A Hundred Years of Solitude*, the collected poems of Borges, a wad of disposable underwear, and socks) and said, "Little Brother." And then, in the same thick accent, "Mom."

This was their first encounter. I thought: *So this is how it happens.* That's when I realized my mother, who'd been so steadfastly calm all this way, even leaning over to murmur a joke or two to me, had now, in the chilly night air, suddenly turned into a feeble, white-haired old lady.

"Hi," she said, which was enough of an answer for this eldest son she hadn't given birth to, whom she was meeting for the first time decades into his life. (Also, there had been some unpleasantness over buying a house a while ago, and they were still a little wary of each other.)

Everyone kept their head down. It felt like we were wandering through a forest at night as dappled shadows fell over us, though actually they were from a faulty flickering fluorescent light (believe me, the whole thing felt as if we'd gone back decades to something from my dad's youth, to some ramshackle army tent or a grimy office at the Ministry of Food or the town hall of some obscure little place) as we walked awkwardly and anxiously into an extraordinarily slow elevator.

※ ※ ※

A first encounter full of misunderstandings. The overture to complete disaster. Misguided hopes and imaginings. Each side knew nothing at all about how the other had lived for the long period of time before our meeting, and so we used the moment of our meeting, almost a ritualized performance, as an opportunity to take these extraneous emotions and gingerly fill in the blanks of our mutual understanding.

It's hard for me not to describe our first meeting with the mainland family in this way. Many years ago, I'd had this thought: sooner or later, my mother would meet this "son" a decade younger than she, whose birth mother was still alive (the peculiar ethical drama triggered by my father's flight from China during the great retreat of 1949). Yet I'd never imagined it would be under these circumstances.

According to the two mainlanders who met us at the airport, when the tour group got down from Mount Lu the night before the incident, my brother and one of the cousins were already waiting at the hotel (having come on the boat from Nanjing for this reunion with my father in Jiujiang). Apparently my father was delighted, urging them to come eat with the group and booking them a room. Later that night, he stayed chatting in their room for hours before heading back to his. ("Could he have gotten overexcited at being reunited with his family?" asked the tour guide.) Early the next morning, for reasons that remained unclear, perhaps because he couldn't sleep, he got up and had a cold shower (a habit he'd had for decades), and that's when the artery in his brain burst. His roommate (another old man from the tour group) was awakened by an enormous thud and found my father, stark naked and soaking wet, flat out on the carpet.

A strange, dark mood slowly grew between my mother and me in the back seat of the van as it rumbled along.

I wonder what that brother of yours said to your dad? Mother murmured in my ear.

In the early nineties, my father returned for the first time to Jiangxin Island in Nanjing. I heard that a provincial secretary accompanied him onto the ferry in an army jeep. As soon as they landed, the firecrackers started going off nonstop ("Like land mines," my father later said). This moved him unbearably, my father who was already retired and slowly becoming a decrepit old man. Of his playmates from a half century ago, only a few old men remained. Father attended three or four banquets every single day, as if to flaunt his generation's long-ago splendor before the island's youngsters, who'd grown ignorant of why these old men deserved respect. Around this time, my brother Yiming, who'd been left fatherless before the age of one (when my father abandoned his wife and son and fled to Taiwan) and spent half his life suffering the stain of being the "son of a Kuomintang agent" and "son of an overseas traitor," and in one struggle session after another, been made to confess and self-criticize for being one of the "Five Black Categories," a rightist—all of a sudden, he went from being one of the island's grape farmers to, by public proclamation, a member of the "Chinese People's Political Consultative Conference, Yuhuatai district."

I have no idea what he thought of this old man, his father, who'd descended into his life out of the blue after more than fifty years.

In the following years, every time my father wanted to "go back," my mother would glumly go to the bank and get the gold chains and bracelets from her deposit box, which she took to a jeweler to be melted down and turned into ten to twenty rings. Then she'd get some American dollars. She grumbled constantly, but would put on her glasses and carefully label which rings were for Yiming's wife, for Jinfang, for the families of Number Two and Number Three and Number Four . . . with molten gold, she took my father's pension and turned it into remittance, so he could rise from the River Styx, into which he'd vanished fifty years ago, and appear before those sorrowful survivors like a god showering gold upon them.

※ ※ ※

The doors opened. The doors shut. This elevator moved slowly, so slowly I'd begun to suspect this whole thing—including my father holding on for us in this desolate, spooky hospital to breathe his last (the image I had in my head the whole time), my mother and me rushing here (as if, impatient to find out how the story ended, we'd flipped ahead to the final pages of the book), standing in an elevator with these old men who now seemed suddenly bashful to find themselves in such close quarters with us—this whole thing seemed too much like a bad joke, a prank whose shoddiness revealed itself in the many details that were just too deliberate.

I wanted to tell myself: I will remember all of this clearly. And yet, I forgot plenty of things almost immediately, because this all felt too much like a dream. Perhaps the dream of an insect who didn't have a linear concept of time. As I stepped out of the elevator like a sleepwalker among these sad, silent relative strangers, down that pitch-dark corridor (later, I learned that the hospital had been shutting down the elevators at night to save electricity; it was only because this gravely ill Taiwanese compatriot's family was arriving that they'd made an exception and left one running), I was already finding that I couldn't recollect all the miscellaneous things that had happened to us en route, as if they'd been peeled from my memory like mold scraped off a wall after the rainy season.

It felt like being in a meticulously crafted film, in which every scene maintained the same atmosphere and mood. As we walked down the dark corridor, on either side of us, as if this were a wartime field hospital, were withered old people on stretchers (they hadn't managed to get beds) who gazed at our group with suspicion and curiosity. Through the open doors were equally gloomy rooms, and as if in a movie tracking shot, one old man after another, shirtless in blue-and-white striped pajama pants, turned to stare at us from where they sat at the feet of their beds, waving reed fans.

Walking into my father's room (finally, the actual room), we found him lying in the center bed shirtless (the electricity saving also involved no air conditioning, which left the rooms extraordinarily hot and stuffy). At first glance, his face seemed disproportionately large (just like, as a kid, when I saw Generalissimo Chiang in his coffin on our black-and-white TV and couldn't help wondering why his head was so huge. It seemed to take up half the space in his coffin. Had the rest of his body been folded away, like a quilt?) and dark purple, almost black. Out of one of his nostrils came a clear tube that passed through a bubbling glass vessel to a rust-stippled oxygen cylinder the size of an industrial gas tank. Mother and I said to him: "We're here. Don't be scared."

(With the specter of death looming, it wasn't clear if we were saying, "Go in peace," or "Don't be frightened, everything will be fine now that we're here.")

Agitated, my father shut his eyes and let his mouth fall open, his plump arms scrabbling in the air like a baby trying to hug its mom. Perhaps because the part of his brain controlling his limbs was still damaged, all he managed to grab was my mother's T-shirt collar, exposing her bra. I timidly shot a glance at those old men, my cousins, and they stolidly turned their blank faces aside.

The other two beds were occupied by locals who'd also suffered brain injuries: an elderly man whose son and daughter-in-law (or maybe daughter and son-in-law) were sitting sadly by his bed, and a young guy with a gaping mouth and staring eyes whose three or four visitors gave off a strong whiff of thuggishness (over the next few days, I would quickly realize that their faces were from the same mold as the shirtless, thick-browed, and large-eyed desperadoes who roamed the streets of this city in packs). For a moment, I thought we'd gotten lucky—didn't these two patients look worse off than Father? Their faces were like fish in a supermarket chiller, frozen solid in a final moment of shock. My father only looked like a sleeping child in the grip of a nasty dream.

All of us barging in at once seemed to plunge the other visitors into the darkness, from where they could watch this performance on a brightly lit stage.

THE HUNCHBACK

Across the road from the hospital was a row of two-story concrete buildings. The ground floor was made up of little restaurants, although "restaurants" might be too grand a name: each consisted of a huge wok over an open flame, a trough for rinsing, various fruits and vegetables laid out on a chopping board, and whatever space they'd claimed on the sidewalk outside, where they would place three or four wooden tables and benches that didn't match. Each dingy interior couldn't have taken up more than four ping, 13 square meters, room for only one table and chairs, which felt like the proprietor's home furniture: laden with leftover food and the children's homework, the screen of an old TV set flashing blurrily above. The one time I made an effort to watch the program, it turned out to be the 1960s anime *Kimba the White Lion*.

On our side of the road, by contrast, was a line of fruit stalls aimed at hospital visitors, though the quality of the fruit was uneven and the prices were about the same as in the average market (or perhaps we weren't as sensitive as the locals to a difference of one or two yuan). Apples and pears were two yuan per kilo, grapes three, and peaches also two. These locally grown, freshly harvested fruits were large and sweet but unevenly sized, and the bruised or damaged ones were left to attract flies. Some imported varieties were very expensive. Sunkist oranges from California were four or five yuan per kilo, and so were monkey peaches (what we call kiwi fruit). A rack at the back of each stall displayed gift boxes of powdered lotus root, oat milk, black sesame pudding, and so on, as well as Wahaha mineral water for one-sixty a bottle. Every stall handed over your fruit in crappy plastic bags that tore apart at the slightest tug, unlike the ones outside Taiwanese hospitals where everything cost a fortune and the fruits gleamed beneath sheets of plastic and packing paper, looking like they'd never go bad.

On the other side of the hospital gate was a cigarette kiosk that looked like a bus ticket booth. Packets of various brands were laid out in an acrylic case, all in striking colors: peach pink, scallion green, dull gold, shiny gold, silvery red, bright yellow—a riotous array. Their names were also peculiar. Apart from the brands you saw everywhere, Ashima, Hong Ta Shan, and Cloud, there were also some local to Jiangxi province or even Jiujiang itself: Southern, Hongyi, Red Plum, White Sand, Moon Rabbit Spring (on its packet: a medieval beauty's portrait), Gan River, Seven Wolves, White Bird (I bought a packet of these; they stank), Flights, East River, Happy New Year.

One time, I bought a packet of Hong Ta Shan for Fourth Brother (the only one of the cousins who smoked). His eyes lit up, and he ripped it open right away to have one. After a couple of puffs, he said, "It's fake. Little brother, you bought fake cigarettes." I said, "Do they really bother making counterfeit ones?" (they only cost ten yuan a packet). The old men snorted and said, "Sure! It happens all the time. There's nothing they won't copy. Even the bottled water you buy isn't the real thing." They said not to buy anything like that from the roadside stalls; nine out of ten times you'd get fake smokes and water. "What about at the hotel or the mall?" I asked. "Or at duty-free?"

"You get fake stuff there too," they answered, faces blank, as if getting "real" items was an impossible task.

One evening, I walked out of the hospital and crossed the road to get some takeout from one of the restaurants there (for the stubbornly thrifty old men, my brother and cousins). The place was run by a young, skinny couple. The wife, in a cambric dress, dark-skinned and wide-eyed, arguing with her husband in a strong Jiangxi accent (I'd noticed that the women here, no matter how young, had the raspy scolding voices of old ladies). When she saw me approaching, she switched on her smile. "What would you like?" Without realizing, I took on her nasal, high-pitched tone as I said, "Four dishes to go." The husband, in suit trousers, flip-flops, and a white shirt with its sleeves rolled up, nimbly set the wok on the flames, looking like a junior civil servant just home from work, showing off his kitchen skills as he made dinner for the family.

On the chopping board were a variety of tomatoes and red and green peppers, alongside grayish slices of pork, some fresh-water fish I couldn't identify but that didn't look particularly fresh, a metal basin of murky water housing river clams and loaches, a bisected chicken, and lengths of lotus root (so thick I thought they were yams at first). All the food was covered in a thick layer of flies, taking off and landing like fighter jets on an American aircraft carrier.

I ordered thick-sliced twice-cooked pork, tomatoes fried with eggs, stir-fried lotus root, and cutlassfish. Then I stood to one side and admired the couple's handiwork. Cars were surging along the road and sand filled the air, tinting everything richly gold, like a potter's glaze.

The wife raised a chopper so large it looked like a stage prop and cut up the ingredients for my order on the dark, glistening wooden board, while calling for her little girl to shoo away the flies with a swatter. The husband seemed to be having some kind of trouble with the gas cylinder. He fiddled with it for a while, cursing to himself, then shouted into the house. Another child came out—a moment later, I realized he was actually a hunch-backed little person. I had no idea how he was related to this couple. He greeted me somberly, then produced a bicycle pump and hooked it to the cylinder. He and the husband began to work it vigorously. (I watched their faces redden to the tips of their ears, and felt the impulse to say, "Are you sure it's not just empty?")

I was completely absorbed in this bizarre scene when Yiming came dashing over, breathing hard (and speaking Nanjing dialect in his agitation) to tell me they'd brought leftovers from their hotel for lunch, so what was I doing here? He said to the wife, "Cancel the order," grabbed my hand, and charged back across the road.

And so we abandoned this family, who stood smiling grimly and sweaty-faced in a tableau, clutching a chopper, a wok, a fly swatter, and a gas cylinder.

THE DISPLAY CASE

I wondered what the people at the classy hotel thought of us. A mother and son. This was the scheduled stop for my dad's tour group after their visit to Mount Lu, apparently the best one in this poor inland town of Jiujiang. And it was here that a blood vessel burst in his cerebellum, and he was carried through the ritzy revolving doors to the ambulance waiting outside by the duty security guard, Eldest Brother, Fourth Brother, and the tour guide, too many people trying to help in a tangle of limbs. Interestingly, this was where Mr. Chen from the travel agency chose to book us a room. Meanwhile, the rest of the group were continuing their tour. Mr. Chen himself had gotten on a plane to Xi'an to lead another one. We moved my father's luggage— the rucksack we'd packed with medicine and spare clothes, plus all the objects he'd indiscriminately bought at various sightseeing spots, fake calligraphy and fake teapots and tea leaves—into our room, for which we were able to get the same 20 percent discount as the tour group. Everyone was provided for.

Each morning, this mother and son went down to the ostentatious breakfast buffet, choosing the same foods from the selection that never once varied. The mother's preference was as follows: first a plate of lettuce, on which she'd randomly place (these things were impossible to imagine when we were outside the hotel in the dusty air, surrounded by carts stacked high with watermelons for sale) desserts made of buttercream and rather stale cake, then a cup of thin soy milk made from powder. The son's palate demanded a large bowl of congee and a platter of fermented beancurd, salted peanuts, pickled mustard greens with pork, and a fried egg (but the staples of Taiwanese breakfast were missing; no salted eggs, century eggs, pickled cucumbers, or gluten balls). Next were two dry, blackened slices of French toast, sweet crullers known as "greasers," or dough fritters stuffed with tofu (no American-style omelets, no French crepes with maple syrup, no fresh milk or yogurt).

Did they know one of us was a widow-in-waiting, and the other an orphan-to-be?

We spent a month there and had the same breakfast every single day, watching the other guests come and go like migratory birds. Most of them were high-ranking cadres from other provinces, in town on official business, or else nouveau riche businesspeople blundering their way across the country looking for things to invest in, the sort who'd learned to wear designer (though perhaps these were fake?) leisurewear, but whose words and behavior remained vulgar. They disported themselves so loudly, with as much abandon as if they were alone, leaving their tables in a filthy state and treating the waitstaff with disdain. Now and then we'd see a table of three or four cadres in the uniforms of the People's Liberation Army (or sometimes Public Security), and it was these who seemed intimidated by the opulence of the dining room with its air of a European concession lifted from such Italian court paintings as *The Muse Terpsichore* or *Minerva Expelling the Vices from the Garden of Virtue*, leaving them silent as they obediently spread their napkins and used the cutlery etiquette demanded. There would also be a handful of Westerners each day, shaking their heads in puzzlement at the powdered milk or excruciatingly sweet coffee. For a few days, we also had the company of an entire Taiwanese tour group, grannies and grandpas in cheap leisurewear, chattering away merrily but also nervous about annoying their guide, with the same innocence and timidity as an elementary school class on an excursion. I wanted very much to go over and "hail fellow well met" these countrymen, then weepingly confess my sorrows: my father, like you, happily traipsed up Mount Lu with his group, but now he's collapsed and we have to bring him home, so we're stuck here (in that broken-down marketlike hospital and this cursed chilly hotel), and also my wife back in Taiwan is almost nine months pregnant, but I don't know if I'll be back in time for the birth.

But nothing at all happened. Everyone came and went, leaving us behind, mother and son.

Each night, we returned to the hotel exhausted in body and soul, in no mood for dinner. My mother would stay in our room, kneeling in front of the makeshift altar on the bedside table reciting scriptures to the bodhisattva statue she'd placed there, while I went downstairs to the ground-floor breakfast room (which became a coffee lounge in the evenings) and sat at the same table, by the full-length window. In the hallucinatory light, I was like an object in a display case. White coffee cup, white sugar bowl, white condensed milk jug, white ashtray, and a little white vase holding an artificial red rose that looked almost like the real thing (in addition, the waitress solemnly recommended an extraordinarily bland cup of "freshly ground Blue Mountain coffee" for eighteen yuan; but everything else about this scene was exactly the same as a coffee shop in one of Taipei's four-star hotels).

On the other side of the display case, a shirtless worker walked past, a scrawny guy pedaled his trishaw with a couple of laborers in the cab, small taxis explosively honked their horns nonstop (these sorts of taxis kept their coolant tanks behind the back seat, where Taiwanese taxis had speakers, so each time they screeched to a halt or turned a corner, passengers heard sloshing behind them), a gaggle of girls laughed arm in arm, so fashionably dressed you blushed to look at them. And across the road, beneath a sign proclaiming "China Maritime Authority," an old man and woman leaned against a maple tree and stared shamelessly at the contents of the display case: you.

three

THE METAPHOR OF THE JOURNEY

I n *Sir Vidia's Shadow*, Paul Theroux remembers Naipaul's words, weary and heavy-hearted:

> There was a strong, almost Buddhist element in writing, he said, in that good writing canceled out what had existed before. Even the second half of a book canceled out the first half, and each book canceled out the previous one and existed as a reincarnation of the earlier work. . . . "I've done my fiction," Vidia said.

(What a shocking pronouncement.)

> "And I've been writing for forty years. I've handled my experience as best as I can. I can't go back to doing this thing which I now reject, because I want to know why one should falsify a perfectly valid experience. . . . In the last century, things moved quickly because of this swift modification that occurred, writer by writer, book by book, and the forms developed quickly. I think now that if your material is so varied, so many cultures meet, and the novel works best when you're dealing with a monoculture—one culture with a set of norms that everyone can appreciate, almost like Jane Austen. . . . But when the world is moving together in all kinds of ways, that form doesn't absolutely answer, and the ability to lie is so immense."

Just as he says. Along the way, the summoned person keeps reliving a similar previous journey. Painstakingly reconstructing the outlines of that past trip through layers of impressions, only to have the fuller experience of the present journey (the one you're on at this very moment) submerge it, crush it, so you remember it only to forget it completely.

This is practically a fable. My father, in a vast and unfamiliar country, collapsing in what looked like sudden death, then my mother and me making our ramshackle journey of a thousand miles to rescue him. How could I recollect such a trip as merely a record of travel? When I read Shu Kuo-chih's "On the Way," that slow, wavering description of a ride on a mainland long-distance train, in a compartment with uncushioned bunks, "glass jars full of hot water, whose lids could be tightened with a single turn," playing cards, eating melon seeds, shelling peanuts, sharing baijiu, walking gingerly down the swaying corridor while holding a scalding-hot bowl of noodles. . . . Memories that provoke a smile of recognition but also unbearable melancholy. On that trip, I wandered like a lost soul through transport, hotel, hospital, and streets, because of a sort of hyperfocus on my lonesome situation of not being able to go anywhere (the tunnel effect of my father's "time of death"?), frowning and cringing (with a sense of neurotic defensiveness), too preoccupied to appreciate the carefree beauty, ridiculousness, and chaos of those around me.

%. %. %.

On our honeymoon six years before this, my wife and I passed through Jiangxi. Not so much a tour as a commute, strictly speaking. We spent sixteen or seventeen hours on an overnight bus from Nanjing to Yingtan, and then another two hours on a train to a little mountain town called Zhixi, to attend the wedding of a close friend from senior high—he was marrying a Jiangxi girl. This wasn't anything like what the wooden boards we later saw hanging from telegraph poles on the desolate roads outside Taipei advertised: "Mainland brides, Vietnamese brides, Indonesian brides, call XXXXXXXXXX." For my friend and this Jiangxi girl, it was a pure love match. Admittedly, by the time he brought her for a visit to Taiwan (and to meet her in-laws while she was there?) he'd already put a bun in her oven. Even so, all of us, his dirtbag friends, made an effort on his behalf: meeting them at the airport, taking them for a European-style buffet meal at Howard Plaza Hotel. Next we went to Badouzi for the view of the sea (this girl was from a mountain town in Jiangxi and had never, in all her born days, set eyes on the ocean). Then a fancy, show-off karaoke lounge (where it turned out this mainland chick knew all the words to Andy Lau and Jacky Cheung's songs).

I brought the couple to a little apartment on Yanji Street, where a fortune-teller worked out their joint birth charts. I remember the old man solemnly telling my friend, "They say there are mynah birds in heaven and Hubei men on earth, yet ten Hubei men couldn't beat one Jiangxi guy. How could a Henan kid like you" (my friend's father was of Henan descent) "ever get the better of a Jiangxi girl in a fight?"

Anyway, we made a big mistake in planning our route (I'm talking about during our honeymoon, when we made a detour to Nanjing to visit my half-brother, then took the train to Jiangxi for this friend's wedding)—we'd blithely assumed transport between big cities on the mainland would be like in Taiwan, with its cities linked north to south by the railroad. The disastrous result of this misjudgment was our itinerary got infinitely stretched in time and space. Almost impossible for your body's instinctive reactions (frustration, dry mouth, joint pain, ringing in your ears) not to overtake you before the end of your long journey (didn't it look like such a short distance on the map between Nanjing and Yingtan?), so it seemed you were eternally in that rickety train carriage with nothing to do but twiddle your thumbs.

You were forever "on the way."

※ ※ ※

We were in the heated first-class waiting room for the night train, which was due around nine. A scene like a deserted stage with a single spotlight, like the first time I saw a Soviet or Eastern European train platform by night in a Tarkovsky film (an utterly different atmosphere from Taiwan's train stations, an orderly line of them through the country): People's Liberation Army soldiers with red armbands on their winter uniforms, fashionable women in fur coats and long boots (a rare sight in Nanjing back then), a cadre on official business in a low-quality suit (as an outsider, I couldn't parse the sartorial difference between him and the street ruffians in ratty suits or the peasants like my brother). Ragged remnants of humanity wearing the heaviness of solo travel on their faces. Despite the inadequate fluorescent lighting and lack of an after-hours guard, as they stood around the wooden display case offering from behind a glass window Wahaha bottled water, foil packets of Shandong honey dates and candied walnuts, vacuum-packed Nanjing salted duck, and all sorts of cigarettes, amid the long wooden benches and public address speakers that seemed to have been placed with as much deliberation as on a film set, the passengers in this segregated space (unlike the regular second- and third-class ones on the platform outside) appeared, like actors on stage, to enjoy how *special* this short-lived time was. The lines of their faces fiercely radiated an individuality that approached depth. I'm sure the film directors

I know, if they'd been able to witness this dreamlike scene, would have gotten excited. "Ah! Don't move, any of you. I want a close-up of your faces as they are right now." Completely different from the noisy, glum-faced souls on the platform outside, exhaling white fog and scheming how best to grab a seat when the train arrived, and even more so from those in the subway stations and Starbucks outlets of Taipei, where a sort of modernity in the flowing crowds deliberately excised any distinguishing traits from their faces.

It felt as if one of these people might look up and say, *Oh yes, that's what I'm saying, that damned General So-and-So*, then another fellow would pipe up, and as if by hypnosis, we'd slip into one of Chekhov's short stories.

Suddenly, with the clarity of an owl's vision, the alien objects hidden in the darkness abruptly became visible. The fragmented, fearful voices of friends at the other end of a long-distance call, warning you to look out for the vicious thugs who'd burst into first-class compartments and lock the door behind them, so you couldn't call for help before they slit your throat or ravished you; to beware, in second class, the "train gangs" who jump to their feet at a signal, forty or fifty of them at a time, faces shrouded; and of course don't call the "Public Security Officers" or "Armed Police," who throw their weight around and turn violent in broad daylight; don't imagine the silent, cruel gangsters and hoodlums of the north are anything like the sweaty, breezy, betel-chewing ruffians and hooligans of the south, the blindly flowing hordes who can only be surveilled and controlled the way engineers study rivers that have overflowed their banks (devoid of any humanity). Huge numbers inspire terror, and when they haven't been chopped up into smaller ones by modernity, it's like approaching a vast snoring creature that's perhaps only feigning sleep, ready to roll over and devour you, so close you can feel the heat of its body in the dark. . . .

I can now look back, full of emotion, and study the scene: a frozen moment, strangers in a cross-section of time. My new bride and me huddling nervously, holding two plastic bags (the thin, low-quality kind) of sesame seed flatbreads and sand pears, pushed into our hands with such vehemence by my sister-in-law that we almost got into a fight trying to refuse. We felt like we'd just come off stage after an epic production in which, at our age, it had taken some effort to sustain our roles—I'd been ordered by my father to make a detour, during my honeymoon, to meet his fifty-something son, my brother, whom he'd abandoned here half a century before. And now we were on our own, having left the gaggle of old people who'd smiled to hear me fussily describing, with many embellishments, the exploits of my father's bachelorhood in Taiwan. Out of the blue, we were (so easily identified as Taiwanese) dropped back into the obtrusive role of foreigners. **We are not like you.**

Did my new bride look up from my embrace and say, puzzled and out of place, "Why did you bring me along on this strange journey?"

Well, because . . . in the gloom I was swimming with great difficulty through a sea of genetic memory, filled with broken limbs, dismembered corpses, and all manner of strange creatures. I didn't know how to connect the oxidized strands of kelp tangling around my hands with the venomous jellyfish that stung the soles of my feet from time to time. What kind of *atavistic era* was being hinted at? **The truth is, I couldn't see the big picture.** Just as, many years later, I stood despairing with my mother in Jiujiang People's Hospital, smelly and dark as a deserted marketplace at night, at my father's bedside, watching his head blackening like an eggplant. Those old men (Yiming and his cousins) hovered timidly to one side, like children who knew they'd done something wrong. I wanted to say, this isn't just a journey. Like the moment we opened the door of our three-star hotel room, to find the man with whom I shared a father (like me and my father, his right eyebrow flicked up sharply at one end) who'd been labeled a "Five Black" during the Cultural Revolution, and next to him a dark-skinned older woman, his wife, holding a bag of oranges. Abruptly, I went down dramatically on one knee. "Eldest Brother!" He raised me to my feet. Through all this, my new bride stood behind me, confused and frozen to the spot. **At that moment, I no longer recognized you.** That bar in East Taipei, smoking pale blue Cartiers, drinking iced Coronas, buying stocks online, then spouting some arid postcolonial theory or dirty jokes. That's when I floated free of myself and into the role my father's words gave me (the grandfather stories that received an airing every New Year's Eve, including his headlong flight from the mainland, the story of **the Lo family**). I was the youngest son of the generation whose names began with "Yi." The young uncle. Women my age or even older, emerging from their concrete houses to run after their children, shyly greeted me with "Young Uncle." And the children called out, "Young Great-Uncle." (I was only in my early thirties then.)

So the train was an excellent metaphor. It allowed a vast landscape you couldn't see in its entirety to be frozen at a particular instant, an interior scene from a journey.

That was many years previously. When I was younger, I used to earnestly copy out the opening of a certain novel. **If on a winter's night a traveler.** Like people hypnotized into a dream state, we followed the other waxworks (the label on our display case would read, "Scene from a train station in the People's Republic, passengers waiting on a winter night"), women in dyed cashmere fur jackets, People's Liberation Army comrades in their smart winter coats, all of us yawning or breathing white puffs of air as we trooped out of the first-class waiting room. Standing on the dark platform, which felt incomparably more huge and empty than any other on which I'd waited. The smell of the station. The distinctive smell of trains. The smell that would linger even after the final departure of the day. **The smell of waiting.** Funny thing was, I couldn't understand the meaning of that waiting room like a display case. As soon as we stepped out, all those impatient, subtly haughty *first-class* passengers were now pathetically strung out on that empty platform, so long you couldn't see either end. Under the stark lighting, it looked isolated and sinister. We could see every one of the second- and third-class passengers in their tattered suits or holding babies wrapped in patterned cloth, rubbing their hands together and breathing on them. No doubt they too were observing the *superior individuals* who'd just emerged from the brightly lit little room. I wondered whether this station really was as my friend described it during the day, "jostling with so many human bodies you can't experience them as individuals, all you can do is study them like flood water as they surge toward the open doors, calculating their pressure and force." At least on this night, looking farther down the platform, we could see at some distance from us, in the desolate light, sad clumps of passengers.

This was, after all, Nanjing Train Station, a key place in the story of my father's escape. In so many images from my memory, like failed reproductions of sepia photo negatives, I was still a kid holding my father's hand, standing on the platform of Taipei Train Station before it was buried beneath the earth, a light rain blowing sideways at us. At the time, I think I was already vaguely aware that every location, including our present one, any solemn train station, harbor, restaurant, or street, was no more than an inferior substitute for the outline of something else in this fugitive's mind.

It felt like a Borges short story. Visiting the city of my father's birth during my honeymoon, then (for unrelated reasons) getting the night train to Jiujiang. Many years later, my father would collapse at the foot of Jiujiang's Mount Lu, and once again I would catch a plane from Taipei and hurry to Nanchang. As if I were sketching a map connecting the cities in my memory, the train stations in my dreams, and the gloomy airports that stared unblinkingly at the unfortunate moment of death. That was why, many years later, I was facing my mother (and Yiming and the cousins, who'd rushed here from Nanjing) as we sat trapped in Jiujiang People's Hospital next to my father's bed, and I chased the memory of the honeymoon night train, with a sense of enlightenment but also broken limbs and shattered bodies. Such a big country, China, and I'd still managed to have my honeymoon take place at the start and end points of my father's "moment of departure."

My new bride was wrapped in a blanket, curled up as far in as she could get on the lower bunk, partly because of the cold, partly out of fear. Almost as soon as we boarded, she'd squirmed into the darkest corner of that aluminum frame and drifted into sleep. I placed my green army blanket and the damp quilt from the top bunk on her, then added her winter coat, but still felt her shivering violently. I placed our luggage on the top bunk and leaned over the edge of hers, a timorous husband facing down something vast and sinister, determined to protect my fragile wife. I didn't know the rules (I was in a third-world country, wasn't I?) and didn't know if a man and woman (even a newlywed couple) were allowed to publicly share a train bunk. There were two other bunks in our narrow compartment. What sorts of people would we be sharing with?

From all of that winter's night, perhaps because my attention was on the body next to mine who, no matter what I did, wouldn't stop shaking, or perhaps due to the enormous fear of *not knowing what sort of creature would step through the doorway*, I retained no recollection of the scenery along the way. Maybe it was nothing but darkness. I remember a low table by the cast iron window sill, on which was an old thermos of hot water and two little cups. The attendant was selling tea leaves, so I bought a portion and produced something like tincture of iodine. The dark brown tint sank to the bottom of the cup, and no matter how I stirred I couldn't get a uniformly colored brew.

Several hours later, at a stop whose name I've forgotten, the door was pulled open and a person *in uniform* entered: a muted grass-green (though perhaps in that murky light and cramped space, my perception of color wasn't accurate) winter military greatcoat. An officer of the People's Liberation Army. He didn't say a word, just flung his rucksack on the top bunk with a practiced swing of his arm, then in a single leap, hauled himself up there too. I had no idea what course of action would be best for the rest of our journey: drawing closer to my wife and pretending to be asleep, keeping my eyes open but ignoring this intruder into our space, or just saying hello and shooting the breeze with him.

In the end, he was the one who spoke first.

From Taiwan?

Yes.

Business? Or pleasure.

Pleasure. This is my new bride. We wanted to visit family in Nanjing. You know how it is. And just like that, I'd revealed everything, all to demonstrate my harmlessness. My face turned guileless and innocent as I ingratiatingly offered up unnecessary details, so nervous that even the truth came out like lies. As if some intricate mechanism inside my body had automatically kicked into gear. I began slurring the ends of my words in an imitation of a mainland accent, like a blind man in a noisy restaurant orienting himself by sound but refusing a Braille menu in a bid to seem "normal." I thought of how, in taxicabs on my island, I would deploy my scanty Taiwanese supplemented with

Taiwan Mandarin to make small talk with my compatriots, so kind but so full of hatred.

And here we were, years later, the descendants of a refugee. Would we, out of self-preservation, allow my father's lifetime of stories to be washed away?

(Like the bat in the fable, neither bird nor beast.)

The deep shadows on the soldier's face and the weak light made it impossible to see if his expression was alert or relaxed. Outside the window, fields lay in darkness. I suddenly realized this must have looked like a comical interrogation: my head sticking out from the lower bunk, addressing his legs that hung down from the upper.

First time on the mainland?

Yes. Visiting family in Nanjing (again, like a docile suspect, trotting out credible details), *and next we're seeing a friend in Jiangxi. He's marrying a girl from there. A few of us from Taiwan are going to celebrate with him.*

Changing trains at Yingtan?

Uh-huh. He's meeting us at the station.

It will be almost noon when we arrive.

True.

The train swayed. Behind me, my wife muttered something indistinct in her sleep. (At that moment, I thought: *Better to share a compartment with a PLA soldier than some scumbag, right?*) To cover the awkwardness, I offered him a packet of 555s from my rucksack, imitating the expansive gesture with which my brother had greeted the riverboat ferryman.

Smoke? I brought a carton for my brother, and it got opened. There's just this packet left, and I can't get used to them.

Oh! No. The soldier seemed very startled. *No way.*

The lines on his face softened. *I don't normally smoke these Western brands either.* After refusing a little longer, he finally stuffed the packet into his pocket, still muttering away.

Anyway, I don't know when I'll be able to get back to the main-land, so I might as well try your local brands. I took the half-full pack of Hong Ta Shan from my pocket and showed him. *I've got a couple of Ashimas in there too.*

Hong Ta Shan is good. Cloud is a local favorite too. I'd thought we were warming up to a conversation, but instead he fell into silence. A man of few words, clearly.

I picked up my cup of pale brown tea, now cold, and swirled some into my mouth.

You Taiwanese . . .

Mm-hmm?

You Taiwanese. He was silent a moment. *A handful of you people are always screaming about independence this, independence that. What do the rest of you think about that? Regular folk.*

(Here we go . . .)

My gut contracted painfully from the cold tea. Another cumbersome enactment of the bat's story. *How can I put this?* I said, *People like me get called "second-generation outsiders" and our opinions don't count. Fifty years ago, the Kuomintang got completely routed, and my father escaped with them to Taiwan. I was born there. Now I'm visiting his hometown to see my brother and cousins like he told me to, but they're old men whose accents I can barely make out. Back home, we're considered outsiders, not Taiwanese. The second generation blends in by speaking fluent Taiwanese and so on. They become Taiwanese. Having gone through all that, with that level of scrutiny, they're not going to have any thoughts about "independence" or "unification." They're cunning enough to say, "Let's keep things the way they are." All they can do is live dull gray lives in a strange "here and now."*

That was my very first visit to the mainland, in between two waves of Taiwanese surging across the border. The first was right after Liberation, when my father and his peers, veterans who'd been exiled fifty years before, showed up with vast quantities of gold rings and necklaces and foreign currency money orders (their pensions and their life savings), like the first rains after a drought, and all those life-and-death legends, those scenes of kneeling before ancestral tablets and tending to old graves, white-haired husbands and wives reuniting in tears, all of that dispersed like a puff of smoke, engulfed by this vast land. The next wave was Taiwanese entrepreneurs, and this time they really did seem like ants moving to a new nest. The former group were on the fringes of Taiwanese society, just "returning home." As the poem goes, "Accents unchanged but hair now white." They were setting out to prove that this notion of *home* that had been suspended for five decades wasn't just a childhood dream they were fooling their wives and children with: those ancestral houses, genealogies, old place names, ferry crossings, small towns, even snacks and drinks they remembered. Their exuberance, starved of fuel, quickly flickered out. It was the Taiwanese businesspeople, manufacturing shoes and hardware and clothes and low-grade electronic components, who came in sufficient numbers and stayed, reversing the flow of people away from the towns near where they set up their factories (such as the friend I was visiting in Jiangxi, whose mainland bride was from a small town in the Jiangxi hill district; she'd gone with some friends to find work in Xiamen and got talking to the engineer at the plant where she found a job, who was my friend). These soldier ants brought with them a bit of capital, and tragic memories of the sullied innocence of their own childhood homes at the hands of the multinational companies brought in by the Japanese or Americans, trampling over the naïveté of the third world: bars, karaoke lounges, workplace fatalities, the exploitation of cheap labor and the sale of women's bodies for equally low prices, knowing the legacy of death but taking advantage of the locals' ignorance and greed to pollute the land all over again.

In this gap, like a crack of light in a carapace, I made my journey. In that first-class compartment, perhaps I was playing the innocent, but hatred and pain were already dogging me like a shadow. The wave of migrations, viscous as glue, was spreading over too much time and space, creating too much complexity, and I belonged to every part of every one of those faces, but not the entirety. Later, during my many future trips to the mainland, I was constantly getting caught by surprise, in different situations, by similar questions: "You people over there . . ." "You Taiwanese . . ." "You guys who want independence . . ." "What do you think?"

My mouth would fill with sour bitterness, like I was the offspring of a chameleon cursed to never be pure-blooded, having to choose between two sides, both of which had rejected me.

I'd smile and reply, "This issue is really too complicated . . ."

And yet, on that journey, as the train passed through the icy, dark winter night, perhaps because of the terror of being in that strange, gloomy country or the helplessness of being solely responsible for keeping my new bride safe, when I faced that straight-backed PLA soldier, I grew cowardly and weak (and in my sorrow, I thought: If my father were here facing this man, he'd surely launch into a spirited rant, spittle flying, that wouldn't stop until we pulled into the station. He'd want a reckoning of how Mao Zedong's Cultural Revolution destroyed history going back eight hundred generations before the Communists even existed. Or my father-in-law, who'd flash a chilly smile and snap, *Have you been to Taiwan, Brother? Do you know the sadness of us Taiwanese? Our president is democratically elected, is yours?*) and said, "Isn't everyone talking about China finally rising up? When that happens, independence or unification won't matter, will it?"

These words were a protective charm—the upper-bunk guy's face brightened, and he almost offered me a cigarette. "You have a point." That just made me even sadder. As if I'd entered a single password and been granted access to a computer program I'd thought it would be much more difficult to get into. So simple. So classic. Like my father. Or my father-in-law. So easy to get to the painful spot, to scratch an itch. And without realizing it, I'd become the last person to look up from the darkness in a group conversation, an unrepresentative person.

The officer (he kept tucking a cigarette behind his ear, now sticking it in his mouth, now twirling it between his fingers and tapping it on his knee) said familiarly, "Think about it: the day will come when both sides are back together. Fine, your Kuomintang" (mockingly pronounced) "navy can guard the southern border. The South China Sea, Southeast Asia, from Vietnam to the Philippines, all of that we can leave your ships to patrol. As for the East China Sea and Yellow Sea, those fleets can concentrate on defending the northern border. The Russians can hold off the Japanese, and we won't let those American bastards keep us out of the Pacific. That will save on defense costs for both of us."

Counting backward, we got married in December 1995. Which means that strange honeymoon trip took place in the middle of December, early winter before the snow came. I remember the best-selling book in Taiwan that year was *The Warning of Taiwan Straits War*, a disturbing novel that combined fake military intel, history, and predictions to create a fantasy filled with dark foreboding about the state of China-Taiwan relations. Yet somehow, it evoked a hysteria in Taiwan that the People's Liberation Army was indeed about to invade. Between July and August of that year, the Chinese Second Artillery Corps carried out missile tests near Pengchia Islet, just 155 kilometers from Taipei. This was followed, in March, by the so-called *Taiwan Strait Crisis*: troops in Fujian carried out live-firing exercises; fighter jets on both sides did target practice right along the sea border; Bill Clinton sent two aircraft carriers, the USS

Nimitz and USS *Independence*, into Taiwanese waters; and Taiwan's stock market plummeted as people felt "the terror of missile shells passing right before your eyes."

And so I sat in that gray reality of fear, the scars of memory still not healed, listening in that cramped carriage as the soldier described, with infinite warmth and innocence, the beautiful time that would follow "China rising up." Behind me, I could hear my wife snoring quietly. The freezing cold carriage felt like a steel womb, so cold even the hidden chambers of my body— stomach, kidneys, marrow—wouldn't stop shivering as the swaying train made its silent way through the vast darkness of the Chinese winter. That image remains stamped firmly in my mind.

We did indeed arrive safely in Jiangxi. My wife woke just before dawn and stared blearily into the faint light. I quickly introduced her to the officer I'd stayed up all night with. On his upper bunk, the soldier looked a little shy. To our gratitude, this unsmiling, low-ranking officer helped carry our luggage from the platform to the ticket gates when we got off at Yingtan Station, his back ramrod straight the whole time. (My friend met us and asked if we'd had a safe journey. I laughed and said luckily we'd shared a compartment with a PLA soldier, rather than one of the thugs he'd warned us so vividly about.) My friend led us to the branch-line train. At the other end, we each got a trishaw pedaled by a scrawny woman, and by evening we were in the hill town his wife came from.

What happened next was like a magic lantern show: events inscribed on thin paper in front of a smoky carbide lamp. Like a jump cut in a film, we sat in an empty room that would soon be the marriage chamber, peeling chestnuts and chatting with the mainland bride's family, copying their startling behavior: dropping or spitting chestnut skins and cigarette butts onto the floor. My wife gaped as she tugged at the yellowing mosquito net around the old wooden bed, marveling at what she called an antique (later on, we discovered they'd folded it up and tucked it into our luggage). That evening, my friend brought us to a state-run hotel his father-in-law was connected to, so we could shit (they didn't have a toilet in their house). Along the way, we passed by a marketplace that had closed for the day and was littered with bamboo baskets and vegetal rubbish. A speaker fixed to a telegraph pole blared, "Hubei province report! Hubei province report! XXX Production Brigade in XXX county, Hubei province, produced a pumpkin weighing five kilograms last month." The sort of thing they broadcast on CCTV.

Early the next morning, my friend brought us to the town market. I remember basket after basket of Sichuan peppers, bell peppers, fried peppers, dried peppers, as well as scarlet, orange, brown, and crimson chilies, and dried spices like fennel, star anise, and peppercorns. Next were the dog meat stalls with rigid canine corpses sliced open to reveal organs, white layers of fat, and darkening blood. Hanging from metal hooks were the only things that showed whether they'd been black or yellow or piebald dogs: their heads, which had not yet been skinned. After that, we went to a silversmith (they didn't have any gold jewelers in town), where we bought several ear picks and a heavy Yuan Shikai "big-head" coin. I followed my wife's lead and, as if we were antiquing, got myself a pair of rubber-soled army boots at the local shoe store, then an earthenware bowl (perhaps for grinding rice) with a design around the rim, from a roadside stall. Next, my friend hailed some trishaws (again pedaled by scrawny women) who took us on a wobbly tour of the town. We'd only gone a couple of streets when we stopped by a vegetable field, where my friend called out a greeting to a man who was busy spreading manure on the ground. We thought there must be something special to see here, but our friend said we'd just reached the town limits.

That was many years ago.

It was barely afternoon, right after lunch, when we had to quickly depart the bride's family home, because getting to Nanchang's Xiangtang Airport would take at least six hours by van. There weren't any planes that night, so the driver would have to return with an empty vehicle, and we didn't want him to get home too late. On the way, my friend casually mentioned that the local Public Security Officers had come to see his father-in-law. When I looked startled, he reassured me it was nothing, they'd heard some foreigners were spending the night. The law here was that if an outsider stayed more than twenty-four hours, you had to report it to the authorities. "But I counted it out for them: you arrived yesterday evening, and left at noon today. That's less than twenty-four hours."

For me, this had just been one of life's many journeys. Only later did I realize it was actually part of my migration story, and full of hidden meaning.

As for the significance hinted at here, when my father, naked and dripping wet, let out a bellow and collapsed many years later, and the pause button was hit on his story, only then did it begin to unfurl within me.

Naipaul was right. Fiction can't possibly cope with this all-compassing, crumbling world, and deception comes so easily.

four

DAY THREE TO DAY FIVE

DAY THREE

With the help of Yiming, Second Brother, Third Brother, and Fourth Brother, I carried my unconscious father from his seventh-floor ward to the ground floor of another building for a CT scan (or what we call a "computer cross-section scan" in Taiwan). We got in the elevator, pressed the button, and were suddenly plunged into darkness. In that instant, I thought, *For god's sake, this is ridiculous.* Everyone was cursing away in dialect when someone, maybe Second or Third Brother, said, "Hey, we're still moving." (The elevator was fine, it was just the light that had blown.) As we approached the ground, the fluorescent tube began to crackle and flicker.

I was filled with rage. An unnameable rage I couldn't have told you the target of.

Father was completely naked, with just a green sheet over him, being paraded in front of everyone in broad daylight. As if the modern conditions in which he'd wearily taken refuge during the latter decades of his life had all been an illusion, and he was back in the chaos of that earlier time when people's bodies were treated with such rough contempt.

This dilapidated hospital building, its corridors lined with grimy, impoverished people, their eyes dim with confusion; the elevator lights that went off halfway through its descent, and the riders who turned on a dime from screeching in fear to arguing urbanely about the cause of the incident; the uneven, sunken passageway—as we pushed Father's gurney along, we encountered one obstacle after another, sometimes a staircase, sometimes a pile of rubble from construction work, and sometimes a rare level stretch we came upon after navigating the previous barricades, only to find it had been neatly paved with bumpy mosaic tiles . . .

These cousins of mine were now old men of about seventy. Sorrowful and withdrawn, they pushed my father (this body that had lost consciousness, lost time) alongside me through this nightmarish place, a ghost city that hadn't managed to vanish before dawn. Several times, I wanted to shout at them, "Slow down, slow down, there's no need to hurry." My father's head wobbled with each jolt from these men who were a generation younger than he, yet already old. If he'd had the strength, he'd surely have hauled himself upright to scream at them.

Yiming held up the drip bottle as he cursed the hospital corridors. The whole thing felt thoroughly ridiculous, like something from a farce. (Was he afraid the narrative would eventually become: he angered Father so much he died?)

A few times, Third Brother got distracted and allowed Father's plump arm to dangle off the gurney, for which the other old men would angrily yell at him. The oxygen tube kept slipping out, and each time I stubbornly picked it up and stuffed it back up his nose.

Then we arrived at the bizarre CT scan room.

How can I describe it? As we walked through the doorway—a white wooden sign with red lettering hanging above it—I felt myself drifting back to elementary school, after gym class, when I and the other duty students would take the giant bamboo basket of volleyballs (in contrast to me and these blood relatives carrying my unconscious father) to the farthest, darkest, dustiest corner of the school, returning them to the storage room. It was also like on Chenggong Hill, when the duty sergeant would lead us to the darkened room of the armory to get our rifles: a heavily locked door, the sergeant horsing around with the bleary-eyed arms officer, the dank air, the sort of lethargy only someone trapped in an enclosed space would have.

In this little room at the end of the corridor (also the only source of light in this cavernous basement), four or five young people in identical white lab coats were talking and laughing. When they caught sight of us sticking our heads in, they immediately scowled and deepened their voices: "What is it? What do you want?" Stuttering, Yiming handed over the letter from the doctor, and one of them read it skeptically (indeed, this yellowing scrap of paper didn't seem particularly persuasive, but luckily Department Head Wan's blue oval ink stamp was at the top). I sensed that every young person here, no matter how low their actual rank, gained a dismissive wariness as soon as they were in uniform, which they deliberately deployed against these folk with mumbling accents, as if they'd taken advantage of many such old people at another unknown time. Still, this young person put his own stamp on the document, yawned, and ushered us into another room (which he bumblingly unlocked with a bunch of keys). He ordered us to take off our shoes and put on hospital slippers, then pushed Father inside.

In the center of that room, rather startlingly, was a large and very modern-looking machine. In a tangle of limbs, the four old men and I lowered Father onto the surface that looked like something from a gym, a reclining machine or sauna bed. He was still naked, with only a thin piece of cloth over his privates. The young people in white (the hospital's radiation technologist and his interns, I later ascertained) huddled in the tiny glass-walled control room, where they operated the machinery (which seemed more like a laser slicer for frozen pork) as it jerked back and forth, circling Father's head.

My undressed father lay with his eyes shut on that strange spaceshiplike apparatus, as if he were a lone voyager and the rest of us had no idea what alien landscapes he was seeing. The four old men and I stood blankly in the gloom around him (I seemed to remember that in Taiwan, no one but the patient was allowed into the computer cross-section scan room, right?). The cold light, the freezing air conditioning, and the rule about removing their shoes and putting on slippers had thrown these old men, my brother and cousins, into confusion.

Through this whole process (the old men and me standing around Father's suffering, diminished body, while the young people in white chuckled and operated the machine that could see right through his skull), a speaker hanging from the ceiling of this sparse room blared Chinese rock music at the highest possible volume. The old men, farm laborers by birth, were incensed at this violent assault of a deathly ill elderly person with degenerate youth music in this bizarre, science-fiction room. Without warning, Third Brother, who was dressed in a Mao suit and had a full head of white hair, abruptly strode over to the control room and banged hard on the acrylic, cursing them (though the music was so loud, I only heard fragments of his rant: "The Communist Party is finished . . . What is your motherfucking music even . . . You're killing your patients . . .").

The uniformed young people stared at us in shock (even after Father's scan was complete, and a doctor came over to tell us to lift him back onto the gurney, the music didn't get one decibel quieter). Second Brother, Fourth Brother, and Yiming urgently berated Third Brother, "What's wrong with you, don't you have a brain in your head? We're completely in their power . . . Why did you . . . Couldn't you have dealt with it some other way? . . . We should be sucking up to them, not yelling . . ."

When the scan was finally done, we pushed Father's gurney out of that strange, basementlike room (back to brushing shoulders with the hurrying throngs, the uneven paths, the hospital corridors baking in the sun). Second Brother's face was still flushed as he continued scolding Third Brother, "You can't do this again, we can't afford to offend them or they'll do something to his head and ruin a perfectly good human being. Are we trying to help him or hurt him?" I'd never seen Second Brother, normally soft-faced and gentle-voiced, reach such a crescendo of rage.

Third Brother seemed both annoyed with himself and resentful of the criticism as he muttered, "Their music was so loud . . . If they go on like that . . . How can they treat their patients . . . This is how the Communist Party will come to an end . . ."

DAY FOUR

Father was supposed to have "minimally invasive" brain surgery on this day—this was our fourth day in Jiujiang, and he was still lying there corpselike, face dark and fever refusing to break. Eldest Brother put it best: "If we go on like this, he's sure to die. It doesn't look like Dad can be airlifted back to Taiwan for the surgery. They won't even transfer him to Nanchang, and that's just an hour and a half away. Now what? We have to flog the dead horse, it's the only horse we have . . ." Father unwittingly threw a spanner in our plan to play roulette with his life: his fever retreated, he started sipping water, and in response to the nurse's bellowed commands, was even able to stick his tongue in and out. We stood in that crowded ward and discussed the situation with the nerve specialist (whom I'd bribed), Department Head Wan. Shamefaced, as if we were causing trouble, we apologetically wheedled, "Please give us one more day to keep an eye on him . . ."

Mr. Wan said, "Is this your mother?" and then spoke only to me and my brother. (From these details, it was clear he really did have a great deal of self-respect and professionalism. He'd accepted my bribe, and now we had a tacit understanding. He maintained the surface haughtiness and distance of all doctors during their rounds, but intangible kindnesses and attentions would seep into the otherwise restricted treatment. He edged out the young doctor who'd initially been assigned to my father and came himself every day to check on the patient and explain the latest developments to us. As a result, we heard many more jargony descriptions of Father's condition. I went each day to the cash desk to settle the bill, and the cost of medication went up from two or three hundred yuan to more than a thousand, in keeping with the promise he'd made: *I'll make sure your father gets the very best meds.* After that, the little nurses swarmed attentively in and out of our ward, constantly changing Father's drip. The two other patients he shared with, both also brain hemorrhage cases, only got a large and a small drip each, morning and afternoon, and nothing further. Even so, he wouldn't talk directly to my mother—even though I'd muttered, "A little something from my mother," as I awkwardly thrust money at him in that dimly lit office—seemingly afraid his professional role would be usurped by a pestering old woman.) Then he took to simply summoning me and my brother to his office, where he explained the risks of "minimally invasive" surgery. Eldest Brother had the nous and retentiveness of a certain breed of village cadre, and began reciting from memory the words on a poster he'd seen opposite the elevator: *The procedure to extract blood clots from the brain, created in 1991, is "unique to this hospital," and after development by a team of specialists, has matured to be the 1999 National Technology Prize runner-up.* Mr. Wan smiled apologetically, face suffused with blushes, "True, we won a little award, but in practice there's still a risk to the patient, particularly someone like your father with blood loss around the brain stem; the smallest tremor might end his life . . ."

All in all, there were six risks:

One, a massive hemorrhage during the surgery itself, which there would be no coming back from. (It was only later that I realized what he was actually saying: *the patient might die on the operating table.*)

Two, this wasn't a craniotomy (a procedure where they cut open your skull with a little saw) but rather a one-millimeter drill bit passing through the bone in order to release built-up fluids or blood clots. Nonetheless, this would still be an assault from the outside world, and there was no guarantee it wouldn't lead to infection resulting in further side effects.

Three, the possibility of related breathing difficulties, or else a brain hemorrhage leading to stomach bleeding.

Four, even if he managed to escape these aftereffects, there was no guarantee this surgery would make any difference to the patient's vegetative state.

I can't remember the fifth and sixth risks, but I imagine they were variations on Mr. Wan explaining how there would be "no coming back from" these complications. Resentment bubbled up in me: *In the beginning, you were so stridently outraged when you ripped apart our plan to move him to Nanchang Second Affiliated Hospital. Why do you seem so feeble now?* I asked Mr. Wan if he could give me, my brother, cousins, and mother some time to discuss the matter, and we'd let him know our decision later. He said that was fine, we could have a day to talk it over, but no longer—my father's condition wasn't great, and he'd need an answer by the next day.

Yiming and I stood in the stairwell at the end of that row of wards (where I noticed the "runner-up for the 1999 National Technology Prize" blood-clot removal poster he'd mentioned, which came festooned with before-and-after CT scans of stroke patients, as well as a picture of Mr. Wan and a team of medics with white masks over their mouths huddled around a "minimally invasive" procedure—boring a hole in the patient's shaved head with an electric drill!), where we gave each other a light and puffed our way through three or four cigarettes without speaking. I knew this was a crucial moment for Yiming too. Who would make this decision? All of a sudden, with unspeakable clarity, I saw myself in the soul of this brother thirty years older than I. We both crinkled our brows when making important choices, looking like we were thinking hard even though our minds were completely blank. After several encounters with Yiming, I knew we had one thing in common: for the sake of smoothing things over or not causing trouble, we said what other people wanted to hear. In that moment, we were perhaps each guessing what the other was thinking, mulling over how to resolve this so as to set the other person at ease. Yiming said, "Looking at Dad now, I don't think he's going to get better. Of course, we're all hoping for a miracle. But in the last couple of days, I've seen Mom getting frailer and frailer. Little Brother, your wife back in Taiwan is having a baby soon. Whatever we decide, we could be wrong, we could be right. Doctors are professionals, so they make things sound serious to scare us—but this guy seems to think our only option is, whatchamacallit, minimally invasive surgery . . ."

I longed to ask him: *What did Father say to you that night in the hotel room? What did you answer?* But instead I said, "Knowing Dad, if he were conscious at this moment, he'd say: *What are you waiting for? If there's a bit of hope, that's good, isn't it? Let's have the surgery right away.* He's a gambler by nature."

And so we decided to go ahead with the surgery. In this broken-down hospital in this unfamiliar little city. Such unfilial, yet pragmatic sons. How much better if I hadn't had to make this decision. At that moment, one floor below us, a worker was putting holes in the stairwell wall with an ear-splitting screech, and I had the sudden insane thought: *Fucking hell, does Mr. Wan use the same type of drill on people's skulls?* (*Hey, dude, lend me that thing for a minute, you can have it back this afternoon after the surgery.*)

That morning, my father had hauled himself back from death's door. The high fever that had persisted for four days finally ebbed. My mother dabbed his cracked lips with cotton soaked in water, and his throat rose and fell weakly as he went through the motions of swallowing. When the doctor came by on his rounds, he shone a penlight into his pupils, slapped his cheeks, and yelled at him to stick his tongue out and in. Father frowned as if he'd just been roused from the deepest of dreams, but nonetheless obediently popped his tongue out. (The old men and I all but clapped and cheered, like the NASA scientists when *Apollo 13* reappeared on their radar screens after circumnavigating the dark side of the moon.)

Finally Father no longer seemed like a dying pigeon we'd picked up by the side of the road, which we'd have to avert our eyes from as we wrung its neck; or the wolfhound we'd once had and brought to the vet with distemper, to be injected with cyanide. "No hope but a quick death."

The hospital had a power outage. The young woman at the next bed got out a palm-leaf fan and wafted some wind toward the older stroke patient (perhaps she was his daughter). Father frowned and began wriggling about uncomfortably (he hated the heat).

DAY FIVE

An insulated cooler served as a stall, and two yellowish light bulbs hung off a power line, illuminating piles of newspapers, cigarettes, and bottled water. The young woman in charge of the stall waved a palm-leaf fan as dim tree shadows swayed and collided. Like a nighttime street in sixties Taipei. Today, the young man in the next bed suddenly stood up, and everyone (including himself) was flabbergasted, as if a roast duck carcass in a restaurant, meat sliced from its body, had flapped its wing bones and risen, dripping wet, from its soup pot. There was a pause of about five seconds before the other youths, wastrels by the look of them, got to their feet in a fluster and wrapped their arms around him.

I was deeply shaken by this scene of a body being "resurrected" right next to me. I'd been absorbed in gently wiping my father's frame as he lay unconscious, and had to force my eyes open as if against a sudden burst of bright light. How could this be? There were three beds in this ward, three patients who'd embarked at the same time on their journeys through the netherworld, traveling at the speed of death. How could this one guy have broken free of his sleeping beauty's curse to step from the fatal shadow, shedding his skin and breaking through his shell?

(This guy had been a zombie, arms stuck straight out, lying there with mouth agape and eyes wide open.)

I felt a jolt of miragelike hope. Perhaps at this very moment, Father was navigating the thick concrete walls of death's maze, sweat dripping from his brow as he frantically sought the way out. Please let him find the exit (as sand trickled, unheard by me, through the hourglass), so he too could, like this scrawny young man with protruding ribs, suddenly rise up with a gasp.

My wife phoned to say she'd gone to see the neurological specialist who'd treated her big sister's epilepsy, and there were several key points:

One, it had been five days since Father's cerebellar hemorrhage, and his condition hadn't deteriorated—in fact, it was slowly improving, which meant we were past the greatest danger. We should find a way to get him the best care and medicine, bearing in mind that surgery or any other "small" procedures should only be an absolute last resort.

Two, if we couldn't be sure the mainland hospital was hygienic or antiseptic, then there was no way to guarantee there wouldn't be infection or side effects, and we shouldn't take the risk of consenting to surgery. The neurosurgeon had once operated on a patient who'd had a procedure at a mainland hospital and found they hadn't even fitted his cranial bones back together properly.

Three, if his condition was stable, then from a medical standpoint he could be moved, although stroke patients need a diuretic drip every six hours to reduce intracranial pressure. We had to be certain he would receive adequate care on the way from Jiujiang to Nanchang Airport, then on the flight to Hong Kong and connecting leg to Taipei, more than ten hours in total.

Four, given his condition, we had to be prepared for the possibility that the patient might worsen and die at any moment.

This information calmed me down quite a bit. For several days now, I'd been like the warrior in Bergman's *The Seventh Seal*, dueling death to prolong the lives of those around me. My head was splitting as six or seven chess strategies floated around my brain (I'm going to bring you back alive, Father).

From the plans I'd made with my mother on our frenzied journey here to retrieve Father's corpse to the present moment, it felt like breaking through death's chessboard defenses one piece at a time. But might this be a trap? What if we ended up losing the entire game? For the first time in my life, I was gambling with an outside force with no room for negotiation, and the stake was my father's life. Every judgment or decision I made determined his survival.

I'd played countless video games in which the mission was to save your father's life, and I'd written a novel about stepping into your father's youth to salvage (change) his tragic fate. And now here I was, living this very scenario.

My brother sent a text message from Taiwan:

One, the insurance company could work with the travel agent to arrange for medical personnel to accompany the patient from Jiujiang to Nanchang Airport, and then on every flight up to Taoyuan Airport.

Two, there was also an international rescue organization that could provide staff and medical equipment all the way from Jiujiang to Taoyuan.

Three, my plan that my brother should ask a Taipei hospital to send an ambulance to the airport probably wouldn't work out, because regulations stated that the ambulance should come from the nearest large hospital (such as Linkou Chang Gung Memorial in Taoyuan).

The night before, Auntie Miao-Yin had phoned our hotel and spoken to my mother for an hour (as I frantically gestured to her from my bed and mouthed the words "international long distance") about the something something Buddhist prayer group they were both in. As soon as they heard what had happened to my father, they gathered sixty or seventy people and chanted the Sutra of the Great Vow for an entire day and night (I imagined dozens of old women in black and sea-blue robes, clutching chiming stones and scriptures, eyes shut and lips murmuring away). Mother began sobbing, which threw me into confusion. All the way from Hong Kong Airport, via Hainan Island, Nanchang, and finally Jiujiang, up till the horrific sight of Father's swollen head and empurpled skin, she'd kept a detached expression on her face. From time to time she even whispered a witty remark to me. Part of me knew that she liked to appear strong. Perhaps she was also doing it for herself, playing the part of someone with no weakness to show. Another part of me understood very well that these last few years, she'd gotten old too, and had developed a defense mechanism against the cruel and violent attacks of fate. Each time

Father exploded without warning with the pent-up fury of a caged animal, her face would take on a comical smile as if this had nothing to do with her, and her eyes would lower to look at her nose and inward to her heart. This expression persisted out of force of habit, even after Father collapsed with a thud (look what trouble you've caused now, old man). As if all she had to do was keep herself aloof, and bad luck wouldn't take her all the way to the heart of tragedy.

five

DEPARTMENT HEAD WAN

The first person I bribed was Dr. Zhang, a well-groomed, decent-looking young man. I waylaid him in the hospital stairwell that looked vast and empty (perhaps due to the starkly featureless concrete wall) in the fluorescent lighting, and stuffed into his hands the carton of imported 555 cigarettes and Rémy Martin VSOP Cognac that Mr. Chen from the travel agency had given me. Mr. Chen's instructions were that no matter what, I had to force these gifts upon the head doctor—along the lines of "find out where you stand with the King of Hell, the sentries just follow his lead"—so this godlike being in his white coat would stop in his frenzied progress between beds laid out like street market meat stalls to patiently explain in Mandarin (rather than the local Jiangxi dialect) how Father was doing.

Honestly, I'd had a huge amount of trouble navigating the maze of irrelevant explanations from Eldest Brother Yiming in his thick Nanjing accent, mixed with his village cadre's discursive rhetoric and ambiguity, which I was supposed to pass on to Mother. I simply couldn't grasp what state my father was actually in, with his bruised head and babbling.

("Father will soon be dead," Yiming kept muttering gloomily. "I'm afraid things don't look good.")

Dr. Zhang declined my cigarettes and cognac in a startled, resonant voice, and for an moment I worried I'd done something gauche, approaching him in this bustling stairwell (unlike the stairwells in Taiwanese hospitals, these weren't dark corners blocked off by emergency doors, but rather like the ones in every government school I'd gone to, brightly lit open spaces bustling with patients and family members—perhaps because the two elevators moved excruciatingly slowly and frequently broke down), but the ritualistic pronouncements of "This is nothing, nothing at all," "You've come all the way from Taiwan, it's no more than my duty to take care of our patients," "You have to accept these, as long as you can save my father's life, we'd be willing to pay any price," allowed him to salve his conscience and wrap his arms around the plastic bag I thrust at him.

What a delicate operation. Like the tacit understanding behind bidding and tossing out cards. Smooth and efficient as any marketplace transaction. As soon as you took your first step, you understood that you were on the right track. Yet it also felt as if you might blink and the whole thing would vanish in a blaze of light, and you'd be back in this slothful, dilapidated hospital where human life was worth nothing. As if none of this had happened.

That very afternoon, Dr. Zhang showed up at Father's bedside with his medical file and CT scan, keeping his face carefully deadpan (in order to fend off the relatives of the other two patients who were drawing closer out of curiosity and envy) as he explained to me (as if he'd ascertained I was the decision maker in this complex situation, while my mother was just a grief-stricken old woman) that Father's condition looked very bad: a severe cerebellum hemorrhage right against the brain stem, in which—thanks to the impermeable skull—blood clots pressed on the brain cells from all directions, causing them to retain water and swell. During this time, the brain cells would have sustained a great deal of damage, as would the respiratory, cardiovascular, and swallowing centers, not to mention the high fever that refused to abate, which might at any moment lead to inflammation or other side effects, including death.

At the time, I didn't have the leisure to imagine whether, had we been in Taiwan, our neurologist would have used such rudimentary language (almost like a high school biology textbook or nursing course) to explain the situation. We were on tenterhooks, as if every single judgment or connection had the potential to determine whether Father would die in a foreign land or be miraculously saved (like one of those heart-warming stories in *Reader's Digest*?).

Amid the confusion and despair, this "command center" felt imitatively dramatic (only later, recollecting this, did I laugh and realize that when giving my brother and sister back in Taiwan instructions over the phone, I'd adopted the tone and phrasing of a Hollywood film—a stranded space shuttle sending a distress call to Houston, a lone surviving special op on a hijacked Air Force One), like I was drowning in tears as I reached up to swat debris off my face, as I told my brother to go through my father's address book and find Uncle Fan who'd gone into business on the mainland a decade ago. This Uncle Fan was from my father's hometown, and I'd heard it was Father who helped him escape to Taiwan as a young man in '49. These days, he had a tennis racket manufacturing plant in Anhui and apparently held some sway with provincial apparatchiks and cadres. I told my brother to ask which hospitals within driving distance of Jiujiang had modern facilities capable of carrying out brain surgery, and if he had a contact there, maybe an official or doctor.

Uncle Fan phoned back almost immediately and told me the best local hospital was Nanchang Second Affiliated (that is, the hospital affiliated with the city's second medical university). "Now you need to go see the Jiujiang mayor, or the secretary of the city council, or the head of the United Front, or the director of the Taiwan Affairs Office. Tell them you're a Taiwanese compatriot and your father fell ill in their city, so they have to provide documents to the First People's Hospital allowing you to transfer him to Nanchang Second Affiliated." He sounded very serious, no hint of a joke, as if I could barge through every door right into the mayor's office and say, "Hi there, Mr. Mayor, I order you to give me these documents right now, no delay." He went through this "procedure" twice, then added that maybe I shouldn't look up the Taiwan Affairs director after all, he might be too low-ranking to persuade the hospital; better to go straight to the United Front.

That afternoon, the tour guide from the agency phoned, a faint tremor of excitement and nasal breathlessness in her voice, to tell us she'd made contact with Dr. So-and-So, Nanchang Second Affiliated's deputy director and incidentally an authority on cardiovascular surgery, and we should get "the elder Mr. Lo" over there as quickly as we could.

I sensed she knew she'd grasped the mechanism by which she could change the fate of my parents and the entire family (or perhaps she was worldly enough to detect my vagabond nature, concealed beneath the formal language we were using), and now switched to a more frivolous way of addressing me: Young Lo.

"Young Lo, you should go talk to the head doctor right now and ask him to come up with some documentation from Jiujiang People's Hospital to say the family wishes your father moved to Nanchang Second Affiliated for urgent surgery." This was a ray of light, of course. Even though my mental image of Nanchang Second Affiliated was decidedly blurry, given the circumstances, it was clearly the only route by which we'd be able to spring my father from this street market of a hospital, which did not have any visible signs of surgical facilities at all. Besides, hadn't Uncle Fan just mentioned Nanchang Second Affiliated too? Just like that, "move Father to Nanchang Second Affiliated" became a concrete version of our ultimate goal, "save Father's life."

I expressed my gratitude fulsomely, whilst remaining cautious enough to raise a question: What if the Jiujiang doctors didn't approve of moving the patient? The doctor had just told me that the cerebellum hemorrhage was close to the brain stem and nerve clusters were coming under pressure from the blood clots, and he might die at any moment. Besides, his head was still bruised all over. What if, on that half-hour drive to Nanchang along bumpy roads, he were to . . .

"That's a judgment for the attending physician to make, Young Lo. All you need to do is encourage them to approve this document. If he can't be moved, we can always get the deputy director to travel from Nanchang, though of course we'd have to provide him room and board. But we'd still need documents from Jiujiang to say there's a Taiwanese patient in a serious condition who urgently requires a consultation with Deputy Director So-and-So from Second Affiliated."

Once again, I was standing on the border between light and dark. Each day, I was unable to work out if there was a "true order of things" behind the languorous atmosphere and the young doctors and nurses who walked past me blank-faced. Was there another meaning behind the tour guide's words, or was she motivated by simple human decency (the milk of human kindness)? Or was this an opportunistic trip for this lofty deputy director, a fancy hotel room (paid for by the family) and a fat bonus to carry out a medical procedure of no practical benefit to my father? Documents, documents, documents. Was I getting the hidden message that people in our situation (relatives of patients who happened to be Taiwanese compatriots) had a secret exemption or extraterritorial jurisdiction that allowed us to make these people temporarily leave the established order of their two-dimensional world and disrupt their strict hierarchy? All I had to do was open my mouth . . .

Yiming and I waited for Dr. Zhang outside what seemed to be a conference room. (Like everywhere else in this building, the door stood wide open. Despondent-looking patients and family members stood around in twos and threes, crowding the doorway and craning their necks to gawp at the doctors at two long tables inside.) At first I assumed this was a meeting or patient discussion—on the wall by the elevator was a Styrofoam-backed poster, "Introducing Our Neurosurgeons," with a photo of some doctors in just such a room, captioned "team discussion of patient conditions"—then I realized they were just hanging out, holding glass teacups and shooting the breeze. This was both the doctors' common room and their shared office. Finally, Yiming went in and asked Dr. Zhang to step out.

I let him know our entire family had complete confidence in these extremely skilled doctors, and thanked them for saving Father's life in the first place—thanks to the rusty oxygen tank that looked like a gas cylinder and the saline solution in its "hanging pouch" (IV drip)—but, with the greatest of respect, this warm-hearted tour manager (I'd decided to give her a promotion) seemed convinced that the deputy director of Nanchang Second Affiliated could operate on my father, and she'd introduced us to him . . . Of course, this would be a difficult decision for us . . . In any case, we hope you, dear doctor, are willing to send a document to Nanchang in the name of Jiujiang People's Hospital . . .

At first, I thought I'd startled him. He listened to me blankly, no expression at all on his refined face. Then he said, "I don't understand what you're saying." Perhaps I was speaking too quietly, or it was my accent, or else I'd used so many diplomatic, polite phrases that the meaning of my words was completely obscured. In any case, Yiming now had to use his blunt-spoken village cadre's words to repeat everything I'd said, and this time the doctor got it. Sadly, I'm unable to reconstruct from memory this wonderful comic performance, the same cajoling voice he'd have used in resolving a land dispute on Jiangxin Island or if someone's chicken had been run over by a tractor. "My little brother's trying to say they're Taiwanese" (he pronounced this like *Tai One Iss*) "and when they find themselves in these sorts of situations, they require surgery, which has to be taken seriously" (*serslee*) "otherwise who'll be responsible if he loses his life? Obviously they want to find the most reliable surgeon, never mind the cost. And right now, over in Taiwan, there's this person who also happens to be my father's good friend, and what do you think he said? If surgery is to happen, then of course it must happen at Nanchang Second Affiliated, it's just a bigger place, you see, don't you agree? There are many good things about Jiujiang, but when it comes to surgery, it's the Nanchang folk who are old hands at it."

That's roughly it. To this day, I can't work out why this young Jiangxi man in his white lab coat could understand my brother's coarse rural Subei-Nanjing accent, but not mine.

He said, "Given your father's present condition, there's no way I can agree to have him moved at the moment. As for your family's request to have the—did you say deputy director?—of Second Affiliated come for a consultation, that can certainly be done. I don't have the authority to approve that, though—you'll have to ask our manager."

And then he led me, as if through a maze, to another part of this crumbling yet majestic Western-style building (which was definitely built before Liberation, during the Nationalist period, because the proportions of the corridors and staircases we were walking down, the filthy terrazzo floors and dusklike light slanting in from overhead ventilation windows, all reminded me of being very young and following my father through public buildings such as Taipei's Tobacco and Liquor Corporation, Zhongshan Hall, or Railway Administration), through various connecting passageways on each story to the next building, until we reached the outpatient hall on the ground floor.

That was my first meeting with Mr. Wan, the department head.

As I walked into Department Head Wan's office, there was only one thought in my mind: how to most efficiently and least offensively persuade yet another link in the invisible bureaucratic chain of this broken-down hospital to quickly place his stamp on a document, so we could transfer my father to a bigger establishment with more modern facilities (at least that's what I imagined was supposed to happen). There was no way I could have predicted the outcome would be exactly the opposite to what I'd hoped, and we would be stuck at this hospital like a boat grounded in shallow water. As I said, ever since the night I arrived and found my dying father lying in this place where time seemed to flow backward, I understood I would have to become acquainted with one system after another, none of which was anything like what they first appeared to be, and if I could just do the right things, say the right words, and go down the right channels, this whole business would be smooth and easy as a conjuring trick. But if I put one foot wrong, all these concealed gateways would immediately slam shut, and I could forget about moving ahead.

Looking back, I must have entered the system from the wrong direction to start with, said the wrong things, taken incorrect turns, and had no hope of grasping how they understood the situation.

This examination room looked like a nursing station in some remote village. Mr. Wan (a youngish doctor of about forty, slightly built, round glasses on his catlike face) sat at a large aluminum desk, hapless yet full of rage as he dealt with the grubby-faced patients who kept creeping into the room from the corridor (I couldn't work out if they were trying to cut in line, or just eavesdropping on other people's diagnoses). He roared at them, not holding back at all, while they met his gaze with respect and fear, yet in their bones was nothing but irreverence and mischief. This doctor-patient relationship was nothing at all like what you'd see in a Taiwanese clinic: cold, impersonal light; neatly dressed patients sitting blank-faced on a row of acrylic chairs, waiting in silence for the singsong computer voice of the display board to chant their number.

This so-called clinic was really no more than one nursing station after another, squashed together along this dank ground-floor corridor. The only difference was the signs outside each room proclaiming different specialties. I stared at Mr. Wan—whose sign read "neurosurgery"—as he lazily asked his patient, "What's up?" The old geezer mumbled with a heavy accent, "Headache." Mr. Wan leaned back in his chair and rolled his eyes. "Headache? Your head aches when you have a cold, so just take two cold tablets and the pain should stop, right?" The old man broke into a delighted grin.

Mr. Wan said, "What's up?" (He hadn't even looked directly at me.) Dr. Zhang bent down and, in a low voice, explained my situation in a jangling Jiangxi dialect. I couldn't understand what he was saying, but I was surprised at the tone of this young doctor's voice—his gravitas had evaporated, and his pitch was much higher. He sounded panicky, anxious. The old man in the patient's chair and the crowd around the door all had vague smiles on their faces. As they listened, they nodded and looked at me (of all the people in the room, I was the only one who couldn't understand what they were muttering to each other).

Mr. Wan suddenly snapped, in a voice he was unable to keep the anger out of, "Which doctor at Second Affiliated? What's his name?"

He spoke in Mandarin, which made me think this was directed at me. Annoyingly, I couldn't remember what name the tour guide had said, and had to mumble, "I think it was a deputy director?"

"Deputy director? The deputy director has a name, doesn't he? You don't even have a name, and you want me to write you a document?"

This was clearly for the benefit of the rank and file. Now he seemed to lose all interest in his patients and tapped the end of his pen on the desk as he read the case notes.

I said I'd find out, and just like an exposed street swindler trying to look trustworthy, I pulled out my phone and ostentatiously called the tour guide in front of everyone.

She answered groggily, as if I'd roused her from an afternoon nap. I said, "Young Lo here" (in the stress of the moment, I found myself adopting this name for myself too), "sorry to bother you, but the deputy director you mentioned earlier—what's his name?"

She said, "What's going on? He's called So-and-So." And then she repeated her instructions about how to get the Jiujiang People's Hospital to produce the right documents. I regretted the situation intensely. From the start, I'd thought this woman couldn't be trusted, and now she'd managed to make the whole business feel underhanded.

Now Mr. Wan rapped his pen on the desk and said, "Oh, So-and-So, is it? He's in cardiovascular, and this patient has a cerebellar stroke. Why get him for this surgery?" The strange thing was, he couldn't have heard what the tour guide said on the phone, and must have known the deputy director's name all along. This whole charade was for theatrical effect.

At this juncture, a ridiculous and extreme image popped up in my mind. I recalled how, many years ago, as my wife and I were packing for our first trip to the mainland, my father insisted with unusual stubbornness that I should bring syringes. I found it comical that he thought I might need such a random object, but he remained firm and even went out to Watsons for a box of ten disposable ones, which he made my mother pass to me. He was getting on my nerves by that point, and I grumbled, "What if they search my luggage at the airport and think I'm a drug smuggler?" But my father's reasoning was, "If you get sick over there and need an injection at one of their hospitals— they don't use disposable syringes, you know—you might get AIDS or something. Make sure they use the disposable ones you've brought."

Now my father's voice was buzzing in my ear: "Disposable syringes." This felt like a metaphor. So many things, in this weightless drifting scene, felt like metaphors: the large, crumpled mass of an elderly man's body; an old hospital building where time flowed in the wrong direction; a ludicrous trip to bargain with death's hourglass. Or perhaps: many years ago, when my father, without my consent, had me transferred to the elementary school across the road from my old one, and I suddenly found myself in the grimy uniform of a government school, hanging my head as I walked past my former private school classmates in their smart aquamarine outfits.

Disposable syringes.

My ears felt like swiveling satellite dishes that could receive sound from 180 degrees around. One picked up the woman chattering on my cell phone, "This deputy director is very busy, it took me a lot of effort to get him to a yes, just tell the doctors these hospitals have teaching demonstrations too, don't they?" while the other picked up Mr. Wan crowing victoriously behind me (I detected laughter in his voice. And in fact, this incident had restored to him a measure of professional authority): "Well? I know every one of the doctors over at Second Affiliated. So-and-So, So-and-So, So-and-So," (he said their actual names) "but the question is, who are you looking for? We're talking cranial surgery here, you can't get someone in just because they hold a high position, can you?" The formerly timid onlookers now cheered, "Exactly! Well said!" as if he were a flamboyant street orator.

Without me noticing, perhaps because she'd heard the commotion around me, or as a result of my stutteringly evasive attempts to placate her, the tour guide had huffily hung up. Even so, I kept the phone pressed to my ear, grunting in acknowledgment as if she were still speaking, pretending the signal wasn't clear so I had to turn my back to the room and press my face against the screened window on the far wall. Through the fog-like green gauze, I could see a narrow space like an air shaft, and among the planks, desks, and chairs with missing legs, and a corroded metal device that might have been some sort of motor, someone had ceremoniously placed a pot of osmanthus flowers. A mouse—perhaps it had just crawled out of the drainage grate that the plant was meant to cover—its entire body dripping wet, lounged as if sunbathing at a beach resort, propped up against the dry earth on the edge of the pot, luxuriantly licking its front paws.

※ ※ ※

As Dr. Zhang and I walked back to the ward, he muttered in a low voice that could have been to himself, or a rebuke, "You should get your brother" (he meant Yiming) "to go talk to the department head. You made everything sound too complicated, and now look, you messed it up."

Before we left Mr. Wan's little room, I'd finally lost control and started yelling at him (though it's always been one of my regrets that ever since high school, when older boys would surround me in the street to try to pick a fight, anger and agitation would make my throat seize up, turning my voice sharp and whiny as a prepubescent boy, in stark contrast to my ferocious expression). I shouted, "My mother and I came all the way from Taiwan to sort out my father's situation, and this is the way you treat visitors? How am I supposed to know who such-and-such deputy director is from First or Second Affiliated or whatever? Who's the cranial surgery expert here? This is an emergency, isn't it? As long as my father can be saved, I don't care how much it costs." (Even in the midst of my rage, I was secretly gleeful at being able to wave this card, flaunting the wealth and influence I had as a Taiwanese compatriot.) "Are you sure you can save my father? If your attitude costs us this chance and my dad—a Taiwanese citizen—dies in your care, are you sure you're ready to take responsibility?"

Unfortunately, the patients around us failed to clap and cheer at my exhilarating performance. Mr. Wan, though, did seem a little stirred by my fury. He narrowed his cat eyes, and in a voice full of meaning (I might have triggered his resentment at being stuck in a dilapidated hospital with inadequate facilities, unable to make full use of his potential, or else roused his sense of worth), he said, "Of course it's our duty to save lives—but what does it matter that you come from Taiwan?"

And that's why Dr. Zhang was so frustrated and fearful (after all, he'd accepted my imported cigarettes and alcohol) as he passed through the crowds of patients, their bodies deformed or damaged to a greater or lesser extent, grumbling away as if I was on his side.

That was the last time he and I negotiated my father's treatment with such intimacy. That evening, I took advantage of a spare moment to barge into Mr. Wan's office (the only room on this floor with a door you could shut). Before he could work out what attitude he should take with me, I'd stuffed two American hundred dollar bills into the pocket of his white lab coat. In order to make sure he didn't mistake them for mere renminbi notes in the heat of the struggle, I made sure that as I grabbed his protesting wrists (his refusal was much more energetic and sincere than Dr. Zhang's), I whispered urgently, "We're so busy dealing with my father's condition, you see, I didn't have time to change money, so I'll have to give you American dollars for now . . ."

He looked like he was fending off a sexual predator in an enclosed space, grabbing my forearms with all his strength and breaking free of my grip.

All the while, he kept repeating in a low voice, "No such thing, no such thing, no such thing, no such thing." I had no idea what he meant.

Finally he accepted the money. We sat there, breathing hard and staring at each other (I had to keep myself tightly under control at that moment—if I'd laughed, the whole thing would have been ruined). As a result of his vigorous efforts to reject my banknotes, his brow was now covered with the sweat of honest labor, and he could tell himself, "I did everything I could." In that instant, I truly believed he was a self-respecting, faithful, and good doctor. "No such thing," he said again. Was this a feeble protest that in this poor hospital (or perhaps in this small inland city), there was no such thing as this ugly capitalist practice? Or an indication that as soon as we walked out of this office, "no such thing" would have taken place inside? What lay between us, the disparity between the positions of doctor and family member, must not be allowed to wobble as a result of what we'd just been through.

I told him, "My mother insisted on this gift, as a show of our respect for you." Then I repeated, "As long as my father can be saved, I don't care how much it costs." How I longed to howl in anguish: *I don't like this either. I don't want to besmirch both of us in this violent way, but this is the only path open to me now.*

Dusk was falling by the time I got back to my father's ward. The lights hadn't come on yet, and everyone's faces were murky in the gloom. Three unconscious figures lay in bed, and from the chairs beside them, the living kept silent watch. The ruined human forms snored loudly, while oxygen from their tanks burbled monotonously through a water filter on its way to their nostrils. Father's fever was still high; his head was covered in bruising like a corpse. My mother sat cross-legged on the edge of the bed, eyes shut, reciting Buddhist scripture with a string of prayer beads in her hand. The old men were taking it in turn— now Second Brother and Third Brother sat to one side, one of them holding down the drip on the back of Father's hand (he kept thrashing his arms and shaking the needle loose), the other dipping a towel into cool water and pressing it to Father's forehead over and over.

None of them seemed annoyed or surprised that I'd disappeared for such a long time. Probably they had no idea what running around various hospital buildings had to do with Father's illness.

Second Brother, his face covered in wrinkles, asked me kindly, "What happened?" I didn't know exactly what he was referring to, but still I said, "It's settled." And he replied, without trying to find out any of the details, "Oh."

The next morning, when Dr. Zhang showed up at Father's bedside to take blood and urine samples and to decide what dosage to put in his IV (they called it a "hanging pouch"), Mr. Wan came up to him, quietly said, "I'll take over this patient from now on," and walked away with Father's chart.

Did I notice Dr. Zhang's expression? He must have known right away that he'd been shafted—I'd gone over his head and bribed his boss. Now I was dealing directly with Mr. Wan, I wouldn't need to ask him for anything. Would he be able to guess how much money I'd put into his superior's hands?

SIX

DAY SIX TO DAY FIFTEEN

DAY SIX

Time began to fall apart entirely. What date was it? What day?
This was like trying to read the tiniest handwriting without my
glasses, all these little incidents piling on top of each other: I
walked down a corridor in the broken-down People's Hospital,
passing by local patients who hadn't been able to get a ward and
so lay in beds on either side, IV drips dangling, until I got to a
building that looked like the empty gymnasium of an abandoned
seaside elementary school, an empty space that could have been
a worksite (the interior of every building here looked under construction) except for two computers, a printer, and many stacks
of paper. Two bespectacled young men in lab coats (a rare and
precious sight in this city) were sitting there. I said I was there
to get the test results for Mr. Lo, Ward 706, Bed 26. They said,
"Please wait a moment. You're from Taiwan, aren't you?" I said
uh-huh. One of them said, "Did something happen on a vacation?" I said yes. Then, like mainlanders in any setting, now that
they knew I was "from Taiwan," they began spouting the usual
questions: "What do people in Taiwan think about Taiwanese
independence? Has your stock market hit rock bottom yet? That
George W. Bush is hoping we brothers start fighting among ourselves, so he can take advantage," and so on. I answered them
one by one. Sure. Yes indeed. It's not doing great at the moment.
I felt exhausted and alone, and the situation had become as sim-
plistic and pointless as those call-in talk shows on that distant

island. Winding, precise strings of language, convoluted as the sewer system of any modern city. City officials being severely punished for drunk driving. Once, late at night, I changed lanes illegally on an empty underground highway, only to get caught by a lurking patrolman and issued a three-thousand-dollar fine (a form of torture no one in this place would ever, ever be able to imagine).

After a while, one of the lab assistants said, "Roughly how much do young people like us earn each month in Taiwan?"

I cautiously (caught between a powerful temptation to show off and an instinct for humility) answered, "About ten thousand yuan."

Two pairs of eyes exchanged despairing glances from behind their glasses, then one of them said, quietly but trying to keep up appearances, "That's about the same as us."

Trying to help the situation, I mentioned that our young people were getting laid off at an alarming rate. Their faces brightened. "Oh, really? But then we lose our jobs too . . ." And again their expressions were those of poor relations hoping to meet their wealthy family but afraid of being hurt, unable to work out when they'd lost that openness and friendship.

Father's condition was worse than it had been the day before. He'd lapsed back into deep unconsciousness, and when Mother and I arrived at the hospital first thing in the morning, we noticed the tiredness on Eldest Brother's face for the first time. He told us Father had been shitting all night long, which he and Fourth Brother had had to deal with, an entire night of mopping up shit. He said, "Don't bring him any more fruit juice, Little Brother, too much of that stuff gives him the runs."

When the attending physician made his rounds, I caught up with him (he seemed to be unconsciously avoiding me after accepting my bribe—probably his inherently honest personality was in revolt) to ask about this, and he said for seven days now, Father had received nourishment only from his drip and ingesting liquids, so naturally his stools would be loose. He said we could try feeding him congee or fresh fruit juice, as long as we avoided the tinned stuff (on the little wooden table was an open can of coconut water Eldest Brother had left there).

Then another tiny clash: Fourth Brother was about to go out with his steel mug to get some congee. I grabbed the mug from him and said not to get it from a street stall, I'd get a taxi back to the hotel. This led to a heated round of us snatching the container from each other and raised voices (it took quite a while for them to realize I wasn't insisting on paying for the congee, but implying that anything they might buy would be less hygienic) until finally, they turned those honest, confused old-man faces toward me and stared in stupefaction. "What's going on, Little Brother? A bowl of congee costs less than a yuan, and you're spending ten yuan on a taxi back to the hotel? What a waste . . ."

At noon, a light rain fell for once on this scorching city, and my mood plummeted to the very bottom. Back at the hotel, I noticed a corner of the lobby had been festively decorated, and high-end mooncakes were on sale there.

Before returning to the hospital that afternoon, Mother and I got a taxi to the People's Great Mall, where we bought baby wipes, a cream for diaper rash, nail clippers (our fingernails had gotten long), and a steel container (from now on, we'd bring hotel congee to the hospital each day). I also picked up a packet of blank paper for writing (like the local toilet paper, it was thin and coarse), and a bottle of Farmer's Spring mineral water (for the fridge in the hotel room, to replace the one I'd emptied out that morning so I could fill it with freshly squeezed orange juice from the hotel's Western restaurant, as the price list on the fridge stated six yuan per bottle, whereas they were only one yuan fifty at the mall).

I felt myself falling between folds of fragmented time. Like Zeno's arrow paradox: if time can be sliced up into individual units, then . . . no, wait, maybe I'm thinking of his tortoise paradox . . . then time can be stopped.

A piece of bad news arrived in the evening: the young woman from the insurance company phoned to say that according to international aviation law, a doctor would have to certify Father stable enough to be moved, and even then we'd have to wait another fourteen days till he could board a plane. Which is to say, the earliest I could be home was the middle of September. By that point, my wife might have already given birth.

I phoned and told my wife, and she started sobbing.

When I bought freshly squeezed orange juice at the hotel in the afternoon, the girl came over with the mineral water bottle I'd given her to fill, and asked, "Are you the family of that old Taiwanese man who had the stroke?" I said we were. She said, "I saw him that morning, when they were loading him onto the ambulance." All of a sudden, I got worked up. "Really? You saw them lift him into the vehicle?" "Yes, quite a few people tried to carry him but couldn't, and there were these old local men, I think they were his nephews? Then someone from the travel agency came to speak with our manager . . ."

※ ※ ※

That morning . . .

A rupture arose between Mother and me in the hotel room.

I said, "Sometimes the thought flashes through my mind, here we are, we can temporarily abandon the jobs we couldn't let go of before, my wife who'll give birth any day now, my cub, all to come to this faraway place, trapped like Father in this unfamiliar city. Why didn't I find a day or two in the first place to arrange a tour? I could have brought Father around . . ."

My mother, seated at the desk, turned her bespectacled face to me. "That wouldn't have been possible. Aren't you always so busy?"

Oh. Silently, I howled as if someone had punched me in the gut. The pain was already starting. Father wasn't dead yet, and we were already behaving like a widow and orphan at the wake, casting blame, expressing insincere words of repentance or absolution, hurting each other. Looking to the absences and violence of the past, seeking a formula of words that would allow us peace.

Now we were stranded in this unfamiliar, chaotic city, marooned in this meaningless time as Father lay choking from a blocked windpipe, unable to advance or retreat. Each day, we hurriedly grabbed a taxi from the hotel to the crumbling hospital. Then again in the opposite direction, retreating to the hotel, while the poor empty-eyed people of this town, and small shops with whitewashed concrete walls instead of display windows, scattered displays of bathroom products or hanging lamps inside, built-in wooden shelves lined with local versions of Coke and other beverages—while these scenes flashed by the taxi windows.

We were stuck, unable to move.

I'd had no idea that all these years, such implacable hatred floated in my mother's heart.

In the ward, the neighboring patients had asked about Father's stroke, then remarked in their heavy Jiangxi accents (were they blaming us?), "How could an old gentleman who'd already had one stroke have been allowed to go on a group tour like this?"

(Hey, isn't this a bit like that film I didn't watch, *The Ballad of Narayama*?)

The lines on our faces grew dark and shadowy. How could we rewind? Who could testify clearly about what happened? Who failed to dissuade Father in the first place from this single-minded idea of a solo journey, this unfortunate trip that would end up being the final one of his life? Back then, didn't we all secretly have the thought: *It's no bad thing to send this bad-tempered, troublesome old man away for a few days, is it?*

DAY SEVEN

Today was the seventh day.

What happened today?

Today the first counterfeit note appeared in my wallet. A fake hundred-yuan note. The strange thing was, all my renminbi came from the money changer in the hotel lobby.

In the morning, I took Father's hospital card and went to make a payment at the first floor counter. The young nurse put the money through a tallying machine (which doubled as a counterfeit detector? That seemed overly evolved, like the sensitive noses of hunting dogs), pulled one bank note from the stack, and handed it back to me. "This is fake."

Since Mother and I arrived at the People's Hospital, we'd already made five or six of these "estimated payments," a process like sleepwalking—early in the morning, I'd take two or three hundred American dollars from my money pouch and change them to renminbi in the hotel's swanky lobby. Next scene: staring with empty eyes at a place like Ximending Central Market, where I followed my mom around grocery shopping as a kid, the unthinking mob of cheap human flesh, the floor always covered in filthy black liquid getting tracked about by everyone's shoes, the Brownian motion of anxiety that arises between people when they're sealed in a large space—that is, at the hospital jostling with its queue-jumping, scrawny, deeply tanned local patients in front of the payment counter, and when I got to the front I'd reach into my wallet for the stack of renminbi and hand it over.

Mr. Lo, Ward 706, Bed 26.

Recited like a chant. Sometimes they'd demand fifteen hundred yuan, sometimes two thousand. In the beginning, my brother Yiming would toughen his voice and try to snatch the bill from me, and once he managed to put in a thousand. But then he got scared off by the cost, and in less than three days, even the two or three thousand yuan the tour guide had left us was gone. We needed to find more cash so Father could continue receiving treatment. Later, pouting like a resentful child, Eldest Brother accepted the thousand yuan I stuffed into his hands. I remember how, early on, he'd patted his fanny pack with confidence and said, "Don't you worry about us, Little Brother. Hey, I just got back from Jiangxin Island—I borrowed ten thousand yuan from your big sister." (that is, the daughter my father left behind on the mainland.)

After a week of looking after Father day and night in shifts, the four old men were showing signs of fatigue. And now I began finding trivial areas of disagreement with them. For instance, they thought it was very improper that Mother and I insisted, despite the extreme situation and unknown length of time, on the luxury of a three-star hotel and daily taxis, but these old men, who'd never been anything but kind, automatically adjusted their expectations and humbly created a gap between us and themselves. They were about the same age as Mother (Second and Third Brother were a few years older), but never dared look her in the eye or speak directly to her, and when she said anything, they would smile shyly and awkwardly, as you might when listening to your uncle's young would-be widow. At the People's Great Mall, I bought the Johnson & Johnson Infant Wet Wipes and Diaper Rash Cream (which cost the same as the ones I bought with my mother on our weekly trip to the Catholic Center in Taiwan, where "Johnson" is transliterated as "Jiaosheng" rather than "Qiangsheng") from the expensive-looking display cabinet. Eldest Brother and the cousins got quite worked up over us using such costly items to wipe up Father's shit. They asked how much per box? I said about eight yuan (actually it was thirty-eight). Later, though, they had to admit these American-made moist tissues were much smoother and didn't chafe Dad's butt as much.

There were so many incidents like this. I realized I was constantly, in tiny ways, hurting them, through the glass wall of incomprehension that cut me off from this country. *But I'm just protecting Dad!* I shouted inwardly. When they shoved a damp towel into Dad's mouth to scrape the white stuff off his tongue, I rudely screamed at them to stop, and insisted on using cotton dipped in water or a wet wipe; when their eyes widened and they tried to stop me feeding him freshly squeezed orange juice (because it was too "cooling"), I carried on because the doctor had said we should try giving the patient liquids with a little bit of fiber. When I smugly mentioned to Eldest Brother that Mother and I were arranging through our insurance company for an international rescue organization to transport Father back home, and even though international regulations stipulated that stroke patients could only be moved fourteen days after a doctor declared them stable, we still wanted to airlift Father back to Taiwan, never mind the expense (like Buddha describing paradise, I spoke of crystalline air and a hundred fragrant plants carpeting the ground, exaggerating how scientific and advanced the Taiwanese medical system was—naturally while also meanly disparaging the street market-like filthy, backward hospital we were currently in), and Eldest Brother's eyes blazed. "What! Two weeks! Little Brother, I was just saying to Fourth Brother yesterday that we ought to get hold of a boat and take Father down the Yangtze River to Nanjing. The hospitals there are much better than this one."

Had I hurt them? Today, Eldest Brother told us that the night before, in the ward two doors down (which was not an operating room!), the head of the neurology department had carried out the "minimally invasive" brain surgery that we'd almost consented to a few days ago, on a female stroke patient.

Eldest Brother went over to have a look (any passerby was welcome to go in and gawk), and he said the doctor was putting a hole right through the patient's bandaged head with the sort of electric drill you'd expect to see on a construction site, *dik dik dik jrr jrr jrr*; then he stuck in a length of tubing and a glassful of purplish blood gushed out. There was fresh blood too, which he collected in a little porcelain dish (for god's sake, this sounded like one of those cooking demonstrations where they cut open a bear's chest, sliced off a sliver of gallbladder, then neatly sewed up the incision).

After seven days here, the hospital felt like purgatory. No one ever cleaned up the vomit in the slow-moving elevators, and on every landing electric drills (had the doctor borrowed one of these for his "minimally invasive" surgery?) and sanding machines produced such a cacophony that you longed for death, just so new façades of crushed granite could be installed around the elevator doors of this rundown building.

Sometimes I'd go out into the corridor to smoke and look down at the hospital yard, in which shrubs had been pruned into the shapes of various musical instruments.

When a voice called out, "Water!" Third Brother, whose hearing was sharpest, would yell, "Quick, go get water, or the others might take it all."

I'd grab the insulated jug, squeeze into a dingy room with a bunch of old women, and hold it up to receive our ration of hot water from a pot. At those moments, I felt the warm fuzzy feeling of "Hey, we're all in the same boat!"

DAY EIGHT

Today I stood in the stairwell looking down at a construction crew demolishing a large house. Brick by brick, tile by tile, they broke it apart and lined the pieces up neatly in a truck.

The scumbag in the next bed was playing a video game.

Another of the scumbags and I went to the lab with stool samples.

During lunch, my mother complained a lot about Eldest Brother.

It was Sunday, and the long hospital corridors had a more relaxed atmosphere than usual. Mr. Wan prescribed a sort of mugwort leaf from the Chinese medicine dispensary. It would be wrapped in gauze, then placed on Father's belly button. This would slow down Father's diarrhea, he said.

I thought back to several years ago, after I'd made myself morbidly obese to get out of the army, during the short time on Phoenix Hill before my discharge. I had to stay in the training camp on holidays too, waiting for the discharge papers to arrive, whenever that might be. Just like now, I found myself among strangers who'd somehow ended up huddled together.

I faxed the insurance company to arrange for the journey home.

When I spoke on the room phone, the son of the man in the next bed looked at me with such despair and envy.

※ ※ ※

Tonight I left the hospital and sat in the back of a taxi, passing through an alleyway thick with slow-moving humanity, and by my side, Mother suddenly blurted out, "How beautiful."

Yes, this was also the first time I was seeing the beauty of this city. Old maple trees lined the sidewalk, and the street hawkers had strung yellow light bulbs between them, but what were they selling? The taxi was going so fast I only got a blurred glimpse, leaning forward and then back, of dull-colored stalls inserted into the street scene. The dazed, filthy old faces that were suddenly so close to ours, the people dragging carts with difficulty (perhaps the local carts had evolved from the ones at the Yangtze docks—two wheels unusually far apart, pulled by a long handle so the boards swayed like a pheasant's tail) on which were piled not particularly appealing seasonal fruits (pears, dates, honey peaches, apples, kiwi fruit, grapes, oranges—or sometimes an entire cart with nothing but little oval dappled melons). The glass display cases by the roadside were stuffed with boxes of cigarettes; only the colorful candy boxes of childhood could be as beguiling. The streets were full of a jumble of people, dressed in such a variety of fashions I would never have imagined any city could contain them all in the same space and time. As if the inhabitants weren't content to wait patiently for this place to expand and develop, so instead used their own bodies as a canvas on which to imaginatively express the city's sense of an era. It felt like taking Chunghwa Bazaar from 1960s Taipei—the side facing the railroad—and placing it next to Miaoli Railway Station in the '70s, plus the gathering point at the fruit and vegetable market on Wanda Road near Huanghe Express-way, or going further back, my idea of the market at the Monga docks, a scene strung together out of several hazy impressions, and they could all have been impoverished handymen (one day from the taxi, I actually did see four or five shirtless men in chinos crouching by the side of the road, selling their labor with cardboard signs proclaiming "cement worker," "plumber," "mover," "electrician"), laborers, vagrants, civil servants after work, high school students still in their uniforms, young matrons in well-tailored patterned dresses (how pretty), street thugs, attractive young things in cheap silvery crop tops and tiny shorts . . . all these people happy to share space, jostling along this dreamlike street by the yellowish light of the roadside stalls.

※ ※ ※

Father's condition continued improving. Although he was still unconscious most of the time, in his occasional moments of wakefulness, he would stir up a fuss like someone who can't hold his liquor getting completely smashed. He would rage and sulk at the three old men (Second Brother had left for Nanjing to sort out the sale of a boat) and kept barking out commands in a slurry voice: "Sit me up!" "Quick, pull me this way." "I want to go have a shit by myself." And the old men, all grandfathers themselves, would smile foolishly, like put-upon children uncertain how to respond to their drunken father. This caused them no small amount of confusion and pain—the doctor had clearly stated that the proximity of the hemorrhage to his brain stem meant any movement at all risked further bleeding, but they didn't know how to resist the petulant demands of this patriarch.

Perhaps in their worshipful eyes, Father was a magnificent celestial creature who'd been possessed by some demonic force.

For the first time, I realized that the contours of their memories of him were completely different than what he'd become: an island-dwelling old man with a steadily withering body. Tremulous with fear, they tenderly cleaned and tended his large, failing body, tears flowing down their cheeks as they wiped his asshole, raw from the diarrhea that seeped from it every ten minutes. As if lifting a large, fallen colt, together they hefted him farther up the bed (so he could sleep more comfortably).

Fourth Brother told me about Father's first return to Jiangxin Island in '91. "We'd never seen anything like it! Every family on the island set off fireworks for him." Even the radio news from Beijing mentioned my father's return to Nanjing.

※ ※ ※

Back at the hotel that night, I couldn't get hold of my wife. I phoned her cell, both of my in-laws' land lines, our home phone, and even my father-in-law's office number—but no one picked up any of them, and her cell was off. Just like that, I was plunged into hysterical fear. Where was she? Had something happened? While I'd been gone, she'd squeezed her eight-months-pregnant belly into the car each day to ferry our two-year-old son and her mother through the city that was growing blurrier in my memory by the day, from my in-laws' place to our home. She had to walk the dog, listen to my voicemails, phone back everyone who called and explain my situation, feed the dog, and while she was at it, sort out all the bedding and clothes we'd prepared for the baby's arrival. Could she have been T-boned by another car at an intersection? As she led our son across the road, like a mother dinosaur with its baby, could the boy have suddenly let go of her hand and dashed into traffic?

Sorrowfully, I thought: *ever since Father had his oh-so-dramatic collapse, the tenuous grasp I had on any kind of normal life has been completely destroyed. As far as I'm concerned, no catastrophe is now too far-fetched to descend upon me—the way a woman who's been raped might feel only disgust and fear toward any man's embrace or erection.*

At this juncture, I couldn't help resenting my brother in Taiwan. He had no family attachments, so why was I the one abandoning my cub and heavily pregnant wife and traveling thousands of miles to be stranded in this fuckhole of a town? Sure, he couldn't leave right away because of his expired passport, so I had to accompany my mother here, but why hadn't he shown some empathy for my situation, the way I was burning the candle at both ends, and subsequently offered to take my place?

Alone in the hotel room with my mother, I gave in to agitation and rage, like a fighting cock locked up in his cage. This was the first time since Father's collapse that I allowed my extreme emotions around missing my wife and son to show in front of Mother. She, in turn, was thrown into a panic by this display of insanity. Following my lead, she started speculating about all kinds of disasters too. At the same time, I felt I was abandoning her, leaving her even more isolated. As if she were now this semiconscious elderly man's only relative, while I was distracted by my other family at the far end of a phone line.

And actually, I wasn't the only anxious person that day. Since morning, the wall phone in our ward had been ringing off the hook with calls from a Nanjing number for Second Brother. Each time the old man would calmly and slowly pick up the phone, then immediately launch into an expletive-filled diatribe in his dialect. (A startling development: he had a combative, prideful side too.) Sounded like he was instructing the caller to make an important decision, with an air of authority and impatience.

When Second Brother hung up, he switched back to his usual humble, smiling face, and quietly explained to Mother and me that they were preparing to sell one of their two boats. The asking price was 520,000 yuan, but the buyer only had 300,000 on hand. He'd instructed his clerk to just cancel the sale. Then the buyer said he'd pulled together 500 grand in cash. Now his sons (he said "your nephews") were worried about accepting such a large number of bank notes—some might be counterfeit. He said, "That's no problem, just get someone to take the buyer to one of the big Nanjing banks, and deposit the money directly into our account. Those banks have cutting-edge counting machines that can detect fake notes" (something I'd personally experienced).

Then Second Brother chatted with me about the good and bad sides of dock workers. Their boats transported goods along the Yangtze River, and the Jiangyin dockers were impossible— dirty and lazy—while the Nanjing ones were even worse. Then you got to Wuxi where they were not bad, and farther on in Suzhou even better. By the time you reached Shanghai, those dock workers were really great. They'd secure anything you asked them to, and when they loaded or unloaded, you didn't need to stand there keeping an eye on them. They were so clean and efficient.

Yet I could see that he was struggling to steady himself. The phone calls kept coming all afternoon, and the room filled with his booming Jiangbei voice. Finally Mother and I suggested he should head home to sort this out.

%% %% %%

Today Father lost his temper in front of me for the first time.

With a violence that was no longer familiar to me, he roared, "Stop talking! Get lost!" (Once again, he'd been insisting on getting up to use the toilet, and I thought that unlike the old men, I could use the civilized language of logic to warn him not to move too much and definitely not to have a tantrum, so we could keep working on getting him safely home, and so on.)

It had been a long time since he'd spoken to me in that tone of voice. Now he was the father I remembered from my childhood and youth.

When he had another bout of diarrhea, I cleaned his bum with a Johnson & Johnson wipe. (He grumbled, "How can I carry on like this?") This close, I could see that his anus was red and swollen from the constant shitting and wiping.

FATHER'S BUTTHOLE

At that moment, I had a sudden realization: my face was right up against Father's butthole—no more than fifteen centimeters away (measuring from the tip of my nose). Like a surgeon, I focused on a little zone that might as well have been circled with a Sharpie. I had the opening pincered in the second and third fingers of my left hand. The sunburst-shaped tissue of the sphincter, swollen beyond recognition, now had little patches of broken skin in among its folds. All of this from the coarse local toilet paper we'd been wiping him with nonstop due to the diarrhea he'd had since regaining consciousness on the second day. Now the ring of purplish, bulging flesh was covered in a thick layer of white lotion (very like the filling of a cream puff), the Johnson's ("Qiangsheng" in China, "Jiaosheng" to us) diaper rash cream Mother and I had bought at the People's Great Mall, and I'd started using Johnson's baby wipes to clean up the little dribbles of liquid shit that seeped from his butthole every now and then.

These wet wipes weren't expensive in Taiwan—each Sunday, Mother used to accompany my wife and me to the Army's Catholic Welfare Center near where we used to live in Yonghe district, to pick up some milk powder, diapers, or this sort of wet wipes. I remember a pack of three refills was 99 Taiwan dollars. At the People's Great Mall, though, they were treated like imported toiletries—make-up, perfume, whitening cream—and placed in expensive display cases where a salesgirl stood ready to serve us. Thirty-eight yuan for a single packet. That was a lot.

DAY NINE

A gray moth on the hotel window. Alarmingly large even through the glass. I could make out the markings on its belly and its complicated arrangement of limbs.

%% %% %%

Today I bribed a doctor.

A Beijing hospital phoned (they'd been notified by the rescue team our insurance company had hired, and wanted to check on the patient's condition to evaluate the likelihood of a medical evacuation back to Taiwan), but Mr. Wan happened not to be around (bad luck—I'd spent all that time bribing him and dropping hints, expressly so he'd take this phone call and tell the insurance company, "Okay, you can definitely come get the patient now." Who could have guessed he'd be absent at this crucial moment?) and Dr. Zhang took the call. Standing in our ward, amid the usual street market chaos, he leaned toward the wall with the receiver clamped against his cheek, flipping through Father's chart and reciting numbers into the phone like a student answering a quiz. Then he raised his head and gave me a dark look (the old men and I were standing anxiously around him) and nonchalantly said, "It's our medical opinion that the patient is not ready to be moved."

The other hospital said something or other and he grunted in agreement, then he said, "But don't all the medical textbooks state that if there's any cranial bleeding, the patient shouldn't undergo any vigorous movements for at least eight weeks?"

He hung up.

And I thought: *Yes, this was a lesson for you. You can hide from the King of Hell, but it's hard to avoid all the little devils.* When I started down the path with Mr. Wan, I thought I'd gotten to the heart of the matter. From then on, it was Mr. Wan who personally came to check on Father during his rounds, examining him and writing out prescriptions. When Dr. Zhang arrived each day, his face blank, to take care of the patients in the other two beds, did he regret delivering us into Mr. Wan's hands prematurely? Nothing to show for it but a carton of imported cigarettes and some cognac.

My heart let out a cry of anguish: *Must my limits be tested at every turn?* My gut shriveled like that of a pufferfish being slaughtered.

We barged into his office, and Yiming raged (in his heavy Nanjing accent), "The family is keen to send our father home as quickly as possible. Dr. Zhang, you've just cut off any chance . . ."

(Wow, he was really at the end of his tether.)

Dr. Zhang stared at us with a half-victorious, half-pitying smile that said, *Don't you see what the situation is?* and at a perfectly even pace (but surely inwardly grinning at his luck that he'd taken that phone call) he said, "That's what it says in the medical textbooks: a severe brain hemorrhage like the one your father had means he can't be moved for at least eight weeks. Never mind an airplane, even sending him to Nanchang in an ambulance could kill him."

Eldest Brother retorted, "But didn't Mr. Wan say . . ."

I interrupted him. "How about this, Dr. Zhang—" and pulled from my wallet a stack (at least twelve or thirteen of them) of hundred-yuan bills, and slid them into the pocket of his lab coat. Naturally, he resisted a little, but I kept pushing them in. Over the last few days, I'd gotten the hang of this ambiguous, secretive procedure. I imagined myself as a drug smuggler, police chief, or mafioso in one of those Hollywood gangster films. Even my voice transformed into a gravelly drawl.

I said, "Naturally, after you've taken such good care of us, we'd hate if we never found an opportunity to thank you properly. We don't mean anything else by this, please don't think that. Just pretend this never happened. A little gesture of gratitude from me and my mother."

He sank back into his chair and began stuttering. All this while, Yiming stared at my face with a strange look. Even after we left the office, he didn't say a word.

I knew that in that moment, I'd not only roughly and successfully humiliated the young doctor, I'd also deeply hurt this man in his fifties who'd been abandoned by my father as a small child in their hometown and managed to survive poverty and famine, as well as being labeled one of Mao's "Five Black Categories" during the Cultural Revolution, this old man, my half-brother.

DAY TEN

Here's what happened today:

First thing in the morning, Mother and I arrived at the hospital to find Father's bed empty. For an instant my stomach plummeted, as if in a flash of bright light the illness was reduced to the simple outline of a bed and window, and the smell of silver bromide. Then one of the dirtbags by the next bed told us, "Your father's gone for a CT scan." We hustled to the elevator. From the landing window, we saw Third Brother, Fourth

Brother, and Yiming in the distance, three old men clutching their lunchboxes like elementary school students, chuckling as they pushed Father down a slope on a gurney.

Mother and I ran to catch up with them, but they didn't see us till we drew level. Right away, I joined in the procession. Looking confused, Father turned his eyes upward to stare at the sky above and the autumnal silhouettes of trees. This was his first trip out of that smoke-filled room while conscious, and by the light of this fall morning, his pupils looked like those of a foreign child, with a dull blue haze from lack of melanin. Back in the ward (for some reason, everyone seemed slow and lazy, yet oddly gleeful that day), Yiming told us Father's diarrhea seemed to have stopped. Then Mr. Wan stopped by to discuss the gap between the latest we'd like to get Father on a plane, which was the following Tuesday (or nineteen days after he first fell ill), and the medical advice that stroke patients were only considered stable after three weeks of recovery. He seemed distracted, though. It turned out he was mainly there to stick a gastric tube down the nose of the Edvard Munch man in Bed 27.

At first I thought he was going to perform "minimally invasive" surgery on that man (put a hole in his skull with a power drill to let the excess blood out). He kept hanging out on the balcony, smoking and playing cards, a crafty grin on his face, as if he didn't dare face this life-or-death decision. Then I found out the patient was just getting a feeding tube fitted. Once again, patients from the other wards, along with their families, swarmed in to see the excitement. Third Brother said the other scumbags had insisted on feeding him the night before, and even though he couldn't chew (but his mouth hung open thanks to the stroke), they kept stuffing it in. Then in the morning, while coughing up phlegm, he brought up a whole cup of Wahaha milk.

In the afternoon, we got the CT scan back. For comparison, Dr. Zhang brought out the ones taken immediately after his collapse and when my brother and cousins carried Dad to the blazing bright room right after my arrival. The first image had four segments with round blood clots, the second only three, and in the most recent, just one coin-sized clot and a sort of shadowy residue. This meant Father's body was absorbing the congealed blood on its own. He was recovering.

The insurance company chose this juncture (as we watched anxiously for minute changes in Father's body as if he were a plant, while fretting about being trapped in this savage city) to silently and meticulously gather more information—they phoned the doctor and got the document they needed. In the small print of the contract we'd signed, there was a single line about "preexisting conditions" being excluded, and without us realizing it, they'd been nudging us toward describing this as Father's "second stroke."

Another thing that happened today: the hospital's elevators acquired wooden floorboards overnight, and paintings of flowers on both side walls. The main lobby now had automatic glass doors (I'd walked through them without realizing they were meant to be automatic). By the entrance was a poster—"A warm welcome to the Provincial Emergency Services Inspection Team"—with large flower displays on either side. Damn them, so this whole rigmarole of apocalyptic drilling and filling the air with stone dust was in aid of some pointless inspection.

(I got into a fight with Mother over my brother not coming from Taiwan to take my place, and she burst into tears in the crowded hotel restaurant. "I'm already feeling very fragile, could you stop making it worse?" When Colonel Buendía returned to Macondo wrapped in his bloodstained army coat after nineteen years of meaningless war, unbearably lonely, he realized his mother "was the only human being who had succeeded in penetrating his misery," but for me the "penetrating" knowledge went the other way, and my mother merely passed over the surface of my self.)

DAY ELEVEN

In the bed to Father's right was an old man (a loud snorer) who had two beautiful daughters, a son, a son-in-law, and an old guy with glasses who turned out to be his little brother.

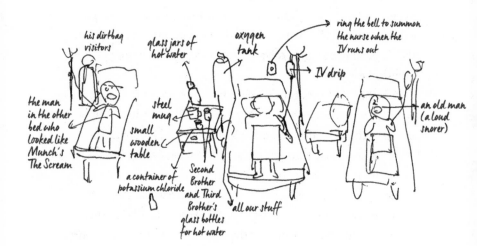

DAY TWELVE

How much did I actually know about this city?

One morning, in a taxi on my way to the hospital, I passed by an elementary school shrouded in thick fog—only when I saw the gateway crowded with children and the red banner with gold words above it proclaiming "A Warm Welcome to Our New Teachers and Students" did I realize what it was. Many of the buildings in this place had a tangle of random objects obscuring their outlines (rotting awnings, illegal wooden structures, bamboo baskets thrust out into the street to extend the shop space, even large trees) and making them lose the identity they had when they were first built, so every street felt as if its organizing principle was to fill every crevice of space, turning it into a single clump.

It wasn't just the buildings. The people too were squashed together chaotically, an art installation consisting of electrical cables, asphalt, and leftover construction materials, scorched and melted together. Despite the bustle around me, I'd hardly seen any elementary or high school students in uniform. There only seemed to be a few basic varieties of people: laborers, military police in dull grass-green uniforms and red epaulets, elderly workers with suffering etched into their faces, street hawkers, crew-cut tour guides with bushy-browed large eyes and fake designer leisure shirts in dark checkerboard prints (very like the casualwear on display in our Zhongzheng district), plus taxi drivers and spicy ladies dressed according to some obscure fashion sense (some truly unsophisticated; some trying to revive the elegance of ancient times; some transcending space and time to appear both reserved and adorable, rather like Shin Kong Mitsukoshi Department Store in Tainan, or the intersection of Mother's Western tailor and fashion magazines; some so hot they had a primeval cheapness about them, everything as short and tight as possible, but falling short of the youthful freshness that escort girls in Taipei or Tokyo possess).

One evening, I sat writing by the picture window of the hotel coffee shop, when through the gloom outside came a spicy woman (plucked eyebrows, cobalt eyeshadow, tight cropped T-shirt with flared sleeves and silvery pink camouflage trousers) who stopped right outside, smiling and waving at me. I froze for an instant before I recognized her: the sweet young girl who sat all alone behind the counter of the hotel's business center in her red shoulder-padded uniform, greeting me with canned phrases when I stopped by every evening to make a long-distance call and complain to my wife about how much I missed home, taking my money and giving me change when I was done.

Another time, I was wandering through the crowds in the People's Great Mall rotunda when I saw the stern-faced head nurse, now out of her white uniform and in a minidress and platform heels, suddenly a spicy woman too.

How much did I know about them? Early on, the family of one of the other patients warned us not to linger at the hospital past sunset, because Jiujiang filled up with drug addicts come dusk, and as a result when we hurried down the stairs at twilight to grab one of the taxis waiting at the entrance with their doors open, the drivers hanging out to smoke and chat, their faces murderous, I'd always have a moment of anemic fear (is he going to drive us to a dark alleyway and steal all our money?).

How much did I know about the two doctors I'd bribed?

Did they go home and sit at the family dinner table or in their staff dorm, and brag to the girlfriend or wife and kids that an old guy from Taiwan had been admitted to the hospital and his son handed them such-and-such an amount of money?

DAY THIRTEEN

Occasionally someone I knew would walk past the coffee shop window, whereupon they'd slow down, or nod and smile, or pull a funny face and wave, throwing me into soft confusion, and in that window bathed in light I'd raise my ass a little off my chair and half-bow to them. And I'd think: *My god, how long have*

I been in this city? In this blurry space, I suddenly had *acquaintances.*

In the last two days, all the hotel staff seemed to have had the same impulse, probably the result of an order from management, that no matter what their role and which floor they worked on, they had to foist the hotel's mooncakes on every guest. At noon, when Mother and I went to the front desk to pay for another day's stay, an attractive staff member asked if we'd like to try their very own brand of mooncake? I asked her when Mid-Autumn Festival was, and she said September 1. I hesitated for a moment, then suggested to Mother that we could bring a few boxes in for the nurses, or perhaps for the other patients' families. How much was each box? She said 88 yuan (that is, renminbi). I said we'd go back to our room and think about it, and maybe place an order in the afternoon. She pouted a little and said in a quiet voice that she wouldn't be there in the afternoon, why didn't we come by the next day instead, anyway whenever we decided we should be sure to buy them through her.

We talked about it back in our room and decided to drop the idea. Eighty-eight renminbi was between 300 and 400 Taiwan dollars! Not cheap at all. If we showed up at the ward with such exorbitant mooncakes, Third Brother and the other thrifty old men would surely give us a good scolding. This morning, the father of the Edvard Munch guy in the next bed asked to borrow my electric razor, and with the front razor extended, he buzzed away at the hairs on his son's scrawny chin (I realized I hadn't cleaned the blade after shaving my father, and imagining his white powdery stubble mixed with the scraggly beard of a strange young man from an unfamiliar place, I marveled at what a mystical place the world could be). Afterward I offered the razor to the daughter of the stroke patient in the third bed. At first she stood on her dignity and refused, insisting she had her own razor and would shave her father later, but the Munch dad urged her to say yes, enthusing about how quick and smooth the electric razor was. And so now the inside of my razor had bits of stubble from three unconscious men.

That's when Third Brother asked me how much an electric razor like this cost, and I said about 38 yuan (I'd picked out the cheapest locally made one from the counter at the People's Great Mall). His eyes widened, and he claimed he'd seen one at the market for ten. How was that possible? We argued a little, but he unloaded a slew of ideas on me in his gurgling Nanjing accent (I often simply didn't understand what he was saying), and where this conversation ended up was: during the Cultural Revolution, while he was hiding in an Anhui village, a donkey came up to him and started gnawing at his chest (which was already nibbled raw), so he lost his temper and grabbed its mouth by the rope harness and one of its hooves, and lifted it right up into mid-air (whenever Third Brother and I chatted while keeping watch over Father, I'd frequently lose the thread of the conversation, partly because I couldn't make out his words and partly because I got distracted; sentences became disjointed, and I never really followed the logic or understood the point he was trying to make).

Which is why we couldn't make any rash decisions about the mooncakes. That afternoon, before leaving for the hospital, we called room service for a fresh Thermos of hot water (Mother liked to bring a flask of tea with her). The chambermaid who came with our water (whom I was fond of because I often asked her for letter paper, and she was happy to bring some even though it was probably expensive here) also murmured, before I could thank her and shut the door, "If you don't mind, sir, I wonder if you'd like to try our very own brand of mooncake . . ."

This kept cropping up. In the evening, after Mother and I returned from the hospital, I slipped off to the hotel's business center (they had a soundproof glass phone booth), and just as I was preparing to dial long distance and tell my wife how homesick I was, the girl who usually sat silent and blank-faced at the counter (I suspected she'd overheard enough from our scraps of phone conversation—Mother and me, or me alone—to piece together the whole ludicrous situation, this disaster we were trapped in along with family elsewhere) opened her mouth for once to push some mooncakes at me. As soon as I stepped into the coffee shop, the girl who told me she'd watched my father being carried through the crowd into the waiting ambulance asked if I'd like to try their very own brand of mooncake.

This all felt like a blind old dog whose sense of smell was still sharp trotting along a familiar path and marking its way with spots of pee. These girls who kept popping up to offer me mooncakes were the same ones whose pretty faces, on any given day in this long, lonely, helpless stretch of time in this vast hotel, I'd picked out with warmth and kindness (and no other motive) from where they floated in the sea of others in identical uniforms, and learned to recognize them.

That evening, in the taxi back to the hotel, the driver went a long distance in silence, then abruptly said, "You leave the hospital at this time every day, don't you?" (My instinctive thought was: *Damn it, we're being watched.*) Mother answered: "Uh-huh, we've made this trip a lot, and we always get a taxi at the same place. Have you seen us hailing another cab?"

"You've taken mine before," said the driver.

I didn't know why I got so excited then, but it felt like meeting someone familiar far from home, and so I said in a completely inappropriate tone of voice, "Really? That's quite a coincidence!"

Today I bribed Mr. Wan again (in the hospital corridor).

My wife phoned to say the insurance company had made their decision, and Father could leave at the weekend. Unsuccessfully hiding her delight, she asked what I wanted to do. Then this morning, Mr. Wan told me even next Friday might be too early—in their professional judgment, stroke patients shouldn't be moved long distances for at least four weeks. I said, "Let's make it next Tuesday then."

I asked my elementary school classmate Chen Wen-Fen to help me get in touch with Dr. Tsai from Taipei Veterans General Hospital, and Dr. Tsai asked me to call and tell him a bit more about the situation, and fax a summary of my father's medical records over. Squatting down by Mr. Wan, I asked if this was possible, and he said no problem, which is when I realized all the nurses around us were giving us sidelong looks because I looked like I was kneeling at his feet. Still talking, I straightened my knees and rose to my feet as unobtrusively as possible.

Today I looked down from the window of the seventh-floor toilet and happened to see Yiming and Fourth Brother, those scumbags, walking along with their lunchboxes, not a care in the world, down the sloping path by the hospital garden.

Today I borrowed Father's camera and snuck off to a corner of the hospital, but I only got a couple of shots before the camera let out an enormous whirring sound and the film started rewinding (and also each snap came with an alarmingly bright flash). I wondered if someone would report me to the authorities for infiltrating a Party hospital and carrying out espionage, and if I'd then get detained. (Perhaps even Father's trip to the mainland was part of my sophisticated plan, and my mother with her prayer beads, chanting scripture by his bedside, eyes shut, was actually Secret Agent Code Name Choshui River Number Three?)

DAY FOURTEEN

The troops were weary and the horses spent, and I was filled with despair.

Here's what happened today:

In the morning, Mr. Wan produced sheet after sheet of doctors' reports and asked if that would satisfy the requirements on our side. I took them from him and went back to the hotel alone in a taxi, where I faxed them to Dr. Tsai at Taipei Veterans from the business center.

When I went back to the hospital with Mother in the afternoon, Yiming, Third Brother, and Fourth Brother were once again waiting for us, wide-eyed, to warn us not to feed Father anything at all. Earlier that afternoon, he'd wanted to vomit but couldn't, and when he strained he produced a huge coil of shit instead. He hadn't shit for three days, and we were starting to worry he might be constipated. Now he was passing soft stools, and everyone was worked up. I got into an argument with Yiming, who said given Father's condition and the fact the doctors had given him an IV drip, there was no problem with his nutrition, so it would be fine if we didn't feed him (what an unfilial son, cutting off his father's food so as not to have to wipe his ass). I retorted that Mr. Wan had said we could give him a little scraping of pear or apple, not so much for the nutrients as to let his gut go though something like the usual motions (he hadn't eaten solid food for two weeks now), otherwise his organs would start to atrophy. Ducking the issue, Eldest Brother said simply that Mr. Wan's words should sometimes be listened to and sometimes ignored.

Our mistrust and lack of respect for one another increased along with the exhaustion of our physical bodies. I continued phoning Taiwan every night, and kept my eye fixed on the date the insurer said we could move Father back. First it was Tuesday, then the local doctors said at least three weeks so we moved it to next Friday, and Yiming immediately lost his temper. Finally the insurance company confirmed next Tuesday at the latest. Now Eldest Brother and Fourth Brother grinned broadly whenever I saw them.

Father still spent most of his time unconscious. Now and then his eyes would half open, and he'd clamor like a drunkard to get out of bed and back to Taiwan. When Mother and I weren't there in the afternoon, he'd scream, "Where's my son? Where's my little son?" Fourth Brother teased, "Little Brother's gone back to Taiwan." Father wanted to know, "Then what about me?" Fourth Brother said, "Why not just come back to Nanjing with me?" And Father sighed weakly, "Fine, then."

Fourth Brother was still grinning broadly when he repeated this conversation to us, but it made me unbearably sad. Deep down, Father actually believed this was something we were capable of—abandoning him in this place and returning home alone.

In fact, everyone (including Third Brother, who'd been steady as a rock throughout) was trying hard to hide the happiness of "finally this is coming to an end."

Then this afternoon, I phoned the insurance company, but Miss Zhang—whom we'd been dealing with all along—had vanished. In her place was a Miss Huang, who told us we might not be able to get him on a Tuesday flight. I asked why, and she said, "Essentially it's the Hong Kong airline who says your father's condition is quite unusual, because we need to bring an oxygen tank on board, and they'll need seven days to apply for special permission because that's an explosion hazard, so they may not be able to get it done before Tuesday." I said, "We've been telling you over and over that we want to get him back urgently for more than a week, and you guaranteed (using that reassuring, professional, and rational tone of voice) that as long as the local doctors agreed, we could be on our way within three days, so how could this seven days rule just come out of nowhere?" She just repeated that it would take seven days, sounding as certain as the erstwhile Miss Zhang (in fact, I was starting to suspect she *was* Miss Zhang) and telling me not to worry, they had a lot of experience assisting in these sorts of international medical transfers. . . .

At night I phoned my brother and sister in Taipei, and they'd called the insurance company only to be given a different excuse: it seemed the discharge letter from the Jiujiang hospital was dated September 2, so there wouldn't be enough time to book a plane ticket for September 4.

Every one of these discussions went in circles, a dog chasing its tail. I was starting to feel like a muddled old woman chasing after a young bureaucrat to list all her troubles, a tangle of grievances, injustices, petty complaints, this or that person who'd wronged her . . . all these tiny details spewed down the phone for a well-trained (how to deal with difficult clients?) customer service officer in a distant insurance office to explain soothingly away.

If Eldest Brother Yiming knew this would drag on till Friday . . . I imagined him throwing a complete tantrum and flipping over the hospital bed.

Today my wife told me over the phone that my brother came by to borrow her identity card. Something about a friend sending him a DVD, and he'd used my wife's name, so he needed her card to collect it. I felt first rage and then exhaustion.

My brother had borrowed my own identity card several times before, all for similarly ridiculous reasons, and one time I told him fairly unambiguously that I hoped he wasn't doing anything that might end up damaging our relationship. I would never ask him for any of his personal documents, and I hoped he wouldn't come begging for mine. Yet here I was, trying to help my father in this distant place, mind and body exhausted, in despair at the Kafka's Castle that was the gap between Taiwan and the mainland, the sheer difference in speed and ways of doing things. As soon as we got here, the travel agency had vanished like a startled animal, and every few days I had to read the tea leaves of whatever passed between the neurology department head and our attending physician to estimate whether I needed to put more money in the next red packet (had all the fuel from the last one already been expended?), and all the while my elder brother back home was up to god knows what monkey business.

Three more things from today:

First, Mother and I put a new roll of film into Father's camera and snapped some pictures around the hospital ward, corridors, staircase, and bathroom. I also took one of Father in his bed at dusk, with Third Brother sitting to one side, as well as his neighbors (Edvard Munch guy and the old mainland man) and their families. Munch guy's scumbag friends were very excited and struck some awkward poses for the camera.

Second, there was a teaching demonstration by a senior physician, so Mr. Wan, Dr. Zhang, and all the other doctors on this floor squeezed themselves with a lot of fuss into our tiny room. They huddled around Munch guy's bed, and the senior physician began prodding at his body, giving his analysis in an unhurried manner, as if he'd already calculated exactly how much time he had between camera flashes. Munch guy's simian friends bobbed up and down between those doctors in their white coats, seemingly agitated at not being able to understand the words coming out of the mouth of this dude manhandling their bro.

(At this moment, Father released a glob of shit, staining the blue bedsheet.)

Third, this afternoon, two young men, medical residents, showed up to take a spine marrow sample from Munch guy.

(Third Brother whispered to me, "That's not good. They're sucking the marrow oil from the dragon bone, but that's where your vigor is stored. At this rate he'll never get well.") The whole process was terrifying (and as always, the hangers-on from all the other rooms came running over to watch. The grapevine was certainly effective here). One of the doctors inserted a thin steel needle many times around Munch guy's tailbone, and though he was shrouded in a white cloth with a hole cut in it, I could see he was wearing the same sort of ant-slip gloves I'd had back in my snooker-playing days, and his hands were trembling violently as he poked the needle in, which made me feel really bad for Munch guy. He tried a long time but couldn't find the right spot. Finally he gave up and handed it over to his co-worker (or should I say classmate?) whose hands were also shaking hard, though he eventually managed to get the needle into Munch guy's lower back by brute force, like jamming a nail into the wall to hang up a picture.

DAY FIFTEEN

Father, in order to bring you home, I've committed bribery, I've committed forgery, I've done every bad thing there is to do.

This morning, Mr. Wan came to check up on Munch guy, and afterward nonchalantly said to the guy's friend: "There's no way he's going to live. We've all done everything we possibly could. Spent so much money, used so much manpower, everything we ought to have done, but we can't find the cause of his illness." Then an older doctor appeared (and after him, as always, a gaggle of younger ones).

Munch guy's wife looked a lot like Gao Tung-Ping, the wife of the anti-Communist hero Zhuo Changren who was recently executed. Maybe a little smaller. Her hair was very dark and rather brittle, and she wore it in two plaits, which made her look a little like a shrunken Native American squaw. I was taken aback when she spoke with a clear, precise Beijing accent, as she told the old doctor what had happened:

"That morning, he went to work as usual on the wall" (was he a bricklayer?) "and came back at noon to have lunch with us. During the meal, he said something about not being able to get the wall straight somehow. I didn't pay much attention. Afterward he had a nap, then went back out to work and came home again in the evening. Again he said he hadn't been able to work properly. Around seven, we had dinner, and he didn't say much" (the old doctor asked if he'd mentioned having a headache, and the woman said no). "At seven-thirty he washed his trousers and went to have a shower. At eight he spoke to the children for a while" (again, I was impressed at how this woman, allowed to have her say in front of all these highly educated doctors for the first time, was able to provide such an accurate list of timings). "Then he said he wanted to lie down, though it was earlier than he'd usually go to bed. Before nine o'clock, he was clutching his head, in the state you see him now."

The old doctor said, "Did you send him to the doctor that very night?" She said, "No, we're not from around here. I called his friends over and they put him in bed to sleep it off. The next day we brought him to XXX Hospital, and he sat in the corridor with water streaming from his eyes and mouth. The nurses there said he was a lunatic and wanted to have him institutionalized."

The old doctor asked, "Had he eaten anything unusual?" She said, "He had a can of traditional Chinese medicine," (a tonic for bones and muscles) "but we all had some." (And here the monkeylike friends chimed in, "Yes, we all had some, and nothing happened to us.")

The old doctor asked, "Are there a lot of mosquitoes where you are?" She said, "Yes, sure, but . . ." He cut in, "But you get bitten by mosquitoes too, and you're fine?"

That's when I felt a shiver of terror, like slugs crawling up my shin bones (how selfish, how human), because Munch guy hadn't had a stroke or brain hemorrhage but some sort of acute brain inflammation the hospital hadn't been able to find a cause for, and I could only think of Father lying all day and night next to a body filled with god knows what germs, the same air circulating between their mouths and noses. I even had the hysterical notion: *What if Father gets safely airlifted back to Taiwan, while Mother or I succumb to this viciously fast-acting brain infection?* (And here I couldn't help darkly recalling Spielberg's film *Saving Private Ryan* because fuck it, doesn't Ryan get rescued from the jaws of death like in a fairy tale, while everyone who goes into the war zone after him is killed?)

⅛ ⅛ ⅛

I phoned my wife and found her utterly depressed and exhausted. (My god, if time kept dragging on like this, would my wife end up weeping all alone as she gave birth to the child in her belly, in that distant city that was growing gradually blurrier in my mind?)

This morning, the hospital room phone rang. It was a woman from the Hong Kong life insurance company, wanting to speak to Mr. Wan—probably to ask for more details about Father's illness, or about his treatment and medication. Mr. Wan had lost his swagger and optimism of a few days ago and now said with great caution in his voice that in their professional judgment it would be four weeks before the patient could be moved, and only the family's urgency had made them insist. . . . Naturally, he couldn't possibly make any guarantees about moving a brain hemorrhage patient such a long distance . . .

For several days now, I'd gotten used to floating around in this swamp, with no sense of time at all, two steps forward and three steps back. If there was good news in the morning, there'd surely be bad luck that afternoon pushing us back in the other direction. The insurance company deployed a rotating roster of women with changing surnames to tell us procedures that switched randomly back and forth, as well as getting a nurse to phone the ward each day to instruct us on how to deal with Father's bedsores and so on, while the attending physician's suggestions lost all value to me—who knew whether his façade of propriety concealed a hint I should increase his bribe? Or was it the opposite, that his guilt at giving in to temptation and surrendering his ethics had made him even more keen to bring his medical knowledge to the fore?

International aviation law stated that cerebral hemorrhage patients could only board a plane fourteen days after recovery. The local doctors claimed that the medical textbooks said acute brain hemorrhage patients couldn't be moved for three weeks. Then the head of the neurology department changed his mind and said it would be a month (having previously declared we could make arrangements after two weeks), and now the Hong Kong airline was saying an oxygen tank would take seven days to be approved . . . All these different gradations of time, and Father was like an old sleepwalker drifting horizontally between various clock faces.

The Hong Kong woman said, "You need to sign some medical documents to get things moving with the airline." Mr. Wan said, "No problem, send them over." Then a moment later, I heard him say awkwardly, "Oh, but we don't have a fax machine . . ." so I snatched the receiver and said, "Please send the forms to my hotel, I'll pick them up from the business center at noon." I gave her the fax number and our room number.

At noon we got back to the hotel and asked at the business center, only to find the fax hadn't arrived. Mother and I wandered over to the hotel restaurant, where we ate the exact same lunch we'd had every one of the last fourteen days: two bowls of vegetable noodle soup, a dish of sizzling tofu, and some stir-fried greens. Mother recalled the various difficulties she'd had when she was pregnant with my older brother, and my older sister, and finally me. ("When I was carrying your brother, we were still living with your granny, and your dad would be furious with her over something or other every single day, while I was just living between terror and pain. Maybe that's why your brother ended up so timid." And I thought: *Is she trying to patch things after our fight yesterday?*)

Back in our room, I phoned Miss Lin from the Taiwanese insurance company (at least she'd remained Miss Lin, and hadn't transformed into Miss Liu or Miss Gu). She said they were still working hard to coordinate things with the airline, though she couldn't go into which fine points they were currently ironing out. Then she brought up the three forms again and said she would fax them to our hotel. Afterward I phoned my brother and sister, and my brother said he'd found out that the Taipei insurance company and the Beijing rescue organization were two completely separate entities, and everything was now stuck at the Beijing end. "Fuck," I swore, "how did we end up here?" At this rate, never mind next Tuesday, even next Friday might not be achievable.

I hung up, and right away the business center called to say, "Is this Mr. Lo in Room 206? Your fax has arrived." I said "Thanks, I'll be down to collect it in an hour."

My head was splitting by that point, and I thought I'd better have a nap before trying again to tackle these problems, which seemed as tangled as the summary of a failed novel doomed from its very conception, but then Miss Lin from the insurance company (still her!) phoned to say, "Did you get the fax, Mr. Lo?" I said, "Yes, the business center called to say it's arrived, I'll go get them after my afternoon nap." Miss Lin got agitated. "Oh no, that won't do, these three forms" (one for the attending physician to stamp and sign, stating what treatment the patient received; a special flight contract from the airline for the family to sign; and declaration from the attending physician that the patient was fit to fly) "are extremely urgent, because the Hong Kong office will be shut on Saturday and Sunday, and the forms need to be submitted forty-eight hours before the plane takes off."

I thought wearily of asking, *So why didn't you send these forms over this morning or yesterday or the day before?* But what I said was, "What time will you need me to fax them over by?"

"3:30."

I looked at my watch: 2:30. Mother and I jumped out of bed, quickly got dressed, rushed down the stairs, and frantically flagged down a taxi.

All the way there, a voice screamed inside me *Fuck it! Fuck it!*

At the hospital, we found Fourth Brother watching over Father alone. Father was having another of his feeble tantrums, and Fourth Brother was teasing him as if he were a dying elephant. I barged into the common room and found the younger doctors hanging out around the conference table (including one of the men who had taken a spine marrow sample from Munch guy the day before). I asked, "Where's Mr. Wan?" They stared at me and said, "He's gone home for lunch." I said, "Where does he live? I have something urgent to ask him."

They must all have thought I'd gone crazy. One of the young doctors called Mr. Wan's cell and stutteringly explained the situation (it felt as if we'd gone right back to the beginning, with them blankly confused at my rage and desperation, fumbling and panicked as they hurried to call the perpetually absent Mr. Wan. Now they chirped at each other in incomprehensible Jiangxi dialect. As if the relationship we'd built up greeting one another awkwardly in the hospital corridors had been ripped to shreds in an instant); then he hung up and, happy there'd be nothing else I could find fault with, said, "He's coming back right away."

I headed back to the ward, still fretting. Mother was sitting on the edge of Father's bed with her eyes shut, running her prayer beads through her fingers and chanting scripture. Fourth Brother wiped the smile off his face and sat in silence, as if afraid of offending me. I paced around the room, and out of nowhere remembered Eileen Chang's recollection of how when she was a little girl, her father would walk around the room after every meal (in order to keep fit), loudly reciting texts that no longer had anything to do with the world, eight-legged essays and imperial memoranda from ancient times. She said he was "like an angry, despairing beast trapped in an iron cage." Then I suddenly remembered: Oh yes, I should probably draft this flight approval letter myself (I was ready to bet the hospital wouldn't have one ready-made), so I sat on the balcony (to one side of me, Munch guy's friends sat shirtless, playing handheld video games beneath the dripping wet underpants and shirts and towels that they'd hung up to dry like the flags of all nations), earnestly writing out my "air travel approval":

Suitable for Flying Certification
　　Passenger Luo Jiaxuan
　　The patient suffered a cerebellar hemorrhage and is currently in a good condition. Due to the special circumstances (a Taiwanese compatriot unexpectedly struck down by a stroke

in mainland China), as well as the urgent request of the family, who are willing to sign a waiver releasing all physicians from personal liability in the case of death or other complications, and on condition that there are medical personnel and appropriate facilities en route, and as there is no risk of infection or inconvenience to other passengers, I certify the patient fit for travel.

Dr. _____, First People's Hospital, Jiujiang City

Mr. Wan soon arrived, and he seemed to be in a calm, approachable mood. His face blank, he listened to my rambling explanation about how the airline company urgently needed these important forms signed (perhaps over the last couple of weeks, he'd gotten used to my mumbling delivery and habit of compressing the passage of time), and without a single protest, he filled in and signed the faxed forms from the insurance company. When I handed him my "air travel approval," though, he studied it for a while, looked up, and asked, "Did you write this?" I said yes. He chuckled. "This is fascinating, really fascinating." With the papers in his hand, he strode over to the treatment station and said to the head nurse and all her little nurses, "Hey, get a load of this, he wrote it. Look at him, so young, and see how he can write. Isn't that fascinating?" At first I thought he was joking (I was in hurry!), but then I realized he actually was very excited, probably because he'd mistaken my traditional Chinese characters for calligraphy. This little misunderstanding altered his attitude toward me, and he now gingerly copied the whole thing out in simplified characters (I was far too shy to tell him that everyone in Taiwan could write like I did). He paused now and then to cross out a few words, including "in the case of death or other complications" and "releasing all physicians from personal liability." Then he led me to another building to get the hospital director's stamp.

An official stamp. Travel documents. Yes, I ought to have predicted this, but I never expected the process would be so slow and convoluted, like Calvino's chapter headings, "in a network of lines that enlace," "looks down in the gathering shadow" . . . I hustled down the pathways and verandas between the buildings of this ancient hospital like I was falling into an old movie where time flowed backward; whether it was the high ceilings and white walls or the slow movement of patients, doctors, and nurses past me, some dizzying force was sloughing away the sharper points of light from everything connecting me to the present moment. In a deserted stairwell, I nimbly slid another couple hundred American dollars into his lab coat pocket (this time out of sincere gratitude). He quickly rejected it a couple of times, then uttered those high-minded words of absolution, "No such thing," but he took the money anyway. He spoke with some emotion, and though he had a few years on me, we were basically the same age, and had I wished I could have treated him like my older brother. He could empathize with Mother and me, having come all the way to this unfamiliar place. He wanted me to be less anxious. Now he asked what other family I had in Taiwan? What work did I do? (I told him I wrote novels.) He then wanted to know, "What kind of novels?" I didn't know how to answer, so I vaguely referred to a few mainland novelists I admired: Mo Yan, Wang Anyi, Han Shaogong. He seemed to have heard of them but didn't express an opinion (I guess he hadn't actually read any of their books).

But then we reached what was clearly the most secret, innermost part of the hospital, and everything suddenly became less smooth. We were in a dingy, silent corridor, probably the administrative center of the institution. Mr. Wan's face grew docile and childlike, and he greeted the medical and admin staff who popped out of the various rooms along the way as if they were his older schoolmates. They in turn teased, "How come a big important doctor like you has time to visit us?" Some fondly tousled his hair, as if he were a promising kid. I abruptly recalled my first encounter with him in that gloomy consulting room (back when we'd hoped he would approve Father's transfer to a larger hospital in Nanchang), when he'd roared, "Oh, the deputy director of Second Affiliated? So-and-So, is it? I know him very well. Tell him to come talk to me, and we'll see who knows more about cerebellar stroke." He was a completely different person now, smiling bashfully and saying hi to everyone.

He led me to a meeting room where we waited outside while someone went in to announce us. After a short while, an older guy of my father's generation (one of the school's senior officials or teachers) came out. Mr. Wan said this was the director of the hospital and explained our situation, then handed over the various forms and my letter for him to examine. The director didn't look too closely, just said, "Fine, fine," and told Mr. Wan to go get Such-and-Such to take care of this. The older man then turned to shake my hand and said he'd heard about us, the visitors from Taiwan, such an unusual situation, he'd given orders that we were to receive the best treatment and care—he wanted to know if we'd had a good experience. Naturally I bowed and thanked him repeatedly. (I had the hallucinatory thought: *When I shake this old man's hand, am I supposed to unobtrusively leave a few American bank notes in his hot and sweaty palm? How much, so as not to be insulting?* Then the moment passed. Would I have lost Mr. Wan's trust by doing that, just as I cast Dr. Zhang into the shadows right at the beginning?)

Mr. Wan led me to another office. The person we were looking for didn't seem to be around, so we sat on a ratty old couch that could have come from a school staff room of my father's era. A pale yellow overhead fan droned in circles above us, and a secretary went through a large folder of documents, copying their contents onto another form. Mr. Wan picked up the desk phone and dialed a few extensions. "Hi, this is So-and-So, is Mr. Zhang in your office? Oh, nothing, but if you see him, please let him know I'm waiting in his office. I have some papers for him to sign." His voice wafted mildly around the languorous room. I began to calm down too, and looked idly at the various objects in this office, which could have been a diorama of my father's youth, rather than a room in the actual hospital where right this moment he was lying unconscious.

After approximately a hundred years (the round clock on the wall, its face smeared with fly corpses and mouse droppings, showed that the insurance company's 3:30 deadline had long passed), Mr. Zhang wandered in blearily (perhaps Mr. Wan's phone call had summoned him from a card game in another department, or whichever rattan chair he'd been napping in). Mr. Wan smiled, apologized for disturbing him, and handed over the paperwork. *The director has looked these over and the family is in a hurry, it would be great if you could stamp them for us, bro.*

Mr. Zhang put on his reading glasses and started reading the documents carefully, one by one. He did this extremely slowly, and the cluster of nerves inside me tensed up again, as if we were trawling the deep ocean and this moment pinged my sonar. I knew there would be some detail I'd neglected. I shouldn't have plunked myself down on his couch like a country bumpkin. I ought to have waited respectfully by the doorway, and the instant he walked through, put a couple of large American bills in his suit pocket. Now everything was being hauled out into the bright sunlit path of regulations and procedures. I kicked myself for placing so much trust in Mr. Wan. They were all the same, taking your bribe only to turn around and treat you like one of their own, warning you not to throw your money in other directions. They always said, *There's no need, those people are just trying to fleece you.* And so the matter got clogged up again.

Sure enough, Mr. Zhang looked up and pulled a metal fountain pen from his shirt pocket. "This is wrong." He scratched out a few words ("and is currently in a good condition"). "No need for this either." Another line through "and on condition that there are medical personnel" to the end of the sentence. Finally, he deleted the conclusion "I certify the patient fit to travel." Then he went back and cut my heading. The statement I'd carefully written out was reduced to a three grubby lines:

Passenger Lo Jia Xuan

Cerebellar hemorrhage. Due to special circumstances (Taiwanese compatriot unexpectedly struck down by stroke in mainland China), as well as the urgent request of the family, I discharge the patient.

Dr. _____, First People's Hospital, Jiujiang City

He looked up, took off his glasses, and smiled. "Is that okay?"

He looked at Mr. Wan, who looked at me. "Is that okay?" (Was this a joke?) I controlled my voice so it didn't shake or crack into a sob. "Sure." Everyone let out a sigh of relief. Mr. Wan carefully unearthed a stack of hospital letterhead from the desk and asked me to write out a clean copy of the text. The paper was very thin, and when my ballpoint pen touched the glossy surface, ink blossomed crudely around every character. The tense, urgent atmosphere had completely dissipated, and Mr. Zhang was shooting the breeze with Mr. Wan. My heart wobbled, and I thought, *Isn't this all about tricking you two into putting your stamp on this?* And so I made sure to leave a blank line on that silk-thin letterhead, and plenty of space between my handwriting and where the stamp would go.

(After getting the stamp and before faxing it from the hotel, I'd add the words I wanted.)

(How idiotic.)

I finished and handed it over for them to check. Mr. Zhang cautiously asked the secretary for a set of keys so he could open the filing cabinet, and rifled around in it until he found a wooden oval stamp (my nemesis!), touched it to the ink pad, turned it over to check, and with great care, stamped it "Medical Department, First People's Hospital, Jiujiang City."

I all but flew from the hospital into a taxi. Before that, I repeatedly bowed and thanked Mr. Wan, while he looked perplexed and embarrassed. *It's fine, I didn't do anything.* He definitely had no idea what I was plotting. At some level, he must have been aware he'd cunningly sold me out with this empty favor. What kind of dogshit certification was this? Yet I felt unexpectedly grateful and excited. He must have been thinking with disappointment and relief, *Silly kid.* This was human nature, all those grandiose words spoken in the shadows, perfectly judged, yet out of this deception and trickery, green shoots could appear, warm feelings and an ineffable connection. I dashed up to my hotel room and, alone at the dressing table, took out my pen, and in the spaces of that stamped document, added all the words I wanted, "suitable for flying certification," "this patient is not infectious, and there is no risk of adverse effects on other passengers," "I hereby certify," and so on.

Traffic noises roiled outside, punctuated by toot after toot from the river boats. I'd never been here at this hour. As I added those words, a restless emotion filled me, so my hand shook as it gripped the pen.

(Father, in order to bring you home, I've done every bad thing there is to do.)

seven

THE CHILD

I said, "Be good, wait here in the car." Once again, I told him don't touch this, this, or that—pointing at the handbrake, the gearshift, and the keys in the ignition—and the child in the passenger seat said, "Okay," but his hands didn't stop moving, tugging the glove compartment open, fiddling with the switch for the electric windows. I thought for a moment, decided to leave the windows open a crack, and took the keys with me.

I locked the child in the car. Through the small opening in the window, I said, "Be a good boy and wait here for me. I'll be back in a short while—I just need to mail this letter."

There was a short uphill path, and beyond it a winding main road on which large trucks full of gravel rumbled by, stirring up clouds of dust. I'd parked by a little ruined Temple of Need, one of those where you pray to stray spirits and other good fellows like that, with none of the usual figurines on the altar, just a sheet of red paper, a small gold censer, and packets of incense sticks that had gotten wet at some point, so red dye now stained the inside of their plastic wrappers. I wasn't sure who had decided to consecrate a dark temple in our little old hillside community. Still, whenever I drove past the gate, I'd murmur a little prayer through the car window as I passed by its emptiness, just to say hello.

At the top of the path, where it met the road, I turned back anxiously and saw that the child had climbed into the driver's seat; his face was half hidden by the steering wheel, looking down at whatever he was busy playing with. At times like this, when I saw that my leaving him hadn't caused him any uneasiness at all, sour misery would well up from the bottom of my heart.

Turning the corner, I could no longer see the temple or car. I recalled a mailbox along the main road not too far from this junction, but after going all the way around the loop, I'd almost reached the next bus stop (Lai Zhong Keng), and still there was no sign of a red or green column.

The farther I walked, the more anxious I got. Maybe I ought to have left the key in the ignition and the air conditioning on, so I needn't worry about the blazing sun slowly turning the interior of the car into an oven . . . But I also couldn't bear the greater risk: that as he horsed around, the child would accidentally start the car and have it roll onto the main road just as a huge truck or bus sped around the bend . . . My brain felt like a tiny square of butter in a foil-wrapped baked potato, returning over and over to the image of the crushed metal frame of a car in the middle of the road, beneath the scorching sun. And the devils that lived in our little hillside development, practically a slum . . . If one of them happened by and saw a car with its lights on and just a small child inside, surely he'd jump in right away and either shove the child out or simply murder him before driving off. . . .

More walking, more distance. Smoke rose off the road in the intense heat, though the melting tarmac was blanketed by a thick layer of sand, only to be glimpsed when briefly exposed by the wheels of a passing truck, reminding you that the scene before you, underpinned by dazzling light, was not as rigidly fixed as you imagined, like a hot pane of glass or a tungsten steel blade. On one side, all the huge tree ferns along the hillside were covered in gray dust. On the other side, a steep drop down to the valley, with the riverbed visible below. Back during the foot-and-mouth epidemic, a news report revealed that a pig farm farther upstream had buried more than a hundred infected pig corpses on a nearby hill. A storm unearthed them, and their rotting rotund carcasses rolled down into this beautiful stream, the corpse water turning the river into a sort of rich lardy soup, eerily pure white.

Now, though, the sun had steamed away this water and its polluted memory, leaving the land completely parched. The road wound its way past unvarying scenery. Driving down this stretch of road with the child, I used to glimpse old people in conical hats sitting on the verge behind bamboo baskets or metal cages, with misspelled cardboard signs advertising their wares: live civets and owls. Gone in a flash. Pets. Slaughter ready.

Nothing at all.

Should I turn back now? But what if the mailbox were just past the next bend? As I hesitated, a spirit car drove riotously by: a pickup truck with the Seventh Lord, Eight Lord, Prince Nezha, and God of Fortune in the rear. Behind it, another pickup on which a sinewy, perspiring young man banged hard and lustily on a drum, shirtless in a red bandanna and black sweatpants. Then one more, from which another youth was lighting string after string of firecrackers and letting them fall onto the deserted road.

I thought: *This celestial procession will shortly pass by where my car is parked. Filled with curiosity and wonder, my child will lean forward in the driver's seat and press his face to the windshield, gawking at these gaudily dressed wooden effigies with giant masks, sailing by as if on a magical cloud.*

Who was I mailing that letter to?

Maybe it was already too late to turn back (I'd now passed three bus stops). The child must think I'd really abandoned him this time. Actually, I was still walking because I had a plan—two bus stops away was a small market town with an elementary school and an OK Mart. I could mail my letter there and get a bus or taxi back. That might be faster then trudging back the way I'd come.

Suddenly I remembered how in his later years, Father began habitually opening my letters. Or maybe not just in his later years, maybe that's something he'd been doing all along. When I'd just started going out with my wife-to-be, she and her friends went on a vacation along the Silk Road, and every letter she sent me was ripped open and read (of course they contained embarrassingly intimate words). Everything else—tax forms, royalty statements, readers' notes, letters from dirtbag friends and former lovers—was handed to me by Father with torn-open envelopes. No attempt to hide. No shame. I didn't even have the energy to protest. "Why did you open my mail?" As if to save me time, Father would matter-of-factly give me a digest of their contents, and sometimes even try to chat about them.

I remember one time when I was a kid, I was having a bath—our old house in Yonghe had a stone bathtub, slate gray with little white flecks, and a half-height wall next to it separating it from the toilet. The tub was old and covered with a dark layer of something like snot, which no amount of scrubbing with a steel brush or powerful cleaning products could get rid of. The stone surface was pitted like coral. When we were little, we would fill an aluminum or plastic basin with water, place it in the tub, then crouch in that to soap and rinse ourselves—and Father would come right in to pee. When that happened, I'd just carry on with my bath.

When Father was done pissing, he'd come over to the tub—looking down at my naked body from above—and I'd instinctively scooch backward in my basin, leaving room for him to wash his hands under the faucet.

This was in our dingy, cramped old house, a small space the family moved gingerly around in, silently and instinctively shrinking our bodies away from each other so as not to get in anyone's way. This time, though, my father didn't stoop to wash his hands. Bizarrely, he held out his index finger and with a rare tender catch of laughter in his voice, said, "Lick this."

I remember hesitating for half a second, then obediently doing as he asked.

All these years later, I occasionally remember this strange scene and still can't understand why he did this. He always played the stern father, but I'm not much younger now than he was then, with a child of my own, and it's only now, like the tide rising up onto the beach by night, that I'm gradually acquiring a faint understanding of the complex emotions of middle age.

Was it a flash of childlike mischief? Or did he catch a glimpse of a little boy bathing in a grimy basin, and that boy was his son, something he possessed? Was he seeking confirmation of his absolute authority when he reached out a piss-stained finger for his child to lick? Or maybe, being in his forties, he was worried about the possibility of diabetes?

I can't remember if my taste buds detected any sweetness. Was it meaty? Salty? Or perhaps the rotten-egg reek of protein in his urine, if his kidneys were already failing?

(Many years later, after my father managed to snatch his life back from the gates of hell, he'd still lurch awake from a nightmare in the hospital, clutching his head and blubbering, "Where's my head? My head's missing! They've taken my head—" Actually, according to the "medical notes" I later received from the dilapidated hospital, the night he collapsed he was: "Losing consciousness. Incontinent. Blood pressure 240/120mmHg. Disoriented. Pupils constricted. Uncooperative.")

Too late to turn back now.

Before me: a sandy wasteland and empty road. In the middle of the road: a vast pit, an excavator held up in mid-air by its own arm, yellow-and-black-striped stone barriers, flashing red police lights, and plastic caution tape randomly draped around.

Gradually, workers began to appear, welding aluminum strips into silvery doors and windows; car workshops; then teahouses and an OK Mart by the side of the road. I reached the bus stop, but no one was waiting. The road was completely empty, with no indication that a bus would show up anytime soon.

Still no sign of a mailbox.

What was going on? Had someone come and uprooted all the mailboxes along this stretch of road? Abruptly, I hated myself for having been so stubborn, walking all this way to mail a letter of uncertain origin, leaving the child all alone in the car. (How was he doing? Had the heat gotten too much for him? Had he instinctively opened the car door like a little animal? Was he now sitting in the gloomy Temple of Need waiting for me, swatting away black mosquitoes with his little hand? Or had he lost consciousness as the car became an oven, was he slumped on the pleather seat, which must be at melting point, his breathing growing shallow?) I ought to have left my phone so I could call him now from a public phone. But no, a two-year-old wouldn't know how to answer a cell phone.

I passed a gas cylinder factory, but everyone there had flocked to the police station next door, alongside a bunch of young reporters, tall and long-haired, cameras at the ready. A car appeared, and the mob ran toward it in a rage. Some tried to climb on top of it, but they fell down right away (the scorching surface and fluid curved lines of the windshield were excellent design features). They smacked the windows hard.

I recognized one of the women in the crowd—she ran a video store I often went to, only I'd lost a tape some time ago and they'd left a ton of phone messages asking for it back, so I hadn't dared go by for a while.

I was embarrassed, but she didn't seem to mind. She told me, "It was them" (pointing at a scrawny woman sobbing her eyes out on the steps of the police station), "that chick's sister-in-law tried to break up with her live-in boyfriend, so he bought a can of gas, flung it at their house, and lit a match. The fire didn't kill any of the adults, but three little girls were burned alive. Her two daughters and a neighbor's girl on a play date.

"It was just on the news, they arrested him on Civic Boulevard, and he's inside the station now being questioned. The parents of the dead children came running over."

Another police vehicle pulled out of the station with five or six uniformed officers forming a cordon around it. A man with a shaved head shouted, "I see him! That's Lin Jin-De!" The crowd swarmed over angrily and started pounding on the roof and windows, though the officers managed to block most of them.

Without quite knowing why, I found myself joining the mob like a sleepwalker, running after the car containing the murderous demon. When my fist came down, an officer with his head lowered caught my forearm and nimbly flipped me away, so I landed limply on the road amid the spattered white chicken shit and betel nut debris. "The police are protecting the bad guys!" Like me, the baldy was slumped on the road. The others stepped over us and continued chasing the vehicle.

I rolled to my feet and started running again, avoiding the other bodies and their eel-like stink, swinging at a uniformed trouser leg. Surprisingly, the officer shrieked like a woman, fell to his knees, and crumpled. As if under a spell, the entire mob stopped moving, but a moment later they had surged through the gap left in the protective ring by the fallen man and were attacking the rear window.

In that moment, I saw the arsonist's face. He was wearing a safety helmet and staring at us through the window with sheer terror. A spider's web of cracks had already appeared in the glass. Just as I was thinking, *Now they're going to smash the glass, and all these hands will reach in to pull this animal out into the open*, the driver suddenly stepped on the gas and the vehicle roared ahead, shaking the vigilantes off as it zoomed away.

"Fuck his mother—" chorused the people behind me as they dusted themselves off, panting and disappointed.

I stood there in that maddening white light and gazed at the impoverished town: those hideous five-story apartment buildings with rooftop tin shacks, those billboards, those telephone poles and illicit cable TV antennae on every corner of each building. In the blazing light, these things took on a beauty like the fluid lines of a fossilized trilobite or nautilus. In this time of disaster, they were revealing a quality completely at odds with their initial regretful aspect, without any depth: the brilliant white light cut off the street scene's shadows, giving it the scattered lines of an engraving.

I remembered my child, still waiting for me in the car by the Temple of Need, several bus stops away. Why hadn't I driven to the mailbox in the first place? When my child was grown, would he hold an implacable hatred for me because he remembered a summer day when his father abandoned him in a car? Why? Because of certain conflicting uncertainties that couldn't be answered?

I had a recollection of one time, as a kid, when my mother took me to have my fortune told. The medium laid out my chart in a notebook, then said to my mother, "Your child is one of the eighteen arhats at the Buddha's feet, now reborn on earth. He will break with his father and mother, his sisters and brothers, his wife and children—but not his friends." This was many years ago, and I can no longer recall what trivial predictions he made next (for instance, I shouldn't go near the water at such-and-such an age because there was a risk of drowning, I shouldn't take a train at such-and-such an age, I would have major surgery at such-and-such an age). Though I've since fortunately survived all those dangerous ages, I still have a deep impression of walking out of the fortune-teller's apartment that day, and as we waited for the elevator, my mother abruptly smiling and meaningfully stroking the crown of my head. "So it turns out you're going to be heartless."

Another recollection from around the same time. I found a scrawny newborn kitten in the schoolyard and hid it in my schoolbag to bring home. Some details linger in the memory like hair and gunk in a shower drain. For some reason, my father was always furious whenever I showed up with a stray puppy or kitten, so in an ecstasy of terror, I surreptitiously stowed the kitten in an attic room, dipping my fingertip in warm milk for it to suck from like a nipple. I thought I ought to teach it to turn in mid-air and land on its feet like a cat should, so I pushed it repeatedly off the edge of the bed.

Those silent, stolen moments in the attic room, drenched in light as soft as milk, were indulgent as a father's love . . . and they lasted till he discovered me. He didn't lose his temper as I'd expected (although he still ordered me to get rid of the kitten), just sighed as if in anguish at his child's unfortunate future. He said, "You get stuck on every creature you catch sight of. Your 'feelings' are going to cause you a lot of suffering in the future."

Two completely opposite descriptions (or predictions?), both leading me astray.

So what could I do, to avoid becoming that unfamiliar version of me they were both gesturing at? Later on, things would indeed rupture between me and my father, mother, brother, and sister (after Father's collapse, my relationship to them became one of subtle enmity). How did it come to this? I'd been so careful, but it happened anyway. The diorama formed: my mother, brother, and sister, standing around my father's bed, eyes glazed, all of them getting gradually older and more odorous. Meanwhile, like an overripe baby, Father was getting fatter and fatter, though his legs were pale and slender as a flower stem, or a young woman's arms. He chuckled and smiled foolishly, lay back in the wobbly bed, and shit his pants (it's fine, we put plastic down on the bed). After so much time with a catheter through it, his large cock head had a dark splotch with a corpse-white ring around it, yet each time the Indonesian nurse wiped him down with a damp towel, it would unashamedly spring erect. During his sleeptalking episodes, when his fever rose, he would babble filthy words. Mother looked on in silence, as if content to watch this child-shaped monster gulping down the offspring it spent fifty years spewing into the world. Like a magic trick, it slowly grew big then shrank again.

My brother contracted hyperthyroidism, which made his eyes bulge and neck swell, while the rest of his body grew skinny as a teenager's. My sister developed an immune disorder that caused her body temperature to hold steady at a slow burn of a hundred degrees. My mother had bipolar disorder, and in addition, the stumps of her teeth beneath her dentures festered and oozed pus.

And I alone, my wife's hand in mine, each of us carrying an infant, stood watching from afar.

(Now I remember who that letter was meant for.)

I remember when my wife was four months pregnant, we went for a blood test, one of those that tells you there's a so many-in-a-hundred chance your child will be born with Down syndrome.

I remember that day, I accompanied one of my dirtbag friends, a talkative guy, to pick up his bride on his wedding day. We had to gather at his home in Sanxia district before the auspicious hour. His uncles and army buddies assembled in their Benzes and BMWs, and when everyone had arrived, we set off together with great ceremony for his bride's home in Keelung City. When I found out that my crappy car wouldn't be included in this procession, I asked my friend if I could go straight to Keelung and join them at the turn into his bride's place—but he insisted I come all the way to his place in the south and head back north together with them. I remember that day, as our convoy sped down the highway, gleaming in the sun, I felt drowsiness overwhelm me and regretted every moment I was abandoning my wife. This was her first pregnancy and she was showing signs of nervous strain, yet I'd left her alone at home to be with these men, most of whom were strangers to me.

When we got to the bridal home, though, I played my supporting role to the hilt. The matchmaker they'd hired was a grumpy-looking woman of few words. We squashed into the tiny apartment, silently accepted the sweet dumplings the bride offered us, then awkwardly passed her the red packets the groom had prepared. There followed a period of utter silence apart from the delicate scraping of spoons against porcelain bowls as we ate our dumplings. Next, like a troupe of delivery men or takeout guys who happened to be dressed in suits, we hefted the large rosewood chests serving as auspicious nuptial items up and down the stairs. To break the silence, I repeated the off-color jokes I'd heard from older men during my own wedding, things like "eat sweet dumplings for a girl, drain your cup for a baby boy."

During the drive back in the scorching sun, I really did fall asleep. I had the vague thought I was hanging out with these guys, but actually I didn't know a single soul except my dirtbag friend. As I bounced along, suspended between sleep and wakefulness, my cell phone rang: my wife calling from home, mewling faintly like a newborn kitten abandoned in a cardboard box. For a moment I thought she was pranking me (I was in a wedding party!). But then she said she'd just gotten a call from the hospital—the results were out, and our child was at high risk for Down syndrome. They would have to do an "amniocentesis." I asked, "What's that?" She said, "I think they take a really long needle and stick it right through my belly into my womb, so they can get a drop of amniotic fluid to test." I said, "Let's talk about it when I get home."

Back in Sanxia, I helped usher the bride into the groom's home (as we turned into his street, startling me awake, I tossed a small string of firecrackers out the window, signaling to the people stationed by his front door that they should light the rest of the pyrotechnics) and then said good-bye to my dirtbag friend. He tried distractedly to make me stay, but I said a household emergency had come up. Even so, he insisted I come back for the banquet. Winking, he told me his dad had gone out and hired one of those techno floats of erotic dancers, and there'd be nakasi and karaoke . . .

Alone in my own car on the way back, I kept screwing up my face and howling, but I couldn't find the switch to make the tears flow. I felt terrified and alone. I had just turned thirty. I still didn't have a steady job. My wife had had a miscarriage just six months before this. I had no idea how many bizarre and unfortunate encounters still lurked in my future. . . . The landscape outside the car at that moment was a swift inversion of the one in which, many years later, I would leave my child alone in the car as I trudged obstinately down the road: harsh light swallowing the depth of all objects, streets as empty of people as after a nuclear strike, one bus stop after another whizzing past, then Earth God temples in the dips between ridges, small pickup trucks with watermelons bobbing in tubs of water on sale for eight dollars each. . . .

Everything quickly flipping by in the blazing light.

I remember turning the key with difficulty in the metal gate (and realizing only then that I'd locked my pregnant wife in the house that morning). The abrupt darkness as I opened the door made me feel as if my swollen tear glands were suddenly emptying themselves. It took me a while to find my wife. She was huddled on the floor at the back of the house. Above her hung a Baroque lamp with three hand-crafted crystal flying cranes. The yellowish bulbs hardly seemed to give off any light.

When I came close, she sank against my chest and started sobbing. My wife was still youthfully slender then (she would soon have two children in quick succession). I could feel her trembling all over, and soon I was shaking too. I tried to comfort her: "Don't be afraid, we're still going to have him even if he does have Down syndrome. Then we won't have any more. I've heard children with this condition live on average twenty years. So we'll take good care of him for whatever time he has here." (*We'll give him all our love*, I said). "And when he's gone, we'll go back to the way we were, just the two of us."

My wife burst out crying again to hear me talk like this. She said, "But the hospital told me there's only a 5 percent chance that he'll be born with Down's. Only a 5 percent chance. . . ."

eight

THE THREE GORGES MIGRANTS

'd originally wanted to write about a journey of banishment (a great migration of millions with a sweeping sense of time and space and a complex history), but in the end I've set down a quiet, still tale. I wanted to capture the sensation of being in an unfamiliar city, everything a stranger would see and hear: boats and cars, bridges and inns, the local harbor, police stations, hotels, hospitals, markets; or else taxi drivers, small hotel owners, bar girls, peddlers of fake ancient coins, even local college students. . . . Without meaning to, I've set my dark scene in a place I feel so unsettled that the ground beneath my feet seems loose, yet one I'd finally realized I might never be able to leave—the melancholy city I'm stuck in, unbearably familiar yet refusing to yield up any more of its stories.

For a while I was enraptured by stories of hotels. I once came up with a narrative about a middle-aged man recuperating in a small seaside town in the northeast, somewhere like Toucheng Township or Nanfang'ao, in a little hotel opposite the train station. Down the alley from the hotel were a shabby Japanese restaurant, an old-fashioned photo studio, a children's clinic with a milky-white acrylic sign so badly cracked the blackened fluorescent tube within was visible, and a narrow, filthy box office window set into a veranda, so dark and empty it seemed unlikely tickets were actually on sale, yet by the patterned curtain of the entrance, improbably, a pretty young woman sat on a bench, fresh as a flower, legs crossed beneath a skirt so short it repelled the gaze. . . . Out the back door of the hotel, past old residential buildings and narrow alleyways, across the achingly slow provincial road, was the railway, and beyond that was a breakwater. My protagonist strolled daily along this dyke. One end was perpetually littered with the dried-out carcasses of pufferfish discarded by the local fishermen, spikes bristling like a sea urchin's, that when kicked went rattling down the slope of the breakwater, like guillotined heads with comical expressions frozen in place. . . .

I've always been enchanted by stories about hotels, but I'm never able to finish writing them. Another time, I wrote about a traveler staying at a small-town hotel who got to know a young priest also lodging there long term. At the time, I could clearly see that the energy flowing so vividly through this story ran right through the hotel itself. The tumultuous passions of the young man, the devout priest trapped in this small town where so many young people sinned out of ignorance (or poverty) . . . but I couldn't finish this piece either.

For the month that Mother and I were confined to Jiujiang, we stayed at a hotel by a six-lane road, beyond which was a wall so long we couldn't see either end, dark gray verging on black, topped with huge aluminum hoardings—simplified-character advertisements for industrial materials—and behind that wall, the Yangtze River. We only discovered this toward the end of our first week there. To start with, we found it odd that around five each morning, we'd hear the faint low cries of steam whistles. At that point, we had completely succumbed to the deferred terror that Father "might soon be dying," and those honks faded to just so much background noise in this strange city. Then one noontime, as we bent our heads in silence as usual over our lunch, I suddenly realized that through the floor-length windows behind my mother, I could see past the road and the wall to a vast body of water, a gray-yellow oil painting beneath a hazy sky, reaching to the faraway horizon, a still-life with ships of all sizes silhouetted against the fog, bodies low in the water, their cabins minuscule. Gazing at them from this distance, they appeared shrouded by vapor rising off that huge body of water, all of them the dull gray of steel or lead. Not at all like the boats we were accustomed to seeing at our island harbor, high and light, their white bodies reflecting blue-green waves.

Shaken by the sight of so much water so close to us, we summoned the waitress and asked if she could tell us what famous river that might be?

The girl giggled. "It's the Yangtze!"

The river ferry dock was not far from our hotel. If you took a taxi, the meter wouldn't have a chance to move.

So the sobbing wail we heard each morning was the final call before the first passenger ferry of the day set off down the river.

We spent almost a month in this strange little city. Occasionally I would draw the thick, heavy curtains and open the window of our room (while my mother, reading glasses on, would kneel in the space between the beds, facing the telephone table, on which she'd placed a Trikaya Buddha the size of a cigarette packet), to stare out at the inky river surface and what I could see of the gray wall in the refracted light of passing traffic. A vague hope would stir in me: that one of these days I'd find the time (rather than going to the hospital) to visit the docks beyond that wall. Dockers loading and unloading goods from river steamers; old sea dogs squatting along each deck, waiting for sedan cars and tractors, old men and women, mothers and children, business travelers and students, gangsters and ne'er-do-wells to swarm on board, smoking cigarettes they'd bummed from the tractor drivers; flotsam on the river, oil slicks and rotting fruit and vegetable scraps. . . . All of this was taking place just the other side of that wall across the road, and yet none of it fell within my field of vision.

Right up to the day we left, I hadn't found a chance to slip around the other side of that wall to witness "a moment stuck in time," one of those docks along the Yangtze.

I remember on the seventh day, or was it the eighth? Second Brother, who'd been the most dedicated in his care of Father, got a phone call from Nanjing. His sons were both in the boat business—the old man once told me with Shanghai rising, it was the best time to be in shipping along the Yangtze from Nanjing to Shanghai, and nothing gave young people better prospects than getting hold of a boat to do that run. First the elder son (he said to me, "Your big nephew") and his wife ("Your niece-in-law") bought a boat and did quite well with it. The younger son got jealous of their success and clamored for a boat of his own. What to do? A secondhand boat cost seven hundred and something thousand yuan (*But that's over three million Taiwanese dollars!* I thought, startled), and they couldn't make it work. Now they wanted to sell, just as the older generation were over in Jiujiang because of Father. The young couple weren't very streetwise (the "young nephew and niece-in-law" were at least a decade older than I) and had agreed to someone's opening offer of just five hundred grand.

That afternoon by Father's bedside, I listened to old Second Brother tell me in his reedy, accented voice all kinds of facts about river boats: *so many tons and so deep a hull would be considered a fast boat; some have a higher tonnage but are cheaper because they sit lower in the water, and therefore can't be used past Wuhan. Fast boats have better engines and sit high in the water—your Fifth Brother has one, though they cost a pretty penny* (he winced), *they get you as far as Chongqing.* He also weighed up the dockers in various cities along the river: *the Shanghainese are the best, a cut above—show up with an entire boatload of loose timber, and without even asking, they'll secure it for you. So disciplined and efficient. The Nanjing ones don't make the grade—lazybones, all of them!*

We could tell how agitated he was and urged him to go back. At first he refused, and it looked like we might have a falling out. Yiming, Mother, and I kept saying, "Second Brother, you should go and keep an eye on the kids, to make sure the sale of the boat goes smoothly. By the time you get back, maybe Father will be out of bed and walking around! Then we'll all go for a beer and celebrate." Talking like this, I began to feel as if I really was equal with these men in their sixties and seventies, with their near-identical faces. Second Brother kept saying no. There were tears in his eyes. ("This might be my last sight of him.") A blank expression flitted across his large, stubborn face for an instant in the afternoon light, and I realized with a start that he looked exactly like Father had when, in his later years, he began his solitary retreat into a closed-off world. You'd think he was deep in thought about something, but actually there was nothing at all on his mind.

"All right, then." He abruptly got to his feet, grabbed his bag and coat from where he'd stowed them under Father's bed (where they lay among the other old men's possessions, Father's things that Mother had brought, her prayer beads, the hot water flask provided by the hospital, and the enamel chamber pot we emptied Father's catheter bag into. The floor was also covered in blades—every day, the little nurses would come to draw blood for testing by breaking a segment off a craft knife, nicking one of Father's fingers, squeezing out a drop of blood, then discarding the sharp bit of metal onto the floor). "I'll head back quickly, sort things out, and come straight back." Elder Brother Yiming and Second Brother spoke in the Nanjing dialect we couldn't understand, probably something about letting the wives know that Father's condition was more complicated than we'd expected, so the other men would have to stay here for now. Fourth Brother was in the worst situation—he had a vineyard that needed harvesting, but his two farmhands were useless, and the grape crop was rotting away. Second Brother pulled out a wad of renminbi and tried to hand it to Yiming, but they ended up rowdily pushing it back and forth (in front of my mother—whom Yiming called Mom and the others called Auntie—they were obliging as awkward village boys who didn't know what to do with their hands). "The old gentleman might have some unexpected expenses." "When you get back, your cubs might end up needing money for who knows what else."

Then they started haggling over transport—the last train had gone, and the bus would be too slow, but maybe he could still get the last ferry to Nanjing? (My ears pricked up.) The younger brother of the stroke patient in the next bed joined in (with the authority of a local), "The ferries stop running at six, you should head to the dock now if you're going."

That's when I ought to have stood up and said, "I'll go to the dock with you, Second Brother." Maybe then I would have seen for myself what lay on the other side of the wall, the Yangtze and its many varieties of boats, but out of caution and shyness I kept my mouth shut. During this whole ridiculous farrago over Father's collapse, Mother and I had come to trust Second Brother the most out of these awkward old men. Now he was going, and only I could see that Mother was quietly panicking as she sat on the edge of Father's bed, eyes shut and chanting scripture. (What if, in the next day or two, all the other old men got word of family crises, and left one by one?) All I could do was smile ingratiatingly and walk Second Brother out to the corridor along with Yiming. . . .

Several days later, amid the fear and uncertainty of our protracted negotiations with the Taiwanese insurance firm and the international rescue company, during which it proved impossible to settle on a day when Father could be airlifted home, Yiming lost his temper and snapped, "We ought to get hold of a boat and take Father down the Yangtze River to Nanjing."

An image flashed into my brain: Yiming, old Third Brother, dirtbag Fourth Brother, and me each holding a corner of Father's stretcher, standing comically yet sorrowfully on the dock, buffeted by the wind off the river, waiting for a boat to slowly putt-putt its way toward us. Perhaps my brother and cousins would coo like old women to soothe my father, "Just a little longer, sir, we'll get you home very soon." Just as I would eventually say to Father, as he lay on a dinghylike inflatable stretcher on the EVA Air flight to Taoyuan, swaddled in the salt reek of diarrhea that still seeped from him, "Just a little longer, Dad, we'll get you home very soon."

I wanted to go a little deeper in describing these old men. Their loyalty, their kindness, the fear and respect with which they treated my father. My father who'd fled alone from his home to another island, where he struggled through half a lifetime before returning with the status of a professor of Confucius and Mencius, whereupon they welcomed him like a celestial being descending from the heavens, an object of worship. (During those years, the island on which he fathered me treated him like a detestable country bumpkin, and drivers kicked him out of taxis. Essentially because by then his wits were already scattered and he was slurring his words, though his indomitable warrior's spirit never once weakened. One time, he got into an argument on a bus with a young guy who refused to give up his seat, and he yelled in front of all the passengers, "You know what? I'm a college professor. Maybe I was your teacher's teacher." That got everyone up in arms. A woman who didn't know either of them sneered, "A professor? Huh, a single mouse dropping can ruin a whole pot of soup.") They treated him like a miraculous fruit to appear high on the otherwise withered branches of the Lo family tree, spread across the arid farmland of Jiangxin Island, and as for me, my brother, and my sister, the offspring he'd half-heartedly popped out (were we bastards? By-blows?) on that other strange island, we were new and improved descendants whose feet would never touch the dirty soil, elite children who'd grown up eating miracle rice, half-brothers and a half-sister like something out of a saga. . . .

Yet their lives were lived in the shadow of my father's irresponsible flight, the "bad portion" he left behind. The first time I visited Jiangxin with my wife, Yiming set up two tables in his empty living room: at one, apart from me and my young wife, were Elder Brother (my father's eldest nephew, only three years younger than my mother), Second Brother, Third Brother, Fourth Brother, (Fifth Brother had to drive his truck to Anhui that day,) all these old men with a "Yi" in their names; and my older sister Xiaxia's husband (my brother-in-law), Auntie Jinfang's brother, plus a local cadre (who might have been Yiming's boss, because later on Yiming handed him the duty-free liquor I'd brought). At the other table were some old women, completely identical to my eye: short, brittle white hair; coarse skin; dark eyes buried in a faceful of wrinkles—my cousins' wives. When I described Father's heroic achievements or shameful doings in Taiwan, they'd titter with their hands over their mouths, patting their chests, like a gaggle of carefree young girls. As for the other young people around my age, they didn't even get seats. Occasionally a couple with a small child would scurry in, and one of the old people would stand and bellow at them to "raise a glass to your little uncle and aunt," which threw me into confusion. I'd have to hand them one of the red packets Yiming had prepared earlier, a hundred yuan in each; then the old person would, attempting to conceal their affection, introduce the newcomer: "This is our Fanghao." (or Fangjun, Fangyun, Fangjie—their names all started with Fang) "The useless bum didn't even finish school, and now he's running a woodworking business with some friends."

I couldn't work out who everyone was. The old people (it was only later, in Jiujiang, that I would learn to tell apart Second, Third, and Fourth Brothers) grew teary whenever anyone mentioned how they'd suffered over the last few decades. They had thick accents and kept interrupting each other, so I wasn't quite able to tell which bad things had happened to whom, but their late father (my uncle) had seemingly had a difficult life, and I began to suspect that the reason these harmless old men had been slapped with the "Five Black Categories" label and made to go through all these hardships was because of the man they called the "old gentleman," my father. I remember Elder Brother sniffing loudly, raising his glass of liquor, and saying, "But now, Little Brother, no one on Jiangxin Island dares to bully the Luo family, there are more of us than anyone else. . . ."

Much later, over many afternoons at the Jiujiang People's Hospital, Yiming and I smoked and chatted in the stairwell littered with empty saline containers, and I caught glimpses of their misfortune in his words. I could all but hear the crunching noises of these old men's backbones being crushed beneath the wheel of fate. Yiming said during the Movement Against the Three Evils, and then the Movement Against the Five Evils, the island's revolutionary committee would try to denounce Luo Jialong (my eldest uncle), but they could never find any grounds, because our family had been innocent and fair for generations, and when the Communist Party entered Nanjing (which is when my father fled), Eldest Uncle immediately gifted all the family's farmland, several hectares of it, to his sharecroppers, so he wasn't even a landowner anymore. When they started working on members of the family, third sister-in-law got confused and went up on stage to point the finger at Eldest Uncle—"my father-in-law interfered with me." ("And that's why, even after all these years, though Eldest Uncle is dead now, none of us has quite forgiven your third sister-in-law.")

(I thought back to the tableful of women. Those giggling old biddies. My aged sisters-in-law—who could have thought that beneath those faces, flashing by as quickly as images in a darkroom, lay such deep hurt?) Another time, Yiming flatly told me, "Dad came to dislike your sister-in-law Jinfang. She knew it too. But there were some things I never told Dad. I was actually matched to someone else before Jinfang, it was arranged by your Uncle Jialong, but then what happened? During those years of one movement after another, who was all of Jiangxin Island denouncing? Your dad, the guy who ran off to Taiwan. There was a white cloth banner hanging in the elementary school: 'Tear down the Kuomintang spy Luo Jiaxuan, tear down Luo Jiaxuan and his filthy foreign connections.' Who was this man? He was my dad. Yet I'd never seen his face. Every two or three days, I was dragged up on stage to explain myself. Like showing up for work. In the end, your uncle himself went to the woman's house to call off the betrothal. At that time, not a single person on Jiangxin Island would have dared marry their daughter to me, Luo Yiming. Only your sister-in-law's father, Uncle Xiang, who was actually of our grandfather's generation, said, 'I don't believe those bad things they're saying, I'm going to marry my little Jinfang into the Luo family.' I was almost thirty by then, a pathetic age to finally find a bride. In '78, your sister-in-law came down with liver disease, and her face got all dark and splotchy. My status was better by then, and Jinfang said to me, 'Feel free to disregard this marriage.' She was illiterate, and now her health was bad; she thought she wasn't good enough for me. I said 'No, that won't do, all we have in this world is gratitude and loyalty, otherwise we'd be no better than pigs or dogs.'"

Yiming went on, "The first time Dad came back to the island, he brought two gold necklaces with him, one for your Eldest Auntie and the other for old Auntie Zhu. Jinfang got a gold bracelet, and your Eldest Sister-in-Law, Second Sister-in-Law,

Third Sister-in-Law, Fourth Sister-in-Law, and Fifth Sister-in-Law got a gold ring each, and one for Big Sister Xiaxia too. Jinfang was worried Xiaxia would feel bad, so she took off her bracelet and handed it to her. I mentioned this to Dad in a letter, but your mom thought Jinfang was implying the bracelet was too small a gift, so she had a gold necklace made and got Uncle Fan to bring it over when he visited."

While all this was happening, what had Father said to my elder brother in that dingy house? And what did Yiming say back? I had no idea. Mother told me that the night before Father's collapse, he'd phoned home to say he was having a great time: they'd gone up Mount Lu, he'd bought an inkstone and some calligraphy, and the rest of the tour group was taking very good care of him. He stayed on the bus if any of the scenic spots were uphill, and whenever there was a toilet he made sure to go (so he wouldn't pee his pants later). When Yiming and Fourth Brother came to the hotel to see him that evening, Father got the tour company to book them an extra room and insisted they stay for dinner; then they had some drinks too. That night, Father stayed in Yiming and Fourth Brother's room chatting till very late. Mother said he sounded very happy on the phone, but said one thing that made her uneasy: "I've told them everything—it feels great. I'll explain when I get back."

Then the next morning, we got the call from the tour operator to say he was seriously ill.

What on earth actually happened?

The night we got to Jiujiang, the local tour guide, Miss Jiang, told us that Father's roommate (another old man) had said Father went into the shower first thing in the morning, then collapsed as he was getting out. Maybe he cried out as he fell, because the roommate was awakened by a loud bellowing, and when he looked, there was Father lying naked on the carpet, dripping wet in a puddle of water.

On the minibus from the airport to the hospital, Mother murmured to me, "I bet Yiming said something nasty to him."

At the hospital, though, Yiming and Fourth Brother were standing there in the dark, apparently just as shocked as us. Innocent as a little girl, Mother said, "Seeing family must have got him all worked up, or else the temperature difference going up and down Mount Lu was too much, and the blood vessels in his brain exploded," for all the world as if she were explaining the situation to the manager and tour guide, none of whose business it was.

Now Yiming said, "Another time, Dad brought twenty gold rings with him. He asked me to pass a few to So-and-So and So-and-So, and do anything I liked with the rest. But of the people he mentioned, some had moved to Shanghai, others had died, and even with the old people who were still on the island—Dad didn't realize, and I didn't want to tell him—the warm feelings he had were from several decades ago; for years now, these uncles have been cold to me and my cousins. When your Eldest Uncle was getting denounced left and right and we asked for help, not one of them was willing. I ended up giving most of those gold rings to Jinfang's brothers. Fourth Brother has the least money, so I also gave some to Fourth Sister-in-Law's family. And for the rest, my mom's brothers got one each. Dad wasn't very understanding—he thought Jinfang was being greedy, taking all those rings for her own family. But actually, that was my idea."

I wasn't sure if he'd said "that was my idea" or "that was my intention." He was an old man of almost sixty now. Short and scrawny, face as narrow as a mole's. Not at all like Father's northern build, five-foot-eleven with a large, square face. Only in the way his right eyebrow flicked to a point at one end did he bear a resemblance to Father (and to me). He must have felt resentful deep down. Fatherless as soon as he was born. No sooner had

Father fled the country in '49 than his wife turned around and married someone else. And now the father he'd waited half a lifetime to meet had finally dropped from the sky (I guessed that with his fatherless heart, he must have wanted more than anyone else to burnish Father's legend in his hometown. For instance, when people said Father loathed his "faithless" former wife, he took advantage of Father being a long way away to blur the circumstances in small ways, until it appeared that Father had forgiven her; when Father was completely indifferent to Jinfang's family's gratitude, Yiming took it upon himself to pay them respects on Father's behalf), only for the situation to so quickly turn to despair. Father said on the phone, "I've told them everything." What could he have meant? He was now swimming alone in the shrinking tank of Alzheimer's, and like a vengeful movie director, was cutting up the few remaining reels, splicing them together into unimaginable scenes. When the vein exploded in Father's brain and the entire room dimmed around him, how heavy was that blow for this old fatherless child?

On Father's last visit to the island, the last of the "Jia" generation, like an old gold-plated earth Buddha, his authority within the family had much eroded. Fifth Brother had apparently hooked up with a young woman on one of his long hauls, abandoning Fifth Sister-in-Law (one of the dark-faced old women at the next table?) and his daughter, who was then in senior high. He only came home three times a year. One of these times happened to coincide with Father's visit. The brothers had set up a big round table at Yiming's home, and they were all there for dinner. Two drinks in, Father decided that as Fifth Sister-in-Law was present, he would give them the benefit of his wisdom, which he did in an operatic speech (first raising a glass to Fifth Sister-in-Law): "All of you gathered here are old enough to be grandfathers. Yigen is seventy-two this year. Normally, who's the head of the Luo household on Jiangxin Island? You brothers. Who gets to say what's what? You boys with 'Yi' names. But your Second Uncle's back now, and I'm going to pull rank for a minute—I mean, as far as I'm concerned, all of you are little children, just babies!" That sent cold sweat pouring down the old men's backs, and they hastily started pouring cups of wine for Father, crying out "Old Gentleman!" like whiny brats. Father went on, "You're the offspring of my poor brother. When I left home, Yifa was just learning to crawl, and that rascal Yicai would run off to swim in the creek till nightfall. Your grandfather would string him up and beat him for that, until I pleaded for him!" In tearful ecstasies, the old men chorused: "Old gentleman, old gentleman, we've let you down we wronged you, beat us punish us, we won't mind, but don't be sad, eat your crab and drink your yellow wine!" My father was completely intoxicated. Where would he ever find such an audience in Taiwan? "You call me old gentleman, so I'll treat you like my own sons. And no son would refuse to listen to his father, so I'll be frank. We're all family here, anyway." And with that, he began ripping into Fifth Brother. To start with he hammered away, interspersing his invective with snide jokes, many of them filthy, until Fifth Sister-in-Law's ears were burning red and Fifth Brother was frantically downing one drink after another, while the other old men snickered and guffawed like children. Then inspiration struck and the lecture grew generously expansive—only I knew what a fearful thing this was, Father being inspired—and his whole world shrank to a closed room. In this little space of loneliness and terror, he rambled to himself. This was no longer a speech, but rather a voyage, an old man among his broken memories, trying to patch the holes in his boat as shameful moments surged through them. In the dim light, the old men's faces were blank, though their mouths hung open. Fifth Brother had set down his glass and was staring at Fifth Sister-in-Law with hatred from the next table. Fifth Sister-in-Law was sobbing. None of them had any idea that Father was on a journey of his own now. Everything slowed down and gently swayed from side to side.

From time to time, I recall the long wall in that unfamiliar city and the muddy yellow river on the other side, along with the harbor I never made it to. What would I have seen? A landscape to match the gray hulls of the ships, or the low dark clouds reflected in the water? A gray cement platform? Wooden jetties with legs down into the water? Perhaps some lonely white waterfowl occasionally flapping their way to the flotsam washing up against the cement breakwater, searching for dead fish among the empty cans? On the island where I live, three or four black-faced spoonbills show up each winter, migratory birds that have been designated a protected species, traveling thousands of kilometers from northeast China, Korea, and Siberia to the mouth of the Zengwen River on the southern edge of this island, where they spend the colder months. One year, the first item on the TV news was an image of bird corpses littering the Zengwen delta and nearby fish ponds. Fifty-six of them had been taken ill, and forty-three had since died. To start with, people guessed that they must have been so exhausted from their long flight that they froze to death in one of the worst cold snaps that winter. But then a vet analysis showed it was botulism poisoning, which meant there was a problem in their food supply or roosting grounds. The wildlife people kept investigating, and discovered that before draining their ponds for the winter, the local fish farmers were using poison to get rid of unwanted fish and shrimp. The carnage was the result of the birds feeding on these carcasses and drinking the tainted water.

Cold, poison, weakened bodies, botulism, eating the wrong thing—while undertaking this great migration, they would have had no idea that death awaited them. These migratory creatures, a little comical with their black faces like Justice Bao, now lay stretched out on our TV screens, pure white against the mud.

Too many, more than our imaginations could grasp, the riddle of death leaving their soaring journeys, like something on an IMAX screen, suddenly bereft of poetry.

Yiming said (in the corridor of Jiujiang People's Hospital, where a poster in the dappled light read "Silence, Cleanliness, Respect"): "When the Cultural Revolution was just getting started, your Eldest Auntie was scared that if they went on torturing people like that, they would eventually kill someone. She couldn't protect all her children, so—like a weary mother bird in peril instinctively hides her fragile eggs with their malnourished, translucent shells in different places to spread the risk—she sent Third Brother, Fourth Brother, and Fifth Brother back to their ancestral home, Wuwei town in Anhui province. Even if all the Luo men on Jiangxin Island were slaughtered, at least there would be a few saplings left in the old house our grandfather had once hastily fled." I didn't have a chance to ask what happened in the decades after this transplanting (a terrified mother trying to keep the next generation alive), what Eldest Brother and Second Brother, Yiming and Xiaxia went through in Nanjing. And what about Third Brother, Fourth Brother, and Fifth Brother, in that rotten little Anhui village? (Third Brother once said to me in his thick accent, "Some years, a bunch of people starved to death.") In the early '90s, after Yiming had planted his vineyard on Jiangxin Island and used the gold Father sent to build a big house, he pulled strings to get Third, Fourth, and Fifth Brothers "deployed back" from Anhui.

Mass migration. I could seemingly only use this ice-cold, anodyne phrase to describe the way these old men accepted their fate and went along with these ludicrous shifts. Climate change. A deteriorating environment. An entire tribe relocating. Just like a telephoto shot on the National Geographic channel of geese or zebras huddling among a vast group of their own species, faces blank, ready to undertake a long journey. Sometimes, panning over newly hatched turtles flopping their way toward the ocean, the camera lingers on an unfortunate few. Some die, some get beached on hidden rocks and are left behind by the rest of the hatchlings, like being put into stasis.

Yiming told me Third Brother was in his early thirties when he left Jiangxin Island, and by the time they were brought back from Anhui, he was well into his fifties. At that time, the Party was opening up and liberalizing. As for Elder Brother's, Second Brother's, and Yiming's offspring, the generation of kids with "Fang" names, some got into the boat business, some set up small furniture factories, some ended up in the city driving taxis or waiting tables. . . . Bustling with activity, they all seemed touched with "modernity." Only Third Brother and his two sons, for all that they were full of vigor and able to carry out any kind of farm work, turned out unsuitable for employment. When Third Brother was working on the farm in Anhui, a mule ran amok and charged around biting people, and took a chunk out of his chest. He lost his temper, picked up the beast, all hundred pounds of it, slung it over his shoulder—where it wriggled like a girl, legs trembling, and pissed all over him—and carried it back to its pen. At the Jiujiang hospital, if we needed to get Father onto the gurney (to get him down to the CT scan room, for instance), or if he shat himself and the sheets needed to be changed, or if he needed to be bathed or rolled over (to prevent bedsores), we'd have to rely on Third Brother to lift Father's large yet powerless bulk, shouldering most of the burden while the rest of us fluttered around uselessly. Later, when Father needed intravenous injections but the little nurses could never find anywhere to stick a needle in because the walls of his veins had stiffened, his arms down to the wrist and the backs of his legs were covered in little pinpricks, a horrific sight. Their repeated jabbing became the most horrific part of each day. Added to that, Father's brain injury caused him to reflexively thrash his arms and legs, and each time he shook his drip loose, it had to be sterilized with alcohol and reinserted into a vein. It became old Third Brother's job to sit ramrod straight by Father's bedside, keeping a tight grip on the arm with the drip. When Father began jerking around, Third Brother had to hold it firm as if in an arm-wrestling match.

After we got back to Taiwan, the hospital nurse (a tiny older woman) tied Father's wrists to the bed rails with soft cotton restraints, restricting his unconscious movements. There was an inflatable mattress pad (to reduce the likelihood of bedsores) and a mattress protector. He wore adult diapers and learned to press the button to raise the bed when he had to eat or drink . . . and I thought of how, for almost a month, Third Brother had sat there like an enormous guardian angel. The memory saddened me. It was as if we were in a different world now, and his strength, the stuff of legends, and the magic circle of protection this strength cast around Father in his "time of difficulty" could be replaced by some tiny items and ingenuity.

The hollow feeling of a human being so easily replaced by insignificant objects seemed like a metaphor for Third Brother's migration story. He came back to Jiangxin Island with his two sons and was confused by the sight of his brothers and their children riotously scrambling to earn money in all kinds of newfangled ways. One time, Yiming proposed to the Yuhuatai district local government that they turn Jiangxin Island into a water park to serve residents of Nanjing. Which is to say, replace the fishing boats and old ferries with speedboats, jet skis, and windsurfing boards. Set up a giant Ferris wheel on the cotton fields behind the breakwater, and perhaps get a permit for a tiger or a black bear, monkeys or maybe a snake, something like that. . . . Third Brother was furious at the idea. But then what should he and his sons do instead? And so they ended up helping all those optimistic, energetic second- and third-generation Luos to build their new homes, carrying bricks and pouring cement. (I remember on my first visit to Jiangxin Island with my wife, how Yiming brought me to a long, straight yellow dirt road like an airport runway, both sides lined with white poplar trees, and he enthused: Look ahead, Little Brother, straight ahead, along this road, this production brigade, are twenty or thirty concrete houses, and every one of them belongs to the Luo family.)

In the dimly lit house, the light so faint you couldn't make out the old men's faces, Father spoke to his elderly son and nephews like a sleepwalker. "This old gentleman left here aged twenty-three, and now I'm in my seventies, I've finally come back." The old men's eyes moistened as they thought unhappily about their bizarre lives. Those migrations that served no purpose at all, except to perpetuate the clan. (Perhaps this place could be thought of as a family darkroom, where the strands of fate crisscrossed?)

I fear that in my description of this "journey," I'm restricted to my father's darkening "Alzheimer's Room," in which the visible space grew ever narrower until it contained only those sighing, white-haired old men. I don't know why, but every time I pick up my pen to describe them, they become foolish, stiff, and regressive. As if a feeling of nostalgia washed back to corrode their features. We always ask: In the brain of someone with Alzheimer's, as a lifetime of memories are pathetically whittled away like a pencil going through a sharpener, what will he be forced to abandon? (Flung into the sea of forgetfulness.) And what will he hang on to, refusing to let go until the moment of death, even as the rest of his mind is being nibbled away, chomp chomp, by little golden worms?

I wanted to record a journey. A passage. A great migration. But then I realized I was just describing this hotel—not even a profile of the unfamiliar, remote city—which seemed out of place in the city and the entire trip. It was up against a wide road and cement wall, and on the other side of the wall, a thick mass of clouds loomed over the vast muddy yellow river, while sails and masts gathered like clouds and the motors of steel-hulled boats putt-putted away, slicing white scars through the water. The dockers, like characters in a silent film, hustled up and down to load and unload the boats I couldn't see. I remember early one morning, Mother and I left the hotel as usual, heavy-hearted, to get a taxi (heading to the hospital to relieve Yiming and Fourth Brother), but for some reason all the cabs were on the other side of the road (windows wound down, drivers waving at us), apparently afraid to approach the hotel. We had no choice but to cross the road and get in one of them, whereupon the driver said in a nasal voice, "Sorry about that. The Three Gorges migrants are arriving today. All the police and traffic cops will be out in force. We're not supposed to U-turn here anyway, but especially not today." He pointed to where we'd come from, and only then did we notice the red banner across the hotel entrance with gold writing proclaiming "A Warm Welcome to the Three Gorges Migrants." We were too dazed for curiosity—I really should have asked the driver more questions—and after a number of days in the city, we still hadn't been to the kiosk for a local newspaper even once, nor had we turned on the TV in our room. It was Yiming who, every afternoon, borrowed a yellowing newspaper from the man in the next bed's brother, put on his reading glasses, and traded views with the other oldsters about the political situation and rumors about certain officials. Their opinions and analysis, to my ear, sounded like the petty grievances or fantasies of village cadres. A sort of distraction and distancing, reeking of the sickroom, seemed to cut us off from those brightly sunlit streets.

I remember the taxi driver getting stuck at a junction. I couldn't tell whether his voice held impatience or exhilaration as he gestured and said, "See? Now we can't move. It's the

Three Gorges migrants." All I knew about this was a small news item I vaguely remembered from a Taiwanese newspaper, maybe one or two years ago. The Three Gorges Dam. All the residents below the waterline would have to be moved. Their homes and land would be swallowed by the water and become the new riverbed. The People's Government had distributed them to farmlands in Hunan, Hubei, Jiangxi, and Anhui. The driver said, "Over the next few days, two hundred thousand people will arrive in our city from the Three Gorges. Afterward, the government will move some of them to the villages along the Nanchang-Jiujiang Expressway." At that point, I was too far sunk into my father's situation and the story of Mother and me being trapped in this small city, and all I could do was stare listlessly out the window, where everything seemed to be suspended in thick golden liquid as the autumn sun poured over it like wine, though I saw nothing at all. Or else I simply don't remember what I saw, or perhaps this brightly lit, contrasting scene, one rumbling army truck after another taking up all the road space, carrying gloomy families in shabby clothes, old and young all clutching their most important possessions, padded blankets and kitchen utensils, village after village emptied out, these erstwhile Three Gorges residents who must have arrived at the harbor on the other side of the high wall in one boat after another down the Yangtze River, two hundred thousand in all, a sea of heads bobbing as they swarmed over the deck railings and jumped down to the dock—perhaps none of this bore comparison with my father's story of his own flight half a century before. As soon as they came off the boats, they were herded into army trucks that set off with no space between them, a closed convoy. The vehicles passed through a gate in the city wall into the urban center. Along the way they'd have seen welcoming banners hanging from shops, government buildings, and street signs. Local people on their way to work or school, waving at them. And did they feel an invisible something separating them from this place? "And it is from the other world that he comes when he disembarks. . . . In a highly symbolic position he is placed on the inside of the outside, or vice versa." And when they entered the city, they were displayed in order to be welcomed, though they were only welcome to pass through, not to clamor for freedom or to jump from the vehicles and vanish in the maze-like streets (they were not allowed to "evaporate" into this city).

I ought to have looked out the window, squinting against the light, following the gaze of the local, the taxi driver, to scrutinize the waves of incomers. These outsiders. These unknown plagues and uncertain threats. Their shriveled yellowish faces, like people who'd starved to death; their wide and terrified eyes. And the rickety old boats of all sizes that had ferried them here, now jostling for space by the dock. Images I had no way of seeing for myself now spilled from their mouths in thick accents: they spoke of thousand-year-old towns emptied out in a single night, then turned into rubble by buried explosives, soon to be turned into underwater worlds of silvery swaying light. They would never again be individuals. As soon as it was decided that they would be moved, they and their descendants would forever be weary, solitary itinerants.

I did look out the window for a moment, but all I saw was the strange city, drenched in golden light and covered in gray dust. Even the trees lining the street were under a thick layer of dust. How could I tell which parts of the scene had been there all along and which were the result of the sudden intrusion? My mother timidly said to the driver, "If we can't get across here, why don't we turn around and take another road? We're in a hurry, we need to get to the First People's Hospital."

%% %% %%

In my country, or I should say in my city, people have a sort of "nostalgia for rough materials and coarse objects." Hotel walls are decorated with bedraggled objects from our years of poverty, such as the metal tobacco and liquor sales licenses that used to hang outside grocery stores (known as "booze shops") in old housing compounds or by the side of the road just twenty or thirty years ago, or metal discs meant to look like bottle caps painted with the names of old brands of soda, or even the "Everyone has a duty to keep secrets and guard against spies" wooden boards from the White Terror, now turned into fashionable playthings. In the expensive kiosks of five-star hotels, they put up the "Fifty Cent Lucky Dip" cardboard signs from our childhoods, with cheap prizes meant to evoke nostalgia: green bean cakes, *Brother Liu and Brother Wang on the Road in Taiwan*, candied sweet potatoes, chocolate toothpaste, tangerine powdered soda, fake meat in red sauce, tartrazine-yellow dried mango . . . though these days it's ten dollars per draw. They also offer low-quality toys: wooden spinning tops, feathered balloon horns, paper dolls, bubble solution with the consistency of superglue, glow-in-the-dark bouncing balls, Styrofoam airplanes propelled by rubber bands . . . none of them cheap, yet they sell pretty well. I know some nouveau riche folk with deep pockets whose living rooms are full of kitschy, gaudy human-sized plastic figures: Mazinger Z, Science Ninja Team Gatchaman, Candy Candy, Ultraman, Little Fairy. I've heard that these sell for twenty or thirty thousand each, and my acquaintances bring them home without blinking (because they're limited editions).

These tattered objects and old cartoon figures have long been removed from their original context. They're like old bank notes no longer in circulation, with no practical function in the real world. And yet, the nostalgia fiends around me insist on dragging them from the garbage heap and assembling them into a tableau that makes it feel as if time has stood still: an old street with a booze shop at the corner (with its liquor license hanging outside, or else the circular emblem of White Plum Blossom soda). Inside the store: a fifty-cent lucky dip and large candy jars made of coarse green glass, with New Paradise cigarettes and Ramune lemonade. Through the entrance of the arcade, you see a Singer sewing machine in black and gleaming metal (a friend of mine opened a pub, using a dozen or so sewing machines with wooden boards atop them as tables, cramming customers into this chaotic yet atmospheric space to enjoy martinis and tequila bombs), and a carefully curated selection of objects including a black-and-white TV set, the sort with legs and sliding doors across the screen, on top of which will be a couple of Tatung Baby collectibles, the rare number 51 or 52, or the single crystal radio set they paid an astronomical sum for, with a clear plastic bubble over a needle pointing to handwritten station numbers, although it won't actually be able to pick up the little league game from Williamsport.

These dead objects, miscellaneous bric-a-brac with no function other than to be heaped up in a dusty diorama of distant history, have been summoned from their original settings, which were much more detailed (these other details can't be plucked from the trash and presented as new, due to the limitations of the nostalgia hounds' memories). They're so expensive, and when put together like this, so very ugly. Even so, my friends wax emotional as they continue collecting them. They say, "This is the era we lived through." An era of such impoverishment and inflexibility (remember those yellow packets of Prince instant noodles, all broken up and full of MSG and pepper, and those "guard against spies" slogans?), so lacking in imagination.

When my friends say, "This is the era we lived through," I never say a single word, just stand among them, because this is "the era I lived through" too. Sometimes we'll be in a room with a glass display case full of cloth puppets in resplendent costumes

(Great Swordsman Shih Yan-Wen, the Yin-Yang Warrior, the Secret Fighter Buck-Toothed Hamai . . . all kinds), or sometimes a bulky retro jukebox, or stained, yellowing posters for old Nationalist films or Taiwanese-language movies. . . . I feel as if I'm being hypnotized when I stand before these nostalgic collages, assembled from the same few key elements (old films, old records, old cartoon characters, old advertisements, old electronics, old toys)—which means, no matter their reasons for putting together these displays, they invariably resemble a junk shop—as if the time and space I once inhabited but carelessly left behind has now been frozen into an arrangement that leaves me dizzy.

Those installations place me in my own past, contemplating bygone times, as if I'm in a hotel. When I enter and leave "the era I lived through," it feels like taking keys with different acrylic tags, only to face an identically decorated room each time. My personal history is no different from that of the other hotel guests. And so the experiences of an entire generation become something that took place in an enormous hotel, one with a historic atmosphere and filled with commemorative objects—all those people wandering the various floors like ghosts; the flirting, squabbling, and gossip in the lobby; the hurtful, tearful, intimate, and lonely stories that take place behind closed doors; the tales of the pianists, chambermaids, bartenders, and majordomo. . . .

This is the citified thinking I brought to the strange little city (where Father lay in mortal danger). The tour company arranged for Mother and me to stay at the very hotel where Father collapsed. The night before, he, Yiming, and Fourth Brother shared a private conversation in his room. Mother reported that in his last phone call, Father happily told her, "I've told them everything." What did he say? Then he had his stroke, and that afternoon Second Brother and Third Brother got the ferry from Nanjing to Jiujiang (landing at the dock behind the wall?), and late the following night, Mother and I changed planes on Hainan Island for Nanchang (and then we sped down the Nanchang-Jiujiang Expressway, along which land had been allocated to people displaced from the Three Gorges?). I'd thought this was a journey, a story of many migrations summed up in an image (the anguished faces of old men huddled around Father's sickbed). The night we arrived in this city, we checked into this hotel. A hotel that didn't seem to fit in this defeated city, like a city of sand built on a fetid swamp. This city was even more backward and impoverished than the "cities of yesteryear" my nostalgic friends built from expensive broken objects, even more enamored of vulgar, inexpensive fashions. From this point until the day we left with Father, our trajectory was only those taxi rides between hotel and hospital.

Some evenings, we'd haul our spent bodies from Father's side and hail a taxi as usual, and the driver would take a shortcut through alleyways thick with slow-moving crowds. I'd stare out in puzzled enchantment at the shabby bars (trying to create a sense of prosperity with Christmas tree lights instead of neon), the pretty young women standing in doorways in glittering red cheongsams slit to the thigh, the young laborers squatting in the street as they waited to haul carts, the bellowing, laughing men in police uniforms, and in those moments I felt a peculiar sensation: *I've somehow blundered into the living, breathing past.*

nine

THE KING OF JIUJIANG

I am thinking of those many nights in Jiujiang. The classy hotel that seemed so unimaginable in that dusty, gray, land-locked city. The night we arrived, we'd planned to spend the night in Father's hospital room, but the old men bossily ordered Mother and me back to our hotel to "rest." As we tried to argue with them, a neighboring patient's visitor (also an old man) piped up, "You should go back to the hotel. You Taiwanese stand out, you'll draw attention. After it gets dark, one-tenth of the people in Jiujiang turn into drug fiends." His words might have been alarmist, but they certainly left an impression. Extending the image of my father's fallen body, sunset turned this dusty little city, with its blurry outlines that refused to cohere into a modern metropolis, into something with the darkness and depth of an oil painting. A scattered writhing of bodies, conveying the poverty and suffering that couldn't find full expression by day.

This warning took root in us. Each evening, Mother and I wearily took a taxi from the hospital back to the hotel and didn't set foot outside again till dawn. Of course, this was a great loss. We were like the most timorous tourists, scurrying into their third-world lodgings at sunset and hiding till dawn, bored out of their minds. The problem was, we weren't tourists, we were a mother and son trapped in this city (because of an old man's ruined body?), and our days were spent trying every means we could to get out of this place. In the evenings, I would leave my mother in our room (the door was technologically advanced and opened with a keycard) and as I walked out, she'd be putting on her reading glasses in preparation for kneeling by the bedside table to chant scripture; sometimes she'd still be there when I got back, sometimes she'd be in the bathroom washing our clothes in the sink, or else lying in bed making long-distance calls to her Buddhist prayer friends back in Taiwan . . . and on the pleated shades of the standing lamp and dressing table light, wet underwear would be draped, both hers and mine. Using an adapter, I plugged my cell phone into the socket under the table. The dressing table was littered with the beverages and instant oatmeal we'd brought to the hospital then back again because Father wasn't up to eating or drinking, as well as local treats from a shop called Sesame Sweets at the People's Great Mall, metal flasks, and various medicines and plasters Mother had brought with her. . . . When the inhabitants of a hotel room have camped out there long enough, it naturally takes on an atmosphere that doesn't belong to travel but is more like the lethargy and inertia of home, an aura that the elderly cleaner is simply unable to scrub away on her daily visit.

When I think of those nights, I can't help connecting them to the many novels in which travelers are forced, for whatever reason, to remain at fancy hotels, novels by Graham Greene, V. S. Naipaul, even Murakami, plus some murder mysteries I can't remember very clearly. The faint dark shadows of palm trees swaying beneath the air-con vents, palatial crystal chandeliers, worldly waiters gliding silently, the hotel owner growing waspish as he watches his magnificent business gradually fall into ruin from lack of customers . . . this world was unfamiliar to me. And I was right in the middle of it.

How can I put this? Even as I became like one of those tourists hiding all night in a huge hotel that might as well have been a foreign concession, afraid to walk into the demonic nighttime city through the bronze revolving doors a uniformed porter would bow and push, I was very aware that at daybreak, Mother and I would make our way to the city center hospital, trying to pass as locals, comically imitating their accents without realizing we were doing it, suspecting taxi drivers of deliberately taking a longer route to inflate their fares ("Hey, we know the way"), trying to cajole stone-faced nurses to change Father's sheets more often than scheduled (he kept smearing his bed with diarrhea), haggling with the fruit hawkers outside the hospital . . . whereas actual tourists would board their bus the next morning and depart forever (visitors at this hotel, both domestic and foreign, were usually here for the sole purpose of seeing Mount Lu), while a new batch showed up ready to check in. Only we stayed, mother and son. We weren't locals; nor had we arrived with romantic notions of exploring this city. This wasn't a journey we had sought out. We'd been arbitrarily flung into this strange place. We hadn't read a single thing before setting out, and even now that we were here, we weren't in the mood to peruse a single newspaper or magazine or guidebook to find out more about the city, not even the free map provided by the hotel.

If someone had noticed us at the hotel ("Oh yes, that mother and son!") and tried to strike up a conversation, they could have called us something more accurate than "travelers": outsiders, visitors.

Every night, I would leave my mother alone in the hotel room full of our outsiderness and stray objects, and go wandering like a ghost through the building that seemed marooned, in exile from some other time and space. I'd bring a book down to the first-floor coffee shop, where I'd have a cup of Blue Mountain coffee for twenty yuan (bland and sour, as if someone had merely poured hot water onto the dregs from a Taipei café, but at least it tasted of coffee beans, unlike the disgustingly sweet packets of local instant coffee). I always sat at the same window table. Lonely and sensitive, I tried recording whatever random events had happened at the hospital that day on the hotel's letter paper.

By the end, one of the waitresses began to recognize me ("A cup of Blue Mountain coffee, right?"), a gesture for which I felt absurdly grateful. Others, though, were stony-faced from beginning to end, treating me the same as the mainland business travelers or foreigners who hung out at the coffee shop late. In the month I was there, I read nothing but the two books I'd hastily shoved into my rucksack before leaving: *A Hundred Years of Solitude* and an anthology of Borges's poems and essays. I went through these line by line (the time I had to sit and read each night was extremely limited), as if the only point of reading was to while away the empty time of this journey. Occasionally I had a hallucinatory thought: weren't these books I was burying my head in also about an impoverished, desolate, damaged third-world country? I forced myself to linger in those descriptions of slums, prisons, massacres in town squares, dirt roads (sometimes I even mouthed the words), and when I looked up, there through the large windows was a living, breathing place of illusions, violence, poverty, and sin.

The coffee shop was very noisy for most of the evening. There weren't many customers, but the two TV sets in opposite corners of the room were always turned up loud. They only showed broadcasts of soccer matches, a little like the British pubs off Taipei's Nong'an Street, though not quite: the commentators spoke with pristine Beijing accents, and the narrative they were pushing was of China's prowess in the Asian section of the World Cup. The battle sounded arduous and ferocious (every time I listened, the opposing team would be some Asian country I didn't know much about, such as Uzbekistan or the UAE). The tone and volume of the commentators filled the coffee shop with the frenetic atmosphere of "a billion Chinese standing up at once." If we were in Taipei, I'd have left long ago to find somewhere else. Here, though, I didn't dare to step outside the hotel. (Walk down the streets where one in ten people were alleged drug fiends, to find another establishment open this late?)

China always won these matches (the Chinese team heroically defeating whatever team they faced from Central Asia or the Middle East), but afterward none of the few patrons seemed inclined to celebrate. There was no cheering, toasting, or singing of "The Internationale," even though the TV had been on so loud and everyone had been staring raptly up at the screen. At this point, the coffee bar would lower the volume (and change the channel to Phoenix Satellite MTV: Chinese pop stars belting out rock 'n' roll), and the row of lights by the windows would go out, replaced by a bizarre multicolored laser display more suited to a disco. The waiters and waitresses, who'd been sitting in front of the TV, would return to work as if waking from a dream (or else sliding into a clockwork dream), expressionless, upper bodies ramrod straight, moving slowly between the tables like fish in a tank.

If I'd stepped out of the door and into those nighttime streets filled with dock workers, unemployed youths, drug addicts, cheap bar girls, and laborers and gone into a local bar, would I have found myself in a scene of riotous celebration, glasses clinking all around me?

I realized that in this big hotel, there was no way I would ever experience the things I'd imagined went on in big hotels: serendipitous encounters and liaisons between travelers, extravagantly odd stories and tales of bravado exchanged by strangers. Like an outsider still in shock, I spent my evenings hiding in a corner of the coffee shop, reading and copying out two great works of Latin American magic realism or scribbling down everything that had happened in the hospital that day while my head throbbed as if it might split in two. My notes were a disorderly scrawl, like the hysterical, melancholy journal entries of a manic patient unable to let go of insignificant details. A thought floated into my brain: when all this was over, I would gather my memories and reconstruct this journey (this city, this hotel) as if it were a novel. In the event, after the international rescue organization finally showed up like celestial warriors descending from the sky, after Mother and I finally were able to bring Father back to our city in an inflatable mattress on a plane, long after all that, the next time I reached for my diary of this tumultuous time (written each evening in a corner of the coffee shop on hotel stationery, white letter paper with the hotel's name at the top and an embossed gold seal, three sheets of which were placed on our dressing table each day), I found that like the silks and satins excavated from ancient tombs, the papers crumbled to dust as soon as I unfolded them. My scribbled words had failed to retain the descriptions I thought I'd captured, "a city of uneven light" or "a camera moving slowly down the corridors of a well-appointed hotel." Like grains of sand in the wind, there were now even fewer words left that I'd set down while on the scene than my mottled memories afterward. The city was just so many mounds of golden sand, blowing away and scattering from the meager, tattered words I'd put down on paper, their shape no longer discernible.

During the first week, I smoked my way through the carton of mild cigarettes I'd picked up from Taoyuan Airport duty-free (my usual Taiwanese brand). After that, I started switching randomly between various local brands, all extremely high-tar (mainly Hong Ta Shan, Ashima, and Cloud, of course, and also some from this province, one named Gan after the river, another called Mount Lu), which left me dizzy and anxious. I got through a whole packet each evening. Soon I had blisters in the corners of my mouth, my nostrils were thick with dried mucus, and the whites of my eyes were turning yellow. One evening, I was copying out Márquez when a bearded foreigner walked by and gently rapped on the edge of my table. When I looked up, he and his three backpacker friends were already paying at the counter, though he turned back and gave me a thumbs up. I had no idea what he meant by that. Later I wondered—could it be that they'd spent a lot of time traveling through this scorching, dusty country full of blank-faced people (more than me, they must have been living in a silent film, trapped in big hotels like this, seeing lobbies and coffee shops and elevators full of people who looked like me in fancy suits and thick gold necklaces, gabbing loudly and vulgarly into their cell phones), and here for the first time was a young literary guy sitting by himself writing in a coffee shop?

Not that I was particularly young, nor was I a local. As I copied out the text of *A Hundred Years of Solitude*, which I'd first devoured in my early twenties, I found that certain demonic and fantastical passages, certain unwieldy phrases and sentences, matched what I was going through as exactly as the fine metal cogs inside a watch, or the thin wires connecting false teeth to gums, the intrusion of an exquisitely crafted foreign object, mysteriously mixing fiction and reality.

I was no longer young. But one evening I copied out how the afternoon before Colonel Buendía's illegitimate son Aureliano José was killed, his mother, Pilar Ternera, saw his death in the cards and begged her impulsive son, "Don't go out tonight . . . Stay and sleep here because Carmelita Montiel is getting tired of asking me to put her in your room." The stubborn boy leaves the house anyway, and sure enough is shot in the street by Captain Aquiles Ricardo of the Conservatives, the bullet entering his back. His murderer is subsequently shot dead too, in another street. I copied out this passage: "More than four hundred men had filed past the theater and discharged their revolvers into the abandoned body of Captain Aquiles Ricardo. A patrol had to use a wheelbarrow to carry the body, which was heavy with lead and fell apart like a water-soaked loaf of bread." I felt that night for the first time that I had reached the age when I could no longer easily recover from hurts like the sudden death of a loved one. Every joint in my body ached, chills went through my lower back, my knees wouldn't obey instructions, and so much hair fell out as I wrote that the coffee shop table was covered in it.

That night, my wife said to me on the phone, "It's raining in Taipei," and I distractedly replied, "So what? It's natural for it to be raining in August." She was silent after that, until I finally hung up. Only then did I realize: wasn't this exactly what Colonel Aureliano Buendía said via telegraph to his old friend Colonel Gerineldo Márquez?

As time was short, I was only able to copy out brief sections each night, but even those few paragraphs yielded the deaths of one or two familiar characters every day. All kinds of deaths. All kinds of burials. All kinds of camera angles, amounting to special effects. He kept jokingly pulling pieces from the bottom and middle of the Jenga tower, and though the blocks teetered at peculiar angles, they mysteriously never fell, but instead grew taller. Like smaller parenthetical asides within larger parentheses, multiple secondary characters died in between the passing of major figures.

This method of dividing my days and nights left me severely depressed. By day, Mother and I, along with my older brother and cousins, prodded and poked at Father's large, broken body in the ill-equipped hospital—wiping away his diarrhea, sticking needles into him, forcing medicine down his throat, rubbing his back, soothing the bedsores around his hip and tailbone—trying to revive him and so drag him back to the land of the living. At night, Mother knelt alone in the hotel room chanting the *Diamond Sutra* and *Ksitigarbha Sutra* to reduce misfortune and increase his life span, while I retreated to the ground-floor coffee shop, copying out one tale of death after another. There were times when I began to wonder: the night I got the news, did I grab the wrong book as I hurried out the door?

One night, I dreamed that I'd run off with a woman. Holding her hand, I frantically scoured a small town, looking for a hotel. The desolate streets made me feel outcast, yet aroused desire. "My window faced on to a wall, piebald with stains, to which a withered moss was clinging." I thought: *This is my hometown.* Walls of packed yellow earth blocked a slate-gray sky. Soil in various shades of yellow, light and shadow spilling across it, filled my entire field of vision. Every shop and home was built on a slant, along the steep slope of the river valley. One store sold charcoal stoves, little bronze hand warmers, rain capes made of palm bark, and ceramic bowls with spiral ridges for grinding rice, these sorts of things. Most of the street, though, had been abandoned. At something like a crossroads, with a winch well that had been painted bright red at the corner, stood three or four old men in padded jackets and felt hats, the only human beings I'd seen so far. They stared at me with strange looks on their faces, as if they knew me very well and had strong emotions about me. With their eyes on me like that, my head felt as if a living creature were jumping around inside it and inexplicably sobbing. Yet it felt as if something slow and violent stood between us, preventing us from speaking.

One of the old men silently led me and the woman into a dirt hut with collapsing walls. "The room was empty" apart from a few wooden chairs and tables, as if before fleeing en masse, its inhabitants had made a last-gasp attempt to change their fortunes by turning their home into an inn. I knew this place, and still holding the woman's hand, climbed "once more up those familiar old bannistered stairs in the corner." The old man didn't follow us, but stopped at the landing, staring at me with exactly the same sorrowful gaze as the others at the crossroads.

What was going on? Were they rebuking me? In the silence I felt a sharp surge of lust, hurtful and lonely, like a short-circuited fire alarm going off loudly somewhere in my brain, completely cut off from any kind of ancestral obligation to reproduce. Now what? Was this wrong? Would this lead to weakening and illness? Was this incest? Was she my Aunt Amaranta? But I didn't remember my father having any sisters. The problem was, I was just a brat giving in to my desires. I'd been interfered with. These shadowy fears you have would never come true, that I'd leave behind an unfortunate child. A baby with a pig's tail.

The old man left. Now it was just me and the woman, standing in the empty second floor. Out of nowhere, I felt violent hatred for her. The woman was very pale, and not beautiful (she wasn't my wife). Full of cunning, she had enmeshed herself in this sticky, filthy web of lechery with me. On the heated bed was a red blanket embroidered with a dragon and phoenix design. At the foot of the bed was an enamel chamber pot, containing several cigarette butts now steeped in piss. And just like that, I no longer felt the slightest urge for my semen to spurt into this pale, mildewed, germ-ridden body, yet the alarm in my brain continued shrilling without pause, and I couldn't find a gap through which I could reach in to silence it.

In the end, revolted as I was, I took the pale woman to bed, in that small-town hotel with the collapsing walls of yellow earth.

"Oh!"

When I woke up, I was unable to immediately work out where I was. Which moment was this, in the life of this "me"? Bit by bit, I pieced together the reality of my gloomy surroundings: in the bed next to me, my mother was snoring as loudly as any man, and on the bedside table, the meditation player flashed its red light, quietly chanting the name of one buddha or another. I felt as if I were on the shore of a dark sea that my father was floating on, the tide gently splashing against me.

The girl in my dream, so delicate and pale, yet from whose soul you could have wrung endless amounts of dirty water, was a college classmate I hadn't known very well. Lying there in the dark, I couldn't even remember her name at first. In the dream, though, we'd been intimately acquainted (I remembered how in the shadows, she seemed to sense my greasy loathing of her and sat on the edge of the bed in proud isolation, dignity intact, unbuttoning her shirt to reveal the crags of her shoulder blades, bra straps tight across them, a tragic sight). The sort of grayish girl who leaves no impression at all. In four years of college, all I remembered was the semester she'd been our class treasurer and spent all her time outside class grimly chasing us to pay our dues to the class fund. What was going on? ("Why her?" "How could I, in such desolate surroundings, have a wet dream?") Out of all the erotica in my mental folder, why had I chosen (so realistically!) this girl at the moment of REM sleep?

Had I been "interfered with"?

My head throbbed, and I thought of a story by my friend Huang Jun set during the nightmarish earthquake in Taiwan, in which the protagonist flees with his wife and children, only to find himself stepping into "a strong sensation of jetlag, as if I'd just crossed the international date line." He keeps replaying the image in his head: "We drove off in our crappy car, far from the ruins, away from that vast gluey darkness, to a place of light. Our whole family. Comforting to know we'd all made it out. Even though many others were still trapped beneath the rubble." But then he notices a stench. First he thinks of the two cats they abandoned in the disaster zone. "The yellow-green eyes of a cat are clearly engraved with the gradations of time, like hands of a clock quickly turning, smoothly or against resistance." He thinks they probably died in the earthquake. But then he watches his two-year-old son drawing on the sandy ground and realizes in anguish that "the bottom half of his body was turning dark. So his movements were a little stiff. Like a puppet's."

Then the child looks up at him, an expression on his face like no two-year-old would have in reality, and says, "Daddy, I can't play with you anymore. Because you're already decomposing."

This was the saddest scene I'd read recently. The story doesn't end There, though. The protagonist goes on to tell us how at a coffee shop one day, he meets an old friend (only right at the end do we find out the twist: this friend was his wife's former lover) who looks like he's been through a rough time—his hair is white, he's fragile and exhausted, "as if he'd looked away and someone had stolen his life from him." What happened to him? Sobbing, he tells the protagonist about a breakup in his younger days. Such a good girl (the protagonist's wife, as a young woman), so pure and good. At this point, Huang Jun's story goes into a long, comical, and rather bizarre erotic passage. This destroyed, hollowed-out man unburdens himself to the silent (jealous? vigilant? sympathetic?) husband, describing that beautiful time and how, behind closed doors, he tried to "have his way" with that pretty girl. Yet whether she was "wearing gauzy underthings at my request, or when we were naked together in the bath," she "refused to let me invade her body."

Next he speaks with frustration about how (one unfortunate moment?) he couldn't stand it any longer, downed several drinks, and fueled by Dutch courage, returned to see her alluring half-naked body, "pressed my hands down on her as if I were falling, and opened her up like a pomelo," thinking, *Now you'll have to show me a good time, won't you?* Out of nowhere, he felt a searing pain right up into his guts that immediately sobered him up. He went limp all over. "And that's when I understood that with nothing but two icy cold fingers, she was able to defeat me. A pair of deep crimson fingernail scars were left on my penis."

Those two "deep crimson fingernail scars" that caused the swollen and unsightly penis to quickly shrivel back into his belly were like metal hooks scraping at the glass of my diseased imagination. Ever since reading Huang Jun's story, I had become like the mystic objects in *Journey to the West*: the monkey king's golden staff, fire-breathing snakes, the celestial army's golden armor, or a golden-haired demon that, with a simple spell, suddenly fall to earth and reveal their true form (as I said, I'd been "interfered with"). Those fingernails seemed to dig into my own unfortunate penis.

I remember how, in old Mr. Naipaul's novel *Half a Life*, he wrote these extremely sad words: "I don't know where I am going. I am just letting the days go by. I don't like the place that's waiting for me at home. . . . And if I stay here I would always be trying to make love to my friends' girlfriends. I have discovered that is quite an easy thing to do. But I know it to be wrong, and it would get me into trouble one day. The trouble is I don't know how to go out and get a girl on my own. No one trained me in that. I don't know how to make a pass at a stranger, when to touch a girl or hold her hand or try to kiss her. When my father told me his life story and talked about his sexual incompetence, I mocked him. I was a child then. Now I discover I am like my poor father. . . . Now we live like incestuous little animals in a hole. We grope all our female relations and are always full of shame."

My friends keep calling me "perverted" (I imagine they're referring to my novels). One time, I was being interviewed by a cute reporter. She started out by politely claiming to enjoy my books, but when we relaxed into the conversation and went a little deeper, she became rather incoherent and angry. She informed me that she couldn't stand how "perverted" my stories were. I said, "I'm not perverted, am I?" She clapped her hands over her jug ears, which were blushing rose red from anger. "That's enough. I've had enough of these perverted things. All your perverted things." I wanted to explain to her that maybe the real reason was that I'd been "interfered with."

None of my friends believed me when I got back and told them everything I'd been through in Jiujiang. When I described the hospital, they were absolutely certain that somewhere among those wards, corridors, gardens, or other hidden spots, I'd pursued, flirted with, and even had my way with the little Jiujiang nurses, ripping off their adorable white uniforms. When I spoke of the lonely, ice-cold, lethargic evenings at the hotel, they accused me with a disturbing amount of detail of barging into the air-conditioned suites, pushing the pleasingly plump chambermaids in their silk blouses onto the white bedspreads, lifting their short skirts, and peeling off their silk stockings. . . .

This game went on for a year. They began calling me the King of Jiujiang and would say, "How are all those kids you fathered in Jiujiang?" They meant that in my month on the mainland, like white men impersonating ancestral spirits, I'd impregnated a bevy of girls (the little nurses and waitresses, I guess?) and become a legendary local figure when, ten months after my departure, a batch of babies with faces identical to mine were born in quick succession. All my offspring.

As time passed, everything Mother and Father and I went through in Jiujiang grew blurry. I started joining in and riffing on my friends' filthy jokes about jade-limbed Jiujiang nurses or our female comrades of the People's Liberation Army with their military boots and leather whips. "Jiujiang" began to feel like a distant, fictitious little city, a place in which I was no more than a boar injected with testosterone, fit to do nothing but endlessly mount those poor young girls with blurred faces, ripping off their uniforms and getting hard, thrusting and ejaculating. One after another, rinse and repeat. (And perhaps they were just crudely made wooden racks, smeared with female pig pheromones and draped with nurses' outfits?)

How come, when faced with the blackness of death, I couldn't help reaching for ludicrous religious texts with gaudy gilt-edged covers? (The Goddess of Mercy, a thousand arms reaching from her flanks and back, each holding an implement of worship, a small goatee on her face, solemn and sorrowful, riding atop a crouched female body, a stiff pose of connection and lovemaking.)

In his book, my friend Huang Jun uses an image from Kenzaburō Ōe's *The Changeling* (which perhaps revolves around the women in his late friend Juzo Itami's life—maybe Itami's little sister, who was Ōe's wife, or else some young lover from Itami's porn videos—getting pregnant by some mysterious means, thus allowing Itami to be "reborn") to create a bone-chilling image: an innocent child telling his mother, who'd just received news of her father's death, "Mom, we can birth Grandpa back to life."

The sperm I'd left behind in Jiujiang, thousands of them carelessly tossed away, seemed to sprout like melons in the night, turning into children. How could they ever understand that they were this way, eyes and noses crooked, hands and feet webbed, created like haploid frogs with transparent skins (abandoned in that strange, gray, poverty-stricken city), because their father, confronted with the ugliness and sorrow of his own father's death, buckled at the knees, unable to face the situation, unable to help ("Birth him back to life! Birth him back to life! Birth him back to life!"), thrust his hands unthinkingly into his pockets, reverting to adolescence: unbearably lonely, self-contained, shivering and scared, whiny and guilt-ridden.

Birth him back to life.

That's when, in solitude and terror, I realized that I faced an empty hotel. (Had I unwittingly taken this icy-cold, unfeeling building, with blank-faced staff silently gliding by, unseen floors and corners hidden in shadow, and turned it into Father's mysterious head, shrouded by Alzheimer's and stuffed with blood clots?) Overwhelmed with feeling, I described every centimeter of that hotel in incredible detail, but managed only to prove it was "no more than an empty hotel." Apart from that, it was nothing at all. Not, as I imagined it, a grand sight rising from the fog, fit to be gaped at by dumbstruck travelers. ("Birth him back to life!") My penis shriveled back to its boyhood size, small and immature, like half a shelled caltrop fruit. Too confused and pure (and lacking in fingernail scars) to understand that awful, epic journey of "birthing Father back to life."

While staying at the hotel where Father collapsed, I dreamed of another hotel, in which I coupled loathsomely with a dull, gray woman. Many years later, my deformed Jiujiang sons would find themselves uninspired to communicate with the real world, and though they didn't know each other and hadn't planned this, they'd find some excuse to check into this hotel, which they'd all converge on at the same time. Like following a river to its end, their sense of smell would lead them to the reality of their dreamscape. That ice-cold, unfortunate dream, reeking to them of damp sawdust, a hard-to-describe tang of sorrow or joy. When they'd found that dream (the same moment I had my arms around a woman's waist, eyes blank, mounting her from behind), they would—this startled me—all be wearing white shipyard uniforms stained brown with rust or black with grease, shaking to an inaudible beat like drug users, dismantling my dream the way they'd scavenge a boiler, pipes, ship's wheel, and mast from a condemned vessel about to be scuttled. Completely unbothered, they pulled wrenches and hammers from their pockets, whistling when they didn't have cigarettes dangling from their lips, movements practiced and graceful (I felt with a pang that I had let down my brood of sons), a team of worker bees laboring away in riotous stage outfits.

Perhaps I should have thundered with rage. "Stop that, don't you dare tear apart this hotel. It's actually the empty insides of your grandfathers' heads after they get Alzheimer's."

Or maybe I should have started bargaining, like a hostage negotiator. "Why don't you leave that big, empty, dilapidated building alone for now, and wait for my (fuck it!) tiny cock to grow up (wait till I've figured out exactly which moment things started going south), but in the meantime I need to go in there and birth my father back to life."

I remember one evening, I'd left the coffee shop and was on my way back to our room (where my mother would still be kneeling and chanting scripture, as if frozen in time), but while waiting for the elevator by the gilt-framed stone wall, I suddenly felt my head spin and my knees soften, and thought, *Am I sick now?* Spending my days by Father's bedside, I was constantly gazing at three stroke patients showing no more signs of life than plants, only their coarse breathing and the tiny bubbles passing through the liquid filter of their oxygen tanks revealing the passing of time. Even our movements—me tapping Father's hip bones (to prevent bedsores), Mother chanting scripture with her eyes shut, Third Brother holding on to Father's forearm to stop him dislodging his drip—felt as if we'd been put under a curse and frozen into statues, or as if our bodies, afraid we'd startle away Father's gossamer-thin breath, had automatically slowed down every indication of life. My mouth dried out, my hair fell out in vast quantities, my breath grew shallow, I no longer needed to shave, and when I touched my ballsack during a shower, my testicles seemed to be retreating back into my body, reversing their descent. . . . Without my realizing it, the image of my father dying had sucked me into a black hole, a gravity-free void. With my accelerated aging, I was comforting my father who'd had a death scare and had his power switch turned off. This wouldn't do! At the end of this journey, I would return to Taiwan probably just as my wife was giving birth to our second child. I would need to return to the role of a young father. I would have to make my body strong again.

With this in my mind, I pushed open the emergency door by the elevator, having decided to climb up sixteen flights of stairs to our room (and I was determined to do this every day we remained here, so at least I'd "get some exercise and strengthen my body" in this drowsy hotel). In that cramped, dark space, I felt as if I'd brought all my hallucinations in with me. The shadows here seemed blacker than the night, wearily dragging themselves up after me, floor after floor.

In this dark, enclosed space like a well, I could hear my own footsteps clearly, their sound amplified by some soothing force that went beyond the senses. Only after our Jiujiang sojourn ended, when Mother and I were finally able to bring Father back to Taiwan (sure enough, my wife went into labor and gave birth to our second child two weeks after my return, I tumbled back into the chaotic life of a young father, and Father remained unconscious with a high fever, still in his "time of death," for another eight months; the only difference was his location was now Taipei Veterans General Hospital, and the exhausted people by his bedside were now my brother and his Indonesian domestic helper, Liyah), was I finally able to give in and forget everything that happened on this trip, dark as a dream of extinguished lights: the hospital, the hotel, the old people, the doctors I bribed (and those Jiujiang nurses?)—until the following new year, when at the urging of a respected older author, I went to the cinema and watched Hayao Miyazaki's *Spirited Away.*

Of course this is a fantastical story of a young girl rescuing her parents. Chihiro Ogino's mom and dad blunder into the spirits' territory, greedily eat the food left as an offering on an altar on a deserted street (though, seriously, the whole scene looks like there ought to have been someone in charge of the place, but they ran off to the bathroom or abandoned their post when a friend invited them to a quick card game), and get turned into pigs. The story of their salvation (like Mulian striking open the gates of hell with his tin staff to free his mother, or Orpheus descending into the underworld to bring Persephone back) revolves around their daughter being stuck in the spirits' bathhouse and having her name taken from her (she can no longer remember what it is), forced to work there in what seems like an indefinite period of servitude (until her parents can be returned to human form).

Of course I trod on a mouse or two in the dark, and something fleshy scampered from under my shoe with a squeak. The hotel's restaurant occupied the second and third stories, and the staff frequently passed between them, so every step was covered in a layer of grease. The sharp stench of the waste food bins permeated the enclosed space: the gamy reek of mutton bones, the allium aroma of green onions, the thick funk of boiled pork, and the vegetal stink of river fish. These varied odors, hard to put into words, left my brain fuzzy. I clambered past them to the fourth floor (where a laser display on the other side of the security doors made me guess the hotel's nightclub was located here, or perhaps they had some sort of karaoke room), then the fifth floor (a sign here read "Sauna").

Had I walked into the dark nucleus of something or other? I was far inland in a strange country, full of empty imaginings and indescribable feelings for this place, but this all felt at odds with the people and streets actually moving around outside this building. I recalled one or two images that left a deep impression on me, like stills from the TV programs like *Wonders on Both Shores* that had been fashionable for the last couple of years—a host and small camera crew traveling to various mainland provinces to introduce the more bizarre aspects of their food culture. One episode showed them at a restaurant in Guangzhou with an unspeakably filthy exterior. This place wanted to show how impoverished circumstances can stimulate the imagination, and had made their name with a weird spin on "eat fresh": on the greasy kitchen counter were mounds of what looked like perfectly normal duck eggs, but when the chef cracked them into a bowl, what slithered out was not an oval yolk but a damp and quivering ducklings. These prematurely hatched little creatures were tossed directly into a wok over a high flame and deep-fried to a greasy golden brown. The host (a household name in Taiwan and a "player") took a bite out of one of these crispy duckling corpses on camera and broke into a shit-eating grin. "Ah! This is so cruel and so delicious, I could weep."

Another episode was set in Chengdu, Sichuan. They were in a fancy hotpot joint, and for the sake of their "business branding image" (the manager actually used this awkward phrase when they interviewed him), all the waitstaff had their heads shaved and were dressed in identical black kung fu outfits, for all the world like a horde of juvenile delinquents with wooden swords from a Japanese yakuza film, though instead they were merely passing between the tables with tureens of scalding broth. The specialty of the house was "live goose guts." The host followed the restaurant manager out to the backyard pen, where they first spent some time bragging that "these geese are fed on a diet of specially selected corn, which keeps their intestines limber and gives them a nice chewy texture." Next, like in one of those porn films where an innocent high school student gets ravished—when they're done too realistically, you can't help thinking: are those four or five thugs doing this for real, actually

raping a foolish teenage girl they lured into the film studio?—
they clumsily grabbed hold of a frantic white goose, pressed it
down on the floor with its butthole facing the camera, and the
good-natured chef stuck one of his hands (I blushed at that
moment, watching him gently tickling the goose's pink butthole
with his middle finger, just as you'd gently arouse a woman's private parts during foreplay) right inside, and pulled the intestines
from the living animal, with no break at all in his narration. "By
doing this while the goose is still alive, we leave the blood in
them, which keeps them very fresh. Sometimes they're still pul-
sating as we bring them to the table." The whole segment had
been edited to feel comedic and a little bawdy, and you could
almost imagine the goose who'd been emptied out in this way
getting a pat on the head for its performance, waggling its feathers, honking a couple of times, and returning to its pond.
"Thanks for your hard work!" Because the customers wanted to
dunk Brother Goose's pale, living intestines into their hotpot.

Just like that, they took a living creature, and with practiced
movements, felt along its body as its breath grew frantic—
belatedly suspicious of what they were up to—found an orifice,
reached right in, and like removing a young woman's silk stockings, pulled this pale, translucent, elastic stuff out, so endless it
seemed like a magic trick. How could that tiny cavity contain
such a long intestine? Was that what was inside? Could the
goose, accepting that its guts had been wrenched out, grow some
more? As each stretch of intestine was ripped out, could it hurry
up and produce another? Or when the guts were gone and the
human hand withdrawn, would the goose be left with a gaping
emptiness and a stretched-out asshole, a cavernous sense of
shame?

With these dark thoughts swirling inside me, I continued up
the endless staircase, which might as well have been a tower, one
step after another, ever upward. Would this ordeal somehow

bring Father back to life? I kept going, aware of my exhausted, burdensome body. My carcass was falling apart, like an over-turned vat of boiled pork spilling rotten, stinking gobbets: white heart and lungs, blanched liver, a whole clump of intestines in different thicknesses, and two kidneys, still twitching. If the leg bones insisted on continuing their motion, up one step after another, those steaming innards would cataract down the stairs. Like in the anime, my parents had been cursed by a god and turned into pigs. I had to keep myself under control, not suc-cumb to terror before this topsy-turvy magical world. As I was the only clear-headed person left, it was down to me to restore them to human form.

In recent years, my father had stopped watching news pro-grams or anything with a connection to the real world. Nor did he sit around in coffee shops in stinky coats like old mainland-ers did, loudly proclaiming their opinions of current affairs in phlegmy voices. Now and then, I'd drop by the old house in Yonghe and see him slumped in his rocking chair in front of the TV, watching a video or broadcast of Peking opera, or else one of those travel programs set on the mainland, *The Journey of Poetic China*, *Mainland Wonders*, or *A Taiwanese Person in China*. He'd always look completely rapt, all his attention on the world inside the box: the Shaanbei farmer with a red bandanna round his head vigorously banging a drum while his waist twisted and his feet stamped left then right and yellow dust rose around him; the team of Hunan craftswomen spending three or four years in an abandoned classroom to embroider a single photo-realistic portrait of handsome, distinguished "Chairman Mao at Yan'an"; the old opera performers in Guizhou offering incense and burn-ing hell money with utter devotion before grabbing a live cock-erel and muttering blessings over it, then slitting its throat and spraying the altar with blood to invite the faces in, that is, to ceremoniously open a chest and bring out the wooden masks that have been used in local nuo opera since the Qing dynasty. And what these old men, women, and children had in common was when facing the camera, without exception they became shy, wooden, and solemn. This closed world, the beautiful landscapes, bright colors, and frozen time sealed in the box of the TV, were to my father (who was elderly, and silently walking into the world of Alzheimer's) a land of the gods, perhaps?

But here's how that story ended: my father collapsed in that land of the gods. One evening, my wife told me during our international call that she and her mother had gone to see a medium in Tainan to ask what would happen to Father. Had his life span run out? Or was there hope? The medium said Father's life span hadn't run out, but during his trip to the mainland, he'd said something he shouldn't have said to his sons (what actually happened, that last night in his hotel room?) and that offended his ancestors who'd been listening in, so these bygone Luos gave his head a gentle knock (the way you might discipline a misbehaving child), but his poor brain couldn't take it and started bleeding, which made him keel over on the ground, unable to wake up.

So that was just another starting point for a story. The first chapter would have to begin something like this: "We got a phone call to say Father had suffered a serious brain hemorrhage in Jiujiang, and began this rescue mission. We got hold of the travel agency and asked them to book us a flight the next day, arrange an expedited visa, and put us in touch with the local tour guide. . . ." This would be a narrative about saving my father.

It was an unfortunate journey. I stepped into the closed world of Father's TV set, the land of the gods. Of course, this was not the serene beauty of Father's imagination, as shown on screen (I imagined Mr. Wan at the hospital, those spiteful little nurses, or the banditlike taxi drivers who terrorized us daily, all suddenly growing shy and awkward when a camera was pointed at them).

When I, his profane offspring, showed up and thought I could use my city sophistication or experience of modernity (through my cell phone's international roaming, I was in touch with the insurance firm, the travel company, and any other "powerful backer" I thought could help) to speak to this land of the gods that had sent Father tumbling to the ground with a single blow, I was to learn in a myriad of ways that nothing was as simple as I'd imagined. I would have to do much more than simply reach into a goose's body and help myself to the infinite string of its guts.

This period of time felt like I was existing within the nightmarish landscape of Father's short-circuited dreams, and nothing could shock me here, no matter how bizarre or scary. A couple of stories above me in the tower of stairs, one of the security doors opened, and a diagonal spill of light picked out this stretch from the darkness. Someone else had barged into this shadowy corner of the building and was coming toward me, step by step. Even if I held my breath and stopped moving now, it was too late to escape their notice or flee.

It was a woman. I could tell from her footsteps. She even skipped a couple of steps, landing with a thud that echoed through the entire stairwell. Now what? Would she think I was the sort of pervert who lurks in dark corners? How would I explain? "Actually, I was . . ." (My father had a stroke in your country, and I'm trying to carry him back to Taiwan like a mail bomb, before he kicks the bucket.) "I was just . . ." (I was just climbing the stairs.) "I'd like to know exactly how my father has been interfered with."

Finally I came face to face with the woman, her back to the light, one of us rising as the other descended. "Oh!" she exclaimed, but then recognized me right away. "What are you doing here?" I knew her too—she was the waitress from the coffee shop, the one who'd run over to say to us, "Are you the

Taiwanese family of that old man who had the stroke? I was here that morning, me and my manager, and those men, I think they were your brothers? They tried to lift him but couldn't, six or seven men and they just couldn't move him."

(At that moment we were somewhere very far from the real world.)

The waitress said, "What are you doing here?" I said, "I got lost." My face turned red in the dark. She said, "Follow me, I'll show you the way out." And so I obediently trotted behind her, heading up the stairs. My face was level with her rump in its high-slit cheongsam, and with each step she took, the white satin material with silver borders would ripple from waist to ankle. At one point, she giggled and turned back to look at me. "A grown man like you, getting this badly lost." This might be the closest I ever got to my friends' lurid fantasies (the little Jiu-jiang nurses, the women in the dark who put up no resistance when you reached for them, the female comrades of the People's Liberation Army with mouths full of Communist slogans, the many babies abandoned by me in so many streets and alleyway through this city). So intimate. So lonely. So like an outsider demanding a moment of tender sorrow, as if from a can with a pull tab. If I'd just reached out in the dark, I could have touched that warm moistness, like plunging into the cavity of a sloe-eyed goose, grabbing hold of the tough, gooey stuff that coiled around my wrist, and with a flick of my hand dragging it into the out-side world.

Out of nowhere, I got the urge to say to her, "Up till now, I was living in a world very far from this. To me, you're like a character from one of my dad's TV shows. Or maybe more than that." (Just as I felt I was living in my father's dream, in the dizzying darkness of that stairwell, I somehow found myself imagining a video that had been neglected for too long, so the tape had gotten all moldy, of my wife and her enormous belly.) From the moment I stepped into this hotel, I'd sensed behind the clipped politeness of every-one in uniform a sort of dismissive enmity: the hotel manager, the chambermaids, the attendant by the revolving doors, the pretty girl at the business center, the waitresses at the coffee shop, and even this girl I was now following. Perhaps this was just a species of fatalism, developed after too much time facing the hundreds of customers who came and went each day (because they lacked the imagination and curiosity to wonder about these hundreds of people from the "outside world"?), and perhaps my oversensitivity to other people's ill wishes was something this city had imprinted on me. Or perhaps I was an aberration, the son of someone who'd left, unavoidably inhabiting a different identity, unavoidably disordering their existence after this gap of time, unavoidably vastly different from them even if our faces were similar, and no matter how I tried to train my tongue to speak differently or simply smiled in grim silence, I would be found out sooner or later. If only we were no more than tourists, like migratory birds. We'd have checked into this hotel, spent a period of time here, then moved on to another one, and then another . . . but here we were, marooned by the tide, and my mother had turned our room (what was it, 206?) into something like home, grubby and full of random objects (like our rundown old house in Yonghe). With a stirring of terror, I now understood that the ending of this story might have the structure of a novel: Mother and I would never be able to bring Father's body, stiff as a mummy, onto a plane and back to our own country. The rest of his life might be spent in a dilapidated hospital in this strange city, as if roots had sprouted from the bedsores on his back and passed right through the bed. When we ran out of money, we would leave this fancy hotel and (for real) look for a cheaper place. I'd find a job, and maybe a local woman to continue the family line here. (Just like my friends back in Taipei riotously joked about, countless chil-dren with my face. The King of Jiujiang.)

ten

MODERATO

How impoverished our conversation is, I thought.

As dusk fell, the woman's features actually grew more distinct, thanks to her makeup. Perhaps exhausted from the day, she was leaning lazily in her seat. A moment ago, her shirt and jeans had seemed rather manly, but now their tiny embellishments—cartoon character patches, little tassels, pleats—winked out of the gloom.

Just like that, she was utterly feminine.

There were only the three of us left. The woman, me, and the sleeping child. The woman's voice was soft and sandy. Twisting around, she idly lifted the cherry from her empty sundae glass and stirred the dregs of chocolate sauce. I felt a sudden stab of something akin to longing. If this child of mine were awake at this moment, how he'd covet that cherry.

The woman looked completely relaxed, and something about the casual ease of her posture made me feel a particularly male form of humiliation. Just like with the rather developed girl who sat next to me at school and treated me only as a friend—she'd happily pluck her eyebrows or spray her armpits with deodorant in front of me, chatting away without any attempt at dignity.

In the dark, I blushed as I did when I was young.

Time shifted. I felt as if I had prepared for this moment very long ago. This scenario. A middle-aged woman. A middle-aged man. A child.

The woman and man sat across from each other, drinking. The boy had been horsing around earlier but was now sound asleep.

She wore a thin, silvery-gray blouse, and the fingers playing with her empty glass were long and elegant. They were both being meticulously tortured by a slow burn of desire. The man looked at the woman with flames in his eyes. He knew she was an incorrigible drunk. From her pale chest came the powerful, arid reek of roses, but that couldn't hide the unfortunate odor beneath.

The waitresses in white shirts with bows on their sleeves breezed by their table. Still in the crucible of desire, they made small talk about inconsequential subjects. The script for a murder movie. Gossip about Such-and-Such and Such-and-Such. "Your husband, is he. . . ." "Do you always drink this much?" The child had been asleep for a while and was probably deep in a dream. If they wanted, they could probably have seized the chance to overstep the costly, messy bounds of middle-aged restraint, like their extremely tasteful designer clothes whose every line, whether crisp or flowing, was exquisitely controlled, and instead said something bold and shameless, a passionate declaration.

"I've waited a long time for you," he said.

I felt I'd prepared for this moment forever ago. But I never expected the child in this scenario to be mine (and not the woman's). I was his father, rather than the man attempting to seduce his mother whom he glared at defensively, like a young beast challenging this interloper who'd evoked a raw hormonal scent from beneath his mother's skirt, leaving him uneasy.

The woman was the interloper.

Any tension between the woman and the boy had evaporated. Far too easily, he'd become her captive (all it took was a cream puff or a cheap plastic toy car from the convenience store). Instead, I was the one who felt uneasy. This put me in mind of a dream I'd had several years ago.

I told the woman: I was in what looked like an abandoned amusement park. It kept drizzling. There were plastic kiddy rides, a zebra, a peacock, and a lion, but the metal springs connecting them to the red earth had patches of rust, and the giraffe was lying flat on the ground—someone had punched it in the face. The seesaw's red paint had flaked off, revealing a wooden surface that looked like dogs had gnawed at it. The little Ferris wheel cars had accumulated puddles of grimy rainwater, as if someone had strung up construction site cement carts and sent them into the sky. A video game arcade was now an empty shell, like the rest of this amusement park, which didn't seem to have electricity or a security guard. All the glass was broken, and at the entrance was a jumble of trampled ticket stubs. I entered the building down a winding slide (I had taken the form of a small child). Inside, for some reason, my mother was playing hide-and-seek with me, running between the whirring chirping grabber claws, revolving doors, slides, and spiral staircases. I only saw glimpses of her as she disappeared around yet another corner. I couldn't catch up with her (after all, I was only a child). Very quickly, I understood: this wasn't a game of hide-and-seek, I was being abandoned.

That's so sad, said the woman. Why would you remember such an awful dream?

I don't know. Maybe I surprised her on a date, and she just wanted to get away from me.

Did you ever see the man? asked the woman.

What man?

I don't know, you were the one who said your mom was on a date. There'd have been a man involved, wouldn't there? Your mother's man.

No. I don't remember. This was just a dream I had as a kid. I was too young to really understand all of this stuff. I can't forget the moment I woke up: alone in bed, my pillow soaked through with tears and snot.

That's very sad. As she said that, though, the woman was actually laughing.

I think my wife has depression, I said.

Oh, what's that about?

I vaguely remembered the woman had once said her father had severe depression, her little sister also suffered from it, and if I remember right, her boyfriend was a long-term user of anti-depressants (one time she said, "Yesterday, my boyfriend and I walked out of a pub, and out of nowhere my mood crashed. I just squatted on the sidewalk and cried. He gave me one of his pills, but the strange thing was, I didn't feel any different. Could it be that my condition is more serious than his medication can deal with?"). It seemed she was surrounded by depression.

Was this a suitable topic of conversation?

I couldn't get away from the enormous sorrow at the bottom of my heart. An unfaithful man invading his wife's privacy to stir up another woman's purely physiological interest. Like taking advantage of the shielding tablecloth to slip off a shoe and run your toe along her ankle, shin, calf, up along her silk stocking. Inner thigh. Our faces impassive above the table. She spreads her legs, and your foot slithers to their meeting point, but then at that moment you abruptly recall your gray toenails, the two toes afflicted with ringworm, skin flaking off.

The woman says, What's going on? Depression's serious, you can't take it lightly.

We're not sure if she has it or not. But all kinds of little things get her down. Take yesterday, for example. This boy's been toilet training for quite a while. He takes off his pants, runs to the toilet, and his little pee-pee . . . I guess he's a little slow for his age, maybe because of all that business with my father over the last six months, and then there's the baby. Anyway he isn't quite able to control his pee. I don't know what came over him, but he took off his pants, ran into the kitchen, took the lid off the trash can, and pissed into it. It was nothing, really, but my wife fell apart. She dashed into the bedroom howling like her insides were being ripped apart.

Oh. The woman toyed with her long-handled spoon.

I suddenly felt ashamed and angry that I'd so easily breached my wife's privacy to amuse this woman, and she didn't seem interested at all. The image of my wife like a wounded swan, head tucked at an impossible angle under her arm as she sobbed, was like a blazing light in the background of this dingy, dark-colored café.

The woman said again: You really can't take depression lightly.

There was this time, I said to the woman, there was this time a group of guys and I, we were high school juniors at the time, planned a trip: we'd take the train from Taipei to Taichung, then with Taichung as a base, we'd radiate out to the scenic spots in that vicinity. I remember one day we went to T'ung-hsiao Bathing Beach, then another day we looked up some friends in Zhushan Township, and spent the night at Xitou Forest Park.

That's weird, a bunch of high school boys. . . .

Yes, a bunch of high school boys. One evening, we went to Taichung Park and rented some rowboats on the artificial lake with pavilions around it. All the other boats had courting couples, but each of ours held two gangly, crew-cut teenage boys, going around that moonlit lake. We felt so restless, we didn't know what to do.

Oh my god. The woman was laughing hard. I noticed the child stirring in his chair. Perhaps he would wake up soon.

Anyway it was a lousy vacation, I said, lighting a cigarette. We had to go everywhere on those old highway buses (back in the day!), and we didn't know enough about the place to make a proper plan. We only went to T'ung-Hsiao because this guy's aunt lived there—he remembered visiting her during summer vacations when he was a kid and said there was a gorgeous beach, so we decided that sounded like fun. But the bus ride took three hours over bumpy roads, and buses weren't air conditioned back then, so we bumped along, getting scorched black by the sun. One of us exploded: Motherfucker, wouldn't we have got to this fucking beach faster if we'd gone directly from Taipei? We'd only been swimming a couple of hours before it got dark, then we spent another three hours getting carsick on the bus back to our hotel rooms in Taichung.

Sounds weird. Were you all gay?

I don't think so, we were just nerds. Someone even brought a guitar along, hefting it up and down the trains and buses all the way, but when we got to the sea it was just left on the beach with our clothes and shoes. Even the best player among us could only manage like three chords, C and A minor and G7. We took turns to wear our one pair of sunglasses, until some bastard got hold of them on the bus and refused to take them off.

What happened at the beach?

The beach? I chuckled. Not one fucking thing. Just some half-grown schoolboys splashing around shirtless in the water. And like I said, soon it got dark and we took the bus back to Taichung.

The woman helped herself to one of my cigarettes and tapped it on the table like a pro before bringing it to her lips. I felt restless again. Was she actually interested in my story? Did she want me to carry on or change the subject? We were sitting across from each other in a fancy hotel coffee shop where they turned up the lights at dinnertime, like we were in one of those billboards you see in front of the sales room at condo construction sites: elongated shadows, an unrealistic garden, and if there's any paint left over from doing the trees and streetlamps, mix it together and use it up on a murky limousine on which you can see every brushstroke. Stark and cold by the halogen lamps.

The child stirred again, and moaned as if he was having a nightmare.

Does he need the bathroom? The woman was so far removed from the child's needs that her ignorance was almost total. I smiled and said: He's too young to be potty trained, he's still in diapers.

Telling the story reminded me of one of the guys in the group, Yang Hao-Jan. I remember when we took off our shirts at the sea, the rest of us were pathetically scrawny, with protruding ribs and pock-marked stick arms, but Yang Hao-Jan had somehow acquired a grown man's physique. His pecs were so firm we couldn't look directly at them, so ashamed were we. Though I have the strong impression that he was much paler than the rest of us.

For some reason, I have a mental image of a body the color of pure white fat, the sort that forms on top of chicken soup when you leave a pot of it on the dining table in winter.

I said, Many years later, something happened to Yang Hao-Jan during military service (thanks to his physique, he got chosen for the marines). I wasn't close to him, I only heard about this from the others. They said, *Yang Hao-Jan has amnesia.* I'm not sure whether he accidentally stood too close to an exploding grenade or if it was just the stress that got to him (I remember people were circulating both versions), but he woke up one morning and couldn't remember anything. After a while, they sent him to a tri-service hospital for treatment, but his memory never came back. (Apparently the rest of his body was just fine, but he simply couldn't remember anything about his past. Eventually they redeployed him as an ambulance driver.)

The pale body that had once stood out among its teenage peers, having lost its ability to remember, became a stiff figure glowing faintly, as if developed in silver bromide or steeped in formaldehyde, in the shadowy memories of people like me who'd had very little to do with him.

I said, There was this other time, one of the guys in the group phoned me and said, *Yang Hao-Jan wants to get the high school gang back together. He's hoping we'll give him some clues about "what kind of person he used to be.*" I said, *Okay!,* even though I'd never been close to him.

We met at a KTV lounge called Locomotive (it was next to Taipei Train Station). I remember I got there early, so I went browsing in a record shop on the first floor. Like a fish in a tank, I allowed myself to be moved around the space by the bodies around me. I don't know how many rounds I'd made when I passed by the automatic doors with the antitheft gates again and saw someone there looking right at me. We paused for maybe five or six seconds, just staring at each other, until the crowd separated us again. It was Yang Hao-Jan. He looked like he didn't recognize me at all.

I said, At that moment, I was completely certain that he was faking his "amnesia." What happened to him in the marines? Maybe he really did lose his memory for a while, but for whatever reason felt compelled to pretend not to remember even after "it all came back to him. I just knew that when we came face to face unexpectedly and he didn't acknowledge me, that reaction must have been the result of a huge amount of effort. Then the others began to arrive, and we sat in a circle. The guy who'd brought us all together introduced us to Yang Hao-Jan, and it was just as awkward as if we really were meeting for the first time. I was among them, smiling and recounting various anecdotes (involving him) from our high school days.

That's the end of the story, I said.

Oh? The woman gave me an odd look. She seemed moved in some way by what I'd said, and a silence fell between us.

I thought that was going somewhere else, she said after a while. I'm still wondering! When your high school gang left the beach and sat on that bus for hours along the highway back to your hotel in Taichung, what happened then? Did the group do something to one of you? Did you meet a woman at the hotel? I thought that would be the high point of the story.

No, I said, nothing happened at all.

That's difficult.

How to love? In our city of yesterday, arid when the sun shines, dank in the rainy season.

The woman said: Your child's waking up soon.

The woman said: It feels like we've just been sitting here waiting for him to wake up.

Another story? No time for that. I wanted so much to say: Let me put my hand against the small of your back and move with the lines of your body. Let's seize this moment while all the waitstaff in this huge, cold room are at the farthest point from us. While my son's breath still reeks of dreams, like the brown stink of a sea urchin. I felt the desire of a fatherless son. I was like the last creature left in the filthy water of an aquarium so overgrown with algae no light could penetrate, unable from fear of extinction to stop myself spewing white froth from between my legs, bobbing gently as a transparent jellyfish. We spoke in the gloom that felt more and more like the bottom of a pond, every word that came from our mouths like the movement of a humming-bird's wings, fragile little bones flapping vigorously behind them. The woman's face turned red, as if she was about to weep.

(But it was too late for that.)

I said to her, simply: I didn't think it would end up like this.

I wanted to place my hand on the small of your back and move with the lines of your body, I wanted to put it on your belly. I thought there might be something there, a glowing silver pitcher (like in Bai Juyi's poem, the silver pitcher trapped at the bottom of a well, its rope cut). Beneath the staticky chiffon blouse and pale midriff like a little girl's, she had a womb made of metal ore. Cold and bright. Empty. Futuristic. Free of those disastrous images—liquid, gooey, horrifically nightmarish.

Like a city of mirrors. Like this city we were in.

I felt my desire dissipate in this icy, gleaming, elegant setting, where all stray noises were absorbed away. Like this fancy hotel, with the air conditioning humming away, where halogen lamps created the effect of an eerily quiet meadow. These gentle whispers ebbed and flowed. They couldn't withstand these violent changes in their surroundings.

I said: I'm a fatherless son now. This city has become a place with no father.

An exceptionally pale body, like that schoolmate of mine splashing in the water, the one who would later lose his memory.

In the dappled shadows of the trees outside and in the beam of light that seemed unable to penetrate the darkness, the woman's face seemed starker and more solid. She was talking about something she'd recently seen on TV, a variety show hosted by Bowie Tsang, who used to date our mutual friend Such-and-Such. When we talked about Ms. Tsang, it was with a sort of melancholy, like she was someone we once knew. "And what's Such-and-Such up to these days?" As if mentioning Bowie Tsang meant we also had to think about Such-and-Such. The woman said in the episode she saw, Bowie Tsang and her mother showed viewers how to eat mitten crabs. Everything from how to pick the right crab from the market stall, where they sat with pincers bound in straw, to cleaning and cooking them. In the most peculiar scene, mother and daughter each held a steamed mitten crab, and Bowie Tsang's mother (who was younger and prettier than the woman had expected) showed off her expertise by reminding viewers in a serious tone that the most important thing was to first remove the crab's heart and throw it away. Bowie chimed in, "That's right. As you all know, these crabs are very cooling, and if you eat their hearts too, the cooling effect will be unbearable." And with that, both women cracked open the outer shells and dug through the exposed flesh and milt for quite a long time, but for some reason, they couldn't seem to find these "unbearably cooling" hearts. The mother used her fingers, then a pair of tweezers, and even described the heart with great confidence: a tiny organ (hence difficult to find), translucent white and star-shaped. Next to her, Bowie frowned with concentration as she kept searching. "We have to find them and get rid of them!" The camera lingered on them, but still nothing happened.

Finally they gave up and (inelegantly) broke the crabs in two, and sifted through the mounds of flesh. "Found it! Found it!" Almost in tears, they held up tiny crab hearts with their tweezers for the camera to zoom in on. "Now let's get rid of them."

The woman said Bowie's mother held up both halves of her crab for the camera and waved them around, then she said something really weird. "A mitten crab like this costs a few hundred Taiwanese dollars, so make sure you get a male. Look, it's all milt inside. It's a shame to eat a female—you get nothing but flesh. You might as well be eating a brick."

"So," the woman said, "after watching this program, the audience all go out and eat male mitten crabs (snap open the gray-brown shell with a crack, and bright yellow milt comes pouring out), until all the males have been eaten and there are only females left in the water. What then?"

The child was still sleeping peacefully.

"What are you laughing at?" said the woman.

I said, When you described the crab broken in two and the yellow milt streaming out, I thought of something else. She wanted to know what. I said, A close-up of my father's butthole.

She laughed so hard she couldn't sit up straight, gesturing extravagantly as she tried to calm her breathing and wipe her tears. She raised her empty glass. "To your father's butthole."

I said I was serious, a while back my father let out a bellow and collapsed in an unfamiliar city, and I had to go there with my mother to bring him back home.

The woman said, "I'm going to the restroom."

I said, "Okay." She stood up and, swaying drunkenly, care-fully skirted the two pushed-together chairs on which my child was sleeping. Looking deep into my eyes, she said, "I'm going to pee-pee."

I said, "Okay." But I stayed seated. Not like those suave men in movies who, at the right moment, are able to follow tipsy, amorous ladies into the chilly interiors of fancy hotel bathrooms. In narrow, hard-to-maneuver spaces, they gently lift these women and place them, like table dancers, atop the toilet bowl. They know how to make these women laugh, how to remove their jeans without annoying them, how to unbutton their silk blouses and reveal the darling little tattoos on their shoulder blades, just as they'd hoped. . . .

Instead, I stayed seated, watching over my sleeping child. (While she was gone, the danger seemed to recede from my child's dream, and the old-man frown on his round little face was replaced once again with innocence.) Just the two of us left. How long had I been sitting there? There was now an entirely new shift of waitresses in white shirts with bows on their sleeves, yawning and looking exhausted. In silent protest, none of them came over to refill our water glasses. I had no idea what time it was. We were paddling through the dark, a gently rocking canoe on a river of night. Perhaps the next moment they would open those blinds made of a hundred strips of white gauzy paper, and we would see sunlight through the window, throngs of cars, and people noiselessly moving through the new day.

This is the story of a son, not a father's erotic adventure. I felt unbearably moved. If the woman had said to me at this moment, "Run away with me," I might have done it. Followed her to another unfamiliar room, opening the window at dawn to see another unfamiliar street. Another different life. And the child would wake to find himself alone in an empty hotel lobby, his father long gone. And when he was grown, he'd discover to his rage that just because his father momentarily had this ridiculous thought, he'd had to grow up a fatherless son.

I remember my father entering a mystical time that contained only the past (when the Alzheimer's was like a cutting room with an erratic editor working to an aesthetic we couldn't understand, snipping the film of his memory into a disjointed montage). In his final days, he regaled us with unseemly stories about women he'd known before my mother. These might have been charming moments, but when murmured throatily by a wizened old man, they grew curdled and inappropriate.

I remember he once mentioned a "Triathlon Queen" (perhaps someone who, as a young women, won a gold medal in her local triathlon? None of us was ever curious enough to ask, and my father never explained, so this "Triathlon Queen" remained only an odd, fleshy erotic snapshot from his youth) with whom he seemed to have fooled around more than once in some private space (his dorm or hers), but whenever things got steamy he'd remember his wife and son on the mainland and slam on the brakes. This went on until the Triathlon Queen's humiliation and frustration reached a boiling point, and she screamed, "Such-and-Such, you are not a man!"

I wasn't sure if it was ethical for an old man near the end of his life to recount so movingly (and also somewhat smugly) his awkward, private moments with the lovers of his youth. I remember how, before receding irrevocably into the form of an "old man," my father had a shadowy "no matter what" love affair. For the first time, I saw the jealous and terrified side of my mother, already an elderly lady. "The other woman" was almost thirty years younger than my father. Whenever he got a call from her, he would take the receiver into the living room and speak as quietly as he could (while turning the TV up loud), "and who knows what kind of sweet nothings they were whispering to each other!" But actually, I believe nothing happened. What could he have done? When I finally caught sight of the woman at my father's seventieth birthday party (my mother tugged my sleeve, "Quick, look, it's *that woman*"), she was dark and unattractive, standing among a group of my father's former co-workers and raising a glass to him. I imagine my mother was disappointed too.

I took the child by the hand and walked out of the hotel's main entrance, where two or three doormen in snow-white uniforms with gold piping and buttons, wearing vaguely Muslim-looking skullcaps, were bending to open the doors of Mercedes-Benzes as they pulled up. The wind came gusting between the buildings, and both of us hunched our shoulders against it, big man and little man. I asked the child, "Did you have a dream just now?" At this point he didn't quite have enough command of language to express himself, and said only, "Yes." I wanted to tell him how very much I loved him, but instead I said, "What did you dream about?"

He said, "Giraffes." No hesitation. No details. No shadow cast on the ground from the light of his description.

※ ※ ※

During a fiction class in college, the young professor came up with a spontaneous writing prompt: devise a scenario full of foreshadowing and narrative hints that could serve as the beginning of a novel. He would call on us one by one to describe our openings in as much detail as possible (though we weren't allowed to write anything down beforehand). This impromptu game was a jolt of real education for me, on my way to "becoming a professional writer." Many clever classmates were called on and confidently stated their scenarios: beautiful settings, a police chase passing through a flea market in front of Dragon Hill Temple, a couple's risky jump off a train as it slowly begins to leave the platform, a taxi driver going where the garbage trucks park beneath Taipei Bridge to prepare for a fight. . . . Like movie stills. Next, our professor pushed them to keep developing a detailed picture: Okay, right, so they run across the road and into the night market's maze of tents, but what stalls do they see? Herbal medicine? National lottery? Pork soup? Tomatoes in ginger sauce? Gradually, everyone stuttered to a halt, looking stunned. They'd tried to summon these places out of thin air, but the more details they added, the blurrier they got.

My scenario was a guy driving a secondhand car (gunning the crappy vehicle as fast as it would go) down an abandoned airport runway, with an ear-splitting ruckus. In the back seat was a woman's corpse.

My professor was stumped by this empty premise. He tried a few questions: Why does this *have* to be an abandoned airport runway? I said because I didn't want any turns in the road, it had to be absolutely straight like in an American movie. And it had to be abandoned because the car should be the only sound we hear. Next, he asked, so going along this "abandoned airport runway," what do you see on either side? I said in the distance surely a couple of huge hangars with curved roofs and tin walls, an orange excavator with dried earth clinging to its chassis, a few scattered black-and-yellow-striped barriers . . . and otherwise just withered grass and exposed red soil with absolutely nothing on it.

My professor told me to sit down. I was blushing, frustrated and resentful. Why hadn't he asked me anything about the corpse? Or the relationship between the driver and the dead woman? Or he could have asked me about the ear-splitting ruckus—what music was the guy listening to?

But no. He only wanted to know about the abandoned runway, and the details I'd contributed were dry and uninteresting.

This was an experience I would have many more times, in other settings. I'd be hanging out with other writers, just shooting the breeze, and someone would casually say: Hey, Lo, how come your stories are so weird—all those characters with blurry faces running around huge, empty, "abandoned" spaces? Baseball fields late at night with the stadium lights on but nobody around, deserted riverside parks, auto repair shops, vacant amusement parks, rooftops high above the city with cement water towers in the background . . . ? They'd give me complicated smiles, as if these were friendly warnings, or as if they really were puzzled and regretful about something. . . .

Many years later, an older writer encouraged me to reread Claude Levi-Strauss's *Triste Tropiques*. Like many classics I'd gulped down in my youth only to find my mind blank when hearing others discuss them, even though I'd dog-eared pages and underlined sections the first time around, on this reading I was startled and wished I could underline them all over again, to make them truly mine. Then I came upon a passage so beautiful it was like being reunited with an old friend:

> An airfield in a featureless suburb; endless avenues planted with trees and lined with villas; an hotel, standing in an enclosure and reminiscent of some Normandy stud farm, being just a row of several identical buildings, the doors of which, all at ground level and juxtaposed like stable-doors, led into identical apartments, each with a sitting-room in the front, a dressing-room with washing facilities at the back, and a bedroom in the middle. Two miles of avenue led to a provincial-looking square, with more avenues branching off, and dotted with occasional shops—a chemist's, a photographer's, a bookseller's or a watchmaker's. Caught in this vast and meaningless expanse, I felt that what I was looking for was already beyond my reach.

(Summoning details from the void that somehow rendered the image more vague and hollow?)

From time to time, for a second or two and over the space of a few yards, an image or an echo would seem to surge up from the past: for instance, the clear, serene tinkling in the little street where the gold and silver beaters worked, as if some genie with a thousand arms were absent-mindedly striking a xylophone. [But those sights no longer exist. The old houses] had in any case been so often destroyed and repaired that they were of an ageless and indescribable decrepitude. . . . I wished I had lived in the days of *real* journeys, when it was still possible to see the full splendour of a spectacle that had not yet been blighted, polluted and spoilt.

I led my child, his eyes still sticky with sleep, across the empty, incomparably wide road. Unexpectedly, it was still night. Once we'd left the dazzling light of the hotel and parking area, it felt as if we'd plunged into a pool of darkness, our entire bodies submerged. The child's feet made crunching noises, as if he were walking across the hollow bones of birds or small animals; then a moment later my eyes adjusted to the dark, and I could make out the withered leaves, each about the size of my palm, scattered across the grass. The child began excitedly trampling them on purpose, those gray-white shapes in the dark. Like a dog walker waiting for his pet to finish peeing, I let him have his fun before telling him to stop. Enough of that, I said, let's go, we still need to get the car.

By that point, I was certain I'd completely lost track of where we were. I could no longer remember how we got to the hotel in the first place. I'd hastily left the car in the basement parking garage of some other skyscraper, then we'd taken the fancy and apparently newly installed elevator to the ground floor (similarly empty, with huge granite slabs tiling the floor and a gilt-edged revolving door). I could visualize the outside of the skyscraper (I couldn't have it wrong, could I?), yet unexpectedly, leaving the hotel and crossing the road, we found a building that seemed ten times larger looming above us, blocking the horizon. It looked like something left over from the Jurassic period, perhaps a brontosaurus's entire skeleton, but no, that would be a science fiction film, Godzilla's bulk towering over the city. It looked hideous in the moonlight, as if its flesh had been stripped away and its fat boiled off, leaving behind stark white bones over which the dinosaur skin had somehow remained intact, covered with thousands of tiny gray-green glass panels like scales. Red scaffolding had been set up next to the giant creature's long neck (a wristband?), and tiny elevators whizzed up and down it, red lights flashing. The head and spine of the dinosaur sprouted several metal arms that made slow movements through the air, looking in the dark as if they really were alive.

The child seemed shaken by this stately nocturnal apparition, and leaned against me in silence as we walked away. I murmured, "Daddy hasn't seen anything like this either." How insignificant I was at that moment.

There wasn't a single vehicle on the road. Defeated, I led my son across the empty street to use the lit-up deserted ATM across the road (my car had been in that ritzy parking lot all evening, and I didn't think I had enough cash on me). I suddenly remembered the "abandoned airport runway" from my college writing class. Those details I hadn't been able to summon from thin air. And now here I was, leading "my child" to the outskirts of this city, gazing up at these skyscrapers like a giant's stacked building blocks, sparse and geometric, beautiful in the electric lights. These vast slabs of stone cut neat rose-colored blocks out of the purplish blue sky.

It felt like we were walking into a scene from the future, and the rest of our species had soared off into outer space without telling us. The child looked tiny, passing through such emptiness. As he walked, he seemed to turn into a translucent gray shadow. I'd never brought him down such an empty street before. Along the way, we didn't see a single convenience store, roadside hawker, or McDonald's, or a single person, a single member of our species, not even a cat or dog!

From time to time we'd blunder into a surreal forest, which I later discovered was actually what Hongxi Gardens apartment complex had instead of an external wall. We passed a fountain built to resemble a Mayan pyramid, with water gurgling from the topmost granite block, and I scooped some for the child to drink (he'd been complaining of thirst). In this way, I led this beloved person sadly through a landscape of true emptiness, the outlines of our faces blurring into shadow in the faint light, crashing into things left and right, unable to find a map, and no mysterious sound reached our ears. Just two small humans, two lonely sons huddling together. "He stood still, weeping bitterly, praying and moaning. . . . Nor was he put to sleep in order to be transported, as he slept, to the temple of the magic animals." Then I had a burst of enlightenment: inside my brain was a granite of pellet compressed to the size of a fava bean, and like a vacuum tube from an ancient radio, it was trembling as it received a jumble of electronic waves, messages, memories, and shocks, and this vast emptiness had turned my mind into an amplifier that couldn't help but spew out all sorts of details. They poured out without end, these silent scraps, so the miragelike city of the future transformed before my eyes, the gold tarnishing and the silver turning to slurry, the pristine surfaces of the granite blocks becoming overgrown with barnacles, shellfish, and moss.

eleven

DAY SIXTEEN TO THE LAST DAY

DAY SIXTEEN

Trapped in this place, I actually began to miss Eslite Bookstore, The Mall, subway stations, and Italian restaurants. Those places in Taipei where capitalism stripped away your humanity as easily as a knife slicing flesh off the bones of a fish, where money flowed and the décor was expensive, clear bulging glass on the side of brightly lit escalators, the empty calories of gossip magazines, chimes as you stepped through the doors of a convenience superstore, parking meters by the side of the road.

Being stuck here was like being in a city where time flowed backward. When I first got here, I was so fascinated by these dull, clay-colored people and streets. The twisted, out-of-proportion bodies in pain, the stark red simplified characters on white metal signs, those faces that looked so like mine but had gone down another evolutionary branch at some point and become an entirely different species. . . . I felt as if I'd spent too long on a scorching beach in high summer—tongue dry, lips cracking, entire body aching and filled with withering terror.

The nouveaux riche who fearlessly lit up cigarettes in elevators; the extraordinarily patient people who put up with the illogical obstacles the system placed before them (such as the patients who cursed the hospital's broken elevators every day, yet obediently took the stairs instead, knowing deep down there was absolutely no way to file a complaint or ask for them to be fixed); the empty violence between human beings, at a distance or close up, caused by those oversensitive, picky individuals who hadn't managed to get all the wrinkles out of their souls. . . .

I felt all the water in my body evaporate away, at a far greater rate than I'd anticipated.

A city where time flowed backward. Like the Taipei of some distant era. In its midst, I suffered with equanimity. Perhaps this had been no more than a folded page or bookmark in that colorful city, until a curse caused a page (or several pages) in the locus of memory to be infinitely expanded, growing to the size of an actual city.

And then placing me within it.

This morning, Mother and I had just got to the inpatient building when we caught sight of Edvard Munch guy's father standing outside looking around in agitation, next to a yellow taxi van (three yuan per two kilometers, cheaper than the five yuan charged by regular radio cabs) with its trunk open. Right away, my heart sank—fuck it, had Munch guy kicked the bucket? But then I noticed his wife on the other side, loading luggage into the taxi, not looking particularly sad. Just my imagination running riot.

Upstairs, we passed by Room 706 (by now, Father had been moved into 708, a premium room with only two beds and an attached bathroom), and noticed that the two beds previously occupied by Father and Munch guy were now empty, leaving only the old man in Bed 25. Eldest Brother and some patients were gathered around the doorway. I asked what happened to Munch guy, and he said, "Discharged." "Discharged?" "Yes, they ran out of money."

In our room, Third Brother was sitting by Father's bed as usual, guarding the drip feed (in the last two weeks, Father's feet, calves, hands, and forearms had been completely covered in needle pricks. By the end, the nurses hadn't been able to find a single spot to inject into, because the walls of Father's blood vessels had hardened, and his legs had been shriveling over the last two years, leaving his veins as fine as a young girl's), while Fourth Brother was asleep in the other bed, fully dressed with his shoes on (Mr. Wan had told us this other bed would only be used during the day by another patient who needed a daily injection, so this room—as old and filthy as the other one—could essentially be taken over by our family). Father was asleep too, looking peaceful. For an instant, I imagined the room bathed in a white beam of calm, contented light.

I was still uneasy about the "authorization to fly." Eldest Brother said Mr. Wan had come by earlier in the morning. I asked what he said, and Eldest Brother said nothing much, just that we should put extra pillows under Father's head when we were feeding him, to prop him up at a forty-five degree angle, so he'd be less likely to choke. Also we should be sure to tell him if we needed anything else.

Which meant there was still no news about the authorization. I'd phoned the insurance company earlier on (the call was answered by a Miss Lu who seemed to have no idea why this might be urgent) to say they absolutely had to make sure our phone number (that is, the number of the neurosurgery ward) got faxed to China Eastern Airlines, so if they had any queries about the authorization, they could speak directly to the attending physician. If they tried getting through the official Jiujiang First People's Hospital Medical Department inquiries line, they'd surely just end up going in circles.

Later, Dr. Zhang came by to ask what sort of "diagnosis certificate in quintuplicate" we needed, but even after I'd spent a long time explaining, he didn't get it. Finally he said, "Okay, how about this, go to the outpatient department on the second floor and buy five blank certificates. Mr. Wan happens to be on duty today; you can ask him how to handle this."

That was more like it. On the phone last night with Chen Wen-Fen, we'd come up with two strategies: first, go to the

Jiujiang municipal government offices first thing this morning and find the person in charge of Taiwanese affairs, thus entering the fantastical arena of "special treatment for our Taiwanese compatriots"; second, come clean to Mr. Wan, and if he complained that I'd added words to his letter after he'd signed and stamped it, emphasize the urgency of the situation (maybe claim the Taiwanese media had got wind of this, and it would soon become a diplomatic incident), and that my determination to get Father home to Taiwan was far stronger than he could imagine. If my father's health suffered as a result of these bureaucratic snafus, who would take responsibility? But when I'd bought the flimsy, yellowing scraps of paper and walked into Mr. Wan's office, he was all alone in an empty room at a wooden desk, looking up at me with a catlike awkward, kind smile. Nothing at all happened. As he lowered his head with great concentration and, in his sloppy simplified Chinese handwriting, patiently wrote out the exact same diagnostic information five times (the hospital lacked a copy machine), I thought that perhaps behind the chaos of bribery, forgery, and second-guessing each other's motivations, there may actually be something noble between us, a hapless young doctor in a dilapidated hospital saving a dying old man trapped so far from home, something that summoned tears to the eyes.

Trying to make small talk, I said, "How come the guy in Bed 277 got discharged?"

He paused a moment, as if seriously considering his answer. He said, "Oh yes, they didn't have any more money. Given his condition, staying longer probably wouldn't have helped anyway, and they were taking such bad care of him, his whole ass had rotted away."

I don't quite know why I blurted out, "So they're taking him home to die?"

This time, Mr. Wan looked up and met my gaze with a sort of sad rebuke, though I couldn't tell whether that was aimed at me or himself. "Yes, they're taking him home to die."

DAY SEVENTEEN

Today they put an old man in the empty bed in Father's room. He wasn't a stroke patient, just elderly (eighty) with a fever that wouldn't go down. A gaggle of his children and their spouses, all flashily dressed, filled the room talking in loud, coarse voices. Eldest Brother and Fourth Brother made a sort of tent on the balcony out of a metal bed frame and went to sleep in it.

Mother asked Third Brother about the wristwatches and pocket watches Father had given Yiming on his last visit, to distribute to the others—had he gotten his? Third Brother said no, he hadn't. Mother asked about another visit, when Father had handed Yiming a stack of American bank notes to give out—everyone was meant to get two hundred and sixty dollars. Third Brother said, "Oh, there was no need for that, we get by just fine. None of us dared to spend the money, so we just put it aside; then when Fourth Brother wanted to build a house we gave it all to him."

We were all silent after that. A long while later, Third Brother suddenly whispered to me, "What I said just now—you can't tell any of that to the old gentleman when he wakes up. He won't like it." I felt a twinge at the thought that my mother had unwittingly cast a tiny shadow across this old man's heart and stirred up who knows what ripples and waves of feeling.

That was the first time this giant of an old man had shown me his vulnerable side (by contrast, during those first nine days, Second Brother frequently wept as he wiped Father's butthole, red and cracked from the diarrhea. While this was going on, Third Brother would sit ramrod-straight and silent at the foot of the bed, eyes fixed on the drip bottle). Still speaking quietly, he told me that during Father's first visit, Eldest Brother's son had plucked the gold rings off the old man's finger, and Third Brother felt he shouldn't have done that.

Then Father choked on the water Mother had been feeding him and couldn't stop coughing, and we broke off our discussion. Third Brother seemed to sink further into the morass of irreparable hurt that these brothers in hardship would unfurl whenever they sat down together, something Mother, Father, and I would never be able to comprehend. After a while, when Father had slipped back into peaceful sleep, Third Brother told me that in the six months before his mother (my great-aunt) died, he noticed she was getting really thin when she came for her weekly visit (she lived with Fifth Brother), so he got some money together (this was back when their lives were still pretty hardscrabble) and asked his wife to go buy a pig trotter (he indicated something the size of his palm) to make stew, and when the meat was falling off the bone he would feed it to his mother. When she was done eating, she could drink the broth. But then she died, he said, and Fifth Brother said it was because of that pig's trotter, but I just pinched my nose shut and didn't say a word to him.

(Third Brother's eyes reddened at this juncture, and I thought my mother really shouldn't have stirred up this innocent old man's emotions, these deep hurts that to us were just scheming and greed happening somewhere else. The distance made these things no more than tiny prickles of unease. Yet to these old men who couldn't move on, nothing would ever return to its original form, and they didn't understand why this "beautiful existence," the central plank of their existence, had been destroyed. Third Brother said, "Those days were hard." One time, he stuffed a hundred yuan into Mom's pocket, and she started crying right away. So many things we couldn't say. After Mom died, Fifth Brother went and had two pairs of trousers made, then he said, "Look, I bought these pants for Mom." And I thought, *Why didn't you buy them when she was alive so she could actually wear them?*)

Today, Mr. Wan led me into a small room and asked if I wanted him to move the old guy in the next bed to another room. (Meanwhile the corridor was full of old people on gurneys, drip bottles dangling, still waiting for a room!)

I wanted to tell him: *One or two hundred American dollars isn't a small sum, you know, not even back in Taiwan.* I felt he thought of me (or of distant Taiwan) as like an international business-man who regularly overtipped astonishing amounts, and of him-self as a powerless minion sent off to smooth out every wrinkle, so his backer could fully enjoy his little imperial privileges. All these doubts meant that whenever I was alone with him, I sensed contempt in the atmosphere. Often, as we talked, I would begin to hate myself, and I guess he did too.

I feared that if I didn't manage to maintain the surface ten-sion, he would realize how despicably and pathetically I was bribing him. He was the one with unlimited power. If he refused to put his stamp on a single document, I would remain trapped here in this rotten place.

DAY EIGHTEEN

The insurance company's promised date felt like a stab in the dark.

My father lay in the hospital, drifting in and out of conscious-ness. Each morning, as Mother and I walked out of the hotel, our bodies twinged all over with pain. You never knew, as you entered the ward, what awful detail the old men would be waiting to pass on: Dad vomited again last night, the diarrhea started up yesterday, and he can't stop coughing (what we feared most: pneumonia). This morning, there was a new bedsore on Father's right hipbone, though the one on the left hadn't healed yet—it looked like someone had left a hickey there, apart from the purple scab in its center. His right side had only ever showed a faint blush of red when we rolled him over, but the old men refused to listen to the nurses and let him sleep on his left side (afraid of making the existing bedsore even worse), so now the red on the right side was turning purplish, and a blister had formed beneath the skin.

The old men were nearing the end of their tether, and I had to make up hopeful stories of progress to cheer them up. They listened with their mouths gaping open, stunned and believing every word when I said there was no problem on the Taiwanese side, and everything was sorted with Hong Kong too, so if we could just convince China Eastern Airlines in Nanchang . . .

In fact, I think this was exactly the spirit in which Miss Lin from the insurance company tried to cheer me up on the phone. I was the elderly Fernanda del Carpio from *One Hundred Years of Solitude*, discussing my condition in letters exchanged with invisible doctors who never once showed their faces.

Often, over the breakfast buffet, I'd listen in silence as Mother recounted events from her youth, though my attention frequently wandered to the other guests, walking by with plate after plate of the food I'd eaten twenty days in a row: greasers (a local snack of tofu dredged in flour and deep-fried), candy (the same deep-fried item, but with a sickly sweet mochi filling), white rice congee with pickled vegetables and shredded meat, fermented tofu, deep-fried peanuts, all that oily food (I feel like puking).

These last couple of days, I'd often rubbed Father's body and his large head.

He'd lost a lot of weight. To prevent bedsores, I had to tap my hands along the line of his body from his armpits, past his waist and buttocks, down to the curve of his thighs. Sometimes I'd forget myself and run a loving hand over his cheek and the edge of his ear. Then a thought would flash into my mind: *Does he realize that's how I normally caress my wife?*

Father's blanket and mattress were soaking wet this afternoon—his external catheter had slipped off. Third Brother, Fourth Brother, and Yiming all screeched with indignation and ripped off his piss-soaked blanket, scolding him in their thick accents (as if this was no longer the old gentleman, their father, but just a ruined body unable to control its bladder or bowels). Father lay completely naked on the wet mattress, beneath blazing fluorescent lights. He looked so lonely, forsaken by dignity. Fourth Brother went out onto the balcony and came back with a mattress pad, dry (but not washed) after being pissed on before. I insisted they go to the nurses' station for a new one, but they hesitated and dragged their feet, because these old men who worked in the countryside planting fruit trees and mending boats (Third and Fourth Brothers couldn't even read or write) were terrified of some department in this backward hospital giving them a tongue-lashing. Finally Yiming went. In the chaos that followed, we managed to shove Father around enough to change his bedding. All the while, Mother and I whispered comfortingly in his ear, "It's all right, it's good that you've peed. Now we're just going to get you on dry sheets so you'll be more comfortable." And like a frightened, shamed child, Father said over and over, with his eyes shut, "Thank you, thank you."

Today, in a corner of the surgical building, I saw hundreds of empty glass drip bottles lined up in rows, their labels still on:

5% glucose solution, 10% glucose solution, 9% saline solution, sodium bicarbonate solution, ciprofloxacin lactate solution (all in simplified characters), a peculiar sight. I'd seen red wine bottles from different vintages slotted into the wall of an Italian pizza joint in Taipei; aluminum hubcaps of all brands piled up at a tire shop under the elevated highway at South Jinshan Road; blown-glass pitchers and vases in all shapes and sizes on the glass shelves of Tianmu Creative Market—but I'd never have thought, in this stairwell littered with phlegm and cigarette butts (all mainland brands with silver simplified characters stamped on the filters), filthy wooden spatulas, and cotton balls, that I'd see a similar display filling the air with the unpleasant stench of disinfectant.

Today I sorted out the next step in the process with the insurance company. Miss Zhang confirmed that tomorrow evening at seven-thirty, a doctor (a foreigner resident in Hong Kong) and nurse (Taiwanese) from the international rescue company would arrive at First People's Hospital. I said all the doctors here will have knocked off by that time, and she said that doesn't matter, our doctor will have his own equipment, he'll just put your father through some simple tests (like sending in the USS *Kitty Hawk* to face down the entire Chinese navy), that's all. I was still uneasy that I'd have to go to the head nurse the next day and ask for her approval to get Father's discharge papers and the hospital bill (which the insurance company required for reimbursement) from the basement office before noon, and I wondered how much money I'd need to stuff into Mr. Wan's hand this time in exchange for his walking me down the silent corridors of the administrative department for another official stamp. Then Fourth Brother remembered that the elevators were turned off after midnight, and we'd have to ask Mr. Wan to intercede with the electricians to please open their doors at five a.m. (which is when we'd have to carry Father down to the waiting ambulance). The two people they were sending would lift Father in and out of airplanes and across borders, guaranteeing his medical care all the way. Fuck, it was almost as though a whiff of the civilized world was seeping in through a nearby crack.

The head nurse was a Ms. Cha, about forty, with fine pale skin and almond eyes. Her stern expression was faintly terrifying when she strode down the corridor, unsmiling, in her uniform (though I'd also seen her casually dressed, strolling through the People's Great Mall).

As usual this morning, Mother went up in the elevator while I took the stairs. Between the fifth and sixth floors, I met the head nurse coming down. She caught hold of me and pointed at her name tag. "Take a look at this, Mr. Lo. What's my surname?" The tag read "Cha ___xiang." This felt like the practiced flirting of a mature woman. I had no idea what was going on, and could only mumble, "That's an unusual surname." I felt exactly as I had back in college when faced with those pretty girls in my class who were universally beloved yet insisted on acting innocent.

Later on, I wondered if she'd meant something else by this. Was I meant to get Mother to add a line to the thank-you note she'd written the night before? "I'd especially like to express my gratitude for the warm and attentive care of Ms. Cha and all her nurses. Their dedication is a clear expression of the close relationship between compatriots on both shores . . ."

Just before noon, the head nurse came in and sat in the armchair by our room door, holding a hanging pouch (IV drip). I hastily went over to ask how she was, and she said she wasn't feeling great. I fetched Mother's note for her to look at, and she stared at it for a long while (maybe she found traditional characters hard to read), her face giving nothing away.

I went back to Father's bedside to keep an eye on him. After a moment, she said, "Your mother's very young, Mr. Lo." This got my mom all excited, and she ran over to say all kinds of foolish things (such as, "We're really truly grateful that you've all saved my husband's life" and "Oh no, really, I'm sixty"). All the while, the head nurse's expression didn't waver.

My mother sat back down, the head nurse silently changed the IV drip, and I felt strangely agitated. Like an idiot, I poured a cup of tea, set it down on the table by her side, and asked, "Are you a descendant of the imperial Manchus?" (I'd noticed the upward flick of her single eyelids, a little like Terry Hu's.) Sounding like a country bumpkin, she said, "What's that?" (She had no idea what I was talking about.) "The Manchu imperial family during the Qing dynasty. Like Jin Yong—his real name is Louis Cha, and he's a Manchu descendant. The surname Cha is so rare. . . ." She said, "You mean am I a minority? No." (A true bumpkin.)

I regretted having said anything. Some glimmerings of culture and complexity among the masses still end up getting thwarted. After a long while, she spoke again. "Do you have a wife waiting for you back in Taiwan, Mr. Lo?" And this thwarting isn't about the loftiness or vulgarity of desire itself, nor even entirely about the paltriness of the flirtations that lie behind influence and the fetishization of capitalism, or the dirt stink an amorous woman from an impoverished town is unable to rid herself of. . . . Often it's just language itself, the confusion that arises when a common phrase goes unrecognized, and the words "What's that?" are spoken out loud.

My mother produced a picture of my son. The head nurse said, expressionless as ever, "He looks like his dad."

Then she added, deadpan, "Just leave the teacup there, Mr. Lo." And with that, she got to her feet and left with the old drip bottle.

DAY NINETEEN

There was a very fashionably dressed taxi driver (about forty-five, looking less like a local and more like a capable and rather windswept divorcee from the Pescadores Islands who'd set up a florist shop after leaving her husband. She was fastidiously groomed, with finely drawn eyebrows and understated makeup. Even her fingernails were immaculate. Her vehicle was as beat-up as every other taxi in this city, but she'd done her best to keep the interior neat and clean) who'd picked up Mother and me three or four times now. She wasn't like her male colleagues, who glowered as they rampaged through the crowded market-places and alleyways as if their one thought was to take us to a secluded spot where they could slaughter us in peace. Kind and respectful, she asked why we went to the hospital every day, and this rare show of concern made us open our mouths and release the pent-up frustration. I worried that Mother's old-woman babbling might be boring her with endless details, but when I looked in the rearview mirror, I could tell she was listening with full attention.

She was nothing like the trendy tour guide we'd met when we first arrived in Nanchang, the one with a mouth full of pleasant bullshit. Nor was she like the coarse, unladylike women in various official positions I'd gotten used to encountering in this city (in this country?). She spoke with decency and sincerity (on such an awkward topic, in which it was so easy to tip over into fake kindness).

Then I noticed that for a couple of days now, she'd been making sure to stop by the hospital entrance at noon, right by the fruit stalls selling pears for one yuan fifty each. When Mother and I came out, she'd open her door and wave excitedly from a few cars back (pushing her sunglasses onto the top of her head).

As if meeting an old friend, Mother and I would happily get into her taxi.

This lunchtime, we rode with her again. As she changed gears and maneuvered the vehicle through the throngs in front of the hospital, a young man suddenly appeared in the bright sunlight and shouted, "You're getting out!"

I didn't recognize him right away. Only when the taxi had got to the other side of the road did I suddenly remember: wasn't he one of the young medical aides in the examination room, from my first few days here? He was still there, by the cooked food stall (where the young couple and pigeon-chested dwarf who ran it were busy chopping vegetables), so I leaned out the window like an old friend who couldn't bear to leave and shouted, "We're going Friday! We've already bought our plane tickets." He smiled and waved in response.

In the afternoon, the head nurse came to our room. "Mr. Lo!" she called, and led me to a desk at the nurses' station. Another woman in a nurse's uniform was holding a little notebook and pen; she had some questions for me. The head nurse explained that this was for the hospital's weekly newsletter. Because it was so unusual for Taiwanese compatriots to be admitted, they wanted to know if we had any suggestions for how they could improve.

I sat blankly in front of all these nurses, a gaggle of girls in white uniforms smiling to themselves and pretending to be busy sorting out drip bottles. It felt like the poem—"What night is this?" I spewed out a whole load of flattering words. It seemed even the head nurse was laughing so hard she couldn't listen. Then they told me to go back and write some more. I asked if traditional characters were all right? Once again, they burst into inexplicable laughter. I had the sudden thought: could some older, influential person in Taiwan be pulling strings behind the scenes to engineer this whole situation?

Back in the room, Mr. Wan came by to say, "Hey, about that thing those girls are trying to get you to write—just ignore them, you don't need to waste your time."

Today Dr. Zhang removed Father's catheter. We were supposed to get him used to controlling his bladder, and only if absolutely necessary should we use this—and here he produced a device that looked like a bag with a condom attached to it (as Dr. Zhang instructed us on its function, and watched as Third Brother and I rolled it onto Father's flaccid penis, his face remained evasively blank).

Third Brother insisted on keeping the sheath in place, and when it looked like it might slip off, he grabbed the white tape that nurse use to secure IV lines and pulled it around Father's cock, both ends in his pubic hair. I began to worry his dick would get inflamed and stop working.

Time for feeding. The question of excretion, the question of bedsores.

Fourth Brother got a crew cut today.

Today I ran into the daughter of Room 706, Bed 25. All of a sudden we seemed very close. She said her father woke up today. I said, "Congratulations, I hope he makes a full recovery." Now they were moving to the six-person Room 710. Who says there's no special treatment?

Today I went with Mother to the People's Great Mall and bought a fifty-yuan set of silver pens for Third Brother's granddaughter Jade. This made him smile in delight.

Today Yiming and I talked about his boat. He earns fifteen thousand yuan a year from his day job, and another ten from growing grapes. The boat brings in a hundred and fifty thousand in rent (but there are debts to pay off, the boat was bought with loans).

Like an infant, Father snuggled in Mother's bosom and whined. His bedsores are getting worse.

DAY TWENTY-ONE

This morning, Mr. Wan carried out keyhole surgery in the next room. The patient's head was shaved bald, and intersecting black lines were drawn across it (paint or felt-tip?). As he prepared to put the drill bit through that shiny head, I realized he was actually very nervous. He stood by the bed with Dr. Zhang and two interns, all of them smoking, chatting, and joking with my three cousins.

Over lunch, Mother told me the story of Fourth Aunt, a child bride who got tortured by her mother-in-law; then her husband ran off and had a daughter with someone else, and only came back home when he was old.

Halfway through our meal, the insurance company called again asking me to go get a letter certifying Father was fit to fly. Apparently these are only valid for forty-eight hours, so I needed the doctors to write another one. I yelled into my phone, "The flight is in sixteen hours, and here you go again! Do you know how hard it is to get a letter validated around here?"

I got back to the hospital at 1:30. The four old men looked panicked and furtive. What were they up to? Eldest Brother said Father had a fever. I got agitated too. Now what? We were ready to go—was something else going to prevent our departure?

Eldest Brother got scared when I said we might not be able to leave, and bundled me off to get the certification.

Mr. Wan led me through the process of getting my father discharged.

First, the young woman at the plexiglass cashier's window counting my money one bank note at a time got the paperwork wrong and had to start all over again.

Next, Mr. Wan brought me to print out the letter, then to the admin department to get a stamp, but no one was there. He made a dozen calls from the office next door, while around him people from the finance department sat in their swiveling chairs chatting loudly and screaming down the phone at patients. Electric ceiling fans droned away. It was like a scene from my father's youth.

Third, the admin officer arrived. He'd given me a hard time before, but now he actually said, "Safe travels."

Fourth, we went back to the cashier's window for another stamp, but the young woman refused. *Fine*, I thought, *forget it, I'll just go get a stamp made when I'm back in Taiwan and do it myself.* (This form was just so we could claim our expenses from our public health insurance.)

※ ※ ※

In the fearful, exhausted afternoon, Father had four or five bouts of diarrhea, and I managed to doze off in the midst of my anxiety.

Eldest Brother talked about the county secretary of impoverished Xie county in Anhui province. When he refused to take bribes (preventing six hundred grand in price fixing), he received threats (a dead duck at his front door) . . . and ended up leaving his post after two hundred and eighty days.

In the evening, the Taiwanese nurse and foreign doctor from the rescue organization finally showed up. It was like that first day all over again, the gloomy hospital corridors, the dazed patients (in their wards) with no medical staff in sight, a ghost town. The fetid atmosphere. The Taiwanese girl forcefully ordered around the bumpkinish little nurses (the same ones I'd been bowing and scraping to).

I felt a complicated, subtle change come over me, and I began to find it intolerable that anyone would look down on this dingy, dilapidated hospital, even as I grew smug at the breath of modernity blowing in from my own country and the superior bearing of the Taiwanese girl (how I suddenly worshiped her). The two newcomers were like a couple of actors staging an impromptu performance in the street, tossing out verse and chorus and stunning the entire floor into silence (later, I would learn that Mr. Wan had actually been in the building at the time, but was hiding). Her skin was so dewy and well cared for, her way of talking so complex and accurate.

It didn't take her long to realize how backward this hospital was. She asked the sole little nurse on duty when the medication was dispensed (she didn't know), which shots Father had had (she didn't know either, but it would be in the record book), if there were any x-rays (no). The foreign man produced some sort of high-tech equipment, extracted some tubes from it, and wrapped them around my father's arms, fingers (with a clip with a red light on it), and chest. The three old men beamed with admiration. If I'd witnessed something like this as a child, my lifelong ambition would surely have been to become an international rescue doctor.

᠅ ᠅ ᠅

I remember, when I was young, reading a Wang Zengqi story about the Cultural Revolution, set in some little inland village where a middle-aged man had been exiled. He didn't say much, just tended the land peaceably with everyone else, digging fertilizer into the soil, raising chickens and ducks, that sort of thing. No one knew about his past. This went on for a decade, until the Cultural Revolution ended, and everyone including him got to go back to their own cities. Several more years passed, then one day the old people of the village were watching TV in the village committee's office and they saw this guy with a towel over his shoulder, gesturing at a pristine field to tell his sweaty young charges how they should defeat their foreign opponents. He was the coach for the national youth soccer team.

At this moment, I felt like that soccer coach. But actually, my English was much worse than my mother's (for several decades now, she'd turned on the radio early every morning without fail, so she could drowsily listen to Doris Brougham's *Let's Talk in English*). In the dimly lit room, the foreign doctor asked us questions about Father. His voice was gentle and warm, but Mother and I could only smile foolishly like a couple of yokels. The girl ended up interpreting (she spoke English with a show-off lilt), and we pretended we'd understood all along, chorusing "oh yes" or "no, no" at the foreigner, though all we knew about Father's condition was the two or three CT scans he'd had since arriving here (when I said "CT scan," the girl said "What?" and I struggled to summon the phrase "computer cross-section scan" from my memory). She took the images, casually flicked through them, and tossed them onto the bed with a snort. "These are very low quality. They really don't tell us much about the patient's condition." I felt such a jolt of despair.

Fourth Brother came close and murmured, "Hey, Little Brother, it seems you don't speak foreign so well either, huh?"

DAY TWENTY-TWO

The night before, Mother and I were up packing till past one in the morning. We had far more luggage than we'd imagined: Father's stuff from a month ago, before a blood vessel burst in his brain and time screeched to a halt (a sad moment, comparing this to his first few visits back to Nanjing around the time he retired or the various mainland tour groups he joined, back when he still had a bit of money and would return to Taiwan after each trip with a huge suitcase stuffed full of newspaper-wrapped inkstones, purple clay teapots, carved stamps, calligraphy, Hunan embroidery, bronze Buddhas for Mother, wooden bodhisattvas, plus a couple of bottles of "drunkard" and "five-grain" spirits. This time around, his denim rucksack might as well have belonged to a ratty old scavenger; it contained some fake calligraphy, quite a few of those cheaply printed landscape postcards from Mount Lu, a couple dozen low-quality cassette tapes of local folk music, the sort they sell at roadside stalls, plus the soap in waxed paper he'd thriftily pilfered from various hotel rooms, a travel toothbrush, toothpaste, an airplane snack of wasabi broad beans, and a few sets of clothes that smelled of old man); Mother's stuff (vast quantities of local snacks and tea leaves, traditional herbal medicines and other pharmaceuticals, all intended as gifts to thank her Buddhist prayer-mates back home in Taiwan for chanting scripture and performing rituals for Father's recovery); all our clothes and other things, including the bundle of inauspicious funeral paraphernalia we'd brought and never had to use: at the bottom of our hearts there'd been an image—the worst-case scenario—of Father being cremated and his remains sent to the ancestral plot in Anhui, so before we set out, Mother hurriedly tossed into a bag (burial clothes?) Father's favorite blue satin robe with the invisibly stitched dragon circles, a pair of new leather shoes, a rebirth blanket, sandalwood incense, and several hardcover volumes of scripture.

And now, at last, we were going back. Mother and I packed all these things away, with every light in the hotel room turned on. Although in the dark hospital corridor, the foreign doctor had asked a couple of times via the Taiwanese nurse, "This patient is clearly not in a fit state to travel. We will have basic resuscitation equipment with us, and we'll keep an eye on his condition all the way, but we can't guarantee that he won't have a medical event in mid-air. Do you insist on him traveling, even in these circumstances?" (And of course, we kept nodding and saying in English, "Yes, yes"), and although we'd signed a release for Father's death (if the patient suffers injury or death in the aircraft not caused by human agency, the family takes full responsibility), Mother and I could scarcely hide our joy. Finally we were going home. This would be our final night at this hotel.

Out of nowhere, Mother looked up from the scattered heaps of clothes and said, "Son, I know we shouldn't count our chickens until we land at Taoyuan Airport, but this isn't too bad an ending, is it?"

I looked at her grizzled hair, and a shudder went through my heart. I thought of the night before my engagement ceremony, many years ago. Mother (and only she) kept me company, in the attic of our old house in Yonghe, laying out on red wooden chests the twelve gifts we would send to my fiancée's home the next day: Jinhua ham, soy sauce chicken, wedding candy, firecrackers, sweet dumplings, longans, rice noodles in red paper, a set of gold chains, and the red bridal outfit, with a red packet stuffed into every pocket and both shoes. She was completely focused but displayed no enthusiasm at all, just doggedly went through each task like an obedient student following her teacher's instructions and finishing her homework. When we were done, she stretched out her legs in the cramped attic space like a high school girl in her dorm and said with great ease, "I suppose they" (she meant my wife-to-be's family) "will be happy with this?"

What should I have said to that? She was an old woman now. For a long time, I'd gotten used to crawling home each time I got into trouble in the outside world and asking her for money. Even after my marriage and the birth of my son, I was still always stretching out my hand to her. Ever since I was a young man, whatever scrapes I found myself in, she would help me conceal from my father, as if she were my co-conspirator. Even now, with my father unconscious, time having stopped for him, Mother and I were scheming away, making all kinds of bold decisions.

I said to her, "Yes, this isn't too bad an ending."

Early in the morning, I went to the hospital in the minibus the hotel had chartered. Everything felt like that very first, dark night. Yiming, Third Brother, and Fourth Brother were waiting by the security post, smoking and looking a little anxious. The ambulance we'd been allocated was parked by the ramp. I went over and gave three hundred yuan to the driver, who looked startled. "Please drive as steadily as you can," I said, "and don't go too fast." Hopefully this would be the final bribe of this trip. By this point, I'd become an expert at palming money. It felt as if, drifting through this ill-defined, grasping realm, only by stuffing every yuan you had into the intersections that made up the outlines of the world could you see where you ought to place your feet next. "Don't worry, sir," said the driver happily. "Mr. Wan gave strict instructions. He said you're a good son."

Then I was back in the hospital corridor, so dark it felt like I was sleepwalking. In the rooms to either side, the patients slumbered silently. Many of them were, like my father, elderly folk who'd suffered brain hemorrhages and turned into sleeping beauties. Here I was, removing Father alone from their shared dream. We walked into Father's room. The foreign doctor and Taiwanese nurse were already there, faces anxious and stern, the self-possession of the previous evening gone. One last time, they took Father's blood pressure and tested his heart and lungs. Next they produced a mass of plastic from a rucksack and inflated it with a pump. Like a magic trick, an orange-red dinghy appeared before us, like the ones on Xiuguluan River. The nurse explained that this was an "emergency stretcher." Clumsily, we maneuvered Father onto it. Moving in the dark was like being at the bottom of a swimming pool—slow motion, the outlines of everything blurry. Father still had a variety of tubes poking out of him (his existing drip, plus the oxygen tank the Taiwanese nurse hooked him up to), and diarrhea was seeping from him nonstop. The foreign doctor tugged at some valves, and Father was engulfed by the stretcher like a hot dog in a bun.

I keep trying to describe this like a journey. Or a dream. Or a movie. As it was happening, I thought: *If this is a film, it must be almost time for the credits to roll. The soundtrack should be swelling.* As the old men and I, with Mother, pushed the stretcher once more through the pitch-dark corridors like on that first day (the point at which I fully entered "the moment of Father's death"), the camera would zoom in on our faces. In slow motion, shoulders quivering, we'd remove Father from this gloomy place. The dilapidated elevator doors would open again, and close again.

"They were young when they arrived in this city, but by the time they left, they had all become old. . . ."

On the way to Nanchang Airport, Mother, the foreign doctor, and the Taiwanese nurse rode in the ambulance with Father, while the three old men and I followed behind in the minibus. The sky was turning pale as the vehicles turned onto the expressway. Landscapes of rolling hills and farmlands appeared, like in the national history books. I listened to the others kibitzing over the occasional small house that appeared on the shifting land, complaining like querulous old women: look, this place is so much poorer than back in Anhui. Surely not? I couldn't understand how these peaceful fields were any different from others in my memory. What faint clues were these men seizing upon to decide whether to envy or despise them? (Was it the crops? Or what the farmhouses were made of?) I had a subtle thought: having spent so much time with these old men, day and night, I'd gradually become one of them, my accent no different from theirs. And now, as the ambulance sped away from the hospital and toward the airport, I was returning to my former self. All of a sudden, I realized I no longer understood the high-speed gabble of their accents. I grew very tired. My head drooped, and I dozed off.

At Nanchang Airport, the ambulance parked by the main entrance, and the driver turned off the engine to save fuel. My father's diarrhea hadn't abated. In the sweltering rear of the ambulance, he was lying down while the foreign doctor knelt next to him, like a couple of trapped beasts. I tried opening the window, but sweat continued to pour down their foreheads.

A short airport police officer in a grass-green uniform came running over to say we couldn't park here. Using their language, I growled at him, "Your supervisor said it was okay. There's a Taiwanese compatriot in the back of this vehicle. He's dangerously ill—if anything happens to him, will you take responsibility?"

The three old men came inside to stand with me by our luggage. When people started going through customs, I didn't know if I should follow them. The old men seemed startled senseless by the elite people in designer clothes wheeling their suitcases through this high-ceilinged space and the uniformed soldiers and security officers roaming all around. They stood silently next to our suitcases, and even when the people in front started walking, they didn't dare to move. I had to go to the counter to ask about our tickets, and when I turned back, they were standing all by themselves in the vastness of the departure hall.

The insurance company hadn't booked seats for Mother and me, so I had to beg the girl at the ticket counter for help. She spoke flawless Mandarin and had a beautiful face, but her manners were coarse.

I asked if we could get seats on the flight to Hong Kong that was leaving soon. She said I'd have to ask inside, but customs told me I couldn't pass through without a ticket, and I had no choice but to return to her window, where someone else sent me to another counter back outside.

This airport was run by three different organizations, none of whom knew what to do with this ragtag group like Tripitaka's pilgrims (a patient in an inflatable stretcher, a foreign doctor and a nurse, a mother and son):

A. The airline (it had taken more than a week of documents whizzing back and forth before we got Father approval to fly);

B. The People's Liberation Army unit stationed at the airport, in grass-green uniforms with red epaulets, some holding machine guns and others walkie-talkies, all looking very stern and murderous;

C. The customs department: a plump little guy in a blue uniform who'd definitely received a bribe from the insurance company via the local tour guide. He seemed quite high up in the hierarchy, because he took care of us all the way through. He was the one who arranged for us to bypass the security line—we just had to pass through a metal detector and x-ray with our luggage and then could get back in the ambulance and drive straight to the runway. This ended with me and the nurse struggling through, laden down (the three old men weren't allowed past the gate), while Mother and the doctor had to remain in the ambulance. I carried the food my father had excitedly brought with him, the cheap teapots and fake calligraphy he'd picked up on the two days of his tour, and his walking stick, plus the various tea bricks and local candies my mother had grabbed. The nurse was weighed down by two heavy rucksacks of medical equipment. When we got to the gate, though, the plump guy and a tired-looking middle-aged plainclothes officer came running over to say there'd be no luggage inspection for us, so we hefted our stuff back to the ambulance. I urged the three old men to go home (they had to get back to Jiujiang to catch the eleven o'clock bus to Nanjing), and we tussled a bit.

Then a girl in uniform came and said we had to put our bags through the scanner after all, so we dragged them back to the gate, where we found the plump guy looking confused. "Didn't I already say you didn't need to do this?"

The three work units at this airport were pulling in different directions. All the little plump guy had to do was have our bags cursorily inspected, and everything would be by the book—we'd be back in the ambulance on our way to the runway. Instead, he probably wanted to show off to the person who'd bribed him just how much power he had, with the flashy move of getting us on the plane without going through any security whatsoever.

Laden down with bags, Mother and the nurse ended up passing through the gate at least four or five times, until the soldier stationed there lost his temper and yelled, "Hey you, do you think this is a market? You can't just waltz in and out. I'm warning you, this is an international airport. Where the hell are you from?" The Taiwanese nurse, who'd flattened an entire hospital of doctors and nurses just the day before by swooping in like the USS *Kitty Hawk*, seemed deserted by her poise. She scowled, and whispered to me that she had no idea what the little plump guy was doing, when the travel company had sorted things out with him. It was Mother and I who'd been here long enough to have absorbed the local customs, and without thinking about it we smiled and bowed at the waist (I was certain at this moment that the little plump guy hadn't shared his bonanza with his co-workers, who as a result were certainly not going to give us an easy time), though it would have made things worse to try to bribe him with cigarettes or cash in front of so many people, and all we could do was keep sweetly calling him "comrade," and my mother nimbly stepped into the role of a suffering old woman while I regaled him with the complicated saga of our troubles (I emptied my pockets and produced the stack of certifications to fly and medical documents, using the most diplomatic language I could summon to sound docile but forcibly hint that getting this desperately ill patient on the plane and back to Taiwan was a complex mission that involved the Taiwanese Affairs Bureau and an international rescue organization, as well as airlines in mainland China, Hong Kong, and Taiwan, and the People's Hospital itself . . .), but I think he didn't actually care about any of this and had just wanted to scare us a little to take the plump guy down a peg or two, because he just waved the papers away impatiently and yelled at us to get in or get out, just do it quick, whichever it was, and not let him see us again. Then he turned on his heel and went over to a group of his machine-gun-toting comrades and said something that made them burst into gales of laughter.

"Bastard," I muttered to myself, and abruptly realized this was exactly the tone of voice Father used when cursing. I recalled the PLA officer, stern and ramrod-straight, in the sleeping compartment of the Nanjing-Yingtan train many years ago. Over this last month, I'd become both jumpy and servile, both detached and hysterical, and I'd learned how to adopt the pose of detached nonchalance that everyone here used, so whatever was in front of them suddenly became very distant. This was a sort of contradictory magical thinking. On one hand, you had to take the attitude of "before anything happens for real, no matter how positive the situation seems, don't let yourself get happy for no reason" (we had to actually carry Father onto the plane, and all of us had to actually get on board, before this was real); on the other hand, in an empty world with nothing to depend on, you had to take a deep breath, steady yourself, and trust that "somehow or other, everything will be okay" (stuff enough money into the right person's hand, and he'd surely find a way out for you, no matter how dire the circumstances).

Who'd have guessed that right at the end, it would be Father himself who found a way out.

By our final round, the little plump guy clearly hadn't managed to get things under control. He came trotting over, looking frustrated, and said, "There's no way around it, you'll just have to go through security." (Did they think we were terrorists with concealed guns and bombs?) The nurse looked like she was ready to blow up. They were already calling our flight. All I could do was haplessly mutter, "You should have done that in the first place." The plump guy glared at me furiously. "I couldn't get past them. What do you expect me to do?"

When I went back to the ambulance to get Father, the foreign doctor's eyes were glazed over, and both men were soaked with sweat. His face was blank as he watched over his patient, a finger over the drip needle where it entered the skin, as if he were guarding a large and dangerous animal. The nurse told him we had to move the patient, and he looked like he might faint. Then the three old men appeared like celestial warriors descending from heaven, and Third Brother said a line that could have come from a Hollywood film, bringing tears to my eyes: "We couldn't go off and leave you." And so they came together for the umpteenth time, and carried Father together into the departure hall.

This was fantastical and magnificent, as if flowers were suddenly blossoming and fruiting out of nowhere around us, attracting thousands of bees and flies, then the fruits rotted and oozed foul liquid. Still unconscious, Father made the greatest effort of his life and expelled all the remaining gas and loose stools in his body at once. The entire vast departure hall seemed bathed in golden light. Everyone here, the workers from different organizations in different-colored uniforms, brought out handkerchiefs or just clapped their hands over their mouths and noses. Like a silent film, I saw them contort their faces in agony, shooing us away. Mother and I, the three old men, the foreign doctor and Taiwanese nurse, were like a procession of child mediums with a god-palanquin on our way to an exorcism. We stumbled ahead, zigging and zagging, carrying Father with a mixture of joy, tenderness, and pain. It felt like moving in a dream. "What the hell is that? It stinks!" came a woman's sharp cry, ripping through this drowsy scene that could have been preserved in amber. Then the little plump guy, hankie over his nose, sweating profusely and face darkening, came bravely (like falling into a shit pit, you could only keep your eyes open, hold your breath, and swim toward the light) running over to us. He said, "I did it, they said it's okay, you don't need to be inspected! Just get your ambulance to bring you straight to the plane. Quick, get this . . . get him out of here."

And so the ambulance hurtled past three or four security posts to the aircraft whose engines had already started. The little plump guy kept yelling, "Don't get too close, don't drive right up to it. Go around the other side and come by the front."

Were they going to shoot us otherwise?

We got out and were immediately surrounded by soldiers. They'd heard we were trying to board the plane without going through the proper channels. Someone who looked like the captain gave orders to search our luggage, and everything got spilled out onto the grass beneath the scorching sun: the doctor's medical equipment, the nurse's clothes and the novel she was reading, Mother's tea and snacks—one officer even insisted that she needed to look inside Father's inflatable stretcher. . . .

twelve

FARAWAY

This time I dreamed about Father in the attic of our old home at Yonghe. Not a real attic, more a crawl space between the tin roof and the false ceiling held up by lightweight steel struts, somewhere to store Father's old books and magazines, extra bedding, old winter clothes, appliances like vacuum cleaners and dehumidifiers, obsolete computer monitors, foot massage machines, and other electronics that no longer worked but we couldn't bear to throw away, as well as huge canvas bags holding plastic Christmas trees, large teddy bears missing their eyes, rusty coat hangers, and the like. You had to climb up a ladder and bend double or crawl on your knees to squeeze in.

In the dream, Father and I, along with my child, and other family members hazily present in the background were all standing amid the junk, in front of the dusty plastic and canvas bags. The attic seemed several times larger than in real life, more like a meat warehouse with animal carcasses dangling in the icy air, or the back room of a laundromat with garments on hangers. To start with, it was just like every time I'd brought my child to see his grandfather in the hospital over the last few months. Father remained bleary and confused, about as aware of his surroundings as a bug (though in the dream, he was as tall and strapping as when he was young, rather than the shriveled figure stuck full of tubes that he was in reality). He looked affectionately at his grandson clambering all over the attic. In distress, I talked to my father as if cajoling a child (silly things to cheer him up: when you're better, we'll go eat at Xiulan Restaurant—vegetable rice, fish jaw, lion-head meatballs, or Ji Pin Xuan soup dumplings). From time to time, I turned and shouted in my father's distorted voice at my unruly two-year-old son, who was growing tired of being treated as the living toy of a foolish old man.

Out of nowhere, my father's brain seemed to clear, and just as when I did something wrong as a little boy, his face grew terrifying and his voice deepened as he said to the child, "I've been watching you. What are you playing at over there? Stand up straight! Behave yourself! Are you asking for a beating?" In the dream, my father, my child, and I were like cartoon monsters hit by a laser beam, frozen in shock for an instant before getting shot up into the sky by a flaming bolt. Our startled faces seemed unable to withstand the endlessly changing surfaces of our lives, both past and still to come, and the whole scene began to jitter.

And so, ignoring the fact that my father's blood vessels were, like frayed wires in a rusty circuit box, liable to rupture at any moment, I began to shake all over (when I woke up, I was concerned at what enormous rage was buried in my subconscious), and with all the energy I could summon from deep in my body, I roared at my father, "How dare you treat him like that!" Then I walked away from my father, my son, my whole family. Strangely, I then ran off to join the China Youth Corps or Boy Scouts in some sort of winter activity, in an elementary school building that had been deserted for some time because of the long vacation. I stood among these campers in their different uniforms, different badges sewn to their sleeves, and it felt like we'd all blundered into an abandoned city, for reasons of our own.

My feelings were complex. I missed my wife and son, whom I'd abandoned in a moment of petulance. I felt a sort of expectation lightly surrounding me like a cold (maybe my wife would show up at this school in a few days, with the child in tow). But

I also had to keep dragging my attention back to this assembly I was now part of (left hand on your waist, take little steps to align yourself with the person in front, eyes right). Go get your basin, toothbrush, and towel. In your groups, discuss the performance you'll need to rehearse for the final night concert. All these little things.

During this time, I kept having fragmented, weary dreams that were invariably set in some forgotten place: an endless gloomy hospital corridor, a retirement home, a public building in some small long-ago town, where I'd have to deal with the meaningless paperwork thrust at me by some sluggish civil servant. And I'd always have the patient, pessimistic thought: this doesn't matter, it will be over soon, and doesn't everyone have to deal with this?

Last night, I dreamed I was in our old house in Yonghe, solemnly discussing Father with my mother, brother, and sister. The previous evening, my wife had told me on the phone that she and her little sister had traveled to Tainan to consult a medium, who told them that Father's earthly life span had come to an end, and it would be almost impossible to save him—he'd only survived the journey back from the mainland by sheer force of will. My brother said the other day, when the doctor was removing the compacted shit lodged in Father's big intestine, he suddenly woke up and, like a plant abruptly bursting into human speech, screamed, "Son, save me! I'm so old. This hurts so much."

As we talked, I could hear my father's voice, so clear and joyous, like when I was a child and he came home in one of his rare good moods, bursting into the living room and proclaiming, "Come here, see what amazing things I've brought home for you."

A sudden thought. In the dream, it was so clear—my mother, brother, sister, and I exchanged looks and hurried into the living room (but Father was supposed to be in intensive care at

Veterans General, tubes protruding from his nose, an oxygen mask over his face, drip bottle hanging above him). Sure enough, just like in the movies, there was an apparition of golden light, a liquid human form glimmering like a million coins, its shape shifting, moving across the walls and ceiling like a shadow puppet show.

We wept silently. Half rebuking, half cajoling the visitation, we said, "You shouldn't be here, you should be in the hospital."

Then we realized: *Father's soul left his comatose body and hurried home, does that mean. . . .*

The body of light knelt before Mother, who was crumpled and sobbing, and embraced her. I wrapped my arms around them both from behind, and in a voice I would never use with my actual father in this lifetime, I choked out, "I miss you, Dad."

And with that, I was startled awake. I was alone in a dark bedroom (my wife was visiting her parents with our child), tears streaming down my face, still muttering: I miss you, I miss you so much.

※ ※ ※

In fact, in this whole series of events, the final scene of me and my father would just be a very long horizon drawn with a drafting pen, and only blank space above and below this line. Nothing there but a long bench. Father and I would be sitting on this bench.

Perhaps this bench would be located in a hospital's inner courtyard, next to a building retaining the marks of colonialism: vaulted passageways, a domed roof, pillars, tall patterned wooden windows, street lamps with conical shades, yellow stone ramps (for patients to wheel themselves up or down). All the trees in this place, maple and parasol and coral trees, or even the recently planted magnolias, would be withered and autumnal.

Father would sit by my side, his body small and weak as a child's after this bout of death, or perhaps like some pre-embryonic stage of salamander or amphibian, lower limbs so shrunken I'd blush and not dare to look directly at them, as if he were a mermaid revealing her nether regions. In reality, Father was supine and would not have been able to sit up like this.

Father had become tiny. He mainly gave the impression of softness, and his face was scrubbed clean. Like a cluster of objects extruded from life, and as my mother, brother, and all those other helping hands tried clumsily to stop him sliding toward death, he managed to slip past us anyway. I sat next to him and didn't feel I could be bothered to conceal my frustration and impatience, the birthright of adulthood. Too many things had happened in the world. And there was so much still to sort out. But because of his willfulness, so many people had been bent out of shape. I glanced at him and felt such resentment I couldn't put into words. Father had shrunk into himself, like a little girl who knew she'd done something naughty. His face was pale and translucent as rose petals. This shyness didn't come from guilt or regret, but rather his utter awareness of his own body's fragility.

There was no way to change anything now.

Only in these circumstances was I discovering the diffident side of Father's nature. All his life, he'd given the impression of a man determined to step forward, one who refused to be silenced. And now I thought: *So he's shy too.* His father died when he was fourteen, and it always felt as if a stretch of time was missing from his life, a father-shaped gap. Now that I thought about it, from my very first story, he always read each draft of everything I wrote with great care. How startled and outraged he must have been to see me transform him into a comical, depraved character. Yet he never directly (looking me in the eye) confronted me about this. Instead, he began all the more urgently to share with me the unfortunate encounters and heroic exploits of his life. In the end, these tales made their way into my work, not as he would have wished, but in bizarre, absurd guises.

And now he was unimaginably free. Meanwhile, the world was crashing down on my shoulders like a collapsing house. Broken beams, shattered bricks, steel struts, and other debris, all landing on my head. So many tears in my eyes that I couldn't open them.

I'm so tired, I said. I'm so very tired.

But how could I whine like this to someone in an even more fragile condition?

I remember in fifth grade, I had an extremely strict teacher. One of the few times in my life I was terrorized for an extended period, by living with this violence. A sort of ongoing terror. Each morning, I'd leave the house with heavy footsteps, shuffling my feet through the gray alleyways and streets to the dull bus stop, past the washed-out adults, all the way to school, where I'd bow to the bronze statue of some worthy person, then pass by the teacher with the duty armband, the dusty gym, the dimly lit classrooms, corridors, staircases, drinking fountains, slogans on the walls . . . and finally to my homeroom. Every other classroom was mostly empty apart from two or three kids lounging around like kittens, but ours would be completely full, and every pupil would be sitting bolt upright, completely silent, staring directly ahead.

At the appointed time, this teacher would march into the classroom, summon two or three boys and girls from the quiet, terrified mass, and demand to see their homework. After this inspection, she would go to the lectern and start handing out punishments that made the other children gasp. These consisted of various repetitive actions, movements as meaningless as getting sweaty pedaling the stationery bike in the gym (she often whacked so hard with the cane that she had to bend over and take deep breaths), a performance in which the torture victim's body would grow limp and deformed. She would hit them across the thighs with a ring binder, or shove eight pencils between their finger joints, wrap her huge hands around theirs, and slowly squeeze (only later did I learn this was a form of torture dating back to the Ming dynasty), or cane the backs of their hands and the soles of their feet and make them pull down their trousers and hit their bare buttocks in front of everyone.

Much later, I began to wonder about these vicious punishments she doled out each morning, these physically ruinous feats that always seemed to land on the same two or three kids—were they human? Or were they robots she'd purchased on the cheap from some futuristic lab? Meticulously constructed to look just like the real thing, but able to withstand these bursts of violence, show up again in our classroom the next day completely unharmed, ready to be brought forward to receive their sentence from the lectern.

Or perhaps this was all a show, intended to put the fear of god into us? (Perhaps this isn't an apt comparison, but when I think back to this period of time, the image that floats to the surface of my mind is the broken limbs and mutilated bodies of Picasso's *Guernica*.) Certainly both she and this performance terrified me.

I resisted going to school. Of course, no one could have known. In reality, I walked each morning, exhausted and miserable, through the school gates, and out of fear, as soon as I got home each day, I would obediently sit at the table by our family altar, doing my homework before the bodhisattvas and ancestral tablets. I wrote very slowly, like walking across the bottom of a swimming pool. I no longer ate dinner with my family. My mother would set aside a bowl of food and bring it to me as I sat alone with my piles of assignments. This happened every evening, like a suspended sentence for the massacre the next day (anyone who didn't finish their work would suffer the same fate as the cut-price robots). I have no idea why, but although I plodded on, the homework never seemed to get done. I asked my classmates, and they said they usually finished around nine or ten. Yet I generally kept writing until one or two in the morning. Several times, my mother couldn't bear the sight and took over while I slumped over on the other side of the table and dozed.

I remember one early morning (sometime in the winter), I set out as usual, tired and despairing, to attend this demonic ritual of cruelty. As I passed by a shophouse, I saw a huddle of grown-ups watching a pig being slaughtered. Maybe this was a new building and the family was just moving in. A housewarming party. The cement area on which they were killing the pig looked moist and faintly green, as if it hadn't quite dried. Two scrawny old men pinned the animal with their legs while pouring scalding water over its face and neck. The fatal knife had already plunged into its body. They'd slit its throat. And yet it remained stubbornly alive, narrow eyes staring, nostrils emitting white steam. Strangely, there wasn't much blood. Maybe it had bled out before I arrived. We stood on the newly laid concrete floor, which was slick from the clear water running over it. The pig appeared to be smiling and didn't cry out when the hot water sluiced over its ears. The old men kicked the carcass (their plastic slippers were marked with bright red, the only bloodstained objects around) and it moved very slowly, as if they were working together in a sort of swimming motion. Whenever they kicked it, it obligingly budged. The old men smiled grimly and shrugged at the onlookers (as if to say, "Would you get a load of this pig?"), then continued drizzling boiling water over the vast bulk of its face.

Wasn't it in the process of dying?

I stood in the crowd, heaving with sobs. Something I couldn't describe, something like dignity, had been completely ripped away. I was crying so hard, grains of rice from my breakfast went up into my nose, mixing with the mucus to form gleaming silver-white globules that spattered onto the ground when I sneezed.

At some point after that morning, I said to my mother, "I don't want to go to school anymore."

I said, "If she dares to hit me like that" (like the faulty robots) "I'll snatch the cane from her and lash it across her face, then I'll jump out of the window and kill myself."

Horrified, my mother ran off to tell my father, and he came to ask me, "What's going on?" (I was sitting by the altar, on which were a couple of red light bulbs, a bodhisattva figure under a glass dome, and two ancestral tablets. In front of me were my piles of homework.) I only got a couple of sentences into my explanation before my body was wracked with weeping. This enraged my father. He reached for a nearby wooden back scratcher and began thrashing me with it, all over my face and body.

(Father, this is where I get confused. What was going on? The awful early morning tragedy I'd been dreading with such mounting fear finally came to pass—but at home, not at school. Were you just enacting violence on my body to echo the violence of the outside world?)

My father said, "I hate it when boys are weak."

The next day, I went out with my father. Without any preamble, he led me to a different elementary school a little farther from our house, a smaller private establishment. Father and I walked into the office, and he spoke to someone, a clerk or teacher, who appeared utterly floored by his authority and way of talking. After a brief conversation (it was only later that I learned the guy bowing and scraping to my father was actually the principal of this little elementary school), my father led me to a classroom, and ignoring the fact that they were midway through a lesson (or that I was wearing a different uniform than the other kids), he pointed at an empty chair in the back row and told me to sit down. He said a few words to the teacher as if he were her boss (I actually heard her call him "Sir"), then swiftly departed.

Just like that, I'd escaped my daily nightmare. I never went back to my original school, not even to sort out the transfer paperwork or to pick up the stuff I'd left in my desk. Such a simple solution. I never saw the sadistic teacher or a single one of my classmates again (and now I suspect they were all robots of varying quality and prices).

In the painting with no background but the straight line of the horizon, I wanted urgently to ask him (my father, lying next to me, shrunk to the size of a feeble child):

"Why did you abandon me?"

"What should I do?"

"Where will I go next?"

My father became fatherless at the age of fourteen. Maybe I would only begin to understand these things when I became fatherless too, having no one to lean on, the bitter solitude of not knowing what you ought to say before the world.

I remember in my first or second year of college, my father and I happened to be home alone. Out of nowhere, he called me into the living room, a dingy place even in the middle of the day. He was in his usual armchair and pointed me to a rattan couch piled high with old books and newspapers. Across from him, a Public Television Peking opera broadcast was showing on the old TV set. Now that I think of it, he was an elderly man by then—he'd just retired. The greedy little worms of Alzheimer's hadn't yet begun to chomp their way through his gray matter, but already visitors hardly ever showed up in our sitting room.

Every cranny in this space, every ornament, was saturated with the moldy smell unique to the aged.

My father seemed to have thought about this a long time before opening his mouth. "I know there are some boys who get to around your age and pick up a bad habit. What's it called? I think it's . . . masturbation. I hope you don't have that problem?"

I felt shocked and angry. What was this? I was past twenty, and it had been a good five or six years since I'd first greedily, guiltily laid hands on my genitals. Why had this old man decided to wait till this moment before discussing sex education with his son? This must have been triggered by something he'd seen in the lifestyle section of the newspaper.

And to make it sound so filthy and shameful.

I remember sitting there in the gloom, blushing bright red, trying to act innocent. Like a little boy, I said sweetly, "What is that?"

"Um, it's a kind of . . . how can I put this . . . it's a sort of harmful thing you do to your body. . . ." He seemed massively relieved (that his twenty-something-year-old son hadn't heard of "masturbation") but couldn't let it go. "Are you sure you don't know what it is? Some people call it 'self-abuse.' Have you heard of that?"

I shook my head guilelessly.

"I'm glad," said my father. With that, he began speaking volubly about all the bad things he'd been through since he was young, the many unkindnesses and humiliations he'd suffered at the hands of other people. And we were back there—ever since we were kids, every time he had a chance to chat with us, he'd go on and on (an endless serial novel occupying vast expanses of time) about his adventures and exploits, his whole life.

He said, "I'm glad you haven't picked up this filthy habit, unlike other boys."

This was one of the few times we actually had an intimate conversation. I had many questions for him but didn't know how to get the words out.

I keep describing everything as a journey: my father's life after he lost his own father at the age of fourteen; Mother and me sliding like paper cutouts into the unfamiliar little city of Father's moment of death after his collapse; or my sleepless nights, thrown out of whack by this twist of chance: Father leaving me, just as I became (I have no idea how to do this!) a father myself, inheriting the role like a fucked-up crown. I'd thought this was a mysterious, complicated voyage. I had no idea that, like in a disaster film, the whole world would carry on collapsing, and in a moment's pause (which wasn't an ending), Father and I would find ourselves on this blank sheet of paper. Sitting on the same bench. Still, silent, filled with an enormous sense of awe and regret for life.

At this moment, I had so many doubts and resentments I wanted to spew at Father. But he was now too small, too weak. If I hadn't been there to hold him up, he would have melted like an ice cube, becoming a little creature like an eel or loach, dripping wet on the frigid floor. I didn't understand—he was clearly the one "currently" facing death, yet he was smiling with expectation like a young girl, while my face roiled with murderous rage.

I remember at the hospital in Jiujiang, his bedsores would often pain him so much that he ripped off the towel covering him, exposing the caved-in lines of his naked old man's body. His penis and testicles like an angry turkey, an unspeakably hideous cluster of red. His deep-brown ass crack, which we'd covered in talcum powder, oozing yellowish discharge from time to time. The old men got all worked up and would play tug-of-war with him over the towel, urging him in their thick accents, "This doesn't look good, old gentleman, there are girls here looking at you." But Father would still insist on wrenching away the concealing towel.

So lacking in dignity.

At those moments I'd deepen my voice, as if I'd seen more of the world than all these old men, like some ancient geezer from a distant era in Father's memory (his own long-deceased father?), and say to him, "Dad, hold on."

His eyes would open wide, and he'd say wildly, "But it's biting me. It hurts."

"Yes, but you have to hold on. Don't embarrass yourself."

And he would weep like a child. "I want to go home. You can't leave me here."

"Yes. But you're here now. So don't embarrass yourself."

"Okay."

%% %% %%

After that, I frequently found myself staring blankly, whether I was sitting or standing. I got into the habit of sighing. Walking down the street, I'd stop dead in the middle of a crowd for no reason. Sometimes I'd sit on the low border of bricks surrounding a roadside tree, or on one of the motorbikes parked along the veranda, or simply on the steps of some apartment building. Squinting, I'd gaze out into the metal stream of cars like a mirage in the roiling white light, a dazzling display with all their different colors of paint. Sometimes I'd see a huge flock of more than a hundred sparrows, circling a drooping banyan tree as if there were no one else around, rising and descending, chasing each other, joyriding. They too changed my sense that the blazing light melting all things within it was fixed and unmoving.

I couldn't have been more familiar with the city. Yet it felt as if something had been knocked off my shoulders.

For a long time now, I had been faintly confused, constantly (by writing novels or other means) describing this world, but always with a sense of incompleteness. At the beginning, I thought it was because I needed more practice, or because I'd swallowed some half-baked ideas whole when I was younger. Then I slowly came to realize that feeling of something being missing was simply a part of the world behind the image. That is to say, right from the beginning, the eyes with which I perceived and understood the world (that's how they were set up) were destined to be a castle built on shifting sands, a noisy restaurant pit stop in the middle of a journey, or an empty station after you'd missed your bus . . . a scene of distraction, not somewhere you could be calm and concentrate.

To put it simply, this was the world I took from my father's dreams. At the age of twenty-five, he was abruptly plucked from this realistically detailed world. That vividly rendered place continued to exert a hold over him for the rest of his life. Like an endlessly shifting dream world. It took him till the age of forty before he allowed me to exist in this world.

I don't know if this was intentional, but right from the start, my father placed me—and my brother and sister, and even my mother—in the lonely, narrow space between his dream and our reality. Naturally, all of us eventually managed, in our own ways, to stumble out of the crevice and leave his dream behind.

At the same time, though, we lost our knack of viewing the world currently unfolding before our eyes and seizing onto its details to remember this other place.

I realized that when I stared blankly at the world whose outlines and depth had been swallowed by that piercing light, I had no way of suppressing the rage that was welling up from some unknown depths of my body. This anger was a well so deep its bottom couldn't be seen. And that shocked me, perhaps even frightened me.

This rage wasn't simply "Father's story has finally been ripped out" or even "Look, Father, this is the bare, still, sunlit world left behind after your story was ripped from it," nor was it a whine, "See how hard it is for me to make my way in the world you described, from beginning to end, utterly wrongly."

At one point in senior high, solely because my friends urged me to, I ganged up with four or five other boys to beat up some guy I didn't know on the deserted roof of the school. To this day, I remember his agonized face trying to look strong. We grabbed hold of his dark blue jacket to prevent him from hitting back, but he twisted and struggled with extraordinary strength. This made us jerk around like spirit mediums carrying a deity's palanquin, the heels of our black leather shoes clacking against the insulated roof surface. Panting, we screamed, "Fuck! Fuck!" One of us pulled off his own jacket and tried to cover the guy's face, but he kept slipping it back off. I remember being squashed among those young bodies as if in a nightmare, my first few punches landing on empty air, then I don't know what happened, but my fist somehow connected with his nose. What a weightless, silent moment. He stared in surprise at the group, then his eyes fixed on me (I don't even know you!), and vast quantities of red liquid flowed like stage blood in a play.

I was scared to death. My voice coarsened as I screamed, "Fuck! Fuck!"

But everyone else had stopped moving.

*% *% *%

This was during my father's absence.

I once hung out with a friend (he was our class hygiene monitor that term) as he stayed behind in the schoolyard after the cleaning had been done. When it got dark, he'd tiptoe into a classroom that wasn't ours. The school was running a cleanliness competition, and the teacher-in-charge went around at the crack of dawn assigning points to each room. Had every last greasy fingerprint been polished off the windows? Were the desks and chairs lined up perfectly straight? Had the floor been mopped to a high shine? Could you run your finger along the blackboard ledge and have it come up spotless?

Purely because of this friendship—not even loyalty—between two young people, he didn't need to say much, just "Come on" when the moment arrived each day, and I would quietly pad behind him into one empty classroom after another. In the dark, we'd move chairs out of line, scatter the tidy boxes of chalk from the lectern drawer across the floor, and spit on the painstakingly wiped windows.

And so, in a silent world, without any motive at all, just because this was a moment my father couldn't witness, I huddled close to and became one with a group of strangers.

Around the same time every Sunday morning, I accompanied Father and Mother on the bus to climb a little hill just outside Taipei. Thinking back, Father was much older than the parents of other boys my age. Their fathers seemed youthful, while mine was an elderly man. I walked up hundreds of stone steps behind him, losing my breath, not saying a word as I listened to him repeat another of his fantastical stories about an impossibly distant place, my true hometown, about the grandparents I'd never laid eyes on, a huge array of relatives I didn't know, and his fatherless existence.

When we got to the summit (where there was a small Earth God temple), my father would take out his handkerchief and dab away his sweat, pour us a cup of scalding dragon well or high mountain tea from his Thermos, then, like always, lift his bamboo walking cane and hit an enormous moss-covered rock.

Rapt, he'd recite poetry that had nothing at all to do with my world:

> I do not fear clouds obscuring my sight, for I'm on the highest plane.

Or else:

> I will walk till the water checks my path,
> Then sit and watch the rising clouds—

Once he recited (I still remember this) something he said was a famous line from the late Qing poet Hu Linyi:

> Faced with the unexpected, they quail not; insulted for no reason, they rage not.

Now I'd been tossed on a vast sea of catastrophe; everyone around me was a laughable puppet but also an innocent sleepwalker. I couldn't have said if I was fleeing or traveling or rescuing my father, Odysseus, after his great voyage. Everyone had returned. Now it was just Father and me in this simple picture, just the horizon and a park bench. Sitting in silence, exhausted and calm, contemplating the memories and recollections that came to us after this tumultuous, terrifying journey.

"I'm so very tired," I said to Father, like a little whiny boy. "Look how we suffered because of you."

But then I realized Father had become very, very small.

(And at this moment, Kublai Khan says to Marco Polo, I do not know when you have had time to visit all the countries you describe to me. It seems to me you have never moved from this garden.

Marco Polo replies, Everything I see and do assumes meaning in a mental space where the same calm reigns as here, the same penumbra, the same silence streaked by the rustling of leaves. At the moment when I concentrate and reflect, I find myself again, always, in this garden.

Then Marco Polo says, Perhaps this garden exists only in the shadow of our lowered eyelids, and we have never stopped: you, from raising dust on the fields of battle; and I, from bargaining for sacks of peppers in distant bazaars. But each time we half-close our eyes, in the midst of the din and the throng, we are allowed to withdraw here, dressed in silk kimonos, to ponder what we are seeing and living.)

I couldn't help thinking of the morning I first heard the bad news. I was with my wife and son (and the baby who would very soon be emerging to face the world) in a hotel by Hualien's Taroko Gorge, blissfully unaware. I remember that morning, we even went swimming in the hotel's heated pool. Just as we got back to our room, hair still damp and reeking of chlorine, the phone rang. It was my wife's sister, calling from Taipei. *Where were you? No one could get hold of you. Uncle Lo had a brain hemorrhage in Jiujiang. We just heard from the hospital there.*

What happened next was as I described at the beginning of this book: I fell into a swamp of time. I drove for seven hours with my wife and son in the car, down the Hualien then the Beiyi Freeway, back to Taipei. The next day, Mother and I took a flight, then a connecting flight, to Jiujiang. A long, slow journey, and this was just the beginning. For some reason, whenever I tried to think back over the whole thing, it felt as if time had frozen in that very first moment, and I was still silently driving my wife and son (as if my wife would never give birth to our second child, and our first son had sniffed out the irretrievable tragedy in the grown-up world and hit his own power switch, and was now sound asleep in my wife's lap) down the twists and turns of that endless mountain road. Outside the window was an illustration from a picture book, a landscape cut out of gray paper. Gray mountains, gray sky, gray road, the faraway gray ocean, the gray steel tower of the cement plant and its mechanical arms. Perhaps, having sustained such a shock, I'd suppressed the moment, and so that wounded, incomplete image kept spinning in place.

"Where the hell am I?" At one point, unable to stand the endless gray, I turned and asked this of my wife in the back seat (she later told me that at that moment, I looked ready to murder someone).

I remember finally arriving at Yilan Plain, but then before reaching Yilan City, I spent more than an hour lost, utterly confounded by the coastal road and the checkerboard of farm fields, having taken a wrong turn and been unable to find my way back. Just rushing along. I remember seeing a sign for a place called Nan'ao and being unable to resist telling my wife: that's a deserted stretch of coast, I used to come here alone (before I met you), I'd get the main Eastern District Railway and get off at Toucheng, then change to a bus. All the scenes I remember are of a winter seaside: the empty beach, abandoned fishing boats rotting below the tidal line, heavy fog over the ocean, the repetitive dull thud of the waves. From a great distance away I took buses and trains to reach this landscape of grayness in all directions, even though all I did here was smoke one cigarette after another, flinging the butts onto the shiny sea roaches crawling through crevices in the rock. Such lonely, despairing images. Buying my bus ticket and waiting amid a crowd of elderly men and women, pressing the bell and alighting on a deserted stretch of road, waving to hitch a ride from a dump truck as it sped by like a deranged beast, a damp cigarette clamped in my mouth against the driving rain. . . . Isolated, broken, meaningless pictures, no clue what connected them. As if our sense of modernism at the time meant we could only send ourselves into those helplessly lonely landscapes, to smoke and clutch our writhing heads and scream by the winter sea.

When I told my wife about this beach, I had no idea I would soon (with my mother) have to travel all the way to "Jiujiang." What sort of place was it? And what would happen to me next?

I remember the year before my wife and I got married, there were several occasions when she snuck me into family gatherings, like a **secret individual being smuggled**. In these crowded, bustling situations, with my young wife-to-be often somewhere else, I found myself standing among her cousins or her father's employees, with no one having any idea who I actually was. They found me an honest fellow of few words and were happy to joke around with me. I remember taking part in at least three of these big gatherings. One was when my wife's grandmother passed away, and I followed the entire family to the Pescadores Islands for the funeral (my future father-in-law paid for everyone's flights, including family visiting from abroad and those of his employees he'd asked along to help out), and I was introduced as "a college friend of their third son" or "second sister's class-mate" and sent to hang out with the male cousins for almost half a month. We put up the funeral tent, got a truck to a nearby temple to borrow round tables and plastic chairs for the guests, picked people up from the airport in Uncle So-and-So's taxi, and even recruited people to make up the numbers as all the cousins knelt at Granny's altar together, chanting scripture along with the monks. . . .

Another time was after a fire at my wife's father's firm, where a large number of plaques and trophies (they were manufactur-ers of gifts and awards) either got burned or were ruined by the fire hoses. My future father-in-law rented another shop around the corner, and I joined the employees in moving the damaged statuettes, glass cases, and huge crates of ceremonial sashes and other paraphernalia in a small cart, down the shaded walkways along Guilin Road and Liuzhou Street (passing by an old hotel where elderly women of the night lounged against the walls outside), transporting everything to the new establishment.

These shenanigans made me a tiptoeing shadow, creeping into my wife's enormous, complex tribe. My wife's cousins and her father's employees gradually came to treat me affectionately, "like one of their own." At big dinners, I was often not seated with my wife and her siblings (they were usually next to the main table with the senior relatives) but instead dragged off to join the guys who drank to excess and enjoyed dirty jokes (and sometimes gleefully exchanged mildly malicious rumors about the boss), while my wife—perhaps because she was shy and awkward, perhaps because of some hazy incident involving the family's long-standing dismissive attitude to women or its propensity to gossip—would send me off on these occasions like a herder setting a bull free to graze, no questions asked. This made me very uneasy to start with. Before me, she'd been with her ex for seven or eight years, and I guessed that he'd been completely at home in these vast, casual, and yet actually quite intricate family functions. And that's why I always felt I was in an odd position, a sort of shadow lover. I didn't know how they all saw me. How they imagined me. What they said about me.

Later on, I came to realize she was "tossing me to a group of complete strangers whom she'd grown up with," in order to give me the space to gradually, in my own way, learn to get along with them and slowly become friends. It was an act of thoughtfulness.

The main thing was, my wife's entire clan had a tendency toward silence, introversion, and a reluctance to talk about themselves. Apart from her branch of the family, which was moved wholesale from the Pescadores to Taiwan island by my father-in-law the year he turned fifty, all the others—mostly the cousins of my wife's generation—peeled away like swans from their flock, getting into the police academy or teachers' college, becoming makeup salesgirls or dump truck drivers . . . all kinds of different identities that enabled them to leave home and "move from one island to another." The story of their family often became about their hometown (now just a summer vacation spot) or childhood. Living among them, I was often mute due to the language barrier (I wasn't fluent enough in the Heluo dialect to speak complete sentences). After some time, my silent smiling presence gained me the affection of this family unused to expressing its feelings. "That decent guy." "Third Brother's foolish Son-in-Law." Sometimes I'd sit quietly among them, drinking and listening to their stories, most of which were about the younger generation: getting odd jobs in Taiwan, changing direction, finding ways to further their education, getting bullied by city folk . . . just some mild, melancholy grumbling. (And bit by bit, I became a part of this introverted family.)

I remember on the trip to the Pescadores, at the reception after Granny's funeral, I sat next to my wife's third uncle and downed many drinks with him. He seemed to like me a lot, urging me to raise my glass again and again while keeping up his constant kvetching (even though I couldn't understand most of what he was saying). Later I found out he'd been a drunkard since a young age, and the police had once phoned my father-in-law in the middle of the night to come and get him—his dear little brother had managed to drive his taxi into the sea by the Goddess of Mercy Temple.

I remember his bleary eyes suddenly opening wide during that conversation. He said my name (as if I were a very dear young relative) and pointed at a ratty old man at a neighboring table who could have been a vagrant. "See that guy?" He claimed to know that old man. When he was still a kid, the old man "went crazy." But actually, "he's your grandpa's" (It was very moving the way he conflated me and my wife, it brought a tear to my eye) "distant relative," though no one knew him anymore, "except me." At a very young age, this drifter found himself unable to remember who he was, so he just started walking across the island, "and walked very far, you know, more than ten kilometers a day. He kept going even after the sun went down. One time, I had a soldier boy in the back of my taxi heading to Xiyu township, and I saw him walking by the side of the road." He spoke of this itinerant old man with such respect and warmth, and I felt he was all but ready to go over to his table and raise a glass to him. Instead, he went on: "Old guys like this will sniff out a funeral dinner from miles away, but he's got no idea this meal he's enjoying today is courtesy of his own family."

That was the first time I came close to confronting and understanding this fact: the reason my wife's entire clan (when did this begin?) was so tight-lipped and unable to express itself, sometimes even tipping over into outright hostility and animosity, was all to do with a sort of fatalistic personality stemming from being only one or two generations removed from the great migration. They all carried themselves very gingerly, choosing words with care, imitating others to gain their affection (or at least to make themselves less conspicuous). They weren't used to this happening the other way around, an outsider trying to ingratiate himself with the group. When they were young, they had to survive in a new place. Now older, they'd returned to gaze upon their homeland (or else they were just visiting because of a wedding or funeral), only to find they weren't quite sure how to repair and extend the family story that had snapped off because of their departure. Besides, in the eyes of an outsider like me, the passing of their clan's oldest member seemed to rouse their instinct to "mend the story," particularly in the way elderly, middle-aged, and young fussed and argued over details of the ceremony—their anxiety and desolation were palpable. For instance, my brother-in-law went around in the ritual garb of the eldest grandson, snapping away with the newest model DSLR camera, capturing ancient Pescadorean practices such as weeping over the coffin, stroking the coffin, circling the coffin. Or the way my father-in-law (at that time still technically my father-in-law-to-be) was very happy to hand out plane tickets in order to get his friends from the Lions Club or Junior Chamber of Commerce to return and attend the funeral, in order to showcase the mourning rituals of Taipei funeral parlors (they also flew in funeral scrolls of various famous figures, and flower baskets from a high-end Taipei florist), bringing them all to the funeral tent on the desolate field outside Second Uncle's coral stone house. Or how, when we were younger, my wife would pull her hand from mine as we got off the plane and abandon me to her male relatives, transforming from a "modern, independent Taipei woman" to one of the gaggle of headscarf-wearing grannies and aunties, sitting so naturally on a bench among them, using a vegetable knife to shell spanner crabs and mud crabs.

I remember the morning we heard the bad news about Father, the shimmering haze of light in the swimming pool, the mystic moment when the sounds of my wife and child suddenly became very, very distant. Then afterward, the three of us (and the unborn child) sealed in a tiny car, hurt and silent as we wended our way along the endless mountain road. Outside, the day slowly darkened, and I kept thinking that this fragile little family "with me as the father" was spinning its wheels as time stood still.

I remember turning off Suhua Freeway and immediately getting lost among the criss-cross village streets and coastal roads of Yilan Plain, until finally we found our way to the city and could follow the signs to the Beiyi Freeway, a landscape I vaguely recognized, and amid the anxiety of finding the way out, I recalled being in a convoy of my wife's relatives many years ago, traveling with great pomp in the opposite direction (from Taipei to Yilan along the Beiyi Freeway) and getting just as lost in this maze of wrong turns, blundering left and right, unable to find our way out.

It was a year before our marriage, back when I was still the "shadow lover" being smuggled into family events, that I went on this momentous journey: less than two months after Granny's funeral in the Pescadores (they believed the family needed to be "washed with happiness" within a hundred days of the death, or the period of mourning would last three years), and so my wife's elder brother (my future brother-in-law) was on his way to his future wife's family home in Yilan, along with all of us, to formalize his engagement. I remember a convoy of a dozen or more cars: a Mercedes-Benz borrowed from a family friend to serve as the lead vehicle, a Volvo, a BMW, and after those flashy cars, a more modest assortment pulled together at the last minute, containing the traditional "twelve gifts" in their rosewood chests, the various wedding outfits and camera equipment for the bride's photo shoot, and the many family and friends who'd come specially all the way from the Pescadores Islands.

My crappy car and I had been dragged into this procession (and placed second to last). Apart from the wedding pastries, it also contained my wife, the husband of one of her cousins, and a couple of nephews. It was a long, exhausting drive. We got caught in gridlock almost as soon as we turned onto the Beiyi Freeway. The two little boys in the back seat grew restless and asked again and again how much longer till we got there, grumbling that if they'd known how boring this would be, they'd have stayed behind in the Pescadores playing video games. Their father started out by scolding them, but eventually he too started complaining about the virtually unmoving lines of vehicles ahead of us. "What's going on? Are we just stuck here?"

I felt isolated and uneasy. I was dressed in the pale yellow trousers that my mother took me to the export clothing store to buy after I won my first literary prize. They were now baggy and wrinkled. My too-tight maroon blazer had been angrily thrust at me by my wife's father (my future father-in-law), who dug it out from a box of clothes he no longer wore, after he saw my usual denim jacket. This odd combination (maroon blazer, trousers the color of uncooked rice) made me feel like a bumpkin appearing before this family of strangers. I hadn't dared tell my mother I was part of the betrothal procession for my wife's brother. That would definitely have had unwelcome associations for her. Ever since moving out for college, I'd rarely gone back home, apart from at the New Year, and as she and my father slowly sank into old age, I continued to remove myself from their enfeebled, gummy state of being. It must have felt as if I was turning into someone else's child. I must have spent four or five hours wandering painfully in that convoy of cars, as if in a dream, along mountain tracks through the surging green countryside with silver-foiled ghost money scattered by the side of the road.

"What percentage of this journey have we actually completed?" Finally even I snapped and exasperatedly asked my wife in the passenger seat.

She didn't answer right away. Getting out her phone, she called her mother (my future mother-in-law), who was in the head car. Before setting out, we'd made sure there was a cell phone in every car so we could communicate. I'd found it hilarious that they were taking it so seriously, at least until we all ended up stuck on this winding mountain road.

Finally my wife hung up, and with her beautiful eyes (this was almost ten years ago) she stared at me in a way she thought was reassuring but actually made me even more stressed, and said: "Don't worry, there's still a long way to go. . . ."

We eventually got past the gridlock (like a blocked intestine) of Beiyi Freeway and onto Yilan Plain, by which time it was past noon. Next, we spent more than an hour going around and around the narrow roads between the fields (many years later, my wife and I would do the same as we rushed from Hualien back to Taipei) before finally arriving in a cloud of dust at my wife's future sister-in-law's house, which was next to a paddy field and a pond. The first six cars, the fancier ones, went down a dirt road and right up to her door; the other, crappier vehicles parked by the field. The kids, bored out of their minds by now, were frolicking like puppies in the paddy, sword fighting with their forearms and splashing in the water. One of them, the son of someone who worked for my wife's father, came running over and launched a flying kick at my ass, using such force it didn't feel like a joke, and leaving a muddy footprint on the seat of my pale yellow trousers. His father stood not far away, smiling as he watched the whole thing, then giving his child the most perfunctory scolding. I made to chase the boy, but he ran far away and shouted hysterically, "Your trousers are torn! Your dick is falling out!"

And indeed, my pale yellow suit trousers had split along the seam all the way from the crotch to halfway up my rear, and I could see my white cotton underpants. At that moment, I hated my mother. I remembered her taking me to buy those trousers, very solemnly helping me to finally dress like an adult. Now she'd left me looking like a clown in front of all these strangers.

(This happened so very, very long ago.)

As I joined the workers in helping move the chests of wedding candy and betrothal gifts from the van to the bridal home, I ran into my wife's father in the living room, which still had an altar and eight immortals chairs. He seemed to have already had quite a lot to drink—his face was flushed red as he bickered with the bride's parents. He called me over, tugged intimately at the shoulder of my maroon jacket (none of them had noticed the huge hole in my trousers), and said, "Am I right? You look much more handsome like this." Then he introduced me to my future sister-in-law's parents, "This is my second daughter's boyfriend, soon he'll be my idiot son-in-law." And this down-to-earth, short, elderly couple stood in the cool, dark interior of their house and said to me kindly, "Good luck, hopefully we'll be celebrating your wedding next year."

That was so many years ago, but for some reason, at that moment I felt like an orphan.

I remember leaving the living room to rejoin the workers and cousins (all dressed in appropriately spiffy suits), and we stowed all the gifts from the bride's family in the van—split-unit air conditioners, a washing machine, a fridge, a TV set, a projector, all still in their cardboard boxes. Then I noticed my future mother-in-law standing by herself away from the crowd on a little ridge of land in the paddy field, gazing at some faraway thing. I walked over and looked in the same direction, but apart from more paddy fields and ponds very similar to these, plus a bamboo grove, there was nothing at all to see. I quietly called out, "Mom?"

She gestured into the distance and murmured, "The general manager just told me that the family big sister first married into is over there. So close, just one village away from us."

I had no idea what she was alluding to. Whether it was this family or the layer of mist shrouding the ground ahead, I couldn't see the farther fields. I hadn't even known big sister had been married before. My sadness and frustration were like a small amount of water at the bottom of a glass, gently quivering.

Had I ever, out of ignorance, said something hurtful in front of big sister? For that matter, had I ever insulted any other member of this family I barely knew?

"I'm very worried," said my future mother-in-law. "I'm scared she'll recognize that place and start thinking about all those things from the past."

That was many years ago. I stood behind her, gazing at her profile, which was very like my wife's but drawn with a thicker pencil. She told this story in the gloom, leaving indelible marks of sadness.

thirteen

GIRAFFE

We stood with the other children behind the yellow plastic tape. At such close quarters, a wave of unrest was transmitted through these squashed-together bodies. We were probably being held like this to intensify the effect—they'd also hired a man to stand around in full battle gear holding a police baton, completely indifferent to the seething crowd on the other side of the line, just stomping back and forth in his rubber boots.

"How much longer will it be?" my child asked anxiously. At this point, even I had been infected by the excitement around me. Soon, I told him. "Very soon."

"But how much longer?" "Very soon." "Why hasn't it started yet?" "Calm down, it will start when they say it starts. Can't you see that everyone else is waiting patiently?"

Suddenly, without any warning, the guy in army uniform furled the yellow tape back into the bronze stanchion (apparently it was retractable) in a single swift movement, and the kids ran free, hollering and whooping. I jogged senselessly along with the child (who yipped in excitement like a puppy) before stopping in confusion.

"Where are we actually going?"

% % %

We were in a huge shopping mall designed to appeal to children. The kids swarmed past a retro soda fountain with a jukebox and a kiosk selling luridly dyed popcorn to the various stands. To my left was a giant Toys "R" Us, and to my right a Discovery Channel shop selling only plush animals. In the blink of an eye, the concourse went from being full of hysterically screaming kids to completely empty—the children had decanted themselves into the booths with shelves of colorful items—and I couldn't help pondering how this scene would look from high above, an alien simulation of Brownian motion, or a probability experiment investigating the random movements of silvery pachinko balls. Standing across from me and my child were three people dressed in animal outfits, with fuzzy bodies and giant heads: a koala bear, a pink cartoon bird (bird head, wings and torso on top, miniskirt and pink leggings below, probably a female bird), and a blue cartoon bird clearly intended to be her boyfriend. Another girl was dressed as a bee, but instead of a mask, she had heavy makeup like a fairy princess. As if she were their guide, she led the three animals in their heavy headpieces toward us.

"What an adorable little boy," said the bee fairy, kneeling down before my child. She and the animals clearly felt embarrassed that all the other kids had run straight past them without a second glance and headed directly for the shops. I guessed they were entertainers hired by the mall and now didn't know what to do with themselves. The bee introduced her friends to my child: "This is a koala bear" (as if that needed to be said), "this is Miss Kiki" (I wished I could tell the bird that she had nice legs), "and this is . . ." (I didn't catch the blue bird's name).

The koala bear touched his black plastic nose to my child's face. Unexpectedly, the child grew shy and burrowed into my arms, pressing his face into my chest, refusing to look up or respond to their entreaties. Now it was up to me to entertain these cartoon creatures. What small talk should I make? Probably not: "Your job looks tough," or "Must be horrible wearing a costume like that in such hot weather," or "How much are they paying you per hour?" or "Once I went to a dinner at Taipei Capital Lions Club dressed as a lion, so I know how much it stinks inside those plush outfits, plus you can barely see through the mouth so even walking around gets difficult."

We all had to stay in character. I told the child, "If you keep ignoring Miss Kiki, she might cry." The girl with the pretty legs raised her wings, as if to brush off tears (and I felt a mild pang of guilt at conspiring with a strange lady who knew nothing about my child), but his face remained pressed stubbornly to my chest.

A moment later, the human animals noticed an older lady by the hot dog stand holding two little girls by the hand and gratefully left us to go talk to them.

Walking among the stands piled high with all manner of expensive toys, I saw one area that wasn't crammed full—it was mostly older children who barged roughly past each other while my child stared with envy and respect, sad to be excluded— selling aquariums: gleaming glass boxes in neat rows, bubbles rising through water containing all kinds of bizarre, dreamlike aquatic plants, colorful sand and special lighting conspiring to make those fat, waving fronds look unnaturally alive in their lonely, cold seascapes.

My child was drawn to a metal tank in the corner, which held what must have been several thousand baby goldfish in shallow water. This goldfish-catching game had been briefly fashionable when I was a schoolboy. Usually it would be an old uncle who set up a lead pool on the sidewalk near our elementary school, with an electric pump to aerate the water, and kids all around would try to grab some goldfish. The nets were made from metal wire twisted into a loop and handle, holding a fragile rice paper mesh that broke apart almost on contact with the water, never mind actually being able to scoop up those swiftly darting fish. Yet for some reason, this roadside game with its near-impossible odds (really, this was just a way for a grown-up to torment some kids!) had become, all these years later, a sort of bittersweet memory of a bygone way of life.

I bought a net from the young woman at the stall, but the one she handed over was, surprisingly, made of sturdily woven cloth and definitely wouldn't rip. She told me the rice paper ones were five Taiwanese dollars each, and you could keep going till they broke, but they were out of stock. The cloth ones were fifty dollars for ten minutes, and no matter how many you managed to catch, they'd give you an additional five goldfish at the end.

But this didn't feel the same, I grumbled to myself. What was this sensation I was after? The feeling of catching goldfish. The feeling of showing my child "how in the past we had to struggle so arduously in our lives."

My child seemed completely unaware of this enormous difference and sat himself on the little stool full of enthusiasm, chasing after the tiny fish. Abruptly, I noticed a dozen or so floating belly up among the darting fish. As if death had blundered into this game of life. I quickly sprang into action, removing the corpses with the steel skimmer they used to clean the pool, only to discover there were actually more carcasses than I'd first seen! Not just on the surface, but also a vast number that had sunk to the bottom of the tank. Having lost the golden shimmer of their living compatriots, they'd taken on the gray or dull pink tint of rotting flesh. The fortunate survivors swam between piles of their fallen comrades as if navigating a maze of stalactites. My child and I had stumbled upon a scene of death. For whatever reason, the tiny goldfish were dying en masse. This ended with my child assuming that the point of the game was to pick out the dead fish, and he began to copy me, happily scooping out cadavers, both floating and sunken. . . .

In a sort of hysterical rage, I turned to bellow at the young woman, "How did these fish die?" (They were all in the process of dying!) She bent over to study the tank, then apologized nonchalantly: Oh, I'm sorry, it's still early and we haven't got around to cleaning the water.

"But what's going on? Why are so many of them dead? Is it too cold in here? Or are they sick?"

The girl reacted as if I'd said something amusing, her eyes crinkling with laughter. "It's fine," she said reassuringly, "it was much worse during the earthquake! When we got to the shop that morning, all the fish had jumped in shock, and all of them, every single one, died on the floor by the pool. The water was completely empty." Then she added, "We had some preschool kids yesterday, and maybe there were so many, they tired the fish out. I bet they all died of exhaustion." She began scooping them out with her hands. They filled half a small basin.

It seemed evident that the game was over. I tried to get the child to ignore the tiny fish corpses like dried leaves, but his net danced and flicked through the water, and even when it managed to nab a live goldfish, in an instant that too had flopped belly-up. That's when I saw that all through the pool were suspended shreds of waterlogged rice paper. I imagined the preschoolers, each holding a rice paper net—a great massacre as the glittering fish splashed and leaped through the water. The ones who managed to escape, no matter how good their evasive skills, were unable to flee the tank, now saturated with stray shreds of paper that smothered them.

I decided to return the cloth net and little plastic basin to the girl. When a vagabond father on an outing with his child hands over a coin for a roadside stall fishing game, an unnameable expectation floats up within him. But when he sees his child enthusiastically and efficiently dredging up a poolful of dead gray corpses, he can't help thinking grimly, *This can't be . . .* Like those people whose job it is to wash dead bodies or clear gutters.

The girl filled a plastic bag with water and generously handed over the "prize" of six or seven little fish. When I firmly rejected this—though, going by my child's catch, this was indeed the number we were entitled to—she didn't seem to mind, just tugged at my child's sleeve. "Hey, this way, I'll show you something cool." I was about to say something when the two-year-old shot a stern look at me, as if to say, "Stop spoiling my fun," intimidating me into silence.

Still holding the basin of dead fish, the girl led my child to a tank that happened to be exactly at his eye level. She opened a door in the acrylic surface and with a pair of tweezers, nimbly picked up one of the dead fish and dangled it in front of the South American horned frog within. There was a moment when I thought this creature, the camouflage colors of a bomber jet, was fake—but then the next instant, as if it had a duty to erase the scene of death we'd witnessed, its jaw flipped open, and in a single gulp, it had swallowed this corpse that was almost the size of its head.

% % %

To tell the truth, during that time of sleepwalking, I was a father who'd lost his script and no longer knew how to proceed. Completely going against the warnings of my elders not to "let the next generation become the slaves of commerce," I threw in the towel and helplessly led my child to his "good friends" in various spots around the city, where they had been precisely placed as if by satellite.

They were found in supermarkets, after-school clubs, and pediatric clinics, and also old-fashioned food markets and malls with a children's department or play zone that took up an entire floor. I'm talking about coin-operated kiddy rides.

Usually these were in the shape of vehicles, or animals, or cartoon characters. Some were painted in bright colors, others were dappled and filthy. My child used to be terrified of those rides that vibrated vigorously and blared children's songs as soon as you dropped in a coin. Then during the month when Mother and I were in Jiangxi trying to bring Father home (and I wasn't around), my wife abruptly mentioned during one of our long-distance calls, "Bai likes those coin machines now." The line was bad, and I wasn't immediately sure what she meant. Apparently it was my mother-in-law who led the child to the market one day, and when she saw a dolphin ride there, hoisted the child onto the dolphin's belly to "play pretend" for a while, until finally she couldn't resist putting in a ten-dollar coin.

From that moment, he was hooked. Wherever he went, he sought out these machines.

When I got back to Taiwan, out of an abstract need to make up for something (what was I compensating for? My father, who could no longer stand upright? Or the love he never gave me as a child? Or perhaps a more intimate fear: one day, you will become like me, a fatherless child, and I want you to remember me at a time full of love and unhurried happiness), I took on the role of assistant to his detective and accompanied him on the hunt to expand his map of "good friends."

Soon enough, those rides were the only landmarks he acknowledged as we went around the city: the McDonald's in Mucha district had a sheep, a Doraemon, an excavator and crane, and a Pikachu; the Burger King at Waishuang Creek had (in addition) a monkey, rooster, dragon, rabbit, and mouse (as bumper cars), as well as a train, police car, off-road vehicle, and helicopter; Guandu Hospital had a little monkey, an airplane, and a double-headed horse; Takashimaya had a catbus and another little airplane (which later mysteriously disappeared, to be replaced by an excavator and a bee); the fifth floor of Taiwan

Adventist Hospital had a trishaw, yet another little airplane, and an English doggy (that is, a brown, long-eared hunting hound that, when you put in a coin, played not the usual Chinese kiddy tunes but songs in English); outside were an elephant and a racing car; the optician at Shenkeng had a black swan and a rotary plane; the entrance to the IKEA in Asia-World had a safari jeep (with a realistic orangutan, elephant, and giraffe in the passenger and rear seats) and construction vehicles. . . .

I would always watch sadly as we drove by one of these spots, whatever district we were in: my child's ears would prick up, his eyes would stare straight ahead, and he'd mutter the names of those metal creatures while his little body twisted impatiently in his kiddy seat. When we reached the deserted spot (because I always took him out at a time when all the other fathers in this city were yawning and arriving at work, and all the other children were tearfully arriving at kindergarten or being dropped off with a nanny; we were a vagabond father and son, wandering the city in broad daylight, heading distractedly toward a distant hospital where an old man lay helpless and ill), I'd help him into the belly of the elephant, boat, catbus, or black swan, put in a coin, and watch him grow rapt in the repetitive and meaningless motion, accompanied by a scratchy and not particularly mellifluous song, until time was up and he immediately scrambled onto another one, into which I'd put another coin, thus starting another round of solo rocking for him while I stood drooping to one side, frozen in time.

The limited time after I dropped in the coin, when his little body writhed within that mass of metal, his uncontrollable enthusiasm and motion, the circular monotony behind it . . . all of this was like (the thought flashed into my mind, and I wanted to say this to him) how many years later, in some form or another, you'll eventually find all the loves you'll encounter in your life, pulling away the layers of secrets keeping them hidden, just as perfect and bewitching, with differences that will linger in your mind—but in the end, they'll grow just as stale and repetitive.

Thus the role of a father. Obligingly following him around as, with the glazed eyes of an addict, he pointed and demanded to be bundled into (so his body could experience the pleasure of motion for a short while) this metal object or that, then I'd put a coin in . . . and silently stand to one side observing. Would he hate me for this one day? The nihilism and fear of having our backs turned to death, as if trying to grab hold of some sort of meaning, inserting coin after coin, jingle jangle. Would he one day realize that his parade of (vibrating, singing) good friends were no more than painted hunks of iron with internal motors, emitting little clanking noises because of metal fatigue? Not the mythological flying creatures of fairy tales, just dead things scattered around the corners and edges of the city that allowed you, for a low price, to purchase pleasure for a strictly limited period.

Would he hate me? They weren't even the carcasses of living creatures.

There was a period of time (before the child was born) when I adopted a stray dog named Spot. I loved that dog and practically treated him like a son. Later I got a female hunting dog named Girlie who'd clearly been spayed, but perhaps her ovaries had been left intact, because whenever she came into heat, Spot would get so agitated that his eyes would brim with tears. Yet there was probably some sort of pecking order in the animal world, because no matter how badly Girlie's hormones were tormenting her, she absolutely refused to let Spot mount her.

On several occasions, I was so bothered by their scrabbling and sparring in the courtyard, and Spot's anguished howls and repeated rebuffs, that I would storm out. After a long time, my wife would get intrigued by the silence from outside and look out the window, and this is what she'd see:

Me squatting in front of Girlie, holding her down by her fore-legs and back so that Spot, whom I "treated like my own child," was able to clamber onto Girlie's rear, although he never managed to actually enter her but just jerked his hind legs around wildly.

From inside the house, my wife would angrily yell, "You animal!" Then the child was born, and less than a year later, Spot died of a heartworm infestation. After the child had learned to speak, I asked if he remembered that we'd once had such a dog? He said, "No."

※ ※ ※

The child and I walked into the zoo as fog rose around us. We were practically the first visitors. Behind us were three or four groups of kindergarten kids, their uniform tracksuits embroidered with the names of their schools. They chattered away, raising quite a ruckus. In every respect—build or head shape, coordination or ability to string words together—they appeared much more evolved than my child.

"Let's go," I said.

"Why?" asked my child. I would later realize he didn't hate them, but actually looked up to and worshiped them, these kids who must have been three or four years older than he. They were rough and merciless. More than once, at one of those large indoor playgrounds in McDonald's or somewhere like that, I'd watch some stinking boy elbow my child out of the way on the slide or plastic steps, then quietly trip him elsewhere in the room. I wanted so much to tell my child that when these kids were older, they'd become the upperclassmen who'd beat you up in an alleyway while still in uniform, or the seniors who'd steal your girlfriend, or your married office manager who'd nonetheless insist on pursuing any beautiful woman you had a crush on, or the senior co-worker who'd call you "bro" in the pub, then cut you to shreds with a couple of sentences at your next annual review

But I didn't have the chance to say any of this. Instead, I hastily dragged my child farther into the zoo (he stumbled along, almost jogging). We even ran right past the "Cute Animal Zone" and "Koala House" that he kept turning back to look longingly at. I just wanted to get away from those noisy, detestable older children so we could have a peaceful moment together, father and son.

I led him to the stop for the "Round-the-Zoo Train" and dropped a copper coin into the little box guarded by a middle-aged woman dressed like a police officer.

"Watch this," I said.

We were the only passengers and sat at the front of the first carriage. This little locomotive was new and painted green, designed to look like something from a fairy tale. Actually, it was just three carts joined together, and though the front one had been done up nicely with gold trim and a smokestack like a real steam train, there were no tracks or awning for the carriages. The seats were toylike and narrow, just like the roller coaster, dragon boats, and horse carriages in the amusement park I'd visited as a kid.

The child seemed excited. But after we'd sat there, motionless, for almost fifteen minutes, the kindergarten kids from earlier showed up, along with other family groups, old people, couples, and children, filling the seats behind us one by one. Evidently they'd already seen the koalas.

I told the child, "If we hadn't rushed ahead, we might not even have got a seat."

The locomotive finally set off (a bell rang at the front of the train), first traveling slowly up a lush hillside. The morning mist had cleared. Sunlight seeped between the clouds, and birds chirped nonstop. The child clutched my hand in exhilaration. Then we turned a corner and could vaguely make out through the trees the animals in their enclosures below. We were moving very slowly, but the animals kept slipping in and out of view. The kindergarten kids hollered, "That's an elephant. Elephant!" And then they spelled out the name in English. I noticed my child was clumsily copying them: e-l-e-ph-an-t. In the enclosure currently flashing past us, we could see in the dazzling light the beautiful rear of a zebra, like some Peking opera character with black streaks across their face.

The children chorused in English, "Zebra!" In the buzz of voices, a particularly juvenile one rang out excitedly, separating itself from the others, "Dad, it's a zibra!" I realized then that I'd taught him the wrong pronunciation.

%%%

The child and I sat on a cement bench beneath an awning. He was drinking something through a straw, a juice beverage called Qoo that came in an aluminum can. By now we'd realized that we'd left his little rucksack behind on the train. I was very exasperated. The rucksack contained his water bottle, a spare diaper, and a packet of wet wipes. "Where's my bag?" But I knew he didn't really care.

In front of us, past a fence and a ditch, was an arid field of short-stemmed grass. The ground rose slightly here. Compared to the limited space allowed to other large savanna animals, this felt wide and luxurious. Giraffe territory. Yet there wasn't a single one around. They were all hiding at the far end of the enclosure, where the zookeepers had built them a cave out of rocks. On the vast swathe of grass stood a lone zebra, looking extremely out of place as it chewed at the grass.

"Why is the zebra in the giraffes' home?" The child was fond of riddles. "It's so mischievous, it got lost."

In sunlight as bright as this, at moments of quiet like this, when it was just the two of us, father and son, a voice in my head would keep talking and I couldn't shut it up. Right next to the giraffe enclosure, there was indeed a herd of zebras (had that lone zebra somehow leaped the fence into the giraffe zone?), and next to the zebras were oryxes, all these bizarre savanna animals assembled before us, chewing their cud. From time to time, they'd glance alertly at us, a human father and son. But we were too far away, and the air between us was still and silent, not a sound to be heard.

In my father's later years, he fell into a particular difficulty. How can I put this? Simply, his condition was one of "having said so many things that you drove everyone else away, and ended up completely isolated." My final impression of him, when he was filled with life and crawling endlessly across the living room of that old house like a bug, is that he was constantly grabbing the phone and spewing vitriol about Such-and-Such to someone else, "Listen up, you mustn't repeat this to anyone else, it's just between the two of us. . . . This Such-and-Such, you know how he got his directorship? You'll die when I tell you. . . ." He could remember with absolutely clarity every shameful thing about any person going back decades, but right afterward he'd call another Such-and-Such and spitefully spill the beans about the first Such-and-Such. In their small circle of withered old men, it was very easy for these bits of gossip to be added to and passed back and forth across the network, so Father often ended up nervously saying into the receiver, "My friend, how could I ever say such a thing about you? Who told you that? I swear to god, if such words ever passed my lips, may there be no more Lo sons or grandsons!" But even I had overheard him say more than once the words he'd just denied speaking, so why invoke me and his at the time yet-to-be-born grandsons in this deadly vow?

There was an even more complicated layer: in Father's world, memory was diffuse and terrifying. He couldn't remember certain things that had just happened. Other events, from decades before, remained embedded in his consciousness, vivid as a movie playing before his eyes.

I don't know how many violent hurts and humiliations it's possible for a person to suppress or forcibly forget in one lifetime. When the metal plate or embolism sealing the cellar in which bitter resentments are stored finally rusts away, the most appalling scenario unfolds: a perfectly good person abruptly breaking apart, like a space shuttle going to pieces in mid-air, hateful bits of the past like corrosion in the electric circuits leading to metal fatigue, so one chunk after another falls off.

Thinking of the final image my father left me—falling through layer after layer of hidden things, too many "dark experiences belonging to him" that had nothing to do with me, but which I also couldn't extricate myself from—I felt rage and sorrow. Was I unwittingly presenting myself before my child as a lonely yet complete person?

Sometimes a feeling drifts into my heart, and I'm not sure if it's resentment or confusion. Here it is: I can't remember a single thing that happened to me before the age of seven. No matter how hard I try, the faint light of memory can only sketch out a couple of images from the first years of elementary school, or perhaps a couple of childhood friends' names. Before that, a blank. Which makes me wonder:

Perhaps my father and mother weren't the most dutiful (or attentive) parents. Back when, like a crawling bug, I had no sense of time, they were completely wrapped up in their own worlds (my father attending those gossip-filled social gatherings), abandoning me in a quiet corner as ordinary as a blank wall covered in rice paper. I crawled and learned to walk on my own, in this long span of time during which nothing would ever happen to stimulate my senses.

And perhaps this created some decisive (though of course you can never really trace any of these things back to their origins) flaws in my nervous system, whether in my personality or my physical coordination.

This version of me now sat next to my child, distractedly keeping him company, and in a haze of low-level anxiety, I worried about his little rucksack that we'd left on a train painted to look like a toy. **I didn't know what all the other fathers were doing at that moment.** When my child was grown, would he realize with a jolt of loathing that his father was in fact an idle vagabond? "Dad, how come all the other dads were at work, but you had time to bring me to the zoo?"

At times my child would notice one of the familiar machines (his good friends) gone from its spot. Or a piece of paper stuck over the coin slot, an explanation scrawled in ballpoint pen: "Blocked." After a while, that animal or vehicle or cartoon character would vanish too. Sometimes an entire batch of machines would be swapped out for different ones, and the child would turn to me in confused terror. "Where did the elephant go? Where did the trishaw go? Where did the little monkey go?"

And I would brush him off with, "They've all gone to the **Flying Cow Ranch**." This was not a place I'd visit, but the child had been there on an outing with my wife and her family (his grandpa, grandma, uncle, and aunts). And I thought with some sorrow: *Ah, already I'm creating for you a nonexistent grave for animals. Fake animals, at that. Fake death.* **It's only blocked.** The workers didn't feel anything when they came here in their truck, removed your friend, and drove off with it. Carting it off to some warehouse with thousands of these machines. A place piled high with all kinds of fake animals and cartoon characters, with broken motors that will never move again. Where the air reeks of grease, paint, and banana oil.

%% %% %%

"I need to pee," said the child.

He only said this when he was practically bursting. When we left the house that day, I'd thought I was being clever by not letting him have a diaper. And now we were looking through a fence at oryxes and zebras on the grassland, lazily chewing hay from a wooden cart. We were on a tarmac road that had absorbed so much heat it felt as if it were floating. At some point without my noticing, a few other visitors had arrived. I picked up the child and jogged away. The empty land was hazy from the blazing light pouring over it, and there was no sign of a toilet or any hidden place where one could pee. One time, I was standing with my child by that same enclosure, looking at the giraffes like paper cutouts on the verdant grass, when the air filled with flying dirt and the sky darkened in an instant. From a distant speaker, a woman's garbled voice warned us of something or other. There was just enough time for a shiver of fear to pass across my heart before the storm broke overhead, and right away the entire veldt, the giraffes, zebras, antelopes, and pygmy hippos, the farther-off elephants, and us, father and son, were all plunged into an algae-clogged gray-green swamp. The swift savanna animals moved slowly through the waterlogged air. I picked up the child and ran, the only living creatures to escape the curse, making quickly for the shelter where the vending machines stood. When we got there, though, water continued to pour down on us—the awning was just black cloth.

(Drenched, I'd simply smiled at the child nestled in my forearm and said, "We're done for now, there's nowhere else to run.")

Now, clutching my child, I ran down the road around the bend from the "Australian Animal Zone." This was one of the more remote corners of the zoo, with golden rain trees and mixed-growth plants. The sun was completely gone. Ducking behind a rock, I pulled down my child's pants, whipped out his little pee-pee, and right away a column of piss spouted onto the rotting leaves and mounds of yellow earth where ants usually crawled.

On the other side of a metal fence, very close to us, was a kangaroo staring right at us with a stupefied look on its face (was it fixated on my child's pale privates?). I thought it was a feral dog at first—I'd never have expected a kangaroo in a zoo to be as disgustingly filthy as the mangy strays who foraged for food in our trash cans. Almost all its fur had fallen off, and its bare skin had some kind of fungal infection that gave it the puffy pink appearance of cheap bubble gum (it also reminded me of the unpigmented skin of sunbathing white Australians), stippled with damp gray-brown patches (for some reason, this made me think of a rubber globe, the pink mass of Australia rising from the blue ocean). At such close quarters, the kangaroo with its yellow unfocused eyes seemed like an actor I'd hired to frighten my child, an unsuccessful attempt that left us staring helplessly at each other.

For a moment, I thought it would get startled and hop away, like those big-footed specimens on the Discovery Channel. Instead, it lay there like an elderly homeless person slumped in a corner of Dragon Hill Temple or Chiang Kai-shek Memorial Hall, silent and indifferent, passing the short time it would have with these unexpected intruders.

The child and I kept going, past the cages and enclosures of giant cassowaries, emus, bilbies, and hairy-nosed wombats. All of a sudden, my child grabbed my hand, as if struck by a thought he wanted to communicate.

"I don't like Grandpa."

"Why not?" I was furious—my guard was down, and this was a stab in my face.

"Because he's dirty." My child stared at me with huge dark eyes. Very seriously, he added, "And because he's already dead."

The long river of life. I stared at my child's face, so like my father's, as if both of theirs had come from the same beautiful mold, while in between, mine had been pinched and pulled out of shape. In the course of heredity, there would always be some genes that hated themselves. Feebly, I said, "You're not allowed to not like Grandpa." I said, "Because he's my dad. And he's not dead, he just sleeps all the time. He can hear us talking by his bed, he just can't wake up."

I don't know what's going to happen next, I said to myself.

%% %% %%

I once came up with a story: a young father spent his days bringing his child to the zoo. Meanwhile his father, the child's grandfather, had for various reasons become trapped on a solo journey in a world of his own. He'd gotten lost in that other world and was lonely and scared, but no matter where he turned, he couldn't find his way back to our world. This young father explored every corner of the zoo with his child—worrying all the while about his father, wandering through this other world. Which noodle shop in which deserted town was he now in? Which dilapidated platform on which train line, which rubbish-strewn street with discarded newspapers blowing by?—looking at caged ducks, swans, Muscovy ducks, rabbits, buffalo, and black-haired Taiwanese pigs in the "Cute Animal Zone"; the "World of North American Gray Wolves" that consisted of a couple of cement caves behind knee-high withered grass, with no actual animals in sight; the pathetic, fat birds waddling through the plastic icy waste of a fake South Pole, twisting their hips like plump women with bound feet, in the blazing fluorescent lights of the "Penguin Tank"; and finally the pitch-dark building that was the "Nocturnal Animal House."

The man held his child (who was frightened of the faintly lit cubes in that cold, dark space, each housing a bird of prey or creature of the night, now stationary as specimens or waxworks), moving past one glass case after another. Owls glaring sternly with eyes like yellow glass baubles, tufts of fur rising from the tops of their heads as if gelled in place; lemurs huddled atop a withered stump in one corner of their display; near-extinct big cats like leopard cats and clouded leopards frustrated at their cramped quarters, pacing haplessly around their enclosures; the crested porcupine that was just a spiky silhouette in the dim light; prehistoric fossil fish, blind and swimming slowly as sleep-walkers through the glowing waters of the giant aquarium set into the wall, including the spineless dragonfish and silver arowana, elephantfish snoozing in the white sand at the bottom of the tank, and the hideous giant salamanders getting the VIP treatment, with a swampy mangrove grove in the middle of the space created specially for them.

This was a dream. They walked drunkenly along. The man knew this led to the maze of his father's dreams. In the dark was one glass case after another, each filled with magnificent creatures bristling with life, the atmosphere no spookier than when, as a child, he accompanied his parents to the underground room of a City Deity temple, where in the shrines on either side were earthen figurines depicting human men and women being tortured by demons wielding all sorts of implements in the eighteen levels of hell.

In my story, I had the child spot his grandfather trapped in one of those glass cases (what a cliché!). The child excitedly started yelling, "That's Grandpa!" And the old man, who was suffering a blockage in the GPS of his pineal gland and had been blundering around the maze of his own dreams unable to find his way out, was now locked in a darkened room in the municipal zoo, transformed into an owl. Or perhaps a palm civet? Or a bobcat? Or a night heron? Or a salamander, crawling around in the mud and squalling like a baby?

I had no idea how the child could have looked at the furry face or hard beak of an animal, or even the eyes on either side of a fish's head staring in opposite directions, and recognized his grandfather. Baffled by the situation, father and son stood before the thick glass, gazing in awe at the creature inside grooming its own feathers or fur, who also happened to be a fat old man currently collapsed in bed, looking drunk and mumbling a constant stream of incoherence. They didn't know how they had stumbled into the old man's dream and needed to find a passage out, a door they could push to exit the grandfather's clogged head once more. Their only choice was to buy a ticket every day and come to this dingy room, father and son leaning against the icy glass, staring at the owl or bobcat or fox or hedgehog that would pant and sink its teeth into the mop thrust through the gap by the cleaning auntie, or claw tentatively at the fresh meat they tossed in, or humiliatingly lift a leg and piss against the glass as they watched.

※ ※ ※

I hadn't thought this would be the ending.

※ ※ ※

I had a splitting headache. After I'd spent so much time in preparation, the intricate deployment intended to get us to the heart of the story, the whole thing was smashed by one sentence spoken by the child (was that the ultimate curse, to make the entire world reverse its course and collapse?). Everything I'd worked hard to bring together, everything I'd imagined and believed, whatever I'd been using to stave off the real world, was now all falling apart. I could all but hear a loud rumbling inside my head, like collapsing scaffolding on a construction site. Now what, Father? Does this mean you're really going to die? Like the story I read in my textbook as a kid, "Sunshu Ao Buries a Snake"? What should I do? At first it was just a rumor, a perplexing threat, and I never thought that one day it would appear in front of me, a living breathing thing.

What should I do?

My child and I had almost reached the far end of the zoo. There were no more enclosures with wooden boards indicating the scientific name and country of origin of each animal. No more animals. Just a dusty hillock with an assortment of trees on the other side of a green chain-link fence. An animal's faint cry in the distance. Low and sorrowful, like a sob. Perhaps a donkey, or a cow? The child huddled close to my leg. "What was that?"

Could it be Ma Lan the elephant?

But no, I thought, isn't Ma Lan dead? Not long ago, the TV news had reported with a great deal of fanfare that Ma Lan's foot injury had deteriorated and become a malignant tumor. To start with, a toenail on her front right foot split and wounded her. The zoo's vet treated her right away, and she began to heal. Later, though, it split again, unable to withstand her three-ton weight. I don't know whether they considered amputating her foot. I saw another news item that said several famous Taiwanese shoe brands were working together to make a fifty-centimeter shoe for Ma Lan. Its sole would have been tire rubber, its laces steel wire, and the interior of the shoe would have had silicone to hold her wound together. There was also an interview with an elderly keeper who said, with great worry in his voice, that they were making a big pot of expensive herbal medicine for her every day. They were afraid her leg would give way and she'd fall over, which was a death sentence for an elephant—their insides couldn't withstand their great weight. If she collapsed, her organs would quickly start failing one by one.

Did Ma Lan fall, in the end? I felt like someone who'd lost their hearing, and though I could see the world before me clearly, there was a constant sense of separation, as if everything was at the bottom of a swimming pool. Close, yet distant. Was Ma Lan alive or dead? It was a bit ridiculous that I didn't know the answer, given that we'd been showing up at the zoo each day. My memory, like an insect's dream, provided only flashes of images: elementary school students weeping as they tied yellow ribbons around trees in the zoo, representing their good wishes for Ma Lan; the Brother Elephants baseball team winning the Taiwan series and rushing to the zoo afterward, where they doffed their caps in remembrance of Ma Lan; the camera lingering on Lin Wang, her widower, looking lonely and refusing his meal of hay. . . .

So Ma Lan was dead.

And yet I didn't have a feeling of "Yes, this really happened."

The same animal was still intermittently crying in the distance, nasal yet resonant. I turned and tried to comfort the child. "Maybe that's just the pygmy hippo—it might be hungry."

A sharp, worldly voice replied, full of expression, "Oh come on, even an idiot can tell they're slaughtering animals over there."

I looked at him, startled. At some point without me realizing, he'd become an adult. Even sadder, he was middle-aged. The cherubic face, once a silver dish with gleaming black eyes, was now puffy, its lines hardened, its expression now solidified into constant caution to guard against hurt—I was sad that this face hadn't moved in the direction of hope. I hadn't realized he'd been walking aimlessly by my side for so long. How much of my distracted mumbling had he heard? I hadn't expected this person by my side to turn out this unprepossessing, like a shade-loving plant.

Did that make me an old man? I tried explaining or apologizing to him but didn't know how to start. Just like that, I understood my father's attempts in his later years to have a heart-to-heart with me, which I'd always impatiently interrupted or fobbed off like humoring a small child, shoving his words back into that dead-end alley where no light ever shone, where the rotting remnants of the past pressed down like layers of fallen leaves. Such embarrassment, such sensitivity, filled with regret and loneliness. I wanted to apologize for turning him into someone who hated the world, someone with such a hard heart, and for all the hurt and humiliation I'd caused his mother—of course, I'd also hurt many other people, including myself—but I was afraid he would coldly reject me and say something like, "Well then, which part of our relationship are you going to use as raw material next?"

My child climbed the hillock, and like a drunkard I followed close behind. Where the soil had collapsed in one spot, we saw a bizarre sight: they'd filled the crevice with concrete to create a little water chute like a shrunken aqueduct. A rivulet ran down this uneven surface, which was thickly covered in moss. Perhaps this was a glimpse of the groundwork from when they'd dug up this hillside to create a zoo. In the distance, several peaks of similar shape were turning purple or dark green as the sun set. Clouds drifted very slowly through the sky. The air seemed to solidify.

My child pointed to the end of the cement slope and crowed, "Look, a giraffe!" What could I say? In this pool of waste water (or I guess you could call it a minilake) at the rear of the zoo lay a lone giraffe, pale as used chewing gum. I knew right away it was dead. It was still a calf. It had all the characteristics of a giraffe apart from the brown markings that ought to have mottled it like the stone walls of a medieval castle, leaving it as pure white as unglazed ceramic. We were too far away to tell if its eyes were open. I didn't see any other carcasses or severed limbs, and couldn't work out what route this giraffe could have taken into the system of drains that led to it being expelled from the waste-water pipe and tumbling through the air into the valley below.

At this distance, we couldn't smell the corpse. But there it was, an authentic white giraffe, at our feet—just like when I was a child, and my father hired a couple of men to come paint our stained walls: they must have had half a bucket of white left that they didn't want to waste, or perhaps they just found our old camphorwood furniture an eyesore. In any case, they painted the old wooden bookshelves in the living room and hallway, and my sister's piano, all white.

The giraffe looked like it had been painted. A coat thick enough to cover up any other shades, any stains or imperfections, leaving nothing but pure white.

AFTERWORD

Lo Yi-Chin

TRANSLATED BY JEREMY TIANG

I wrote this book almost twenty years ago, and now it feels like a film being projected in a dream.

After the events of this story, my father lived on in a unresponsive state for four more years, before passing away in 2004.

When I was writing it, I hadn't yet seen Miyazaki Hayao's *Spirited Away*. I later watched this fairy tale of a father and mother becoming human again after being turned into pigs, and was deeply moved. The absurdity and awkwardness captured in *Faraway* is something I feel many people have experienced, in this story of a father being rescued.

In 1949, as a young man in his twenties, my father retreated to Taiwan at the end of the Chinese civil war, along with Chiang Kai-Shek and millions of defeated soldiers, civil servants, and teachers.

From a young age, I sat in the living room of our old house in Yonghe district, listening to him describe his hometown, a sandbank on the Yangtze River. I always felt as if my brother, sister, and I were just single chromosomes, unfertilized, floating in the gray dreamscape left when he inexplicably became a foreigner. As far as he was concerned, the latter fifty years of his life, the wife and children he had in Taiwan, his old age and the onset of Alzheimer's—all these were like blurry images seen on a deep-sea diving trip, a lonely, desolate landscape. In his final years, he seemed to live only on the sandbank of his youth and childhood, somewhere within himself.

I am a child of Taiwan. When I went to China as it was back then, the experience had some of the novelty and unknowing of *Alice's Adventures in Wonderland.* In the two decades since, I've been to China many times, for various reasons, and I've gotten to know some excellent creative, educated people. The strange thing is, all the characters I encounter in this book seem to be from a different planet altogether. And yet, now in 2021, the entire world seems to have gone back twenty years in their treatment of China, back to the time of my mysterious arrival there, all that hatred and fear, when everyone I met was like the officials in Kafka's *The Castle,* just gossipy bystanders. I couldn't figure out how to break through the impasse, and so I remained stuck, spinning my wheels in that nonsensical landscape, like something from a farce. As for my father, this place was somewhere he, like Odysseus, could never return to, the most lyrical homeland in the world. I returned to this dreamscape of my father's, where he lay trapped, and brought him back to Taiwan.

After that, whenever I was faced with bureaucracy, or dealing with organizations and hospitals in China, I grew fearful that the shadow of this Kafkaesque experience might once again have fallen over me. As in the ending of *The Catcher in the Rye,* "about all I know is, I sort of miss everybody I told about." I'm very grateful to Jeremy Tiang, the translator of this book, and also to Professor David Der-wei Wang of Harvard University, without whose constant encouragement I think I would have found it hard to persist in something as extravagant as writing novels.

TRANSLATOR'S NOTE

With every translation, I take on what feels like a grave responsibility: becoming an author's voice in another language and context, transforming every word of their text while ensuring it remains the same, which is of course impossible. With a book as personal as *Faraway*, this responsibility is multiplied many times over. In a lot of his writing, Lo Yi-Chin blurs the lines between life and fiction, history and imagination. This novel takes an intimate, vulnerable time in the author's life and builds upon it a meditation on family, belonging, and exile. As I translated, I was aware of adding a further layer to the careful craft of the book, yet another structure on top of an artifice made from his life.

Of course, the political and cultural circumstances that form the context of the book are very real, and for all that Mr. Lo's family has one foot on either side of the divide, there are still concrete differences to be navigated. For instance, China and Taiwan use different systems of romanization, so while the family share a surname, those in China spell it "Luo" while those in Taiwan spell it "Lo"—just as Taiwan hyphenates given names but China doesn't, hence Mr. Lo is "Yi-Chin" while his half-brother is "Yiming." I have gone with the principle of calling each person by the name they would call themselves, and each place by the English name in general use in that country. This has led to a certain amount of inconsistency, but no more, I think, than is present in life.

Mr. Lo makes copious use of quotations from other texts. As not all of these are identified in the novel (and even where the authors are, their translators into English are not), I am listing some of them here: Fyodor Dostoevsky, *The Brothers Karamazov*, tr. Richard Pevear/Larissa Volokhonsky; Paul Theroux, *Sir Vidia's Shadow: A Friendship Across Five Continents* and *Half a Life*; Gabriel García Márquez, *One Hundred Years of Solitude*, tr. Gregory Rabassa; Italo Calvino, *If on a Winter's Night a Traveler* and *Invisible Cities*, tr. William Weaver; Michel Foucault, *History of Madness*, tr. Jonathan Murphy and Jean Khalfa; "Upstairs in the Tavern" by Lu Xun, from *The Real Story of Ah-Q and Other Tales of China: The Complete Fiction of Lu Xun*, tr. Julia Lovell; Claude Lévi-Strauss, *Tristes Tropiques*, tr. John Weightman and Doreen Weightman; Wang Wei, "My Retreat at Mount Zhongnan," tr. Witter Bynner.

Faraway was originally published in 2003, and it is hard to believe it has taken this long for the book to find its way into English—and, indeed, that this will be the first book-length translation into English of this prolific and beloved author, whom many regard as the most important currently writing in Taiwan. I am grateful to Christine Dunbar and all at Columbia University Press for making this happen, as well as to my translation collective Cedilla & Co., Chi-Ping Yen of the Taipei Economic and Cultural Office in New York, and Professor David Der-wei Wang for their support, and above all to Lo Yi-Chin for entrusting me with his story.